DM

Anathema

OTHER BOOKS BY COLLEEN COBLE

Abomination

Midnight Sea

Fire Dancer

Alaska Twilight

The Aloha Reef Series

Distant Echoes

Black Sands

Dangerous Depths

The Rock Harbor Series

Without a Trace

Beyond a Doubt

Into the Deep

ANATHEMA

COLLEEN COBLE

THOMAS NELSON
Since 1798

NASHVILLE   DALLAS   MEXICO CITY   RIO DE JANEIRO   BEIJING

Published in Nashville, Tennessee by Thomas Nelson. Thomas Nelson is a registered trademark of Thomas Nelson, Inc.

Thomas Nelson, Inc., books may be purchased in bulk for educational, business, fund-raising, or sales promotional use. For information, please e-mail SpecialMarkets@ThomasNelson.com.

Library of Congress Cataloging-in-Publication Data

Coble, Colleen.
Anathema / Colleen Coble.
p. cm.
ISBN 978-1-59554-247-2 (hardcover)
ISBN 978-159554-557-2 (IE)
1. Amish—Fiction. 2. Parents—Crimes against—Fiction. I. Title.
PS3553.O2285A84 2008
813'.54—dc22
2008004094

Printed in the United States of America

08 09 10 11 QW 6 5 4 3 2

For my Amish friends,
thank you for the lessons
you've taught me about peace,

and

for my aunt and uncle,
Don and Edith Phillips,
thank you for the constant
encouragement in my life.

PART ONE

o n e

"Hannah, why do you fight back? Always you kick against the goad. We're told to turn the other cheek."

PATRICIA SCHWARTZ

Hannah Schwartz quickened her pace along the path from the farm-house until she stood on the hillside peering down at the covered bridge. The Indiana winter wind pierced through the black wool cape she wore. She played nervously with the strings on her bonnet.

Had he come already? Oh, she shouldn't be here. *Mamm* would be so unhappy with her. But Hannah had made this choice for a good reason.

Though only seven o'clock, the darkness deepened with the storm clouds building in the southwest. Thunder rumbled, and she heard the strains of her cousin Moe's yodeling as he went to the barn. She couldn't let him see her. Slipping past the bare branches of an arching goldenrod barring her path to the road, she hurried the last few feet. Flanked by bare maple trees, the opening yawned ahead. She stepped onto the planks of the bridge. A lingering odor of gasoline exhaust made her sneeze three times.

Pausing, she waited until her eyes adjusted to the deeper gloom. She didn't need light. The interior of the covered bridge was as familiar to her as her own bedroom. Reece would be along in a few minutes. She shivered, but not from the February chill that swept down off the hills of Parke County, Indiana.

It was wrong to be here. If her parents knew . . . and Noah.

She paced the wide wooden boards of the covered bridge, pausing occasionally to listen for the sound of Reece's truck. She'd expected him to be here waiting for her like usual. Perhaps he'd had to attend to a con-venience-store break-in or some minor law violation. She leaned against one of the massive crossbeams supporting the bridge and looked through a cutout in the siding that formed a window overlooking the water. Still there was no sign of Reece. If he didn't come soon, she would have to go back.

She heard an engine and turned with an eager smile, only to face two men she'd never seen, approaching in a small four-door car. She stepped up onto the footpath of the bridge and waited for them to pass, but the car slowed. The window ran down, and a man who looked to be in his thirties leaned out as the car stopped. He hung his arm, covered with a red and black plaid jacket, out the window.

His blond hair was thinning on top, and his pale blue eyes gleamed in the light from the car's dash. "Hey, pretty lady, need a ride?"

"No, I'm waiting for a friend," she said.

"Well, your friend's not here, but we are." The door opened and he got out. The other man hopped out as well. He was about the same age and wore an orange hat. They approached where she stood.

Hannah shrank back. "My friend will be here any minute."

The man's smile turned predatory. He grabbed her arm and pulled her toward him. "We can have some fun."

"No!" She struggled to pull her arm from his grasp, but his other hand snaked around her waist. To her horror, she felt him grappling with the snaps on the back of her dress. "Let go of me!" Panicked now, she began to kick and strike at him.

"Whoa, we've caught ourselves a little wildcat." He pinned her hands down and began to drag her to the car. The other man held open the back door.

Where was Reece? She opened her mouth to scream, but the man clapped his hand over it. She smelled tobacco on his fingers and beer on his breath. He tossed her like a rag doll into the car and began to crawl inside with her. She kicked him in the face and scrabbled for the other door, only to find the other man there. A shriek tore from her throat. Hannah's limbs froze. This couldn't be happening.

The first man's face twisted into a snarl, and he grabbed her ankle when she tried to kick him again. He managed to climb in next to her. "Get us out of here," he told the other guy.

The man in the orange cap ran around to the driver's seat and jumped in. He accelerated toward the end of the bridge. Hannah shrank against the door and fumbled with the lock.

The blond man grabbed her arm. "No, you don't."

He tried to kiss her on the neck, but she bit him on the ear. Bile rose in her throat at the taste of his blood. He swore and pulled away, holding his ear. His face darkened, and he raised his hand. His arm and hand cast a shadow in the light of the overhead dome. She cringed just before his slap landed on her cheek. Her vision darkened, and she saw stars.

The car was nearly to the end of the covered bridge. The man in the front seat swore, and the brakes began to squeal. The car fishtailed as he tried to stop. Over the top of the seat, Hannah saw a truck blocking the end of the bridge. Reece stood between the vehicles, gun drawn. The car's headlamps caught the gleam of his badge.

"Get out of the car!" he shouted. "Hannah, get out of the car."

Hannah found the strength to grab the lock and flip open the door. The blond man made a halfhearted attempt to grab at her, but she slid out of the car. He slammed the door shut, and she heard him shout to the driver, "Let's get out of here!" The car reversed and backed quickly toward the other side of the bridge.

She lay on the wide wooden boards with the stink of car exhaust filling her lungs. She could see the glimmer of water through the cracks in the boards. What had almost happened? Shudders racked her shoulders, and she rose painfully to her hands and knees. Her palms stung, and her neck muscles throbbed. Running steps sounded on the boards, and Reece called her name.

"I'm here," she said, her voice trembling as hard as her limbs.

Then his strong arms were lifting her. He held her close to his chest, and she felt the way his heart pounded in her ear. His breathing sounded ragged, and she knew he'd been just as frightened as she. "You saved me," she whispered. "Again. You always are there at the right time."

He cupped his palms on each side of her head and kissed her. "I'll always be here for you. No one is going to harm *my* Hannah."

The possessiveness in his voice thrilled her. No one had ever made her feel she was so precious. "The first time we met, you chased off kids who were throwing tomatoes at me," she said, a smile finally finding its way to her lips.

"Stupid kids," he growled. "Just because you Amish don't fight back is no reason . . ." He broke off, his voice choked.

"I got in some licks this time," she said. "I'm ashamed to admit I fought back. But they—"

He put his fingers over her lips. "Don't think about it. You did the right thing."

In spite of what he said, she'd actually *bitten* a man. The shame felt too heavy to bear. All her teachings told her a Christian shouldn't fight back, should meekly accept whatever God sent her way. She'd have to carry this choice without telling her parents.

"Let's go to the jail and file a complaint against those two."

"No!" She shuddered at the thought. "I don't know who they were anyway. You got here in time. That's all that matters. Where were you?" she asked. "I was about to go home."

He slipped his arm around her waist. "Got hung up at work. I'm here now."

"And just in time." She dared to put her arm around his waist, too, and he grinned. His smile was the first of his many good traits to attract her. A smile that reflected a zest for life. He was *Englisch*, which made him taboo. And maybe that was part of the attraction that spread over her at the sound of his voice. He was older too—nearly thirty. Experienced. She liked that about him.

The emerging moon gleamed on the badge pinned to his shirt. "I wasn't sure you'd come," he said.

Hannah's free hand went to the strings on her bonnet. "I promised I would." The word *promise* mocked her. Honoring her word tonight had caused her to break even bigger pledges. "I shouldn't have come."

"You belong with me." His hands came down with a possessive grip on her shoulders.

Big hands, softer than *Datt*'s. As a sheriff's deputy and a detective, Reece didn't chop wood or handle a saw like the men in her community. He smelled good too. No odor of perspiration, just the spicy fragrance of oriental woods. She'd spent a whole afternoon at the department store last week, trying to identify what he wore, before deciding it was a fragrance called Contradiction.

And that pretty much summed up how he made her feel.

She dared a glance at his face and smiled back. "I can't stay long. Someone is at home buying *Mamm*'s quilts. They'll miss me in a few minutes."

He pressed a kiss onto her forehead. "What are we going to do, honey?" he whispered against her hair.

"Come to meeting with me this Sunday," she said. "It's at our house. Visitors are welcome."

He smiled. "Trying to convert me?"

"It would solve a lot of problems," she admitted. While it was unusual for an *Englischer* to convert to the Amish faith, it had happened. Her own mother had walked such a path. And it would keep Hannah from having to make an impossible choice between her family and the man she was falling in love with.

He tugged her toward the shadows. "Come sit in the truck with me." He took her hand and led her to his pickup, a black Dodge he'd bought just last week. He opened the door for her, and she slipped inside. It still smelled new, and her cotton dress slid across the leather seats. She ran her palm across the supple leather. So beautiful.

Reece got in on the other side and drove under a walnut tree, where he parked. He clicked on the auxiliary power. Music spilled from the radio, his favorite, Creedence Clearwater Revival. "Bad Moon Rising" blared from the speakers behind her. He slid out from under the steering wheel and pulled her into his arms. His lips came down on hers. She wanted to savor the sensation of his strong arms, let the music blot out her misgivings. Noah had never even embraced her. It wasn't allowed. This was wrong, too, but in this moment, she didn't care. All she knew was the touch of Reece's hands and the scent of the mint on his breath. She relished the mastery of his hands on her.

Reece lifted his head, and his breath whispered across her face. "You know how I feel about you. Marry me, Hannah. We can leave right now. I'll take care of you. You'll never have to worry about anything. You're mine— you know you are."

The bright joy beating against her ribs exploded into panic. She put her palms on his chest and pushed. "The bishop would put me under the *Meidung*." Why couldn't she have met Reece three months ago, before she was baptized? But even then she would have been faced with an impossible choice. She slid away to brace her back against the door, but still she couldn't bring herself to open it and walk away from him.

She was weak, so weak.

The thought of leaving her family made her lungs ache. Being Amish was as much a part of her body as the bone and sinew that kept her upright. Her life was about laughing and talking around the dinner table with loved ones, working side by side with her *mamm*. She'd never expected to find herself in this place, loving one of the *Englisch* when she was engaged to one of her own people.

"You could convert," she whispered.

"I'd have to give up my job, my life. I can't do it, Hannah. I wish I could. But I'll take care of you. There's a world out there you know nothing about. An exciting world of new experiences."

He was right. The Amish faith forbade military service or a job in law enforcement. If she went with him, she would have to give up everything. If he came with her, he'd be in the same position. It was an impossible situation. Oh, but she wanted to be with him! His power and strength made her feel safe when her world seemed filled with uncertainty. He knew so much—all about the world she'd seen only glimpses of.

The day after he'd saved her from some neighborhood bullies, he'd come into the café where she worked and ordered coffee at one of her tables. She'd been drawn to him from the first. She watched the way the other deputies deferred to him. And every minute she was conscious of his eyes watching her.

She shivered. Noah would be so hurt if he saw her in Reece's arms. She should have been stronger.

"Hannah?" Reece reached his hand toward her. "Come back over here, honey. It's okay. I won't push you. I just want to take care of you."

God would punish her if she accepted the invitation in his voice.

From somewhere, she found the courage to grab the door handle and yank it open. She found the motivation to turn and run toward home. Reece called after her, but she didn't slow. The Bible said to flee temptation. The cool wind brushed against her face and shivered down her back. It slowed the blood pounding along her veins, throbbing in her head. Her feet grew lighter as she sped from the bridge toward home. Harsh breaths heaved in and out of her chest.

Scalding shame swept through her veins. What had she become? Could this relationship be good if it caused her to sin so grievously against her parents, against Noah?

Her soles slid over gravel, and she stumbled, nearly went down on one knee. Daring a glance behind, she saw that Reece hadn't followed. She stood and hurried on, stopping on the road to catch her breath. Up ahead, the gaslights glowed yellow through the window. She hoped her parents thought she was still in the barn.

Composing her features, she stumbled toward the house, though she doubted serenity would do her much good. *Mamm* would take one look at her face and see the guilt etched there. Her mother could almost read her mind. Mamm knew what it was like to struggle against the strictures of their faith. Maybe Hannah could talk to her. *Mamm* would understand. She'd tell Hannah how to deal with these emotions.

The thought of leaving her Amish faith left a hollow sensation in Hannah's soul. She'd been taught—and believed—that they'd found the true path to God.

The house was quiet when she opened the back door. Where were her parents? She walked past the wringer washing machine in the utility room and stepped into the kitchen. The empty lemonade packets she'd left by the sink still lay there. Her mother had promised to clean up while Hannah did the barn chores.

"*Mamm*?" Hannah called. Only silence answered her.

Her feet stuck to spilled lemonade on the floor. Her mother never would have left the kitchen in such a state. Had someone taken ill? Alarms began blaring inside her head, and she quickened her pace to rush into the living room, still calling for her mother.

Her eyes fixed on a bumpy quilt hugging the middle of the living room floor and, oddly, a jumble of feet poked out from under it. Her mind fought to sort what her eyes saw. A quilt she'd never seen lay on the floor, black but bright with her mother's trademark hummingbird pattern. *Datt*'s size 13 black shoes extended from one side of the quilt, while *Mamm*'s size 5 shoes peeked out on the other side.

"Mamm?" she asked. Could this be a joke? Her father loved to tease. They'd hop up any minute, laughing at her gullibility.

No one moved. She bent down and touched her mother's exposed leg. It was cool. Hannah scrabbled back on her haunches. A scream built behind her teeth, then blared out with such force that her throat went raw. She couldn't stop screeching. The room began to swirl as she rolled onto her stomach and began to crawl. A red symbol had been painted on the wall. The wheel-and-spokes pattern imprinted itself on the backs of her eyes. A strange word was written just below it. Bile rose in the back of her throat, and she choked it back before stumbling out the door. She had to get to the greenhouse.

BUBBLE LIGHTS ATOP the four squad cars parked outside the farm-house strobed into the night. All available Parke County deputies had responded to the call to the Amish farmhouse. Deputy Matt Beitler parked his SUV behind his partner's truck and got out. He buttoned his coat against the wind. When the call came in, he had been enjoying his day off with Analise. He'd not been happy to be summoned to work.

He opened the back door and let Ajax, his year-old K9 search dog, out of the back. Taking a firm hold on the German shepherd's leash, he walked toward the house. The odor of manure from the barn wafted over him as he strode over the rough ground. Double homicide on an Amish farm. The Amish were peaceable and model citizens. Reece had sounded almost incoherent when he called, which made Matt break every speed record getting here. His partner wasn't often anything but calm and methodical. O'Connor loathed losing control of anything.

Generator-powered floodlights illuminated the yard. The sheriff had already called in the state boys, and technicians were busy looking for clues left by the perp. O'Connor was comforting a young Amish woman. In the dark, it was hard to make out more than her white bonnet.

O'Connor glanced up and saw him. With his arm around the young woman, he led her to the porch and seated her in a rocker. "I'll be right back," he said to her before turning to join Matt.

Matt watched the woman put her face in her hands. Her shoulders heaved. Her family or friends must be the murder victims. O'Connor would give him the details.

"Stay," Matt told the dog. He looped the leash around a hitching post and met his partner halfway, near the front door.

"Thanks for getting here so fast." O'Connor took off his hat and swiped at his blond hair.

Thirty, O'Connor was already showing signs of early balding. He wore a distracted expression. The detective was one of the most dedicated in the sheriff's department. He'd helped Matt get the job and had been quick to partner with him, even though he was the senior officer.

"Bad scene?"

"Worse than you can possibly imagine." In the glare of the lights, O'Connor looked deadly white. "Both of the parents." He nodded toward the young woman. "She found them covered with a quilt." He hesitated. "Their limbs are contorted, backs and necks arched."

"Strychnine poisoning?"

"Maybe."

Matt winced. Strychnine was nasty. The victim suffered muscle convulsions that got worse and worse until the poor victim was worn out and the lungs quit working. He wouldn't want to go that way. "You interrogate her?"

O'Connor looked away. "Not yet. I—I was in the area and heard her scream. When I got here, she was outside, in shock. I think she passed out briefly."

"We'd better talk to her." Matt started toward the woman, but his partner grabbed his arm.

"Go easy on her," O'Connor said. "In fact, let me handle it. She's all alone now."

Unusual in an Amish family. They bred like rabbits. "Easy? We need the truth before the trail goes cold. What's going on with her, boss?" Matt stared from his partner to the woman rocking with her arms clasped around herself. "Can I at least ask her some questions?"

O'Connor dropped his hand from Matt's arm. "Just be careful."

Matt approached the woman. "Ms. Schwartz? I'm Deputy Beitler. I'd like to ask you some questions."

In the brighter wash of light, he guessed her age between twenty and twenty-two. She looked almost colorless between her white bonnet and shapeless gray dress.

O'Connor stepped around him and took Hannah's hand. "Can you handle this now?" he asked the witness.

Matt shot his partner an incredulous glare. Since when did they tiptoe around witnesses? The media would be swarming the area any minute. But it was O'Connor's call. "Ms. Schwartz?" he said again.

She looked up. In the glare of lights, her eyes took on a golden glow, eyes like those of a tiger. He could see clear down to her soul, and there was only goodness. Matt shook off the thought. In his experience, the first place to look for a perp was among a victim's family and friends. Though in this case, he suspected a hate crime. But maybe she hated her parents. It happened.

She rocked back and forth, back and forth.

"Can you tell me what happened?"

"I came home from—from a walk and found my parents." Her voice was hoarse.

He could see she was still in shock. "What about before your walk? Was there anything out of the ordinary, anyone else you saw while you were out?"

She rubbed her head. "I—I don't remember."

He straightened from hunching over the notepad in his hand. "You don't remember?" O'Connor kept patting the woman on the shoulder. Matt had never seen his partner behave this way.

"Everything is a blur. I can't think." She rubbed fiercely at her temples as though trying to force her brain to cooperate. She looked up at him with a piteous expression. "It was my fault."

He clicked his pen on again. "What do you mean?"

"Of course it wasn't your fault, Hannah," O'Connor said, his voice a little too loud. "You need to rest. You'll remember more tomorrow."

Matt poised his pen over the paper. "How was it your fault?"

She raised her gaze to his then. "I mixed up the lemonade. It was a free sample we got in the mailbox. The poison was in that, wasn't it?"

"What makes you think they were poisoned?"

"The—the way they looked. Poisoned rats look like that." She shuddered. "We use it in the greenhouse."

He and O'Connor exchanged glances. O'Connor called over another deputy and asked him to check out the greenhouse.

Matt turned back to Hannah. "You prepared lemonade before you went for your walk?"

She nodded. "With lots of sugar because my *datt* has a sweet tooth. I poured glasses for everyone, including an extra for the guest. Someone was coming to look at *Mamm*'s quilts."

"Was it a man or a woman who came to buy a quilt?"

She scrunched her forehead and went even paler. "Oh, why can't I remember?" she moaned. "Let me think." She sat quietly a moment. "Cyrus. Cyrus Long. At least I think he was here tonight. My memory is all jumbled up. Maybe he was here last night. I can't remember."

"Can't or won't?" he asked as O'Connor rejoined them.

"Matt," O'Connor said with a warning in his voice. "I want to talk to you." He retreated a few steps from the woman.

Matt joined him. "What is *with* you, man? I've never seen you act like this. You're mucking up the investigation."

O'Connor glanced at Hannah, then back to Matt. "She was with me."

"With you? What does that mean?"

"I mean she slipped away to meet me." He crossed his arms over his chest. "We were together. That's all you need to know."

Matt couldn't wrap his mind around it. O'Connor was a good eight years older than the Schwartz woman, and as one of the *"Englisch,"* he should have been the last man she'd consider getting involved with. "I see," he said. "A little cradle robbing?" He knew he was pushing it. O'Connor was his boss, but that was hard to remember when they were friends, practically brothers, before they were partners.

"Shut up. You know nothing about it. I've been waiting all my life for someone like Hannah—sweet and good. When I'm with her, I'm better than I am alone. She had nothing to do with this crime," O'Connor said, his voice firm.

"You know as well as I do that the perp is usually known to the victim. You need to tell Sturgis. You can't work this investigation."

"This is *my* case. I know my limits, and I can handle it, Beitler."

"O'Connor, think about this. You're already on thin ice with that brutality charge."

O'Connor ran his hand through his hair. "And you think about how you got this job. And where you'd be if not for me."

It went against Matt's strong sense of right and wrong, but he finally shrugged. "Have it your way." Both men went back to the girl. "I'm going to take a look at the scene," Matt said.

Hannah trembled. "I don't have to go, do I?"

"No, you stay here with Detective O'Connor." At the house, Matt ducked under the yellow tape at the door and entered the living room. Halogen lights mounted around the room illuminated the bodies lying on the wood floor. "What have we got?" he asked Sturgis.

"Two adults, I'd guess in their early fifties. Poisoning, maybe strychnine from the contortions of the bodies. The autopsy will tell us." He nodded toward a heap of cloth. "A quilt was over them. The daughter removed it before we were called."

"Who called it in?" Matt asked.

"The daughter. She went out to the greenhouse and used the phone there."

"They have a phone?"

The captain shrugged. "The Amish use phones in their businesses. You ever notice the little phone booths out by the road in their communities? Some of the families will share a phone, but they only use it to make appointments or do business. They don't want it intruding on their personal lives."

Matt depended on his cell phone. He barely glanced at the quilt before allowing his gaze to wander the room. A sofa with worn seat cushions sat against the middle of the wall. Sturdy wooden tables, most likely handmade, flanked it with gaslights flickering on top of them. No rugs, no wall ornamentation or pictures.

A red symbol and words on the wall caught his attention. "Blood?" he asked.

"Paint." Sturgis stuck an unlit cigar in his mouth and chomped on it.

Matt wanted to chomp on something himself, anything to get the vile taste of murder out of his mouth. "It's a peace symbol. We know what this is all about?"

"Well, the Amish are all about peace. Maybe it's a hate crime in some twisted way."

"A hate crime against the Amish?"

"That was my first thought. It seems very well thought-out. The killer brought in everything he would need."

"Not everything," Matt said, his gaze lighting on a spilled pool of liquid. "Hannah Schwartz mixed up some lemonade that came in the mail."

"Might be coincidence."

"Maybe." But Matt would lay money on finding poison in the drink. "What about the foreign word? We know what it means?"

"Not yet. I think it's Greek."

Parke County was a quiet area, and murder was uncommon here. The largest town in this west-central Indiana community was Rockville, where Matt lived, with a population of 2,650. The joke in the area was that they had more covered bridges than residents. Driving through thick forests and hills was a peaceful pastime of Matt's. He'd been on the force less than a year, and this was his first murder. Seeing something like this was a shock he could not imagine getting used to.

Matt dragged his gaze from the bodies. "Let's get the Schwartz woman in here and ask her some more questions. I'll have one of the deputies take Ajax out and see if he can get a scent on the perp."

t w o

Sitting on the porch of the plain white farmhouse, Hannah couldn't quit rocking. The cold wind laden with the scent of water from the lake behind the house tugged at the strings of her bonnet and lifted the hem of her long skirt. The rocking calmed the screams still hunkering in her throat. *It's not true. It's not.*

The chant echoed in her heart over and over. This had to be a nightmare. She'd awaken any moment to find herself helping *Mamm* make noodles or shoofly pie. She'd hear *Datt* yodeling on his way in from the greenhouse.

She'd expected God to punish her for her sin. Even when she'd put her black shoes on the road to the bridge, the knowledge settled over her like one of her mother's heavy quilts. The heart commits sin first, and her heart was as black as the night. This punishment, though, was too much. She couldn't bear it.

Reece stayed close, but she huddled inside herself, undeserving of his comfort.

"Hannah, *liebling?*"

Hannah looked up to see her aunt Nora and her cousin Moe standing by the steps. "You're not yodeling now," she told Moe. Confusion contorted his face, and she knew she wasn't making sense.

Her aunt rushed up the steps with her arms outstretched. Hannah rose to meet her and practically fell into her arms. "They're dead," she sobbed. The screams she'd been holding back built in her throat, moving closer to her mouth. She clamped her teeth closed again.

Nora held her, their tears mingling. Hannah became conscious of Moe's big hand on her shoulder too. He wouldn't know what to say, but his presence calmed her. Nora had to be grieving too. She'd lost the brother she loved. How could a loving God allow something like this to happen? Hannah didn't understand.

"Ms. Schwartz?"

Hannah lifted her gaze to meet that of the young cop. She struggled past the cotton wool in her brain to find his name. Deputy Beitler. He was a merciless hunter, his blue eyes assessing her for any weakness. His gaze softened for a moment, then hardened to flint again.

He couldn't blame her any more than she blamed herself.

"Come inside with me a minute. There are some questions we need to ask, and we want you to see if anything is missing in the home."

"I can't," she whispered. Her gaze went past his shoulder to the black body bags being wheeled out of the house on gurneys. A scream rose in her throat, but she locked it behind her teeth. Her mouth and eyes watered with the effort of holding in her grief.

"Be strong, Hannah," Moe said. "We'll go with you if you need us."

Before she could answer, she heard the sound of buggy wheels and the deep vibration of her cousin Luca's voice calling to her. The blood rushed to her head, and without realizing she was moving, she found herself by the buggy as Luca swung his boots to the ground. He was more like a brother than a cousin to her, having lived with the Schwartz family since he was five.

The Amish didn't hold much with hugging, but in her desperation for comfort, she hurtled herself into her cousin's arms. He smelled of sweat and horse as his arms came around her awkwardly, though he hugged her as tightly as she clung to him. His chest heaved, and she knew he'd heard the news.

She lifted her head and saw his shocked gaze on the body bags being loaded into the emergency vehicle, but she couldn't turn and look too. One glimpse had been too much to bear.

"Both of them?" he whispered.

She wet her lips, but no words could make it past the tight constriction of her throat, so she merely nodded.

His gaze roamed her face as though to seek out some glimmer of hope. When he found none, his shoulders drooped. "It is God's will," he said. "Will we not accept both good and evil from his hand?"

It was the way of the Amish to accept whatever came, to turn the other cheek when injured. But both of Hannah's cheeks felt brutalized, left raw and bleeding. She had no more to give. Seeing the bodies of her parents had shattered her innocence. The pain in their faces had driven a spike deep into her heart and left a wound that would never heal. Why should they have had to suffer on her behalf? And there was another death, one few people knew about. *Mamm* was going to have a baby after many years of trying.

Luca released her, and she followed him as he went to where Reece stood with Deputy Beitler. Nora and Moe were a few feet away, and Moe was comforting his mother. Even if Luca was unaware of the detective's speculative stare, she was not. How could the man suspect they might be capable of such a horrible deed? He must know nothing about her or her people.

Luca stopped in front of the detectives. "I am Luca Schwartz, Hannah's cousin. I live here too. Can you tell me what has happened?"

"I'm Deputy Beitler. This is Detective O'Connor. I'm sorry to tell you that your aunt and uncle were murdered tonight." He paused when Luca made a soft moan. "I'm sorry for your loss. Can you tell me how you happened to be living with them?"

"My dad and Abe were brothers. My parents were killed in a buggy accident when I was five."

The deputy nodded toward the house. "I was about to ask your cousin to examine the home and see if anything is missing. I'd appreciate your cooperation as well. If we can pinpoint the motive, it might lead us to the killer."

Digging her feet into the dirt, Hannah prepared to tell him again that she couldn't go back in there, but Luca nodded and turned toward the house. Her gaze collided with the young deputy's, and she could have sworn she saw triumph in his eyes. Her dislike of him mounted.

Life wasn't a game, and it shouldn't be about power. Her heritage emphasized the good of the many, not self-interest and power. The *Englisch* persisted in getting the focus of life wrong. She clutched her wool cape more tightly and followed the men. Duty called, and she would do her best to answer it.

She glanced at Reece, and he answered the plea she put in her gaze by taking her elbow. The warm touch of his hand strengthened her. "I couldn't get through this without you," she whispered.

He gave her elbow a reassuring squeeze. "I'll protect you, Hannah. No matter what it takes. You can count on me."

She nodded, knowing he meant the words from the heart. With him by her side, she didn't feel so alone. His presence was better than her aunt's or her cousins'. Maybe because she knew how her family would react if they knew why she'd survived this night.

She wet her lips and forced herself to step through the door. The spot where she'd found her parents drew her gaze, but they were gone.

Cruel. Deputy Beitler was as cruel as the devil himself. She averted her gaze from the spot, and the room blurred as she blinked back moisture. She was overreacting. He was doing his job—finding out who killed her parents.

"Anything missing?" Deputy Beitler asked.

Hannah forced herself to study the room. The harsh glare from the lights the detectives had strung around the room threw everything out of focus. The stark illumination forced its way into the shadows, showed every defect with glaring detail, and made the room look small and forlorn. Was the couch really that worn, the wood floor that scuffed?

She knew what it must look like to these *Englischers*, even Reece. A modest home with the bare necessities. Their home had been filled with love and laughter, good food, acceptance. These men chased after fireflies that escaped their fingers, always pursuing bigger and better. A place like this held true riches.

The men sought what was in this very home, but they didn't know it.

A large wooden chest, six feet long and eight feet tall, occupied the east wall. The doors stood open—and the shelves were bare. A gasp escaped Hannah's lips.

"What is it?" Reece asked.

"*Mamm*'s quilts." Barely aware that she put one foot in front of the other, Hannah walked to the chest. At last count, there had been ten quilts, each worth at least fifteen hundred to two thousand dollars. But it wasn't the lost money she mourned. Her mother had a special touch with fabric, an unusual method of juxtaposing color and design that no one else could duplicate. The hummingbird design she'd stitched into many of her quilts had never been matched and was admired in their community and in the state.

Hannah could pick her mother's handiwork out of thousands of quilts. She turned her head to the men who had followed her. "They're gone, all of her quilts." Whirling, she went back to the center of the room. "Where's the quilt that covered them?"

"It's been taken in for evidence."

"I've never seen it before, but it was *Mamm*'s."

"How do you know if you've never seen it?" Reece's partner asked.

"The hummingbird pattern stitched into the quilt. No one else does that. You have to look close to see the fine detail, the tiny stitches, the design."

"Maybe it was made when she was younger, or when you were too small to remember," Reece suggested.

"Perhaps." Uneasiness tugged away the composure she'd begun to gather around herself.

"Anything else missing?" asked Deputy Beitler, his voice clipped.

Hannah glanced at her cousin. "Do you see anything, Luca?"

He shook his head. "I checked upstairs. All is in order. Why would anyone take the quilts?"

"How many?" Reece asked.

"Ten. Close to twenty thousand dollars." She winced inwardly at how flat her voice sounded. The deputy would think she cared about the money, when in fact it was the last thing on her mind.

"They'll probably start turning up on eBay," Beitler said.

"Or in shops that sell Amish quilts," Reece said.

Deputy Beitler pointed to the wall. "That symbol mean anything to you?"

Slowly she dragged her gaze to the garish red symbol she'd avoided since entering the house. She forced herself to study it, but it just looked like a cross with the beams sagging. The word under it contained letters she'd never seen before. "No." She swayed where she stood, and Reece took her arm.

"She's about dead on her feet," he said. "She needs to rest. No more questions tonight, Beitler."

The other deputy's scowl darkened. "I'm not through yet."

"You're done for tonight." Reece's voice was firm. "She's had all she can take."

He put his arm around Hannah, and she leaned into his embrace in spite of the raised eyebrows the action was sure to cause.

Luca shifted from one foot to the other. "Can we stay here?"

Beitler gave him a sharp look. "Not until we're done gathering evidence."

The last thing Hannah wanted was to stay here. "I want to stay with Aunt Nora," Hannah said. "She needs me too."

Luca nodded. "I'll come too."

Deputy Beitler took out his pen and pad. "What's the address? I'll likely have more questions tomorrow." Luca gave him the address, and he jotted it down.

Another deputy poked his head in the door. "We've got another body. Down by the pond. Ajax led us right to it."

THE BODY LAY half-submerged in the pond along the back of the property. The contorted limbs told Matt the man had died the same painful death as the family inside. "Any ID?"

"Yeah," one of the deputies said. "Driver's license belongs to a Cyrus Long."

Only when Hannah gasped behind him did Matt realize she and Luca had followed him and O'Connor. He swiveled on his heel to face them. "This the guy who was here tonight?" In the wash of the halogen lights, Hannah's skin held no color. Her gaze stayed fixed on the body. He moved to obstruct her vision, and the horror in her eyes began to recede.

She looked up at him then. "Yes. He's our neighbor." Her mouth dropped open, then closed. "He said he wanted to buy one for his wife, Ellen." Her gaze focused on Matt again. "Her birthday is next week."

Matt took the pad and pen out of his pocket. "How well did you know them?"

Luca answered. "As well as any *Englisch* neighbor. We were friendly, but our lives went in different directions."

Hannah nodded.

"How did he get this far?" O'Connor asked, still inspecting the body. "If the perp poisoned him, too, how did he get out of the house?"

"Good question. Maybe the coroner can tell us." He stepped away to talk to O'Connor in private. "Let's start canvassing the neighbors, checking Nyesville and other towns around the county. See if anyone has heard threats directed toward the Amish."

O'Connor nodded. "We had that rash of barn arsons five years ago. Three Amish barns were torched. Maybe it's related. We never found the offender."

"Hey, look at this, Matt," one of the deputies called.

The plastic bag the deputy pointed to held chocolate chip cookies. Matt glanced around the area. No quilts, but the pond was right here. "Maybe this is the murder weapon. And maybe this is the perp. Let's dredge for the quilts. Maybe he tossed them in the water."

HANNAH'S WORLD HAD gone dark even though sunlight streamed in the windows of her aunt's home. Through unblinking eyes, Hannah lay on the bed looking up at a water stain on the ceiling.

Downstairs, Aunt Nora clanged pots. She could smell the aroma of coffee and shoofly pie, something that would normally have her scooting down the steps. No one made shoofly pie like Aunt Nora.

The upstairs felt quiet, almost as though it mourned with her. The Amish community had circled around the past week, trying to love the pain away. Their kindness wasn't working.

A tap sounded on the door, and she tried to ignore it. She felt no hunger, felt nothing more than the slight weight of the blanket on her body and the beginning thump of a migraine in her left temple.

"Hannah? Are you awake?" called her best friend, Sarah, through the wood panel.

She struggled into a sitting position. "Come in, Sarah." She'd thought Sarah would come this morning. She lived two farms over.

Her friend eased into the room as though she feared her footstep on the bare wood floorboards would cause a fresh spate of sobs. She carried a tray of steaming coffee and a sliver of shoofly pie on a saucer. "I brought you some breakfast." Her dark blue dress and white apron were pressed and starched, and her hair wasn't drawn back quite so tightly as usual under her *kapp*. Sarah had a crush on Luca, and Hannah wondered if he was downstairs too.

The aroma of the molasses pie filled the room, but Hannah turned away from it. "I'm not hungry." She swung her legs over the edge of the mattress. She had to get up, face the day.

Sarah shut the door behind her with one foot. "Try to eat, Hannah. You can't mope. God's will be done."

"If one more person says that to me, I will scream." She swallowed against the constriction in her throat and composed herself. "I know God is sovereign, but it's not fair, Sarah." She rubbed at her temple.

"You have a headache?" Sarah moved to sit on the bed. She took Hannah's hand and began to apply pressure to the fleshy pad between the thumb and the first finger.

Hannah's headache began to ease almost immediately. "Thanks, Sarah. Why couldn't God punish me instead of them?"

"How is it your fault? The poison was in the cookies Cyrus brought."

"But it was my sin." Confession trembled on her tongue. "God's punishment is more than I can bear."

"You haven't . . . done something . . . with Noah, have you?"

If only it were that simple. She and Noah could kneel at the next meeting and confess. "No. He's been a perfect gentleman." She lifted her head. "I—I've been seeing someone else, someone *Englisch*."

Sarah put her hand to her mouth. "Oh no, Hannah! You must turn away from him. Confess it to the bishop. It will all be forgiven. Who is it?"

"It doesn't matter." Hannah stood and went to grab her dress from the hook on the wall. "I'd better get dressed. The funeral begins in two hours." She went down the hall to the bathroom and made herself presentable.

Hannah had lied. It *did* matter. She was lost, abandoned. How could she stay here among her people and be reminded daily that she'd caused something so bad? And what if God wasn't finished? Maybe he would do more to harm her loved ones because of her sin. Besides, she longed for Reece, for his strength and take-charge attitude. He'd only been able to see her in his professional capacity, but when their eyes met, she knew he ached for her pain.

Sarah had gone by the time Hannah entered the kitchen, a big rectangular room occupied by cabinets along the far end and the table and chairs at the other. Aunt Nora stood by the sink. About five feet in height, she was nearly as big around as she was tall, and she turned to envelop Hannah in an embrace smelling of mint from the meadow tea she'd likely gathered minutes ago.

"My dear," Nora crooned.

"I want them back, Aunt Nora," she whispered.

Her aunt smoothed her hair. "I know, *liebling*. So do I."

At least Aunt Nora wasn't offering platitudes. "Why would Cyrus do this?"

Her aunt pulled away and turned to the refrigerator. She shook her head. "You must eat."

Hannah stared at the older woman's back. What was that brief expression of disagreement in her aunt's eyes? "Aunt Nora, do you suspect someone other than Cyrus? He had the cookies in his hand. The clerk saw him make them in his bakery."

Moe stuck his head in the door. "The buggy is ready. We need to go."

Her aunt turned to the door. "Let's go, Hannah. We'll be late." She snatched a wool cape off the hook and went out the back door.

Hannah followed, but her thoughts swirled. Did her aunt know Cyrus?

three

"Hannah, you're going out to work in the world. Make sure you hold yourself separate. Always remember your traditions and your faith."

PATRICIA SCHWARTZ

They were four lone survivors in an unfamiliar world. The heavy *clop-clop* of the horse's hooves struck the pavement like a death bell clanging as Hannah huddled in the back of the buggy beside her aunt. Luca sat in front with Moe and guided the horse past bare winter fields whose only signs of life were the remains of cornstalks sticking through the muddy soil. The black horse-drawn hearses, two of them, in front of her cousin's buggy crawled under a leaden sky. The dark seemed to press down with a heavy hand that she could not escape. The cemetery was on the edge of her father's farm. Narrow wooden stakes bearing only the initials of the deceased dotted the hillside just past the tall maple trees that protected the grave sites. The grave diggers had left a trail of mud across the wet grass.

At over two weeks after death, the burials were long overdue, but they'd had to wait until the autopsies were completed and the bodies released. The funeral service itself was a long blur held at the church—a few hymns sung without instrumental accompaniment, some Scripture, and a sermon. The service was hardly different from any other Sunday gathering, yet it was not the same at all. Everything was changed now, as radically different as if Hannah had awakened in some strange world. Friends mouthed sympathy, but not a word penetrated.

For an instant she longed for a service like the *Englisch* had, a memorial where friends and family were allowed to speak their minds about their loved ones. The minister had mentioned her parents only in passing.

She spoke to her hands. "I couldn't have survived this without you, Luca."

He didn't look at her. "*Ja*, they were like my own parents. I have no one now. No one but you."

Luca turned his horses into the cemetery lane behind the hearses just as the first cold drops of rain began to strike Hannah's face. He pulled back on the reins, and the horse slowed, then stopped. He clambered down and held up a hand to assist her. The serenity of his expression gave her pause. Wasn't he just as tormented as she was?

The wind whipped her skirt and tugged tendrils of hair loose from her bonnet, but the chilly air wasn't nearly as disquieting as the icy cold inside her body. Hanging on to his arm, she followed her cousin to the yawning graves. Hot moisture sprang to her eyes at the dark holes scarring the earth.

She couldn't bear to see her parents put down into the black earth. Not them. She looked away, stumbling under the weight of her doubt. Had she absorbed so much of the *Englisch* way of thinking in her little contact with them? When her grandparents had died, she was able to accept it. They had lived good, long lives. But this loss left Hannah longing for the touch of her mother's hand, for the sound of her father's yodel as he walked from the greenhouse.

If anyone deserved to be in heaven, it was her parents. She knew that was true, but heavy mourning muffled her conviction that they were in a better place.

Aunt Nora embraced her, and they both nearly toppled, but Luca righted them with a steady hand.

"Hannah, you're making a spectacle," he whispered. "Pull yourself together."

"Hush, Luca," her aunt said. "She's the one who found them. Can you not have some compassion?" She hugged Hannah tight. "Go ahead and cry, *liebling*."

A few wayward tears slipped down Hannah's cheeks, but she managed to choke back the sob that bubbled in her throat. How could Luca be so calm, almost serene? Pulling away from her aunt, she drew herself erect, tipping her chin into the air. If they could do it, so could she. Others would be looking to her to be an example. The bishop would expect decorum.

From the corner of her eye, she saw Noah Whetstone coming across the sodden grass toward her. Strong, both in body and in spirit. Such a good man. Why then did she turn her head and pretend she didn't see him? Why did dread coat her limbs with lethargy? She'd promised herself to him. Their wedding was only three months away.

He was so . . . boring. The thought of listening to his slow voice across the dinner table for the next fifty years made her shudder. He never talked of anything but lumber and building materials. Reece spoke of exotic places he wanted to show her—Hawaii at sunset with its flood of color, the scent of Irish bogs, the sound of the chimes at Big Ben. A world out of her league and out of her reach. She'd asked her father to continue school because that was the only way she'd ever see some places. The Amish forbade air travel. But her father had refused. Reece wanted to show her everything, let her chase every experience.

She forced a smile of welcome at Noah when she could no longer pretend, then her gaze tracked the crowd—mostly her own people but some reporters and a few *Englisch* neighbors as well. She longed to see Reece's face. She knew he would come. His worldliness strengthened him, and she could draw from his wells.

Her gaze fell on the caskets being carried to the graves. Her sin had caused this. She hated that she still yearned for the *Englischer*, for the exciting world he offered.

She was wanton, evil.

Noah's big hand fell on her shoulder. "Hannah?"

She turned her head, moving so his hand fell away. "Hello, Noah. Thanks for coming."

"Did you think I would not?" His hazel eyes held worry and questions. He took her arm to escort her to the open graves.

"No, no, of course I knew you would come," she said, falling into step beside him.

He'd been by the house nearly every day since the murders, and the strain between them had grown instead of lessened. He had to know something was wrong. Steeling herself for what must come, she tightened her hold on her emotions. She must not disgrace her family this day.

Two women hurrying over the uneven ground caught her attention. For a moment she forgot to breathe. The older woman looked like her mother dressed in *Englisch* clothes. The same auburn hair as Hannah's own, cut in a stylish layered cut, barely touched her chin. Only when the women neared did Hannah draw in a breath. Of course it wasn't *Mamm*. It must be her sister, Cathy, the aunt Hannah had never met.

She stepped out to meet them. The older woman embraced Hannah, and it felt like hugging *Mamm*. Hannah clung to her, closing her eyes and pretending for just a moment that the woman was her mother. But her mother never wore strong cologne, and the clothes were all wrong. Hannah pulled away.

The woman kept her hands on Hannah's shoulders. "You must be Hannah. You're the spitting image of Patty."

Hannah had never heard her mother referred to as Patty. She liked the informal, breezy nickname. "You're Aunt Cathy?"

Cathy nodded and dropped her hands. "I'm so sorry, sweetie." Tears flooded her eyes. "Your mother was a wonderful woman."

"I know," Hannah whispered. Her gaze went to the younger woman, about her own age. "Are you Mary?" She'd seen a picture of her cousin when she was about ten.

Mary nodded. "We look enough alike to be sisters," she said.

Subtle touches of makeup enhanced Mary's skin and eyes. Hannah stared into Mary's face and saw what she could be if she were *Englisch*. The stylish clothes, the cute hairstyle. She was aware of how she must look to these two women: a frumpy dress, lank hair wound up on top of her head and covered with a prayer kapp, sensible black shoes.

She didn't deserve the life she led now, a life supposedly devoted to a God who had punished her beyond what she could bear. It was hard to even form her lips around acceptable words, to manage a smile. "Thank you for coming," she said. "How did you hear about it?"

"Your aunt Nora called me." Cathy's eyes reddened. "I wish I'd come sooner. I never got a chance to tell Patty I was sorry. Now it's too late."

Hannah caught the movement of Luca's arm from where he stood near the grave site. "The service is about to start."

The short service passed in a blur. When it was Hannah's turn to drop dirt onto the casket, as was the custom among her people, she came to full awareness. Noah gave her a little shove forward. She scooped a handful of mud. The earth clung to her fingers, the cold penetrating to the bone, and refused to drop onto the casket.

It was like her own refusal to let go of her family.

She shook her hand and finally succeeded in tossing down clumps of mud. Holding her head up, she turned from the open graves and found herself facing Ellen Long across the field. When Hannah inhaled sharply, her cousin Luca glanced at her with a question in his eyes.

In Hannah's mind, the strychnine in the cookies proved Cyrus's guilt, though no one could understand the reason he would take two lives and then his own. The detectives were still investigating. They'd questioned his wife, who'd tearfully proclaimed that she knew nothing about it.

Luca turned to look. "It's Mrs. Long. We need to talk to her."

Hannah shook her head, her gaze still on the young woman in the sky-blue suit. "Not me. Luca, her husband killed my parents." She couldn't tear her gaze away from the pretty blonde. She embraced the bitterness and anger rising in her chest. The man had some sick and twisted reason to kill her family. It wasn't Hannah's fault.

Didn't Ellen realize her presence here would cause them all pain? The young woman was struggling to walk in inappropriate heels that sank into the mud. Her hair drooped in wet strands around her face. From here it looked as though black ringed her eyes. Hannah rejected the pity struggling to emerge from her emotions. Surely the woman had known her husband hated the Schwartz family. Maybe she had participated in the murders. Cyrus had to have had an accomplice, someone to run off with *Mamm*'s quilts.

The bishop approached. "How are you doing, Hannah?"

She wanted to scream that she couldn't answer that question one more time, but she just hung her head and said nothing. If she could wish herself away from here, she'd leave in a heartbeat. Everyone expected so much from her, but she had nothing left to give.

"Hannah, Mrs. Long is here. You need to speak to her, tell her you forgive Cyrus."

Luca took her forearm in a firm grasp. "We'll do it now. Both of us."

"No!" Hannah jerked her arm out of Luca's grasp, and he let his hand drop. "We have no one left. I don't want to talk to her." With a shock, she recognized that the hatred she felt toward Ellen Long was a thin veneer over her own self-hatred. Hannah, not Ellen, was the one who was guilty. God had merely used the Longs to punish her.

"You have to forgive, Hannah. You know it is required." The bishop took her firmly by the arm and began tugging her toward the woman, who stood with a pleading smile, watching them approach.

Noah flanked Hannah's other side, his hand on her arm as well. She felt as though she were being dragged to the gallows. Something broke in

Hannah. She dug her heels into the soft earth that had received the earthly remains of her family. "No, I won't," she said, her voice rising above the shriek of the wind. She tore herself free from their grips.

A flash of light caught her eye, and she saw a sheriff's car pull to a stop on the soft shoulder of the dirt road. Reece got out of the driver's side. He saw her and jogged to meet her. "Are you okay?"

Luca moved toward her again as Hannah shrank against Reece. "Come, Hannah. It must be done."

Reece's strong arm came around her. "Don't touch her. She doesn't want to go with you."

"Please stay out of this, Deputy. It's something Hannah must do for her own good." Luca attempted again to tug her away from Reece.

Reece's other arm came up, and he tore Luca's hand away from Hannah's arm. "She's free to go if she wants, Mr. Schwartz, but I won't have her forced. Hannah, do you want to go with him?"

"No!" She burrowed closer against Reece's barrel chest.

"You heard the lady." Reece turned away with his arm still around her and moved her away from Luca. Only Hannah saw his smile.

If she had to talk to Ellen, she would babble out her own guilt. She couldn't forgive the Long family any more easily than she could forgive herself. They were all in this together, if everyone just knew the truth.

Reece moved her away from the rest of the group. "You're still shaking. What did he want?"

Hannah couldn't talk about it. She couldn't face what she'd become. Inhaling the spicy scent of his cologne, she knew he would rescue her. She had to be brave enough to let him. "I'll marry you," she gasped. "But we must go now, quickly, before they can stop us."

Reece's hands tightened on her shoulders. "Are you sure, honey? There's no going back."

"I'm sure." She'd chosen her course. God had rejected her. She was anathema.

four

The new clothes Reece had insisted on buying Hannah were alien, strange to her skin. The skirt just touched her knees, and her arms were bare for the first time other then when she bathed. She tugged on the V-neck of the blouse and wished for a shawl in the dimly lit Market Street Grill. Trains chugged around the bar, but she kept her gaze averted. Bars were where the devil and his crowd hung out. Why would her new husband bring her here? Wabash. She'd never been farther than Nyesville.

She stared out the window. The trees hadn't leafed out yet, and the small downtown looked as barren as she felt with *Englisch* all around her. The breaded pork tenderloin sandwich in front of her nearly covered her plate, and she had only managed a few bites.

This wasn't the way she'd pictured her wedding day. It was supposed to be on a Tuesday, with a church service followed by a daylong celebration of food and fellowship. She should be wearing a blue dress and black kapp. Even the food they'd eaten today was alien. There was no chicken and stuffing with lots of celery, no creamed celery. All the extra celery seed *Mamm* had saved to plant in the garden this year for her wedding would go to waste.

She chewed food she couldn't taste and sipped chlorinated water. She glanced down at the golden band on her hand. She was a married woman. No, more than that, a married *Englisch* woman. Even during her *rumspringa*, her running around time, she'd never been tempted to desert her faith. Yet here she was.

"Pretty ring, isn't it?" Reece said, reaching over to squeeze her hand.

"Never have I worn jewelry," she said. Reece beamed proudly until she added, "It feels very strange. And sinful."

His smile faded. "Finish your dinner, honey."

He sounded as tired as she felt. She picked up the sandwich and tried to chew another bite. All she really wanted was to flee the place, run back to the comfort of her family. But they were dead, all dead. Her duty was to obey her husband, to love him and be as good a wife as her mother had been.

He smiled at her. "We'll have a good life, Hannah. I've already found a job here in Wabash. Our apartment is across the street. It's just been renovated, and I think you'll like it."

"Downtown? Not in the country?" She'd rarely even been to town, and the constant hubbub of cars disoriented her.

"Do you always mean to question me, Hannah? I know you don't like to be told what to do, but I'm your husband. We'll be happier if you follow my leadership. This is a strange world to you, but I know what's best for us."

"No, no, I'm sorry. Of course you do." She was doing this all wrong. "You are my husband. I always plan to obey you. But so many things are foreign to me. Be patient, please, Reece." Her rebellion was what had killed her parents. She needed to be more submissive.

His gaze softened. "You'll learn everything, sweetheart." He gestured at her plate. "It's obvious the food is not to your liking. Let's go see our new home."

She stood so hastily she nearly knocked over the chair. Staggering a little in the unfamiliar heels, she held on to his arm all the way out to the curb. Quaint Victorian buildings lined the street. Knowing the name of the town—Wabash—made her feel still connected to her roots in the Wabash Valley three hours west of here. Dodging the cars coming down the one-way street, he helped her across to the other side. She stepped onto the curb beside the stone elephants.

He led her to the left to a set of glass doors.

He stopped to dig in his pocket. "I've already got the key."

She went past him through a large glass door at the end of a store called Modoc's. Inside, the entry was spacious, and a wide staircase ascended to the next floor. The Victorian woodwork looked freshly refinished. "I like this," she said.

"Finally, something meets the approval of the princess." He was smiling, but there was an edge to his tone.

She tried to push away the hurt as she hurried up the majestic stairway. It would take time for them to adjust to one another. They were practically strangers, even taking into account their snatched moments together. It was the pressure of the past few days that had changed things. Once they settled in, he would be the sweet Reece with whom she'd fallen in love.

Reece caught up with her at the top of the steps and pointed to a doorway on the right. He unlocked it and swung it open for her to enter. She glanced around and smiled. "The sitting room is small, but it's cozy."

"Living room," he corrected. "You need to start getting the terminology right."

"Living room." She walked through the furnished space to the tiny kitchen. No window at all, but she kept a smile on her face. "It's all new."

"So's the bathroom." He showed her the miniscule bathroom just past the kitchen.

She spied another small room off the hall. "A nursery!"

He frowned. "A computer room. Let's get one thing straight right now. I don't want any kids, hon."

Her smile faltered. "Oh, Reece, you don't mean it. I want lots of babies."

"I'm serious. If you get pregnant, you can have an abortion."

Her limbs turned to ice. "It would be a mortal sin. That's taking a life."

"That's a matter of opinion. Enough about sin, Hannah. I'm sick of hearing the word. We don't need children. All we need is you and me, happy together."

"Why don't you want babies, Reece?" She edged closer. "They bring so much joy to a house."

His expression turned stony. "I was a foster kid with nothing that was sacred, nothing that belonged to me. I was always the last person anyone cared about. I knew someday I'd find a woman who would love me only. Aren't I enough for you, Hannah?" His gaze searched hers.

"Of course you are, Reece!" She cupped his cheek in her palm. "I love you. We won't talk about it now."

"I won't change my mind, hon." He turned his head and kissed her palm. "But we'll have a good life without kids." His smile turned tender. "Let me show you the bedroom."

A DREARY GRAY day held Rockville in its grip. It was a shock after the sunshine in Hawaii. Matt glanced around the room of assembled deputies. "What do you mean Reece is gone?"

"He ran off with the Amish chick," one of the men said. "After the funeral."

Matt sank onto a chair. That's what he got for taking off two weeks for his honeymoon. "What about the investigation?"

"The poison was in the cookies. Long was seen making the cookies, and he's dead."

It seemed too easy to Matt. "Motive? And if he knew the cookies were tainted, why would he eat one?"

"According to the coroner, he likely either inhaled the strychnine or absorbed it through his skin during the baking of the cookies. It was accidental." Captain Sturgis cleared his throat. "The motive is unclear, but that's the way it is sometimes. People do crazy things and we never figure out why."

Matt had seen plenty of that over the years. "You find the quilts?"

"We dredged the lake, but nothing turned up."

"Then he had an accomplice."

"Probably, but we have no leads. No one saw a thing. It's been a frustrating case. It's your baby now, with Reece gone. If you can find anything, you'll be a hero. How was the honeymoon?" A sly grin crept out.

"Great." He left the other deputies and went to his office. Maybe Reece had left him a note. It was unlike his partner—his foster brother, in fact—to take off without a word. Matt rummaged through his desk but found nothing but a new report on a burglary of a local convenience store. Maybe Reece had left something with Trudy, their grandmother. Matt dialed her number.

"Matthew, I never even got a postcard," she said when she picked up the phone.

Stupid caller ID didn't even give him a minute to get an explanation in. "Analise was sick a lot. Migraines. I took care of her and didn't get outside much."

"She should have that checked."

"That's what I told her, but she's had them for years. Hey, did you know Reece ran off with an Amish girl? Hannah Schwartz." Silence on the other end. "Trudy?"

"When did this happen?"

"I guess after the funeral. I just heard about it. I take it he didn't come to tell you good-bye? Or leave my gun with you?"

"What gun?"

"He borrowed my revolver." And Matt planned to get it back when he found Reece. It wasn't the gun that upset Matt, though. It was the way Reece had just disappeared without a word.

"After all I did for that boy," his grandmother muttered.

At nearly thirty, Reece was hardly a boy, but Matt said nothing. She needed to vent. "He'll probably call you once he gets settled."

Matt used to be jealous of the relationship Reece had with Trudy, but he'd accepted it long ago. There was no use crying over something he couldn't change. If she wanted to love a foster kid more than her own grandson, he'd let her.

THE SOFTLY GLOWING candles on the table scented the room with cinnamon. Hannah paced the living room, pausing occasionally to listen for Reece's footsteps on the staircase. She willed herself not to cry. The special dinner was ruined. The pasta sat in a milky, soggy mess in the bottom of the pan, and the spaghetti sauce had burned in spite of the low heat. She should have shut it off and warmed it up when he got home.

She'd wanted tonight, their first anniversary, to be perfect. Reece should have been home nearly three hours ago. He'd called from Scotty's Bar two hours ago and said he'd be there in fifteen minutes. She should have known better. When he got to swapping stories with his friends, he lost all sense of time. The outfit she wore should please him, but she was tempted to change out of the short, tight skirt into something more modest and comfortable. He didn't care anyway. She tugged on the plunging neckline. Her feet ached from the spiky high heels. These revealing clothes embarrassed her, but he always reminded her she was supposed to please him, not herself. At least he hadn't made her go to the bar with him tonight to show her off like he did sometimes.

She dragged herself to the tiny kitchen to begin cleaning up the mess. Her eyes burned, and she wished her aunt Nora had a phone. Here in Wabash, she felt so isolated. Reece refused to take her to church or let her meet anyone other than the leering men in the bars. Was this normal for an

Englisch family? She had no way of knowing. One Sunday she'd slipped away while he was working to attend the Presbyterian church up the hill on Miami Street, but when he found out, he'd been so angry he'd frightened her and she never tried it again.

She heard the front door open and wiped her hands on her apron. Taking it off, she drew a deep breath, then walked down the hall to the living room to meet him.

He wore a smile and held a bouquet of drooping flowers. "There's my girl," he said, his voice slurred. His eyes were bright as he stared at her. "Come give me a kiss, honey. You look good enough to eat."

The thought of his drunken kisses made her shudder, and she stopped where she was. "Did you eat?"

"Of course not. I wanted to eat with my beautiful wife." His smile widened. "Come here, Hannah."

She turned and headed back toward the kitchen. He wasn't going to come home three hours late and then expect her to be happy to see him. "I'll fix you a hamburger or something. Dinner is ruined."

"Ruined?" He trailed after her into the miniscule kitchen. "If you loved me the way you should, you'd have held it for me."

She whirled. "You were supposed to be home three hours ago. Even if you'd come home two hours ago like you promised, it would have been okay. But there's nothing left now. It's all ruined." Tears ran down her cheeks, and she swiped them with the back of her hand.

His gaze rambled around the kitchen and took in the soggy pasta, the crusted-over sauce, the mushy vegetables. "I had things to do," he said. "You have no right to question me. Don't I give you everything you want? I buy you pretty clothes and makeup. Perfume and jewelry."

"And I *hate* it!" Unable to stop her voice from rising, she tugged the earrings from her ears. "I feel like a harlot most of the time. Like all you care about is my looks. If you loved me, you wouldn't keep me cooped up in this apartment with no friends and nothing to do."

From the way his color rose, she knew she'd gone too far, but she couldn't bite back the hot words that continued to spew. "You won't even let me have a baby!" She picked up the pot of pasta and dumped it in the sink. She wished she had the nerve to throw the sauce on the floor, but then she'd just have to clean it up herself.

He grabbed her by the shoulders. "Get hold of yourself, Hannah. How dare you talk to me like that? I'm your husband. You promised to love and obey me."

Her rage evaporated as quickly as it had boiled. Yes, her duty was to love this man no matter what, but why did it have to be so hard? He shook her when she didn't answer, and his face turned a more mottled red.

He shoved her away from him. "After all I've done for you, this is the thanks I get?"

Her back hit the counter, and she reached behind herself to grab it so she didn't fall. Her face flamed. "You shoved me." Her voice shook. He'd never lifted a finger to her.

"I'll do more than shove you if you don't obey me." The color drained from his face, and he advanced toward her.

She cringed and lifted her hands in a protective move, but before she got them high enough, his hand lashed out and his palm smacked her cheek. Pain flared on her face, but shock stole her whimper. His gaze bored through her, and a muscle jumped in his cheek. She stared into the face she'd kissed and caressed, into the warm brown eyes that held no trace of a smile or love. Did she even know him? Had she ever? The Reece she thought she knew never would have lifted a hand to her. His face crumpled then, and she caught a glimpse of her real husband.

He reached toward her. "I'm sorry. I can't believe I did that." He folded her into his arms and whispered in her hair. "Forgive me, Hannah. It won't ever happen again."

Even as she mouthed the words, "I forgive you," she wondered if life would ever be the same.

f i v e

"*The world will tell you to serve yourself first. But don't listen,*
Hannah. Serve others and you'll find true happiness."

PATRICIA SCHWARTZ

How'd he ever let her talk him into coming up here? Reece eyed the
Amish women strolling through the flea market with a gaggle of
children following them. Seeing all the Amish here in Shipshewana was
likely to make her discontented, and he'd had enough of that to deal with
over the past four years.

"Isn't this fun?" Hannah said, smiling up at him.

When she smiled like that, all was right in his world, and he let his irritation drop. "Want some caramel corn?" When she nodded, he stopped at
another vendor.

The flea market at Ship held every Tuesday and Wednesday through the
summer was famous all over Indiana and Michigan. The large space was
packed with vendors hawking everything from purses to yard ornaments. He
was bored already with the items. He'd rather look at guns or something.

When he turned to hand Hannah her popcorn, he found her deep in conversation with an Amish woman. He'd die if she ever left him to go back to her people. His gut tightened until she turned back around with a huge smile.

"There's a big quilt display the next row over." She grabbed her popcorn and lit out down the aisle without even waiting for him to say it was okay.

He would never understand her obsession with quilts. Why did she never look at him with the same concentration she gave them? His thoughts were always of her first, and he'd hoped for the same from her. He darted after her, intending to grab her arm and insist they go back to the car, but a man with a wagon got in his way, then three children darted in front of him. By the time he disentangled himself, she was nowhere in sight. He bit back a curse and stalked down the aisles. Nearly half an hour passed before he found her.

She sat at a picnic table with her shoulders slumped and tears on her cheeks. When she saw him, she rose and brushed at her wet face. "They weren't there."

"Would you just stop looking? The quilts will never show up."

She would never find her mother's stolen quilts, but that wasn't what concerned him. He hated catching that faraway expression on her face. Maybe she wished she'd never left her people, wished she'd married the yodeling farm boy Noah. He couldn't abide the thought.

"What? They have to be somewhere, Reece."

"I forbid you to go looking anymore, Hannah." He said it as sternly as he could with other people close by. She bit her lip, and her face took on the mulish expression he hated, but she just bowed her head and nodded. "Let's go," he told her. "We're done here. I want to get back to Wabash."

It had been a mistake to bring her here. She needed to forget the old life. Concentrate on him and being a good wife. After four years of training, he should have managed to eradicate the last traces of her defiance. She knew how her obsession bothered him, but she continued to search anyway. When the quilts were on her mind, he took second place.

She followed him out to the truck. "Can we stop at Blue Gate Restaurant for lunch?" she asked when they got into the hot cab.

He glanced at her bowed head. All he wanted was to get out of town before she stopped and talked to every Amish woman around. "Sure, honey. Just give me a smile first." He waited until her head came up and her smile broke out, then drove to the restaurant. They joined the throng of people flooding into the place. It had been expanded to seat more than six hundred people, and the crowd annoyed him.

He ate a whole jar of the peanut butter spread and asked for more while Hannah just picked at a piece of homemade bread. "I thought you wanted to eat here, but you're hardly touching anything."

"My stomach is a little upset."

He caught the longing on her face when she engaged their Amish waitress, a young girl, in conversation. So much for learning something from the scolding. He shouldn't have brought her in here. She needed to be as far from these people as possible. She'd nagged him for years about finding an Amish community. Of all things, she wanted him to convert. He'd nixed that idea quickly enough, but she wouldn't let it rest.

After the girl brought their meals, he bolted his down. "Let's go."

She left her spoon in the half-eaten bowl of homemade chicken-noodle soup and followed him out to the truck. For the whole ride home, she drooped against the door and stared out the window. When the truck zoomed around a buggy, she tensed and stared at the occupants.

"Riding in a buggy is different from riding in a vehicle," she said.

"Yeah, the truck's faster." The last thing he wanted was to talk about the Amish. He didn't want her longing for her old life. He'd given up everything for her.

"You're not insulated in a buggy. You're part of the community. We would call to friends out the open windows, smell the flowers, feel the breeze."

"Do you always have to disagree with me, Hannah?" His hands gripped the steering wheel. There wasn't an ounce of gratitude in her. After all he'd done for her, she still longed for her family. It wasn't right.

They drove in silence until the truck got out of Shipshewana. She fiddled with her seat belt, adjusting it across her stomach in a weird way he'd never seen. He was about to tell her to quit it when she folded her hands in her lap and tipped her head to look at him.

"Reece, I have something to tell you."

"What is it?"

"I'm pregnant."

His foot came up and jammed on the brakes. He steered the truck to the side of the road, and a car zipped around him, blaring its horn. The male occupant thrust out his middle finger and shouted something as he flew past. On another day, Reece might have gunned the truck after him and tailgated him, but he was too shaken to react.

He turned to stare her in the face. "What did you say?" Maybe he'd misheard. His pulse was thumping in his ears, and he could hardly draw in a lungful of air.

She shrank away from him with her hand up for protection. "We're going to have a baby, Reece." Her smile was too bright. "Don't you think it's time? We've been married over four years."

"No, it's not time. I'll take you to a clinic for an abortion." He clenched his fists but had the self-restraint not to hit her. Maybe it was an accident. If it wasn't, she'd have to be taught a lesson for her own good.

"I'm not having an abortion." Her chin jutted out. "I'm not, Reece. You can't make me. I—I'll leave you first." Her voice trembled just a little.

He couldn't believe he was hearing those words from her mouth. "You think your family would take you back in? After leaving your husband? You know they won't."

She grabbed his arm with both hands. "Don't make me choose between you and the baby. You think I'll ignore you for the baby, but I won't, I promise. I love you."

"You've already chosen the brat over me." He couldn't believe it—couldn't comprehend that she'd defy him so completely. The unfamiliar emotion shaking him was fear. Fear of losing her love, fear of their perfect life changing.

She squeezed his hand. "No, I haven't. I can balance things. Give me a chance, Reece. Give *us* a chance."

Staring into her pleading face, he weakened. Maybe she was right. She was too soft to do what had to be done. "Okay, but you have to have your priorities right. I'm the man of the house and I expect you to pay me the respect I deserve. Understood?"

"Understood." She threw her arms around him and rained kisses on his face.

Which was just the way it should be.

HANNAH YODELED A tune under her breath as she cut the thread on the last curtain panel. The baby's room would be finished as soon as she hung the curtains. With difficulty, she rose from the chair and carried the panels from the sewing room into the small room off the hall. Everything was in place. The tiny sleepers and Onesies lay folded in the dresser drawers, and she'd finished the last pair of knitted booties. The hand-stitched quilt she'd made lay folded at the foot of the crib. Soon her little one would be safe in her arms.

The sunlight streaming through the window lit the yellow walls with even more color. A crib mobile swung in the breeze above the bed. It was all perfect, or rather, it would be in two weeks when the baby arrived. Hannah put her hand on her swollen belly and felt the child kick against her hand. "Soon, little one."

Reece had chosen for them not to learn the baby's gender, but she felt in her heart it was a girl. Her smile faded. She'd never imagined marriage could be like walking through a field of buried explosives. Reece had a lot of pain inside, pain she'd failed to soothe. If inflicting pain on her soothed his, maybe it was her lot in life. A lot she deserved, after what she'd done.

Moving carefully, she climbed onto a chair and hung the curtains. The soft color looked perfect against the walls. It was only when she glanced at her watch that she caught her breath. It was nearly six, and she hadn't even started dinner. Reece would be furious. As if on cue, his whistle sounded on the stairs outside the apartment door, and she heard Reece call her name. She should have had dinner ready. He was always angrier when he was hungry.

Holding the back of the chair, she managed to get down in one piece. She knew she looked as big as a beached whale. Reece hated her cumbersome size. A sharp cramp struck, and she bit back a groan so he wouldn't hear. He hated complainers. Could this be labor?

He pounded on the door. "Hannah, I forgot my key."

When had dread replaced delight at his appearance? After that first slap, she'd been sure there would be no more. He was always so sorry, but not sorry enough to keep his fists to himself. Her mother would have said she'd made her own bed. And she had. But she'd never expected that bed to be so full of nails. There was no going back. At least he'd let her get her GED the first year, and now, after five years of marriage, she would soon have her college degree as well. He was a good man at heart.

The baby would make everything better. They'd be a real family. Maybe Reece's obsession with her would ease. She would have joy in her life that eclipsed the heartache. The baby would change everything. It was her only hope.

"I'm coming," she gasped out, still in the grip of the contraction. The strength of it surprised her. Maybe this was the real thing. She managed to get to the door and fumble with the dead bolt. It was always a little stiff. She threw open the door to see him stalking away in his police uniform.

She rushed after him to stand at the top of the wide staircase down to the street. "I'm here, Reece."

He turned around and mounted the steps again. He kissed her, and she clung to him as another contraction took her. *Breathe, don't let him see yet.* She couldn't explain her panic. Reece would take care of her. He was a take-charge kind of guy. He'd get her suitcase and make sure she got through this.

He nuzzled her neck. "I'm starved. What did my little wife fix me?" He raised his head. "I don't smell anything cooking. Dinner isn't even started, is it?" Disapproval dripped from his words.

"I—I think I'm in labor," she gasped as another contraction hit. She grabbed the top of the banister for support.

"Don't make excuses. The baby isn't due for another two weeks. You were too busy playing in the baby's room to think about me, weren't you? I'm disappointed in you, Hannah."

"No, really, Reece. Here. Feel. I think it's really labor." She tried to put his hand on her belly, but he jerked away. Fear battered at her, but she tried to stifle it. He wouldn't hurt her when she was pregnant.

"Is this how it's going to be when the baby comes? You all wrapped up in the kid and never paying me any attention?" His eyes glittered, and he grabbed her arm. His fingers pressed into her flesh.

She managed not to wince. "No, of course not." She knew the expression on his face. If she had somewhere to go, she'd leave here and never look back. Her anger simmered, but she had to keep it from boiling over. If she lost control, her punishment would be greater. She should soothe and placate him, but she didn't have the energy. "You're hurting me, Reece."

He dropped his hand, and the flare in his eyes banked to a dim glow. He raked his hand through his hair. "Hannah, you always know how to push my buttons. If you'd honor me like you should, this wouldn't happen. It's my duty to train you up properly, but you make the job harder than it should be."

Even though she knew he was only manipulating her, she dropped her head. It was true she'd forgotten him today. Some days she wished she could forget him forever. Tears blurred her vision.

His hand reached out again and caressed her bare arm. He backed her against the wall. His head came down, and he nuzzled her neck again. His touch made bile rise in her throat, and she escaped his grip instead of raising her face for his kiss. She knew it was a mistake when she saw the manic anger blaze into his eyes.

He stepped toward her, but he didn't touch her. "I told you right from the start that I wasn't father material. I want a wife, not a nursemaid. A lover, not a nanny. When that kid comes, we're not keeping it."

Too late she realized he blamed the baby for her brief flash of defiance. She couldn't let him take her baby. "It won't happen again, Reece. Really. I'm so sorry," she babbled.

Love and anger vied for control of his face. She backed up until she stood at the edge of the stairs. She should have watched her tongue. She lifted her face to him. He could hit her there and not hurt the baby.

Mottled red had crept up his face. "I should have seen that rebellious streak in you. I'm your husband, Hannah. I know what's best, but you never seem to listen."

"I know you do." She put her hand up to cup his face. She forced herself to smile. "I've got steaks out for dinner. I'll have them ready in fifteen minutes."

His hands gripped her shoulders. "You promised me you wouldn't put the baby ahead of me, but you're already doing it."

She wrenched away from his painful grip. "I'm not, Reece! You're the most important person in my life." Too late, she realized she teetered on the top step. Hannah's arms pinwheeled out as she struggled to catch the banister, but the staircase was too wide.

His hands rushed out toward her, but she lost the fight to regain her balance. His hand struck her shoulder, then she was tumbling down the steps. She thought to protect the baby, and she tried to curl into a ball. Her head slammed against the railing, and she saw colors as brilliant as fireworks. Everything rushed by in a blur, the rails and the carpet alternating in her view.

Protecting her stomach proved impossible. At least she and the baby would be together. In seconds she lay in a crumpled heap at the bottom of the stairs. Reece's footsteps rushed toward her, and she tried to scoot away. A vise of pain gripped her stomach, and her vision faded to black. Reece cried out her name in an anguished voice. Something warm trickled between her legs, then the pain blotted out the world.

THE MACHINES BEEPED in the hospital room. Reece sat in the chair beside Hannah's bed. His gaze went to the monitors, and he put his head in his hands. She couldn't die. He'd be lost if she died.

She stirred, and he looked but her eyes didn't open. Her hand swept across her stomach, then settled there. A grimace twisted her lips, and he was sorry for the pain she would experience. It might be hard for a while, but she'd come to realize it was better this had happened. His gaze touched her face. Hannah's long lashes lay on her cheeks. Even pale from the trauma, she was so beautiful. Her tawny hair spread out over the pillow. He loved to plunge his face into her long locks. They were so like his real mother's, the only happy memory of his childhood. He laid his hand on her forehead and smoothed her hair. It was time for her to wake up. "Hannah," he said in a firm voice. "Wake up."

Her lashes fluttered, and pain contorted her features. "Sleep," she muttered.

"You can sleep later. Open your eyes." A commanding tone usually worked with her.

She sighed, and her eyes finally opened but remained bleary and unfocused. "Look at me, Hannah."

She blinked, her gaze sharpening when she took in his face. "Reece. Where am I?"

"You're in the hospital, hon."

"Hospital? The baby came?" Her hand moved over her stomach again. "Was it a girl?"

"Hon, the baby died."

She rolled her head from side to side. "I want my baby. Give her to me!"

"She's dead, love. I'm sorry."

"A girl?" Her gaze sharpened again.

"Yes, but she didn't make it." An expression he couldn't read passed over her face, but she didn't argue with him again. "Are you in pain? Do you need anything?"

She struggled to sit up. "Can I have some water?"

He knew she'd turn to him for comfort. He started to pour some water, but the pitcher was nearly empty. He'd been drinking it through the night while she slept. "Let me get the nurse. I'll be right back."

No one was at the nurses' station, so he wandered down the hall looking for ice. All he found were patients' rooms. He finally found an aide in the last room, and she ordered him to cool his heels in the hall while she finished checking her patient's vitals. She led him back the other way, and he waited while she went to a small room he'd missed.

He'd been gone nearly twenty minutes by the time he made it back to Hannah's room. When he pushed open the door, the bed was empty. He thought she was in the bathroom, but the door was open and the light off. "Hannah?" He whirled to look in every corner of the room. The clothes locker stood open, empty of her things. A hospital gown lay on the floor.

She couldn't have left. No way could she have passed him in the hall without his noticing. He sprang toward the door and looked down the hall in both directions. An exit sign beckoned from the end opposite the nurses' station. Beneath it, a door was just closing. He ran down the hall and shoved the door. When it opened, he saw Hannah stepping into an elevator. "Wait!" He rushed to intercept her, but the elevator doors closed before he could get to them. He caught only a glimpse of her stony face looking back at him.

Where was her obedience, her respect? He jabbed the elevator button several times. "Come on, come on." When no elevator appeared, he glanced around for the stairs and found the exit. Plunging down the flights, he planned how he would punish her for this. She would be sorry she crossed him. He threw open the first-floor door into a lobby looking out over the parking lot. On the other side of the glass, Hannah was getting into a vehicle—*his* truck.

"Stop!" He ran through the lobby and out the door. He had his hand on the truck's door handle when the vehicle peeled away, tires screeching. His wife turned to look out the window at him. It seemed impossible she'd done this to him. How dare she openly defy him? When had she gotten a key made? Had she been planning this in the past weeks when she'd coaxed him into teaching her to drive? She'd said she would sometimes need to take the baby to the doctor. She'd tricked him.

Swearing, he dug his cell phone out of his pocket and called his partner on the police force. She had no place to go but home.

His partner met him in fifteen minutes. They drove at top speed to the apartment and parked on Market Street. Reece bounded up the steps but found only an empty apartment. She'd already been here and left with her suitcase, probably the one packed for the hospital. She'd escaped him, and somehow he knew finding her wouldn't be easy.

An unfamiliar sensation washed over him, and he touched his eyes. They were wet. He and Hannah belonged together. He knew with certainty they'd be together again.

PART 2

Five years later

six

*"The Lonestar Quilt is a reminder that we aren't created to be loners.
The Amish prize family and community above all else."*

HANNAH SCHWARTZ,

IN *The Amish Faith Through Their Quilts*

Hannah's gaze wandered the living room of her home, a modern ranch that rambled over a postcard-sized Milwaukee yard. Quilts hung from every wall and also lay draped on quilt racks in every corner. She knew the history of every one, who had made it, the year, the purpose for its creation. They were her children, the only ones she'd ever have. The thought depressed her.

Asia Wang, Hannah's publicist and assistant, ticked off the items on her list. "You've got an interview with *McCall's Quilting* magazine at nine. A camera crew from Channel 6 is coming in forty-five minutes. Tomorrow is even busier with packing to fly to New York to film *FOX & Friends*." Near Hannah's age of thirty-two, Asia looked slim and elegant in her gray pantsuit and coordinating shoes. But then, she was always put together.

Hannah nodded. The whirlwind success of her book had stunned and humbled her. And sometimes the demands on her time exhausted her. "But what about the book? And the quilt for the cover? You've got to slow down the publicity stuff, Asia, just for a few weeks until I can catch my breath."

"This opportunity won't come around again. We have to make hay while the sun shines. You'll get it done." Asia dismissed Hannah's fears with an airy wave of her hand.

"Yes, I know. We have so much to be thankful for, but I've got work to do at the office too. I need to figure out how to work it all in without going insane." She forced a smile in spite of her fatigue.

Asia consulted her notebook. "Interview first. The auction isn't until eleven. We'll go in long enough for that. I think the staff is throwing a farewell party for you as well."

A pang pressed against Hannah's ribs. The museum had been her family, and she'd miss them all. She'd never guessed that the success of her book, *Amish Quilts: a Factual History*, would catapult her to such fame. It had been on every major best-seller list for six months, and her publisher was clamoring for the new book's publication to be moved up. It was like being hit by lightning.

"You'd better get changed." Asia stepped to the window and glanced outside. "The mail is here. I'll get it while you change."

Hannah nodded and dumped Spooky, one of her four cats, off her foot. Black with a white marking at his neck, the cat loved to lay on her feet. She quickly changed into the clothes Asia had laid out, a black skirt and chunky gray sweater with tasteful pearls. Asia had tried to get her to spice up her wardrobe, but Hannah insisted on maintaining her image as an academic, and her publicist eventually quit hounding her. Hannah checked her hair and found the French twist still intact.

When she stepped back into the living room, she found Asia going through the mail. "Anything interesting?" she asked.

"Looks like a personal letter," Asia said, holding out an envelope.

"It's from my aunt." She opened the envelope and discovered it held another envelope and a letter. She pulled them both out, and her gaze fell on the inside envelope—one bearing familiar bold handwriting. Reece's writing. The envelope burned her hands, and she dropped it onto the floor as the familiar bitterness burned like bile.

The dark letters shouted at Hannah. Her limbs froze.

"What's wrong?" Asia asked. She stepped to Hannah's side. "Who's it from?"

"Don't touch it!" Hannah had hoped never to see that handwriting again. Just looking at it brought Reece's harsh voice to her head. Her hands curled into fists. If she ever saw him again, she'd kill him. If not for him, her baby girl would be with her now.

Asia's dark eyes widened. "Is it that bad?"

"My—my husband." Hannah's limbs trembled with the strength of her rage. "I don't want to see anything he has to say. I'd hoped he'd never find me here."

Asia gave her a speculative look. "You're married? You've never told me."

"We've been separated for five years. I guess it's possible he filed for divorce and charged me with desertion." She should be so lucky.

"You'd better read it." Asia scooped it up off the floor. "What do you have to be afraid of?"

Hannah didn't reply. She stared, immobile, at the letter.

"Oh, Hannah, was he abusive?"

Hannah took a step back. "I can't talk about it."

"Let's make some of your fabulous meadow tea before the reporter gets here. We'll read the letter together and it will be okay. You'll see. He can't hurt you now."

"You don't know Reece," Hannah blurted. She took a deep breath and held out her hand. "I'll read it now." The paper crackled in her hand. When she removed the single sheet of paper, a picture fluttered to the ground, and Asia retrieved it. Hannah didn't look at it. She just put it facedown on top of her desk. First things first. Reece was sure to plead for her to come back. It had taken him five years to find her, and she'd begun to hope that her hidey-hole would stay secure. Or that he'd moved on. She'd been strident about protecting her location from the media.

She unfolded the letter. He'd handwritten the note. Every day for five years he'd left her instructions for the day on the kitchen table. She'd grown to loathe the sight of his penmanship.

"Want me to read it?" Asia asked when Hannah let her hand containing the letter drop to her side.

Hannah held it out to her friend without a word.

Asia took it and began to read. "'Hi, hon, it's been so long and I've missed you so much. We need to talk. There are things to discuss. Isn't our daughter cute? She looks just like my beautiful wife. Give us a chance to be a real family. Call me, Hannah. My cell phone number is 317-555-1212. I promise it will be different.'"

Hannah put her hand to her throat. What did he mean? Hysterical laughter bubbled in her throat, but she choked it back.

Asia looked up. "'Our daughter'? What is this, Hannah?" She glanced down at the envelope. "There's another note in here."

"From Reece?"

"No, it's signed 'Aunt Nora.' Want me to read it too?"

"Sure." Why would her aunt send a letter to her from Reece? Nora knew Hannah wanted no contact with him.

Asia cleared her throat. "'Hannah, my dear, Reece has assumed I'm still in touch with you. He's right of course. This letter showed up addressed to you. I opened it and was torn over whether I should send it, but in the end, I thought you should see this since it mentions your daughter. I hope it's not too upsetting.'"

Hannah wrapped her arms around herself. The memories of her fall began to flood back, but she refused to think about it. He was just trying to twist the knife. And doing a good job. Her daughter was dead. Her gaze went to the picture. She picked it up and turned it over.

A little girl of about five stood looking into the camera. Her auburn curls sprang from her head. Her golden brown eyes smiled along with her mouth. She was in front of a familiar covered bridge. Squinting, Hannah could make out the words above it. It was the Narrows Bridge, just two miles from her old home. Hannah could have been looking at a picture of herself at that age. "It can't be," she whispered. She tried to find another explanation. Maybe it was Luca's child. She'd tried to call him at work several times, but she always lost her nerve before he got to the phone. She glanced at the photo again. No, that couldn't be right. Aunt Nora wouldn't have sent this if it were a picture of Luca's child. Besides, the child wasn't dressed Amish.

She pressed her fingers to her head. "Oh, I'm so confused."

"Let me see." Asia took the picture from Hannah's fingers. "Hannah, she looks like you. You have a daughter?"

Hannah shook her head slowly and began to recount the story.

Every muscle screamed in agony. Her mind replayed falling down the steps. She thought he'd pushed her, but even if it had been accidental, the fall killed her baby, and it was his fault. The horror of that knowledge nearly made her vomit. She'd shared her bed, her dreams, with that man. He'd taken everything she had to give and then destroyed what she treasured most.

"Could I have some water?" she whispered from the hospital bed. She had to get him out of the room.

When he left to get the water, she threw back the covers and staggered from the bed. Ignoring the pain that gripped her, she managed to get to the closet. She had to hurry. He'd be back any minute. She had to escape him once and for all, or he would kill her too.

She managed to pull on her skirt and blouse, to thrust her feet into her shoes. Her purse was in the bottom of the locker. If she could get to the shelter, they would take care of her, she'd been told. When he'd broken her arm last year, the nurse had insisted Hannah take the information about a shelter.

It took her way too long to get dressed with the agony slowing her movements. He'd be back any second.

Nearly bending double with the pain, she peeked out the door. To her left, Reece had his back to her and was haranguing a nurse. To her right was another exit. She slipped out of the room and hurried to the door as fast as the pain would allow. Glancing behind her, she saw Reece starting back to the room. She slipped into another doorway and waited until he entered her room. A patient behind her asked a question, but she had no strength to answer. As soon as the coast was clear, she darted back to the hallway, through the exit, and rushed toward the elevator. It dinged and opened almost as soon as she punched the button, and she breathed a prayer of thanks.

She stepped inside and pressed the lobby button. As the doors closed, she heard Reece's angry shout. Her last glimpse of him caught the murderous expression in his eyes.

When Hannah finished her story, she found Asia wiping tears from her cheeks.

"I'm so sorry," Asia whispered. "Have you seen him since?"

"No. I made it to the shelter. They helped me change my name to Hannah Miller, which I've used in my private life, hid me while I got a legal separation—I don't believe in divorce. I finished my master's degree and got this job three years ago with their help. I always thought he'd find me again." She'd spent the last five years watching children on the street, wondering what her daughter would have looked like if she'd lived. The pain had never gone away. She knew better than to let herself hope. Reece's manipulation had caused her pain too many times in the past.

"Do you think he pushed you on purpose—to kill the baby?" Asia asked.

"I—I've never been positive. I thought I felt a hard shove. It was enough to send me running away before he killed me." She looked back down at the picture. "Surely she's not still alive?" Just saying the words made hope spring to life.

"I can't tell where this is," Asia said, looking at the picture again.

"Parke County, Indiana." The place she missed above all others. But it wouldn't be the same now, not with her family gone.

"So he's trying to say the baby didn't die from the fall? That when she was born, he took her to Parke County? How is that possible? He was with you in the hospital."

Hannah hadn't thought of that. "Maybe he had someone help him." It was stupid to try to argue this into being. "Oh, I don't know what he would do. I could never second-guess Reece." Though she'd tried for five long years. "But she's not with my family."

"How do you know?"

"She's not dressed Amish."

"What are you going to do?"

Before Asia asked, Hannah hadn't been sure, but she lifted her head. "I'm going home to find out."

"Hannah, you can't. We've got a full lineup of publicity events." Asia crossed her arms over her chest.

"Reschedule them. This is important."

"Your book sales are important. You owe this to your publishing house. This time may never come again, Hannah. Be smart about it."

Hannah hesitated. Maybe Asia was right. They were riding the crest of a wave. "I'll do today's, and I'll do *FOX & Friends*. But reschedule the rest."

Asia must have recognized the inflexible tone of Hannah's voice, because she nodded. "This journey might make the news if we let it out."

"I don't want anyone to know what's going on." The odds were against the child's being her daughter, and Hannah would look foolish for thinking otherwise. Besides, her loss was too painful to talk about.

"Everyone would sympathize with your plight. And the publicity might help you find the little girl faster."

"No. I couldn't do that to her. I expect Reece is just messing with my head anyway." She should put it out of her mind. Tear up the picture and get on with her life. She looked down at the picture in her hand again. What if this child really was her daughter?

"I don't know the guy," Asia said. "But could this be his way of flushing you out?"

"Maybe, but it doesn't matter. I have to know." The desire scorched her. If there was even the slightest possibility that this little girl could be hers, Hannah would follow any rabbit trail, walk on nails, climb mountains. She'd even face the devil himself—Reece. The man she suspected might have killed her parents.

seven

"The Sunshine Diamond Quilt is simple but has a beautiful message—look for the good everywhere."

HANNAH SCHWARTZ,

IN *The Amish Faith Through Their Quilts*

A lightning rod rode the crest of the roof, and as the breeze shifted, a rooster weather vane swung around to face Matt Beitler. He approached the freshly painted red barn. The sliding door stood open, spilling out the scent of hay and horse.

His dog, Ajax, strained at the leash. "Stay," Matt said. The dog fell back, then sat on his haunches. His grayed muzzle pointed up toward Matt in a hopeful gesture. Matt looped the other end of the leash around a hitching post and glanced around the property.

"Let's check inside." His partner, Blake Lehman, stepped around him.

"Wait a minute—we haven't secured the scene!" Matt grabbed at the deputy's arm, but Blake shook him off. "The geocacher who found the body said it was in the woods behind the barn."

"But the perp could be hiding here." Blake moved through the barn door.

Matt didn't object. Maybe it was better to have him out of the way. "I'm heading to the woods," he called. "Backup should be here any minute."

He turned and surveyed the sparse grass between the outbuildings and the house. Laundry hung from a line strung from the house to the top of the barn. He noticed a pulley that allowed the occupants to run the clothes up the line and back. A buggy sat parked partway under a tree.

"Amish," Blake said with a twist to his mouth. "Our schools are in trouble because of them. We've lost funding since they moved into the area."

Matt stepped to the back porch and pounded on the door. "Sheriff's department," he called. Only silence answered. Nothing stirred in the yard. Matt veered across the lawn, grabbed Ajax's leash, then headed toward the back. Dry grass crunched under his shoes, and the wind moaned through the treetops. He eased behind the barn, but the area was empty. No back door here. He darted across the empty pasture to the woods. Blake sounded like a herd of elephants following him.

Matt turned and frowned. "Keep it down!"

"Maybe it's a prank call," Blake said.

"I don't think so. Look at Ajax." He pointed to his dog. Tension showed in every line of the muscular German shepherd's body. Ajax strained at the leash. "The caller said about fifty feet inside the woods, on the other side of a meadow."

Matt couldn't hear anything above the wind and the crunch of dead leaves. Ajax dragged him on. A loud buzzing began to ring in his ears, and he knew what he'd find before he stepped past the meadow into the shade of a large oak tree.

Flies rose in a cloud at their approach, then settled back onto the body, a man dressed in the typical Amish garb of dark pants, a white shirt, and a straw hat. The man was smooth-shaven, so he must not have been married. The heat had caused the body to begin the decay process, and the stink of death coated Matt's nose.

"Looks like poison," Blake said. "Probably strychnine from the way he's contorted."

Matt retreated. "Don't disturb him until forensics gets here. Call it in."

Blake nodded and stepped back into the clearing. Matt tuned out his partner's yammering on the radio and glanced around the wooded area. A few fallen maple trees stretched across a dry stream. Newly sprouted leaves danced in the wind, and a brilliant cardinal fluttered over his head.

Nothing else stirred. Considering the strong odor and the flies, the perp was long gone. He needed to talk to the guy who found the body. The man had been too freaked-out to wait for their arrival. He had given his name, address, and phone number, though. That would be Matt's first stop when he was finished here.

Blake's heavy footsteps tromped back through the brush. "They're on their way. Weird case. Wasn't there something similar some years back?"

Matt nodded. "An Amish man and woman were poisoned. Their only kid, a daughter, found them. This setup looks the same. Except their bodies were covered with a quilt."

"Were there any leads?"

"We found a neighbor dead from the same poison he'd supposedly used on the family. Though it never made sense to me. I was never sure the guy we found dead was the killer. I think he might have been another victim. The case is still open, but we never found a motive—or the quilts stolen from the family's home."

"What happened to the daughter?"

"She married the detective in charge of the investigation and left town." Matt's voice grew clipped. He should have tracked them down. He was still mad about Reece's rude departure. And the gun he'd never returned.

Blake jerked a thumb toward the body. "You think it's connected?"

The thought had been hovering in Matt's head. "It's been ten years. You'd think the killer would have kept on killing." If they were connected, maybe he'd be able to close two cases at once.

Blake's cell phone rang, and he pulled it out.

"Nice phone," Matt said. "Expensive, though." He'd had his eye on the iPhone but had never been willing to plunk down that much dough.

Blake grunted, then answered the phone. "Hi, honey," he said.

Matt listened with half an ear. It was probably Matt's sister, Gina, Blake's wife. He stooped and studied the ground for clues.

SPEAKERS BLARED OUT the names of passengers with messages waiting for them. Her cell phone in her hand, Hannah sipped her latte in the LaGuardia Airport. The show had gone well, but she was exhausted and wanted nothing more than to sleep in her own bed tonight. Asia had gone to the restroom, and Hannah toyed with the idea of calling Luca. He'd be shocked to hear from her. Maybe he'd heard of her book. She hoped not, though, knowing that by writing it she broke every principle of *Hochmut*.

The concept of self-promotion was alien to the Amish. Her cousin would be grieved to know she even had a publicist and sought to promote herself and her book. He would tell her to let God be her publicist or, better yet, to choose a career that didn't put her in the limelight. Luca and Hannah's father had built their greenhouse business by providing good service to the community. They'd never taken out an ad in their lives.

Her hands shook as she flipped open her cell phone and punched in the number. She'd never forgotten it, though ten years had passed since she'd spoken with anyone at that number. Settling the phone against her ear, she took another sip of her hot coffee to wet her dry throat. What would she say?

The phone continued to ring until the answering machine in the greenhouse picked up and Luca's familiar voice instructed her to leave a message. She hung up without doing it. This was a conversation they needed to have in person.

She watched the people walking past. Mothers with children clinging to their hands, fathers carrying babies. Her heart ached with emptiness. How ironic that all she'd been taught since childhood focused on the importance of family and community, and now here she was at thirty-two without anyone. No close friends other than Asia, who was an employee. Oh, she had acquaintances from the quilting society and at the museum, but no one she could pour out her heart to. No one who understood why she kept herself aloof.

Sometimes she didn't understand herself. It should be easy to put down the wall and make herself vulnerable again. But it wasn't. Living with Reece had shown her how a mask could hide the real person. Trust was hard to find, maybe because she'd never been able to let go of the bitterness and anger she felt toward Reece. And toward Cyrus Long, who had ruined her life. If her parents had lived, she never would have been brazen enough to run off with Reece.

Her life would be so different today.

SOME DAYS, LIFE had a way of mocking him. The first day of the investigation had turned up nothing, and all Matt wanted was to take pizza home to his daughter and watch VeggieTales after the sitter left. But when he pulled into the driveway, he saw Gina sitting on the porch swing with Caitlin. Every marriage had conflicts, and she needed to work out hers with Blake, not run to him with every little problem.

He stifled a sigh and got out of his SUV. "Hey, girls," he said, smiling down at his daughter. She was the one bright spot in a world gone gray three years ago, when Analise died.

"I brought pizza," Gina said. Her smile was tentative, as though she feared he would be upset.

"I was craving it." He ruffled the top of his daughter's hair. "You got a hug for old Dad?" When Gina was around, Caitlin had eyes for no one else. Poor kid missed her mother's touch.

Nothing was said about why Gina had come until two hours later, after

Caitlin had been bathed and put to bed. "Spill it," he said when he came back to the living room where Gina sat with Ajax's head on her lap.

"Spill what?" She rubbed Ajax's ears. He wore a blissful expression.

"The long face. You haven't said a word about Blake. Where is he tonight?"

"I have no idea." Her lips quivered, and she didn't look at him.

Matt flopped into the recliner. "Did you try calling him? He's probably working late."

"What time did you leave him?"

"About two hours before I came home. I was going over the murder." He glanced at his watch. Over three hours ago.

Her lips quivered. "I—I think he's having an affair, Matt."

Matt balled up his fists. "I don't believe it. Blake loves you." He got up and went to the sofa. He started to put his arm around her, then dropped it back into place. They didn't have a huggy-kissy sort of relationship. But she turned into his embrace and wailed against his chest. He patted her back, but he was bad at this kind of thing.

"Trust him a little, Gina. He'll be home soon."

She lifted a tear-stained face. "Well, he can come around and find an empty house. I'm leaving him. Can I stay with you for a while, Matt?"

He dropped his arm. "You know you can, but it would be better for you to go home and work out your problems. Give him the benefit of the doubt. Are you sure this is what you want?"

"He's having an affair! I found a hotel bill. And a receipt for a five-thousand-dollar ring. He didn't give me any ring."

"Where'd he get that kind of money?"

"I have no idea. But you're missing the point! It wasn't for me. He has to have a girlfriend." She swiped the tears from her face with an angry hand.

Until now, Matt had thought his sister was overreacting. He didn't want to think about where Blake had gotten that kind of money. A rash of burglaries had occurred over the past two months. But no, this was *Blake*. His partner and friend. He'd never do anything like that. "Maybe it's a surprise and he borrowed the money."

"I don't care about the money! Would you quit worrying about that? We're okay financially. Blake never lets a bill go. The receipt was for two months ago. If the ring were a surprise for me, he would have given it to me already."

"Want me to talk to him?" What could Matt say? This mess wasn't his business. But he couldn't believe Blake would cheat on Gina—he loved her. "Divorce isn't the answer. Especially leaving him without giving him a chance to explain."

"The Bible says it's okay when it's infidelity, if that's what you're worried about."

"Just because it's okay doesn't mean you should do it. Analise and I had some rough times too, but we weathered them. I just keep thinking about what would have happened if I'd given up. We would have missed out on some important times together. We wouldn't have Caitlin either."

She gave a huge sigh. "I should have known better than to ask you, Mr. Perfect," she muttered. She shoved Ajax's head off her lap and stood. "It's hard not to give up. He's never home."

"Look, go home and at least talk to him. I'm sure there's an explanation. Give it a shot anyway."

Her gaze came up and tears sparkled in her eyes. "Didn't you hear me, Matt? When am I supposed to talk to him? He's never home." She grabbed her purse with quick movements. "I've got to go." She stopped by the door. "Pray for me. I don't think I can get through this." She vanished through the door.

The human spirit could take more than one ever thought it could, but Matt wished his baby sister didn't have to go through this.

FIRST THING IN the morning, Hannah and Asia hit the road. Five hours later, they were nearly to Parke County. They'd crossed the Illinois line into

Indiana half an hour ago. Hannah's four cats prowled restlessly in their carriers in the back. Their yowls had grown more outraged in the past hour.

The last time Hannah had come through here, she'd been peering out the back of Reece's truck as the world she knew fell away. Then, the landscape was still in the grip of winter with an early spring beginning to poke through. Now spring blossoms dotted the green hillsides, and she caught glimpses of covered bridges down several narrow lanes.

Home.

The word evoked both dread and longing. She knew what would face her, and the thought was something she'd pushed down into the darkest recesses of her mind for ten years.

"You okay?" Asia asked from the driver's seat.

Hannah slanted a smile her way. "A little scared. I don't think I could have done this if you hadn't come with me." She looked back down at the quilt piece in her lap. Working on it kept her mind from peeking into corners she'd closed off for years.

"It's what friends do. Besides, we've got to get that book delivered." Asia's grin was cheeky. "They won't eat you, will they?"

"It might hurt less if they did." Her heart squeezed at the thought of the reception that awaited her. There would be no slow smile from Luca. And her friends might not talk to her. She missed Sarah. Hannah took a last sip of her iced vanilla coffee.

"Which way?" Asia asked.

"Let me look at the map." Hannah opened the atlas and found the Indiana state map. "I always get turned around with all the roads."

"Girl, you grew up here. Your sense of direction is hopeless." Asia pulled to the side of the road, consulted the map with Hannah, and pointed. "We turn left here." She resumed driving and took the next road.

Hannah gazed out the window. "This looks familiar." The woods crowded along the road, the sun disappearing ten feet into the thick trees. She rolled down her window and breathed in the scent of forest and river.

The fields had been freshly plowed, and soon corn would grow so close to the road it would be like traveling through a green cornstalk tunnel. But she'd be long gone by then. The thought hurt.

"So what is this shunning thing? You're still family. How can they turn their backs on you?"

The world never understood. Even though Hannah was about to put herself on the receiving end of a very painful circumstance, she didn't begrudge her people the right. "They want to make sure the corruption doesn't spread. If I hadn't joined the church, there would be no *Meidung*, but I knelt before the entire congregation and promised to be faithful to our way. I broke that oath when I ran off with Reece. And they love me. They don't want me to continue on the wrong path."

"Have you been in touch with anyone since you left?"

"Just my aunt. I tried to call my cousin at work the other day, but he wasn't in."

"Why didn't your aunt follow the ban? She still corresponds with you."

"She's a bit of a rebel." Hannah laughed remembering her aunt's small rebellions: curtains at the windows, a landscape picture or two in her bedroom, sending her son, Moe, to the public school. For some reason the bishop had always allowed her the small indiscretions. *Mamm* said he'd been sweet on Aunt Nora once upon a time.

The car crested a hill, and in the valley ahead of them lay the old homestead. Hannah caught her breath, and her lungs constricted. The ten years hadn't changed it. Luca had given the house a fresh coat of paint recently, and the white siding gleamed in the spring sunshine. The redbud trees along the pond bloomed with purple flowers. *Mamm*'s bed of jonquils had spread out to take over more of the side yard. Hannah could almost see her mother on the other side of the screen door, her white prayer cap bobbing and weaving as she kneaded bread.

Laundry flapped in the breeze from a line stretched by pulley from the house to the top of the barn. Two buggies were parked under a big walnut tree. She could imagine it was yesterday she was here last instead of ten years ago.

"Who inherited the property?"

"My cousin Luca and I. I'm not sure what he did about that. Likely just took over the farm and greenhouse and is waiting for me to show up someday." Hannah knew Luca would never take it to the law to try to gain anything.

"Do you think he'll turn you away?"

"I don't think so. He and his wife won't be able to dine with me, though. I'll have to eat alone."

"If you haven't been in touch with him, how do you know he's married?"

Hannah drank in more of the sights before answering. The garden had been turned over and planted, but nothing grew yet. The greenhouse billowed with colorful flowers and leafy plants. She could smell the aroma of phlox from here. Horses grazed in the pasture, and she strained to see if Lucy was still there. Her soul leaped when she saw the appaloosa's familiar spots.

She dragged her gaze from the familiar sights. "The small clothes on the line. The Amish cherish children and welcome any that God sends them. We don't use birth control. If he's married, he has children." Hannah held the picture of the redheaded girl in her hand, and she studied it again. She longed to find the answer to this riddle today.

Hannah had no idea whom Luca had married. He'd once had his eye on her best friend, Sarah. The thought of facing Sarah as well as Luca made a sheen of perspiration break out on her forehead. She opened her mouth to tell Asia to drive on past, but it was too late. Asia was already pulling into the driveway behind one of the open black buggies.

"I thought buggies were enclosed," Asia said. "The ones I've seen in northern Indiana even have lights on them."

"My ancestors are Swiss Amish," Hannah said, her gaze riveted on the screen door that offered a glimpse of movement. "Too much comfort is bad for the soul." She leaned out the window. "They refused to use lights or warning signs until the state made them. They believe if they have an accident, it's God's will. It's all part of *gelassenheit*. Calmness in the storm of whatever God brings."

"There are the kids," Asia said, gesturing toward a trampoline in the backyard.

Two towheaded children bounced on it, both girls, the strings on their bonnets flying in the breeze and their dark blue dresses fluttering around their calves. Hannah guessed their ages to be about five and six. The screen door opened, and a young woman stepped out onto the side porch. Hannah would have recognized those blue eyes and pink cheeks anywhere. Sarah could have been a poster child for a healthy farm girl raised on fresh dairy and vegetables.

She squinted at the car, then her gaze locked with Hannah's. Her mouth dropped open, then closed. Those perfect pink cheeks paled. Her hand left the screen door, and she took the first step down.

"Hannah?" she said in a faltering voice. "It's you, isn't it?" She moved quickly down the remaining two steps into the yard.

Hannah put aside her quilt block, then thrust open the car door and got out. For the first time in years, she felt naked without her prayer bonnet. And the sleeves on her blouse were too short. Why hadn't she taken more care with her clothing this morning? Her attention had been on the child's picture, and she hadn't thought about what her family would say. At least she wore a broomstick skirt that came down to the bottom of her calves.

"Hello, Sarah," Hannah said. She made an awkward move to embrace her friend, but Sarah stepped back with an alarmed expression and a quick glance at her children.

"You are all right?" Sarah asked, her gaze going past Hannah to the car. "Where is your husband?"

How did she explain it? Sarah would never understand. "We're separated," was all Hannah could manage.

Sarah's already-wide eyes did a slow blink, and her mouth twisted into a frown. Asia got out of the other side of the car, and Sarah glanced at her. A formal smile froze on her face.

She wouldn't be rude to a guest, Hannah knew. It might have been smarter than she realized to bring Asia. "Sarah, this is my, ah, good friend Asia Wang." She'd nearly introduced Asia as her publicist. That wouldn't have gone over well.

"Hello," Sarah said in a forced tone. "Could I, um, get you some tea or coffee?"

The Amish prized hospitality. Since Asia wasn't under the *Meidung*, she was welcomed, though Hannah was a pariah. The thought hurt.

"No, thank you. We stopped for coffee on the way," Asia said. "Your kids are cute."

Sarah's distracted glance went to where the children still bounced on the trampoline. "Naomi and Sharon." She looked back at Hannah. "Why are you here after all this time?"

Sarah wasn't going to make it easy. Hannah would give anything for things to be the way they were ten years ago, before everything changed. "Is Luca home?"

"No, he's on a trip to Indianapolis to sell some plants. He won't be back until next Monday night." Sarah bit her lip and looked as though she was about to cry. "You should go, Hannah, before the bishop knows you're here."

"I need some answers first," Hannah said. She might as well make this quick. There was no welcome for her here. She reached into the car and grabbed the picture of the little girl off the seat. "I wonder if you know this little girl. Maybe you've seen her around the area? The picture was taken just down the road."

Sarah frowned, but she took the picture and stared at it. "She has the look of my Hannah. She could almost be your daughter." She gave Hannah a quick glance. "Who is this child?"

"I'm not sure." Hannah longed to pour out the story. Once upon a time,

Sarah would have listened to every heartache, cried with Hannah over every painful moment. Now they were like two strangers.

Sarah handed back the picture. "I've never seen her."

Hannah pressed for an answer she wanted to hear. "You've never seen her around? She's standing by the covered bridge down the road."

"She's a stranger. What is this about?"

Before she could answer, the sound of an engine and tires on gravel made Hannah turn. The bubble lights atop a blue SUV made her stomach dip. A familiar set of wide shoulders exited the driver's side of the vehicle. She had no trouble putting a name to the tanned face under the hat. The firm lips and piercing blue eyes sometimes haunted her nightmares.

Detective Matt Beitler. After living with Reece, she thought of him as Matt now, though her husband's former partner still terrified her. She forced herself to stand her ground when those eyes that noticed everything looked her way. If she hadn't been so frightened, she might have laughed at the way his nostrils flared like those of a dog at a fresh scent. His lids came down into a squint that told her he hadn't forgotten her any more than she'd been able to rid herself of memories of him. His gaze pinned her in place.

"Hannah Schwartz." He drawled the words. "Where's O'Connor? He took my favorite gun when he vanished."

She remembered the gun. Reece probably still had it. "I have no idea," she said. "We've been separated for five years."

He raised his eyebrows at that, then shrugged. Another deputy got out of the passenger side, and Hannah caught a glimpse of a dog in the back of the SUV. She struggled to remember the dog's name. Ajax. The other deputy was putting away his phone. He walked with a swagger that announced his importance. He probably was attractive to the ladies, with his young Elvis look.

Matt looked her over. "How long have you been back in town?" he asked.

"About ten minutes."

"Where were you yesterday?"

She put out her hands, palms up. "What—I'm under suspicion already?"

His gaze sharpened. "How did you know we have another murder?"

"I—I didn't," she stammered. "I mean, you were acting suspicious of me. Isn't there always some crime happening?"

"Not like this. And not in Parke County. This is Indiana, not Chicago." His gaze dismissed her and went to Sarah. "Do you have a minute, Mrs. Schwartz?"

Sarah took a step back. "Luca isn't here right now. He's in Indianapolis. He won't be back for another week."

"I need to talk to you," Matt said in a gentle voice.

When a man as hard and focused as Matt Beitler sounded sympathetic, something bad had happened. Hannah and Sarah exchanged frightened glances, and Sarah edged closer to Hannah. Hannah slipped her arm around Sarah, and her friend didn't pull away this time.

"What's wrong, Matt?" Hannah asked. She bit her lip when he frowned. Maybe he didn't like her using his first name. Some people could be touchy about that.

"Maybe we'd better go inside."

Hannah fought against the panic bubbling up. "Is it Luca?" She forced the words out past her tight throat. *Please, God, not Luca.*

Surprise flickered across his face. "No, it's not Luca," he said.

Hannah and Sarah exhaled at the same time.

"Look, Deputy, can't you see you're scaring the women half to death?" Asia put in. "Just tell them what's wrong."

Matt pressed his lips together and directed his gaze at Sarah. "It's Luca's cousin, Mr. Honegger. Moe Honegger. We found him in a meadow on the other side of the county yesterday."

Moe. Hannah could still imagine him yodeling as he milked the cows. She'd been hopeful Moe, if no one else, would listen to her when she came home.

"Moe?" A bead of perspiration dotted Sarah's upper lip. "He was supposed to go with Luca until he got sick."

"We know," Matt said with a gentleness that was out of keeping with his sharp glance around the yard.

"What's happened to Moe?" Sarah whispered.

"He was poisoned."

Hannah would have fallen if she and Sarah hadn't been clinging to each other. Poisoned. Just like her family. How could it be coincidence, right when Reece had found her again?

eight

"Amish Plain clothing promotes humility and separation."

—HANNAH SCHWARTZ, ON *Good Morning America*

A chain-link fence barred Reece from the playground. He snapped a few pictures when he thought no one was looking. The kid looked just like Hannah. He'd been amazed and shocked the first time he saw her. And the plan had been born.

Settling on the bench by the street, he pretended to read the newspaper until the bell rang at two thirty. Kids began to pour from the school, escorted by the teachers who saw them off. Five minutes later, the kid said good-bye to her teacher and ran to a red Neon. Gina got out and opened the back door for her. The little girl climbed into the car, and the woman buckled her into the car seat.

By the time they drove away, Reece had jumped into his car. He followed them through Rockville and out US 36. His car weaved a bit as he jotted down the license plate number. He'd thought Gina would take the kid home like usual, but this wasn't the right direction. The car turned north by Billie Creek Village and continued on down a gravel road. He let his car fall farther behind. The plume of dust would tell him which way to go without his staying close enough to call suspicion on himself.

The dust settled at a house and barn near Nyesville. As he idled past, Gina and the kid walked to the front door and disappeared inside. There was surely a chink in the armor somewhere, something that would prove the kid needed rescuing.

He pulled behind a tree and watched. A little while later Gina came out carrying a suitcase. She and the kid got in the car and drove off. He fell a ways behind them and followed them to Matt's house. Was Gina moving in or something? That could complicate things.

But not so much he couldn't handle it. He had to prove his love to his wife, show her how different things could be. He'd made a mistake five years ago, but it wasn't too late to fix it. His grandmother had told him it was never too late to do the right thing. He could give Hannah the family she craved.

MATT'S KNEE ACHED from his old football injury as he walked slowly to his vehicle. Ajax trotted beside him and hopped into the backseat when he opened the door. The new case was going to ruin his day off. They had nothing. The guy had been poisoned with strychnine just like the victims a decade ago, but there were no prints, no clues. Just a body in the woods.

He had no idea what to do with himself tomorrow. Maybe take Caitlin out to see his grandmother. It had been nearly a month since he'd gone by the old house. His mind would be too busy thinking about the new case to get anything productive done at home.

He called his sister at his house. "Hey, I'm just getting off work. You get Caitlin all right?"

"Of course. We're baking chocolate chip cookies. I stopped by home and got my stuff."

"Does Blake know you're moving in with me for a while?"

"I told him this morning. He didn't even try to talk me out of it." She ended on a muffled sob.

"Did you ask him about the ring?"

"He said he'd bought it for me, then took it back after a fight."

What a lame excuse. "Do you believe him?"

"No. I'll move in with you for a while. Hey, Matt, there's something I noticed today. It might be nothing, but it left me uneasy."

"What's wrong?"

"There was a guy outside the school watching the kids. He was there on Monday, too, when I got Caitlin. You might ask Mrs. Downs if he was there when she got Caitlin on Tuesday."

"Maybe it's a parent." But his gut tightened.

"I've never gotten a close look at him. He wore Amish clothes with his hat pulled down low, so I couldn't see his face. Something about him seemed familiar. I think he followed us today."

"In a car? An Amish man drove a car?" Matt quit searching for his keys in his pocket. "You're sure? Maybe it was a Mennonite."

"Well, he had a beard and hat like an Amish guy. I thought I saw him get into a tan truck. One followed us to my house and then on to here too."

Matt didn't want to believe someone could be stalking his sister, but it was a possibility. Could it be someone masquerading as Amish? "Could Blake have asked someone to watch you?"

"Why?" Her voice dropped to a whisper. "I'm not the one cheating."

"Sorry, Gina. I wish I could fix it."

She said nothing for a long moment. "You helped, Matt. It helped to have someone to talk to. Listen, I need to get the cookies out of the oven. Don't forget to ask Mrs. Downs about that guy."

"I won't." He clicked off the phone and rang the neighbor who watched his daughter two days a week. She hadn't noticed any man, she told him. Maybe the man's behavior was innocent, but Matt planned to talk to Caitlin's teacher about it. He remembered when he was growing up, how he played outside all day without Trudy knowing where he was. She didn't care, for that matter. Thirty years ago there was no need to fear the possibility of some sicko snatching a kid.

Time pedaled back as Hannah clipped meadow tea leaves from the patch at the side of the yard. The cats prowled at her feet in the dark. She breathed in the cool spearmint fragrance. Nurturing came naturally to her, but there was so little she could do for her grieving aunt.

"Don't go far," she told her cats before opening the back door. They never wandered away from home. When she went inside, the kettle of water was boiling on the woodstove. She tossed the leaves into the water and turned off the flame, then covered the brewing tea. She could hear Aunt Nora weeping in the living room and the soft sounds of comfort Sarah made.

It should have been her job, but Sarah thought Aunt Nora didn't need something else to upset her, and Hannah had agreed. Once the weeping stopped, she planned to bring in tea and reveal herself to her aunt.

Asia was getting cream from the propane refrigerator. "This milk looks funny." She gave the pitcher a suspicious sniff.

"It's raw, straight from the cow. The cream rises to the top. You just skim some off for the tea."

Asia's brows raised, but she used a coffee cup to skim some liquid, then poured it into a creamer. Hannah turned from the stove to find two sets of big eyes on her.

The oldest little girl, Naomi, was the first to speak, and the familiar German-Swiss dialect sounded strange. "Are you really our cousin?"

Hannah nodded and smiled. She answered in German, but the words rolled awkwardly across her lips. "*Ja.* You are not in school yet?" Amish children spoke German until they went to school, where they learned English for the first time.

"Next year," Naomi said. "I'm six. Sharon is five."

Asia had that frozen smile on her face that people wear when they don't understand anything. Hannah held up a finger to signal she'd switch back to English in a minute.

Naomi crept closer and put her hand in Hannah's. "Your hair is pretty. *Mamm* says beauty doesn't matter, but I wish mine looked like yours."

Hannah squeezed her cousin's hand but didn't answer. She wished for a prayer bonnet to cover her bright hair. Her rich auburn locks had singled her out for attention from the *Englisch* when she was growing up, and she didn't want to experience that again.

The sobs were tapering off in the gathering room. Hannah transferred the tea to a teapot, then arranged it on a tray with cups, sugar, cream, and spoons. Just as she lifted the tray, she realized none of them would receive it from her. She'd forgotten in the grief of the moment.

"Can you take this in?" she asked Asia. "I'll stay here with the children."

"Why can I go but not you?"

"They aren't allowed to accept a favor from someone under the ban. I'd forgotten." Her eyes stung. She so badly wanted to help. Asia lifted the tray from her hands and disappeared through the door with it.

There was still some tea in the pot. "Want some tea?" she asked the girls. They both nodded, so she spooned sugar into cups and added the pale yellow liquid of meadow tea. She sipped her own, and the spearmint flavor brought all the familiarity of home to her: the horses neighing outside, the homey welcome of the farmhouse kitchen, the fresh herbs growing on the windowsill. She'd missed it all, and only now did she realize just how much.

The sound of a buggy crunching along the gravel outside caught her attention. She rose from the table and peered out the window. The sun caught the strong face under the wide brim of the black hat.

Bishop Samuel Kirchhofer.

THE OLD QUILT was getting threadbare. Matt tucked it around his daughter and kissed her sleeping cheek. He left the door partway open and went down the hall to join his sister in the living room. Ajax stayed behind to keep watch. He passed the computer room. The steady blue glow lit the dark office and beckoned to him.

He sat in front of the monitor and clicked the Firefox icon, then typed in the URL of a forum where people searching for missing persons gathered. The ad he'd put on the bulletin board hadn't brought a response in the year it had been up, but every time he sat down here, he hoped and prayed for a lead, anything.

A figure blocked the light from the hall fixture behind him. Gina pulled up a chair. "Aren't you ever going to give up?"

"No." He studied the screen displaying the old photo he'd uploaded. She was probably twenty-six in the picture. His eight-year-old self gazed up at her with naked love. Two weeks later she'd left him and Gina and never looked back. So why then did he think she'd come running just because he was looking?

His sister sighed. "You can't find someone who doesn't want to be found." She clicked through a few of the links and read the posts. "Look at all these, Matt. Hundreds. And one in a thousand finds a clue. Why bother?"

"I'd just like some closure. That's my job." He attempted a laugh, but it came out flat. "I'd like to ask her why she left us. Why she never called or wrote. I've got a daughter myself now, and I'd never do that to Caitlin."

Gina leaned back in the chair and shoved away from the computer. "Everyone isn't like you. Some mothers get tired of kids nagging them all day long. It happens every day. I pray to God every day that I never turn out like her."

Matt turned his head and looked at her but didn't say anything. It puzzled him that she didn't seem to care. Weren't girls supposed to be close to their mothers?

She pushed her hair out of her face. "Don't look at me like I'm some kind of heartless witch. *She* left us, Matt, remember? Pretending not to care is the only way I can get through knowing we meant so little to her."

"Do you remember her?" He could still smell her perfume sometimes in the night. Hear her voice. It wasn't natural that he couldn't get over the abandonment. He wanted to forget, but the memories dogged him.

"Not much. Aunt Irene was a good mom to me, in spite of her mental state at times. She loved me and made sure I didn't lack anything. You'd be happier if she'd kept you too." Her gaze gentled. "I know it must have been hard staying with Trudy."

His aunt hadn't wanted a rowdy boy. Neither had Trudy, for that matter. And neither had his mother.

nine

"The Irish Chain Quilt is a popular pattern in which the colorful blocks are all connected. In the same way, the Amish community is a long chain of fellowship and love."

HANNAH SCHWARTZ,

IN *The Amish Faith Through Their Quilts*

The murmur of voices in the other room settled, and Hannah heard the soft clink of spoon against cup. Maybe the bishop would go to the front door and not enter through the kitchen. He didn't have to know she was here. While she'd always liked the man, she knew he would gently urge her to reconcile with God and come back to her Amish faith.

She saw the wide brim of his hat pass the kitchen window and head to the front door. Her hands shook as she took a sip of her sweet tea. The confrontation would come sooner or later, but she'd put it off as long as possible. She set her tea on the table as Asia came back from listening at the doorway.

"They're calmer now," she said. "Some guy showed up."

"The bishop," Hannah murmured. Her hands itched to work on her quilt. The activity always soothed her.

"He's the head of the church?"

"This division, yes. Does my aunt know I'm here?"

Asia shook her head. "Sarah didn't say a peep about it. I think she's waiting for a better time to mention it."

"Did anyone see you?"

"No."

Asia glanced at the children. "Is the tea good?" They looked up at her with blank faces and went back to sipping their tea.

"They only know German until they go to school," Hannah said. The cell phone inside Hannah's purse rang. She grabbed it before it could disturb anyone in the other room. The number flashed across the front, but she didn't recognize it. "Hello," she said.

Reece's gravelly voice sounded in her ear. "Hang on," he said. "You can hear our little girl's voice."

Seconds later, a child's voice called out, "You can't catch me!" Hannah's heart leaped at the childish voice. She gasped and pressed the phone tighter to her ear. The child laughed and chattered to someone, and the voice imprinted itself on her soul. Was this her child? Or a horrible joke?

Reece's voice came back on the line. "Doesn't she sound sweet, Hannah? She misses you. I miss you. We can be a real family, hon. It's all up to you."

She struggled to speak past the invisible band around her throat. "Leave me alone, Reece. You killed our baby."

"She's not dead, Hannah. You just heard her voice. Come home and you'll see. I'll give her back to you. We can put the past behind us, start fresh. Your running off nearly killed me. I need you. Your daughter needs you. I even converted to the Amish faith too. We can be everything you always wanted."

"You're lying." She shuddered with the desire to get in the car and drive to where he was. To see if he really had the child. But it wasn't possible. Her daughter was dead. She still didn't know who the child was, but she knew Reece. He would never willingly care for a child. "Were you baptized?"

"Not yet, but soon. I'll send you a picture. I joined a community in Shipshewana."

"You don't even know German!"

"It's all in who you know. Some teenagers were harassing the bishop's son, and I stopped to help. He's been tutoring me in German and helping me learn all the rules. This can work, Hannah. I'll even switch to your old district. Just come home."

Reece the protector. He was always rushing in to help and then expected eternal gratitude. She hardened her heart to resist the plea in his voice. He had to be lying. He'd sworn he'd never become Amish. "How'd you get this number?" she asked.

"I still have friends," he said.

And he did. His background in law enforcement was one reason she'd resisted getting a phone for so long. Then when the book hit big, she'd had no choice, but she had an unlisted number. That hadn't slowed him down long. Saying nothing at all, she quietly closed her cell phone, then pressed the button to shut it off.

Aware that Asia and the children were staring at her, she managed a smile. "Anyone want a cookie?" Her aunt always kept cookies in the jar on top of the refrigerator. She didn't wait for an answer, since the girls wouldn't have understood, but reached up and pulled down the jar. The girls each accepted a cookie, and Hannah turned to pour them some milk. Once she set the glasses on the table, she moved to the sink to stare out the window.

Asia's vanilla scent told her that her friend had moved closer. "Was that Reece?" she asked.

"Yes. He says he has our daughter. That he's raising her Amish in a district in Shipshewana."

"But she wasn't dressed Amish."

"I know." Hannah glanced into Asia's worried face. "He'd taped a little girl laughing and talking. He said it was our daughter. I think he's toying with me, but I can't get it out of my head, Asia. What if he's not lying? What if this little girl really is my baby? Maybe he converted after the picture." Hannah couldn't let it go. Everything in her longed to hold that little girl, to smell her hair, to hug her close and kiss that soft, round cheek. Maybe she was losing her mind. Life with Reece might have driven her over the edge.

Asia sighed. "Find her, then. I bet she's here somewhere. Reece doesn't have her. He probably saw this girl and realized she looked a lot like you. He's playing games, trying to get you back. He couldn't have had her all this time. You said he wanted nothing to do with fatherhood."

"I know. He told me to come home if I wanted to see her." Hannah inhaled as a thought struck her. "You don't think he's already taken her from her home, do you? What if he kidnapped her? I can't let her fall into his hands!"

Asia grabbed her forearm. "Think, Hannah. He's not going to risk jail. He's just trying to lure you home."

Hannah's panic calmed as she recalled that the girl's voice had mingled with other children's. "You're right—I know you're right." Shuddering, she leaned against the counter. "I thought this was all behind me."

"It will be if you let it."

Hannah glanced at her then. "Could you just walk away, Asia? Look that little girl in the face and walk away without knowing?"

Her friend hesitated, then sighed. "Probably not. But there's no way I'd go back to the guy who beat me."

"I'm not going to." But would she? If Reece had her daughter, she would have no choice but to go back long enough to grab the little girl and flee. "Maybe I'll go talk to the sheriff. He might know something about the child."

A woman's voice Hannah recognized as her aunt's raised in a sharp protest, though she couldn't make out any words. Asia exchanged a long glance with her. "I wonder if Sarah told her I'm here," Hannah said.

Footsteps sounded on the wooden floor, then her aunt burst through the doorway, followed by Sarah. Tears marked Aunt Nora's eyes with puffiness, and she swiped a hand at her wet cheeks but only succeeded in smearing dirt on them. Her bonnet was askew, but her dark blue dress and white apron were neat and pressed. She had to be fifty now, but she looked older.

Hannah took a step toward her, arms open. Aunt Nora rushed into them. She hugged Hannah with a desperate grip, and a keening cry burst from her lips.

"I know," Hannah whispered, rocking the older woman a little. "I know." Tears rolled down her cheeks too.

How well she remembered the grief, anguish, and disbelief. The emotions had never left her. The horror of that night colored everything she'd done since. Every time she thought of the monster who'd destroyed her baby, her anger and hatred grew. If she was right and it was Reece who had killed her parents too, she'd spit in his face, rake at his eyes with her nails. No punishment would be great enough for all he'd done.

Every time she thought of her hate, the insistent voice of conviction came. Forgive. A voice she'd gotten good at ignoring. She knew her hate hollowed out her insides and drove nails into her compassion. She should pull it out by its roots, but the thought of justice was the only thing that kept the tears at bay. If she suffered for it in the end, then so be it.

If that man was Reece, he'd killed her parents to get to her. And his plan had worked. Was it her bitterness that made her want to believe he was guilty? Or could she be on the heels of truth? What if he'd struck again, killing Moe this time? A tremor ran through her, and she tightened her hold on Aunt Nora until the older woman managed to choke back her sobs.

Her aunt pulled away and dabbed at her face. "Thank you for coming, Hannah. I know it wasn't easy for you." She straightened her shoulders. "I know my Moe is in God's hands. I must accept God's will. I shouldn't have meddled." Fresh moisture flooded her eyes.

"Meddled?"

"I was warned to stay quiet, stay out of it. But I saw the child." She bit her lip. "I knew then the sins of the past would come out."

"You saw *my* child?" Hannah tried to keep her emotions in check. This was no time to push her aunt.

"Later," Aunt Nora whispered. "Oh, why didn't I listen?" She wiped her cheeks with her apron.

Rebellion stirred in Hannah's heart. Why had God allowed this? He could have kept Moe and her own family safe, but he didn't. If this was his will, it wasn't fair. She didn't understand how her cousin and now her aunt had been able to just shrug and accept it. She was never going to forgive the man who had done this.

Who had warned her aunt to stay quiet? And about what? It seemed impossible that Aunt Nora knew something, but maybe Hannah's mother had confided something in her sister-in-law. *Mamm* had no close family of her own, and *Datt*'s family had taken her under their wing.

Nora tugged on Hannah's hand. "Come say hello to Bishop Kirchhofer."

Hannah hung back. "I—I don't think I'm ready." She knew what was waiting for her, and the thought of a lecture at a terrible time like this made her want to run. But her aunt pulled harder and led Hannah to the living room.

More than ten years had slipped away since she'd been in this room she used to love. She and her mother had come over every week for tea and quilting, fellowship and belonging. The same hand-crocheted runners topped the end tables. The overstuffed sofa was looking a little threadbare. Everything was spotless, just like always.

The last time Hannah had been here, her mother and father were still alive. Her mother sat in the rocker by the window so she could see to stitch the quilt block she worked on. The light gilded her blond hair and made her look angelic.

It had been two days before she went to join the heavenly choir.

Hannah tore her gaze from the scarred wooden rocker to face the bishop. The last time she'd seen him, he'd ordered her to repent of her unforgiveness toward Cyrus Long.

He was looking at her again with the same loving sternness. Her entire life had trained her to submit to authority, and the need to do it was like an itch she couldn't reach. Her knees weakened with the desire to fall to them and confess her sins. She reminded herself it was a trained response. He didn't know her any longer. She was a different person from the pliable, easily deceived girl who had left here at twenty-two.

"Hannah, you're well?" he asked in his deep voice.

When Hannah was a child, the tones and cadence of his voice always made her think she was hearing God's voice. The bishop had always looked as old as the limestone along the creek, and his flowing white beard and weathered face under the broad brim of the hat brought to mind Old Testament prophets.

"Yes," she said.

"We've missed you. Your family needs you."

She stepped back a pace. "Please. Now isn't the time to bring pressure. We need to help Aunt Nora get through this."

"It's never the wrong time to do right," he said in a gentle voice.

Hannah didn't answer. She turned to her aunt. "Have you heard any more from the sheriff's office?"

"They've managed to get the autopsy scheduled for tomorrow, even though it usually takes much longer. Matt is a sweet boy who seems to care." Aunt Nora wiped her eyes again. "The Lord's will be done."

"Indeed," the bishop said. He turned his gaze on Hannah again, and an uncomfortable silence followed.

"I guess we'd better go," Hannah said. She couldn't stand much more silent pressure from him.

Sarah had been standing silently by the table with her children. "Do you have a place to stay?" she asked. "Or are you going back home?"

"I'll find a motel room somewhere," Hannah said.

"You'll stay here," her aunt said. "You understand I can't eat with you or accept any favors from you. But I won't turn you out on the street."

"I know the requirements," Hannah said. "Thank you. I'll bring in our suitcases." With Asia in tow, she fled the presence of the bishop and Sarah.

"What was that all about?" Asia asked. "Gosh, the tension just vibrated in the air. Did he expect you to say you wanted to come back to the Amish faith?"

"That's exactly what he wants. And it's even tempting," Hannah said. "It will be hard to be here as an outcast."

"Could you ever go back and give up your life?" Asia shuddered as if it was the worst thing she'd ever heard.

"Family is important," Hannah said. "We try to preserve that as much as possible and lock out the world. When I didn't have the conveniences, I didn't miss them. Even now, there's not that much to miss. I don't watch much TV, and we always had gaslights and propane-powered appliances."

"So why not go back?" Asia smiled. "You said 'we.' Like you are still Amish."

"It's too late. Divorce is never accepted—not for any reason. But I'll always be Amish at heart. Even if I reconciled with Reece, I'd have to forgive the murderer, too, and I'll never do that. Never." She thought about her aunt's words. Who could have warned her? And about what?

THURSDAY MORNING, TWO days after the murder, and he was already getting an autopsy. It paid to have friends in the right places. The cold in the coroner's lab penetrated Matt's bones. The rank smell nearly made him gag, but he stood his ground near the door. Ajax whined and pawed at his nose. Matt rubbed his dog's ears. "It's okay."

Whit Grout had done him a favor and pushed the autopsy to the top of his list, so Matt decided to meet him here in the basement of the hospital, though it was never a pleasant experience. The coroner came through the door peeling off his rubber gloves. Matt didn't want to speculate what the stains were on the man's lab coat. Whit shucked it, too, revealing khaki shorts and a T-shirt that read "Greenhouse Gas Coming Through—Hold Your Nose." About forty, he was so thin the only thing that cast a shadow was his blond hair, bushy as a porcupine. In spite of Whit's appearance, Matt had never met a smarter person. Whit noticed things. Important things.

Matt and Ajax fell into step beside him as they went to Whit's office. "What'd you find out?"

Whit didn't answer, plowing on ahead through the door and straight to the coffeepot. It smelled burned and stale, but he smacked his lips as he gulped half a cup. "Ah, that hits the spot. Want some?"

"No thanks. You figure out what killed Moe? Was it strychnine?"

"He had enough poison in his system to kill ten people his size." Whit dropped into his chair, a wooden piano stool that let him twist in any direction.

Matt took the more comfortable wooden folding chair, and Ajax curled up at his feet. The coroner had a big enough budget to get some decent furniture but seemed to relish putting guests at a disadvantage. When he came in here, Matt felt like a bug under the microscope, and he suspected Whit was always analyzing how people reacted to his environment.

"He inhaled it. Check any flowers at the house."

"We did. They were loaded with poison. They were sent to his mother. He was the one who put them in water and must have gotten enough of a whiff to kill him."

Matt had hoped for something easier to track down, but the flowers didn't seem to have come from any local florist. And Moe was dead and couldn't tell them who delivered the box of roses. Nora had no idea either. He rose and moved to the door. "Thanks, Whit."

"Got a Jane Doe that you might be interested in. About the right age. Drowned, natural causes looks like."

Matt's fingers tightened on the door handle. "Hair color?"

"Light red with gray."

The right hair color. "Can I see her?"

"Sure." Whit drained his coffee cup and rose.

Matt followed him down the hall to a room that held the cadavers in cold storage. When Whit pulled out a drawer, Matt drew in a deep breath. The rasp of the zipper sliding open on the body bag sounded loud in the cavernous room. He focused on a spot on the wall, probably the spray from a soda can.

"Well?" Whit prodded him on the arm.

Matt looked down into the woman's face. His gaze took in the sharp nose, the narrow-set eyes, the wide forehead. "It's not her." Relief and disappointment did a two-step. Why did he even think it might be? Only Whit knew of his secret search. "Thanks, my friend."

"No problem." Whit zipped the bag closed before shoving the drawer back into place.

Back outside, Matt drew in a lungful of clean air. But the taint of death stayed with him. His cell phone jangled at his belt, and he flipped it open. He noticed he'd missed several calls while he was in the dungeon. "Beitler."

Blake's voice came over the phone. "Where you at, partner? I've been trying to reach you."

"Talking to the coroner. My cell doesn't work in the basement."

"Your grandma called. She said she saw something the night Moe Honegger died."

"I'll meet you in front of headquarters." Trudy probably was one of his missed calls. He put Ajax into the backseat, then drove to the sheriff's office, where he slowed down long enough to allow Blake to jump into the passenger seat.

"She say what she saw?" Matt asked Blake.

Blake shrugged. "Someone cut through her corn patch, knocked down some stalks."

"Might be kids."

"Maybe. She seemed adamant she had to talk to you."

She was always adamant. Matt drove west out of Rockville. When he passed the road toward Nora's house and the other Amish farmlands, he wondered if Hannah had stayed in the community or gone home. And why had she come? She'd never explained.

Blake ran his window down. "How's Gina?"

"Fine. You two need to work it out."

"I'm working on it."

Matt's grip tightened on the steering wheel. "Is it true, Blake?"

His partner didn't look at him. "Is what true?"

"You having an affair?"

"That's none of your business."

Matt closed his mouth. He wanted to ask where Blake had gotten the money for the ring, but he feared to hear the answer. If Gina's suspicion wasn't true, wouldn't Blake deny the charge?

He turned down his grandmother's road. Trudy's house was the only one on this narrow way. She came to the door before Blake's raised fist could fall on the door.

"Don't just stand there—come in," she said, standing aside so they could enter. "Not the dog." She pointed her finger at Ajax. "Stay."

Ajax's tail drooped, but he settled down with his head on his paws and a mournful look in his eyes. "I'll be right back, boy." Matt pressed his lips together but didn't say anything. This was an old disagreement, and one he wasn't going to win. Trudy's ways were set by seventy-two years of footsteps encased in concrete.

She wore her gray hair loose on her shoulders. Even at seventy-two, her skin held a pink bloom. Tiny wrinkles crouched at her eyes and around her mouth, but she didn't look her age. The flowing red caftan gave her frame an elegance that matched the proud tilt to her head.

Matt followed her past stacks of old newspapers and magazines. He'd tried to clear out the clutter for years before finally giving up. Trudy was who she was. There was no changing her. She settled in a worn chenille rocker. He and Blake took the matching sofa. The crocheted doilies on the arms and the back of the sofa were starched and spotless.

"You've been neglecting me, Matthew," she said, fixing her blue gaze on him. "It's been three weeks and four days since you were here last."

Sheesh, did she keep a calendar? "I've been working a lot of overtime. You know how it is when there's been a murder. It will calm down soon." The guilt was a familiar companion. His job demanded so much of him. There were only so many hours in the day.

He took out his pen and notebook. "So you said someone trampled your garden?"

"More than trampled. Destroyed it." She began to rock. "And there's white powder on the ground."

He and Blake exchanged alarmed glances. "Don't smell it. Moe died from inhaling strychnine. Hang on." He called headquarters, and his boss promised to send out a car. "We'll get it checked and cleaned up," he told his grandmother. "In the meantime, stay away from it."

The coils of the chair seat screeched with Trudy's every movement. He could still hear that sound in his dreams. He would never forget the nights she locked him in his room and sat outside his door, rocking and rocking.

He took out his notepad and began to write. "Footprints?"

"Plenty of them. All one man, I think. You can check them for yourself. They lead across the field toward Nora Honegger's house."

"Did you see anyone?" Blake put in.

"If I'd recognized someone, don't you think I would have said that right off? But I saw his truck parked down the way under the old sycamore tree by the river. Just before the covered bridge."

"Make and model?" Matt asked.

"Tan. That's all I know."

Gina had said the man who followed her and Caitlin home drove a tan truck. "Anything else?"

She stopped rocking a minute. "I heard him whistling." She pursed her lips again and blew out a tune. "Like that."

Matt recognized the tune. "'Bad Moon Rising.'"

"If you say so."

Blake wouldn't know it, but Reece was a big Creedence Clearwater Revival fan. "Thanks for your help, Trudy. I'll go take a look at the footprints and the powder." He stood and started after Blake, who was already heading to the door.

Trudy caught his hand. "You found her yet?"

"No."

"And you won't," his grandmother said. "A woman like that can just disappear. She was never worthy of David. It was good riddance when she disappeared."

"Not for me." Wrong thing to say, and he knew it.

"She could wrap men around her finger like yarn. You're just as stupid as your father." She waved her hand. "Go ahead, get out of here. You're dying to escape."

Matt's guilt wouldn't let him just walk away. He brushed a kiss across her hair and inhaled her Suave hair spray. The scent reminded him of a time when he was lost and afraid. He wasn't that little boy anymore.

t e n

*"You see windmills at many Amish homes. They're used
to bring water up. The Windmill Quilt is a quaint
reminder that God provides all we need."*

—HANNAH SCHWARTZ,
IN *The Amish Faith Through Their Quilts*

The bird wall clock in the kitchen chirped the time. Nearly midnight Friday. No wonder the quilting stitches appeared blurred to Hannah's tired eyes. The cats curled up at her feet added to her sleepiness. She had wandered through Nora's house, looking at the quilts. Some were so worn and threadbare they made her wince. Quilts should be treated with care. One had been tossed carelessly over a chest, and she folded it up and laid it in a chair. The ones she recognized as her mother's handiwork, she'd caressed. The memories were almost more than she could bear.

She'd wanted to talk to her aunt about her strange comments, but her aunt was tight-lipped and tearful with the funeral looming tomorrow. Hannah, too, found it hard to concentrate since Moe's body reposed in the traditional white clothing in the closed dining room. The coroner had released his body yesterday for burial, and they'd been busy with preparations and visitors.

She heard a creak on the steps and glanced up. With a long gray braid over one shoulder and dressed in a pink nightgown, her aunt swayed at the foot of the steps. She came toward Hannah with a book in her hand.

"I'm sorry I was so bad tempered tonight," she said. "I was so shocked when the detective took away the flowers. They'd been delivered to me while I was visiting my friends down the road. Moe must have smelled them when he put them in water. It should have been me who died." She shook her head. "But God's will be done."

"Can I get you anything? Warm milk, tea?" She offered even though she knew she shouldn't.

Nora settled onto the sofa beside her. "I'm fine, or at least, as fine as I can be." She fingered the quilt block. "Really lovely stitching, Hannah."

"Not as good as my mother's."

Nora smiled. "Ah, your mother. I couldn't have loved her more if she'd been my own sister. I still miss her." She examined the stitches more closely. "You're every bit as good, my dear. You must love it like Patricia did."

"I do. It's my way of holding on to my mother," Hannah whispered. She'd never admitted to anyone what fueled her obsession.

"Your mother always said it was her way of making sense of the chaos in the world." Nora pointed to the basket on the floor. "Looking at the jumble of fabric and thread, there seems to be no pattern, no order there. But little by little, quilting brings order."

"You're right. Maybe that's why it calms me." Hannah wanted to bring up all her questions but worried over her aunt's fragility.

"What pattern are you working on?"

"It's a Triangle." She showed her aunt the brightly pieced square. "I use black fabric for the background and border, just like *Mamm* always did.

"This one is supposed to be photographed for the cover of a pattern quilt book I'm writing. It will illustrate the three things important to our way of life."

"It's beautiful." Her aunt's hand stroked the fabric. "I'm very proud of you."

Pain encased Hannah's heart. No one had said those words to her since her parents died. Reece had been quick to point out her failings, and praise from the museum was scanty until her book came out and she'd been catapulted into fame. She didn't feel worthy of any praise. She'd turned her back on her heritage and fallen into a relationship straight from a suspense movie. Now here she was with a failed marriage. Hardly a person to be proud of. But that was her aunt Nora. She saw the best in everyone.

Maybe that was why the success of her book frightened her.

Hannah put down her quilt block and reached for her bag. She pulled out the picture of the child. "This picture you sent me. Look at the quilt she's sitting on."

Nora carried it closer to the sputtering gaslight. "It's hard to see. What is it I'm looking for?"

"I recognize the quilt. It's the one *Mamm* was working on the week she died."

"Oh, Hannah, my dear, are you sure? The Sunshine and Shadow Quilt isn't uncommon." Her aunt's eyes held strain when she passed the picture back.

"I'm positive. I helped her choose the colors." It was the last quilt her mother had finished, and Hannah's favorite. "*Mamm* called this her 'almost Amish' quilt."

Her aunt took another look at the picture. "Because of the yellow in it."

"She loved to push past a bit of tradition." The design radiated green, turquoise, yellow, and red against a navy background. "She let me decide which colors to set against one another. And she let me buy some yellow fabric for it even though that's not a normal color for us." Even Hannah could recognize the stubborn tone of her voice. And honestly, was she sure that the quilt was *Mamm*'s? She *thought* she was. But was it wishful thinking? Only finding the child *and* the quilt would answer those questions.

Nora handed back the picture. "Did you tell Matt?"

"No."

"Why not?"

"He's a cop. He won't be interested in helping me find my—the little girl."

Nora patted her hand and settled onto the sofa beside Hannah. "You're not sure this is the same one, are you, dear?"

Hannah picked up her quilt block again. "I want to see it to make sure," she said. "Aunt Nora, Reece called me this morning, right after I got here. He said he has our daughter and that he's raising her Amish. He said he's converted. I think he's lying. Oh, I'm so confused. Are you up to talking?"

"I thought that's what we were doing." Her aunt laid her book beside her on the sofa. "I know you've been dying to ask me about what I know about the little girl and Moe's death. There are things you need to know, Hannah. A powerful enemy isn't through with this family yet. When the letter came, I went to see—" Before her aunt could finish, the window glass beside the sofa shattered. Shards of glass spilled out onto the wooden floor. The cats yowled and ran for the kitchen. Hannah and her aunt jumped up and turned to look as a glass bottle shattered and burst into flame. The fire spread quickly from the accelerant.

"The extinguisher!" Her aunt ran to grab a fire extinguisher in the kitchen, then returned to smother the fire.

Hannah called 9-1-1 from her cell phone as she roused Asia from sleep.

HOURS LATER, THE fire department and the sheriff's department left, and the women wearily cleaned up the soggy mess. The burn marks on the floor couldn't be hidden, but they mopped up the water and scrubbed away the soot in preparation for the funeral only hours away. None of them had heard or seen anything to indicate who had tried to torch the house. But Hannah feared she knew—Reece. He was sending her a warning that he'd found her. And that anyone who stood between the two of them would suffer the consequences.

SMOKE STILL LINGERED in the air from the ordeal the night before. Hannah slept restlessly in the old bed, the single window in the room looking out over the Indiana hills. She was back in her hometown, yet she wasn't part of her family, her people. Did she even want to be? Her life here was a lifetime ago. She coiled her thick braid at the nape of her neck. She'd forgotten how hard it was to see in the small mirror that only showed part of her head. Her gaze stared back, and she wondered who that woman was. She didn't know anymore.

Asia spoke from behind her. "Do I look okay? I have no idea since this place only has that teeny mirror. What's up with that?"

Hannah turned. Her friend's black skirt touched the top of stylish boots. The lacy black top plunged farther than Hannah ever wanted to wear again, but it looked good on Asia. "You look lovely. We don't hold with vanity. A full-length mirror would encourage us to put too much emphasis on our appearance."

"Yeah, but I can't even tell if my slip is showing." Asia twirled on heels high enough to give her a nosebleed.

"Not a sliver of it." Hannah gave her hair a last pat.

"You sure you want to wear that old shapeless thing?" Asia pulled on the loose waist of Hannah's dress. "It's like a gunnysack."

Her aunt had hung one of Hannah's old dresses in the bedroom closet, and she'd put it on. She looked down at the plain blue dress. "You're right. I think I'll change. The bishop might think I intend to confess at the next meeting." Besides, it seemed she was a girl again, and the clothing brought back the horror of the night she'd found the bodies of her family.

She stepped past two twin beds with no headboards. They were neatly made up with white sheets and blankets. She opened the closet, her hand hovering over a plain black dress with three-quarter-length sleeves. So severe and unflattering. Was it a sin to want to look nice? She'd tried to cover up after the way Reece made her dress, but maybe she'd gone too far.

After changing her shoes to low pumps, she defiantly added a simple locket to the outfit. Her family and friends would think she was a heathen for wearing the jewelry, but she needed some space from them, and this would create it.

Asia shook her head. "It's better, but sheesh, Hannah. I wish you'd let me take you shopping sometime. You've got a terrific figure, great hair and skin, and you do nothing to enhance your assets. I know you think you need to look the part of a matronly quilt expert, but you're only thirty-two. Live a little!"

"Reece used to make me wear slinky dresses that plunged to my navel, and high heels," she said. Her skin still burned at the memory of the way men looked at her.

"You're kidding! You?"

"I hated them." Hannah smoothed her skirt with her hand. "Has Aunt Nora come out yet?"

"Nope. Not a peep from her room."

"I'll check on her." Hannah went to her aunt's closed doorway down the hall off the living room. There was no sound from the other side. She tiptoed to the door and listened. Nothing. Rapping her knuckles softly against the wood, she called to her aunt. At first she thought the older woman would ignore the summons, but the door finally opened.

Her aunt was fully dressed in her usual dark blue dress and sensible shoes. The prayer bonnet looked a bit askew, but her features were composed as she tucked a hanky up her sleeve. "We should probably go down. Everyone will be arriving."

Hannah nodded and followed her aunt downstairs. Buggies were beginning to pull into the drive, dozens of them. Men hauled in backless benches and lined them up around the living and dining rooms and the kitchen. Women carried covered dishes for after the burial.

Her back erect, Aunt Nora accepted their handshakes and thoughtful words.

An hour later, they were all assembled. Hannah followed her aunt to the dining room and sat on the bench beside her. Moe's coffin was a plain pine box. The split top was hinged, and the upper portion of it had been folded back to reveal Moe's face. Hannah clasped her hands together as the usher seated people on the benches. She barely noticed Sarah and the girls come in. Luca would grieve that he'd missed the funeral. He likely didn't even know yet. He had no phone with him.

Asia sat on the bench behind Hannah and her aunt. Hannah turned around and whispered to Asia that they would sit through a regular church service, not a real funeral as the *Englisch* knew it. The bishop removed his hat, and in unison, the other men in the line of ministers removed theirs, as did all the men in the house. The bishop began to speak, an exhortation from the Old Testament. Preparation for death was the main theme of the sermon, and that theme was continued thirty minutes later by the second minister. When he was done, the minister read Moe's obituary in German, then dismissed the men to prepare for the viewing.

In spite of the number of people attending, the rearrangement went forward in near silence. The house emptied of mourners, and the men carried the coffin to the entry. Friends and neighbors filed past Moe to say their good-byes. Several people nodded to Nora and murmured condolences as they left to get in their buggies and go to the graveyard.

Hannah whispered to Asia that she wanted to go to the grave site in a buggy. Slipping away from the crowd, she hurried to the barn and hitched up a spry black horse to Moe's single-seater. She waited until the last of the buggies pulled out, then fell into the line behind them.

She needed to be alone to think. Life had come at her too fast in the past week, and with it, memories of her earlier life in this place. Was it as idyllic as she remembered? She believed it was, and she mourned the loss of her innocence.

With her thoughts swirling, she fell behind the rest of the buggies. The sky darkened, and rain began to patter onto her head. It grew nearly as dark as dusk. The air took on a greenish cast, and she feared a tornado might be in the swirling clouds.

She slapped the reins on the horse's rump, and he picked up the pace. As the rain fell harder, she wished her people believed in buggy coverings. She could barely see the road with the water dripping in her eyes. A dark shape loomed ahead in the downpour, and she realized a car without lights was bearing down on her. Did the driver see her? She directed the horse to the side of the road and kept going forward, but the car swerved toward her side of the road. She couldn't see the make or model, just the shape coming closer.

It was going to hit her, and her gut told her it was a deliberate move. She didn't want the horse to be harmed but didn't know what to do. Then she saw a path cut into the newly planted field of corn. Just as she turned the horse into the path, the car brushed by so closely that it rocked her buggy. Perspiration popped out on her forehead, and her hands began to shake. All she could see were the taillights flashing as the car slowed at the next intersection and went on.

Someone had tried to hit her.

She gulped back her fear and backed the buggy out of the lane to continue on to the grave site. The sun began to peek through the clouds as she finished the trip. She'd be late and a bedraggled rat, but she was alive. Still shaking, she stopped the buggy behind the long line and stepped down into the mud. She realized she was right in front of the graves of her parents.

Plain wooden stakes marked their sites. There were no flowers on any of the graves, and she longed to put just a single carnation on her mother's. She'd loved beautiful flowers so much. Keeping them from her didn't seem right.

Did *Mamm* ever regret her decision to join the Amish church? It wasn't done very often. It helped that her parents were German and she was already bilingual, but she gave up so much for *Datt*. Hannah wished she could talk to her mother's family, but the brief glimpse of her aunt and cousin at the funeral had been her only contact with them. Maybe she could find them again. Aunt Nora might know how to contact Aunt Cathy and Mary.

Had Reece really converted to the Amish faith? And if he had, where did that leave her? She couldn't go back to him. What if Reece was indeed behind everything—her parents' deaths, the fire at Aunt Nora's, the attempt on her life? Or was it her bitterness blinding her? Could she be wrong about Reece? But no, she'd felt his hand shoving her down the steps. A man who would do that was capable of anything. Her hatred swelled.

Hannah saw Asia's car parked along the road and waved to her. Asia jogged over to join her. "What happened to you?" she asked. "You look like a drowned kitten."

"Someone tried to run me off the road." Hannah told Asia what had happened, and immediately her publicist wanted to call Matt. "I don't want to spoil the funeral. We'll go see him later."

They stood on the edge of the crowd. Hannah tried to be as inconspicuous as possible. A blue Saturn rolled to a stop in the line of vehicles, and a woman got out. A sense of déjà vu rolled over her when she recognized her cousin Mary.

Ten years older now, Mary had lost the fresh bloom of her early twenties. Her auburn hair was cut short, and the style did nothing to flatter her face. She'd gained a few pounds as well, and the blouse she wore strained across her stomach. Hannah stepped out to meet her.

"Mary, I don't know if you remember me. I'm Hannah."

The other woman smiled. "It would be hard to mistake you since we look so much alike."

"Is your mother here too?" Hannah remembered how her mother and Aunt Cathy also resembled each other.

Mary fell into step beside Hannah, and they moved toward the throng of people around the grave. "No, she's in Maine again. After your parents were killed, I ended up moving here to Indiana. I read about Moe's death in the paper and thought I'd come pay my respects. I know he's not a direct relative, but I still feel part of the Amish side of the family. I thought you left town."

"I did. I came back for a visit a few days ago. Where are you living? I'll stop by if you don't mind."

Mary gave her the address. "I'd love that."

"Are you married? Have kids?" When the question sprang from her lips, Hannah wondered if the child she sought might be Mary's.

"Nope, no husband. Or kids." A shadow darkened Mary's eyes.

They rejoined Asia at the edge of the crowd. The interment service proceeded without incident, but watching Nora's pain hurt Hannah. It was all she could do to stand back and let closer family comfort Aunt Nora.

Mary had to get back to work after the service, and Hannah promised to visit. Once her cousin got in her car and drove off, Hannah wanted to do the same. "I can't eat with them," she told Asia. "I don't want to embarrass Aunt Nora or Sarah. Let's go to the jail. I need to see Matt and tell him what happened on the road."

She told her aunt they were leaving, then she had Asia follow her to return the horse and buggy to her aunt's house. Once she cared for the horse, she and Asia headed for Rockville. When they got there fifteen minutes later, Hannah stood five feet away from the car, staring at the big boxy building. The jail repelled her, reminded her of the questioning she'd endured ten years ago. She could still smell the cleaning solution used in the room where she'd been grilled for four hours, and the scent made her stomach churn. What made her think they'd help her now?

She glanced down at the picture in her hand. The little girl smiled up at her, but the gap-toothed grin failed to move her. This couldn't be her child. The wind ruffled Hannah's hair, swirling it around in her face as a sign that she shouldn't go in.

Confusion gripped her. She retreated to the car and put her hand on the door handle. The best thing was to get back in the car and not draw attention to herself.

"Hannah, what the heck? I thought you wanted to talk to Matt."

"I probably imagined the whole thing. Now that I think about it, I'm sure it was an accident. And this whole daughter thing is probably a mirage."

Asia pointed her red-tipped finger at her. "You get right back in there and talk to him. We haven't come all this way not to pursue every avenue."

"You're right. I know you're right." Hannah turned and forced herself to march to the door and yank it open.

THE JAIL SMELLED like someone's roast beef sandwich. Matt walked past the deputy manning the front desk and proceeded down the narrow hallway to his cramped office, last room on the left. Blake followed him. The guy whistled through his teeth, and the annoying ditty set Matt on edge.

"Hey, Beitler," a young deputy called. "The Rockville police reported a big heist from the Ace Hardware store. The alarm wasn't triggered and we've got nada."

Great. The rash of break-ins was getting worse. He wondered—for the umpteenth time—if it was an inside job. Someone smart had been pulling the robberies. He pushed away his doubts about Blake and stalked on to his office.

Attending the funeral had been a waste of time. He'd seen nothing suspicious and caught only one glimpse of Hannah. She hadn't seen him.

He dropped into the chair behind his overflowing desk and pulled his keyboard to him. Calling up the files, he ignored Blake, who was pacing the room.

"The white powder at Trudy's was insecticide dust, nothing lethal to a person," Matt said. "But the flowers that were delivered to Nora Honegger were loaded with poison. So far we haven't been able to discover what florist delivered them. The box they came in was in the trash, but it was plain white cardboard with no business name." Leaning back in the chair, he flipped open the file containing the printouts of what they knew so far. "The funeral was this morning. I went for a little while. Some people from town came, but it was mostly Amish."

Blake finally quit pacing and came to sit on the other side of the desk. "I think it's a family member."

"Of course you do," a female voice said from the doorway.

Matt looked up to see Hannah standing in the hall. Her cheeks were flushed, and her golden brown eyes sparked with fire. Her hair looked wet, and so did her clothes. With that titian hair, she probably had trouble hanging on to her temper. "You have something to say?"

She advanced into the room. The black dress only partially concealed her figure, and he wondered if it shamed her that she was so beautiful. He realized he was enjoying seeing her agitation.

"You've trained your partner well," she said. "He's just as quick to jump to conclusions as you."

"The murderer is generally someone close to the victim," he said.

"We are *Amish*. We abhor violence." She pointed to the computer. "If you look through your files, I doubt you'll find a single case of one of us breaking the law. No one in our community killed Moe or my family."

"Are you okay?" he asked when he realized she was shaking. He thought more than anger lay beneath her nerves.

"Someone tried to run me down in the buggy."

He stiffened. "Why didn't you call me? What did the vehicle look like?"

"It was during the storm, and the rain was coming down too hard for me to tell." She gripped the back of a chair, and her voice grew steadier. "Maybe I'm jumping to conclusions. It could have been an accident, but I tried to move out of the way and the vehicle matched me."

"The next time something like this happens, *call me*!"

Blake's cell phone rang. "I'll be back in a minute." He disappeared through the door.

Matt kept his gaze on Hannah. "There's not much I can do without a description of the car, but you need to be careful."

She nodded, the hectic red in her cheeks draining away. "I—I came for another reason too." She swallowed hard.

There was something so vulnerable about her that Matt wished he didn't have to question her. His job was to push and prod until he got at the truth, and he knew there was a lot she held back. Getting at it might hurt her. "So what's up?"

She blinked, exhaled, then slowly opened her bag. Rummaging inside, she withdrew a photo and held it out. "I wonder if you've seen this little girl."

A child? Matt took the slick paper. His sweet daughter's face looked back at him, and he almost smiled. "Where did you get this?" He tried to think of what Caitlin might have done. Thrown rocks? Darted in front of her? He lifted his coffee cup to his lips.

She bit her lip. "Reece sent it. He says it's our daughter."

Matt choked on the sip of hot liquid. "Wait, let me get this straight. You've never seen this girl before, yet you say it's your daughter? How is that possible?" He looked down at Caitlin again. It *was* Caitlin, wasn't it?

She didn't look at him but rushed on. "I was pregnant, and Reece wasn't happy about it. About two weeks before the baby was due, he shoved me down the stairs. I just remember pain and coming in and out of consciousness. When I finally woke up, he told me the baby girl had died."

Matt found it hard to get his mind around what she was saying. A shiver of fear tickled his spine. "And now he's saying the baby didn't die? That this child is that baby?"

She nodded. "I left him as soon as I found out. I thought that was the end of it until I got this picture last week. I want to find my daughter," she said with a stubborn tilt to her chin.

No way. Maybe Reece had seen a picture of Caitlin and recognized the resemblance, then chosen to use it. It was impossible her daughter was his baby girl. "When was this?" he asked before he could stop himself.

"Five years ago. April fourteenth."

The day before Analise had found a tiny bundle on their front porch. Horror stopped his tongue. He wouldn't believe it. He swallowed hard and managed to feign indifference. "And you believe him? Maybe he's just yanking your chain."

She nodded. "He might be trying to hurt me. He says if I come back to him, I can have her back. He says he's raising her Amish up in Shipshewana, but this little girl is dressed *Englisch*. So it's hard to believe what he's telling me."

Matt forced himself to breathe, to act naturally. He couldn't let on how upset he was. At least he knew it was all a lie. "I think he's bluffing." He knew he should tell her, but he had to know more first. His child's future hung in the balance.

Tears hung on her lashes. "He called me yesterday, and I heard her voice. She sounded darling."

Reece had taped Caitlin's voice? Maybe Gina wasn't overreacting and someone had been following her. Maybe Reece had seen Caitlin and realized how much she looked like Hannah. He might have seen this as a way of getting to her.

Matt had to gain some time, figure out what to do. No one was taking his daughter. "You think he's in town?"

"I'm sure of it. He sent me this picture to flush me out so he could find me."

"I'll try to find him, talk to him."

She shook her head. "He's crafty. He won't tell you anything. But can we look for the child?"

"What makes you think she's in Indiana?" He was total slime to try to confuse her.

"See here?" She handed the picture back to him. "There's a covered bridge in the background."

He peered at the picture. She was right. He remembered the picnic by the bridge, too, just a month ago on an unusually warm April day. "That doesn't say for sure it's here. There are covered bridges in other places."

"Yes, but look at the name on the bridge. It's the one by my—my cousin's house, the Narrows Bridge. So we need to start here."

By some miracle, he kept his voice steady. "There's no crime yet. I'm not sure what you expect me to do."

"Isn't it a crime to steal a baby from her mother?" Her voice rose. "How about murdering a child?"

"You don't know this little girl is even yours. And did you ever press charges against Reece?" He didn't even have to wait for her to shake her head. Of course she didn't. She'd simply walked away from him like so many battered wives without making him pay for what he'd done. "So we have no proof of anything."

"Then what do I do?"

"I'll find Reece and talk to him." He waved the picture in the air. "But I think you're chasing a dream. This little girl probably just has red hair." He had to believe it for his own sanity, to keep panic from sweeping him away.

"I understand that. But I have to do something. I have to find her, discover the truth for myself."

He nodded. "I'll keep you posted. Give me your cell phone number." As she dug for a pen and paper, he glanced at the photo again. His blood ran cold at the thought that Reece had been watching his baby. The man had to be somewhere nearby, and Matt would find him, force him to tell the truth. Force him to go away and leave them all alone.

eleven

"Take a look at the Amish Bars Quilt. Less is more in the
quilt and in the Amish way of life. They're able to escape the
plague of materialism sweeping the country."

—HANNAH SCHWARTZ,

IN *The Amish Faith Through Their Quilts*

Asia had the radio turned up and was singing along when Hannah got back to the car. Perspiration trickled along the back of her neck, and her pulse still raced from the effort to convince Matt to help her. If she'd had anywhere else to turn, she wouldn't have gone to him.

The smile on Asia's face faltered when she saw Hannah. "It didn't go well?"

"That man could make a bishop swear." Hannah slammed the door behind her and fastened her seat belt as Asia laughed. "He's going to look around, but he's still looking at our community for the murderer. Just like he did when my family died. One of us was his first assumption. I thought he might have learned something, grown up some."

Asia started the car and pulled into the line of traffic. "Don't you watch *CSI*? It's generally someone close to the victim. He's just following standard procedure."

"But does he have to be so obnoxious about it? I want to talk to my aunt, but not while she's so upset. She seems to know something about this."

"Well, you can do that later. *Publishers Weekly* called, and you have a phone interview with them in an hour and a half. They want a quick quote from you for an article they're running on why Amish books are so popular."

Hannah wanted to shake her head and refuse, but Asia was just doing her job. "Asia, I don't want to do any promotion while I'm here. Please don't schedule anything more."

Asia didn't seem to hear. "We've got to maximize the opportunity while we can. I plan to call some women's magazines next and set up photo shoots here in the area where they can see you interacting with the Amish."

"No, absolutely not. No photos here. You know the Amish don't like their pictures taken. They don't tolerate graven images or vanity." The very thought made Hannah want to pace. If her family were fully aware of her fame, their disapproval would soar. When had she so fully disassociated herself from the concept of *Hochmut?* Her people had a horror of elevating themselves into the limelight, but she'd welcomed it when it had come. Perhaps she had even been a bit prideful of her success. No wonder the bishop warned against how easily worldly ways could creep in.

They reached the turnoff to Nora's farm, and from the corner of her eye, Hannah saw a truck go by. The man's head swiveled, and their eyes locked. It was Reece. She saw recognition come into his face, and he smiled.

"Step on it, Asia, quick!" Her pulse thundered in her ears. Five years wasn't long enough to get rid of the metallic taste of terror that came at the first glimpse of his face.

"Who is it?" Asia stomped on the gas. She did a U-turn in the middle of the road and sped away in the opposite direction.

Hannah peeked over the top of the seat behind them. "He's turning around to follow us!"

Asia accelerated. "Is it Reece?"

"Yes." Hannah barely breathed. "Go back to town, and we'll go to Matt." She glanced behind them. Reece had nearly caught up to them. "Get out of here!" The tan truck stayed on their trail. "There's a little lane around the next curve. It goes across a covered bridge. There's a thick hedge on the other side. Maybe we can hide there."

Asia held to the wheel with both hands. "Call Matt!" The car went airborne over a hump in the road, but Asia maintained control.

Hannah grabbed for her purse and dug out her cell phone. "The battery's dead!"

"Get mine."

Hannah looked around for her friend's bag. "Where's your purse?"

Asia groaned. "It's in the trunk."

They crested the hill, and Hannah kept her gaze glued on the truck behind them. She lost sight of it as they went down the hill. "Right there," Hannah said, pointing out the narrow lane.

Asia spun the steering wheel, and the car plunged down the overgrown road. They entered the covered bridge, the dark coolness a haven. The tires rumbled over the wooden planks. Then they were out the other side. Still no sign of the truck. Hannah directed Asia to the thick copse of trees and shrubs where she used to play with her siblings.

Asia ran the windows down and turned the key to off. The sound of the engine died, and Hannah heard the chatter of birds overhead and, in the distance, the whine of a vehicle tearing down the hill. She caught her breath and waited. Would he notice the turnoff? He'd grown up around here too, and he might remember this place.

She opened the car door and peered through the foliage hiding them. A flash of metal showed through the other side of the covered bridge. A tire thunked on wood. "He's coming!" Panic closed her throat, and she looked wildly around for some place to hide.

"Get back in the car! I'll get us out of here." Asia started the car.

Hannah jumped back inside and closed the door with as little sound as possible. She didn't put her seat belt on in case she would have to jump and run to escape Reece. The thought of him laying hands on her again made her head swim. She pushed away the weakness. Never again would she let a man hurt her like he had.

Holding her breath, she watched the truck rumble past up the narrow dirt road. Maybe he thought they'd cut through to the other road that way. "Hang on," she said. "Maybe he won't see us." But even as she spoke, she saw his brake lights flash. "He's spotted us!"

Asia accelerated away from their hiding spot and back onto the covered bridge. "You sure this bridge is built to take us running back and forth?" she muttered.

Plunging into the river would be better than facing Reece again. Hannah turned in her seat to peer behind them. "Yes." Would she ever really escape him?

The car emerged from the bridge into the sunlight. "Back to town," she said. "Let's try to make it to the jail."

Asia's speedometer hit seventy by the time they crested the hill. The truck followed them, gaining every second.

"Faster!" Hannah cried. Her pulse battered the flesh in her throat. It seemed inevitable that she would have to face Reece. Maybe now was the time.

"I've got the accelerator clear to the floor."

The city limit was just ahead. "We're almost there."

The truck gained on them until their bumpers were almost touching. Asia made a sharp turn down the street toward Matt's office, even running a red light. The truck didn't manage the turn, though the tires squealed as it tried. Asia turned at the next street and wove around until they were in front of the jail.

Just as she slammed on the brakes and parked, Reece's truck came from a side street. He pulled in behind them and ran his window down. "Are you okay, hon? We need to talk," he called. "I'm not going to hurt you."

Hannah's hands shook, and she trembled all over. She threw open the door and tottered out. Breathing deeply, she tried to gather enough strength to run into the building. She couldn't bear to look at his face.

The car door slammed behind her, then Asia was at her side, taking her elbow. "Let's get inside." She turned and faced Reece. "I've gotten a restraining order on you—get out of here before you're arrested."

Hannah dared a peek at him. He had a beard coming in. It was about an inch long. Was it to give weight to his lie about converting to the Amish faith? She could see the slash of dark suspenders against the white shirt he wore.

He waved and accelerated out of the parking lot. "You'll have to talk to me sooner or later, Hannah." The words rang through the open window before his tires squealed on the pavement and the truck zoomed away.

Hannah's shaking began to wane, and anger took its place. He couldn't do this to her, not anymore. Men like Reece always got away with their crimes. And she could have kicked herself now that it was over. She'd let her fear drive her. If only she'd mastered it and confronted him, maybe she would know more about the little girl. She needed to find some backbone.

MATT STUDIED THE women. Both were clearly shaken. Hannah was pale, and she stood twisting her hands together. Tears pooled in her eyes. Even her friend Asia paced the sidewalk, her black hair bouncing and her brows drawn together as though she wanted to bite someone.

She stopped and pointed a red-tipped finger at him. "So, Officer, what are you going to do to protect Hannah from that madman?"

He thought about correcting her. Detective. He'd fought hard for that title. "I'll put out a warrant for his arrest, bring him in, and talk to him."

"*Talk* to him? What good will that do? Talk rolls off the back of a man like him. You're just protecting him because he's one of you!"

Matt spread his hands out, palms up. "He's not one of us. We'll bring him in and tell him he can't break the restraining order." His gut said Hannah needed protection. He had one dead body, and he didn't want another murder on his desk. "I'll arrange for a car to drive by." Besides, he wanted Reece out of commission and as far away from Caitlin as possible.

Hannah tipped up her chin. "Surveillance isn't going to stop Reece." Ajax pressed against her leg and whined. She rubbed his ears, and her shoulders relaxed.

"It might discourage him," Blake put in. He put his pen away.

She shook her head. "He has total contempt for law enforcement. He thinks he's above it all because he was a deputy himself once."

Maybe he still was. "What's he doing now?"

"Last I heard he was a guard for a big corporation in Detroit. He lost his job on the police force there after he beat up a drunk. If it's true he joined the Amish church in a district in Shipshewana—which I doubt—he would have to be doing something else."

"Do you believe him?" he asked her.

She didn't answer right away. When he thought she was going to refuse to talk about it, she finally gave a tiny shrug. "I don't want to believe him, but he might have."

"Why would he do that?" The man Matt knew hated being told what to do. Matt couldn't see Reece taking orders from a bishop.

"He thinks it would add to the pressure to make me go back to him."

Matt didn't ask her if the pressure would work. The torment on her face made it clear that such a circumstance would make her decision harder. "So where are you staying? You still at your aunt's?"

"Yes, but I don't want to bring more trouble on her head. She has enough with her son's murder and the Molotov cocktail last night." Hannah glanced down the street. "I could stay at the bed-and-breakfast out at the maple farm."

"Too remote. And it's probably not good to stay with your aunt either. She's in the middle of nowhere too." He thought for a minute. His rental cottage was one block over with plenty of nosy neighbors. It was empty right now. Digging in his pocket, he pulled out his keys. "I own a rental close to the station. There are two bedrooms and neighbors who would shoot an intruder on sight. You can stay there."

She shifted from one foot to the other and looked down at the keys in his hand. "Thank you. I'll pay you for it."

"It will only be a few days." He pressed the key into her hand. "It's over on Water Street. 303. White with blue shutters. Wait, I'd better go with you so the neighbors don't call me to tell me someone has broken into the place." He walked to his SUV, then got Ajax loaded in the back.

"Hope you know what you're doing, partner," Blake said.

"You got any other ideas?"

"She's not your responsibility. We do the best we can."

Matt shot him a look of disgust. "And maybe get another dead body. I don't understand what's happening yet, but I intend to."

Blake shrugged. "We can't play bodyguard for everyone."

"You're all heart, Blake." But what did he expect from a guy who would cheat on his wife? He pushed away the thought of his lies to Hannah. That was different. "Follow me," he told the women. He got in his vehicle, then waited until they climbed back into their car before leading them the short distance to his house.

Parking in front, he saw that the grass needed to be cut and the shutters could use a new coat of paint. Funny how he hadn't noticed until he was bringing guests. He let Ajax out, and the dog raced to sniff at the other car's wheels.

Hannah got out of the car, and her gaze swept the house. "It's charming." She sounded surprised.

"I'll let you in." He opened the gate to the picket fence and walked to the door, which he unlocked and pushed open. "After you." The women stepped past him into the foyer. He'd just cleaned it on his day off in hopes of renting it, and he could still smell the Lysol in the air. "Where's your luggage?"

"At my aunt's."

"I'll go get it for you. I don't want Reece following you here." His mind still raced about how to hide Caitlin now that he knew Hannah was looking for her. And what was Reece's game? By now Reece knew where his sister lived. At least she lived with a sheriff's detective.

"Oh, my cats are there too." Hannah bit her lip. "I—I should probably go back there instead."

"Cats? I hate cats." The thought of the sneaky creatures strolling through his house made him wince. "Can't your aunt keep them for you while you stay here?"

"She just lost her son. I don't want her to have to worry about them. I need them with me. It will take Reece a while to figure out where we are."

"If he's as guilty as you say he is, he might have been the one to throw the Molotov cocktail through the window. Just how many of them are there?"

"Four."

At least she had the grace to look a bit ashamed. "You have plenty of litter? And food?"

"Yes, I brought all their things with me. The stuff is at my aunt's too."

Now that he looked a little closer, he saw that her eyes were almost cat-like. The golden brown color and the almond shape reminded him of a tabby's eyes. As he'd often told Caitlin. He shoved the thought away. "I'll go get the felines. They can stay here."

"Are you sure? Will Ajax be okay with them?"

Ajax looked up at the mention of his name and came to sit at Matt's feet. "I'll leave him here for now. Anyway, Ajax loves cats. It's his one flaw."

She smiled then, and he thought she should do it more often. The flash of white teeth and the light in her eyes made him smile back in spite of the way he wished he could boot out the felines.

"Maybe I should go with you. They'll be out of sorts in a strange place without me around."

He knew the feeling. Leaving the two women in his house made him want to stalk around and swish his tail too—if he had one. "I can handle it. I don't want him watching your aunt's house and following you back here."

He stopped to get Blake to help, then drove out to the Honeggers'. Buggies still lined the road and the driveway. "I wish we had something new to tell Mrs. Honegger," he told Blake as he parked and got out. He nodded to several Amish men sitting around smoking on the front porch. Another woman came to the door when he knocked, then Mrs. Honegger pushed through the crowd to step out onto the porch with him and Blake.

"May I help you?" she asked.

"I apologize we don't have any news yet, ma'am."

"We wait on the Lord's will, son."

"We plan to see justice done, Mrs. Honegger. I'll track down the killer."

"When you do, let me know. I need to go to his family."

Did she plan a tongue-lashing? "Why do you want to see his family, ma'am?"

"I will accept this from the Lord's hand, young man. I've already forgiven the one who did this, and I want to comfort his family."

Matt didn't understand how she could be so calm and accepting of what had happened, but her attitude intrigued him. "I'm here for another reason. Your niece and her friend were followed today by Reece O'Connor. And someone tried to run Hannah down in the buggy on her way to the grave site. I'm having them stay at a home close to the sheriff's station."

Mrs. Honegger put her hand to her mouth. "Hannah! Is she all right?"

"She's fine. She escaped without incident."

"Oh dear. I need to talk to Hannah, explain what's happening." The woman literally wrung her hands. "I should never have sent her the picture."

"Tell me, do you know who threw the explosive through your window?"

She looked up at him, her brow smoothing. "I'll talk to Hannah. It's not your concern. It's a family matter."

"If you know something, it's your duty to tell me."

"I'll talk to Hannah only."

He scribbled down the address and phone number where Hannah was staying. "Here's her contact information. Don't wait too long. I believe she's in danger." He pressed it into her hand. "I'm here to get her luggage and cats."

Relief flooded her face. "They've dug up my flower bed trying to get some poor chipmunk."

"You let them outside?" He had a vision of trying to corral four cats. It wasn't pretty.

"I had no choice. They stood at the door and meowed until I wanted to cry." She stepped through the door, and he followed. "Their carriers are on the back porch."

He saw them stacked in the corner. "I'll get them." He grabbed two. Might as well get started. One black cat with white paws sat licking its paws in the flower bed. He approached with caution. "Hey there, kitty." The animal looked up with obvious disdain in its green eyes. Matt set the animal containers on the ground and opened the doors. "Want to go see Hannah?" He rolled his eyes at his own stupidity. Like the dumb things could understand.

To his surprise, the feline gave one last lick, then calmly walked into the closest cage and curled into a ball. He clicked the door into place before the cat could change its mind. Glancing around, he spied a white cat under a blooming crabapple tree. He scooped up the second carrier and walked toward the cat. The animal scampered away and leaped onto a branch about face high, where it hunkered down among the white blossoms that gave off a sweet scent.

He set the cage down, then scooped up the cat. It meowed and squirmed, but he managed to stuff it inside and get the gate closed. When he turned around, Blake came toward him with the other carriers.

"I've got them," he said.

Matt caught a glimpse of a calico face and a ginger tabby. At least he didn't have to chase them down. Once they loaded the cats and the girls' luggage in the SUV, he nodded toward the woods. "Let's take another look around while we're here." He ran the windows down and headed out back.

The crime scene tape still marked off the area in the clearing. He ducked under it and glanced at the spot where they'd found the body. The technicians would have gone over that area with a fine-tooth comb. But maybe something else was here. Birds scolded from overhead as the men picked their way through the underbrush.

He caught a glimpse of movement between the leaves. "Hey!" he yelled.

A man's face peered through the foliage. Ruddy cheeks bloomed above his black beard laced with gray. Matt guessed him to be about forty. Dressed in jeans and a bright red shirt to alert hunters to his presence, he stepped from the concealing bushes and came toward them with a backpack slung over one shoulder and a GPS unit in the other. A woman about the same age followed. Her jeans had muddy patches on the knees, and she wore a red long-sleeved blouse. Her long hair, streaked with white, held twigs and leaves. A plethora of patches covered their vests.

Once he got nearer, Matt recognized the man as the geocacher who'd found Moe's body. Kevin Brainerd.

"Is there a problem, Detective?" Kevin asked. He stood with his feet planted apart.

"You live near here?" Matt asked.

Kevin shook his head. "Me and my wife"—he thrust a thumb at the woman—"we got a place on the other side of the county."

"I'm surprised you're back over here considering what you found the other day."

Kevin shifted and glanced at his wife. "With all the hoopla, we never found the cache we were looking for."

"Did you know the victim?" Matt asked.

Another quick glance at his wife. "Well, we bought vegetables from his mom every summer, and we talked to him occasionally."

"Find your cache this time?"

Kevin smiled then. "Yep. A nice assortment of coins and DVDs. We took a coin and left a shirt patch." He pointed to a patch on the shoulder of his shirt. "Had them specially made."

"All right, then, stay clear of the taped-off area."

"Yes, sir." The two headed north, away from the meadow.

Matt turned to Blake. "If they found the cache, what are they still doing here?"

twelve

*"The Postage Stamp Quilt is a beautiful example of intricate work.
And you might be surprised to know that many Amish love to travel.
They hire drivers to take them on vacation. They refuse to fly and
will only travel by boat, train, or automobile."*

—HANNAH SCHWARTZ,

IN *The Amish Faith Through Their Quilts*

Reece stalked the roadside, kicking at dandelion blossoms and other blooming wildflowers. All he wanted to do was talk to Hannah, but she thwarted him at every turn. She never even gave him a chance to say he was sorry.

The kid was the key. He knew his wife, and she'd do anything for a child.

Her gentle nature had attracted him, but once he'd married her, he'd found her tough as shoe leather under that sweet smile. She had a way of defying him that most people wouldn't notice because of its subtlety. Who would have thought she could have hidden herself away from him so completely for five years? She had to have had help.

But now he'd found her. He'd been so lonely without her. No one else looked at him with stars in her eyes. No one else turned to him for love and protection. She'd always made him a bigger man than he was. He wanted her to love him completely again. It was her duty anyway. The minute he'd met Hannah, he'd known she was the missing piece of his soul. If anyone could understand the demons that sometimes took him, it was her. She'd disappointed him, though. Sorely. But things would be all right again. He could explain, make her see he was only thinking of her and of their marriage.

He turned his thoughts back to the kid. Maybe they really could be a family. His head filled with notions of throwing a baseball on Saturday afternoons and taking her for ice cream. Fatherhood might not be so bad. They'd be the perfect little family. But he'd have to make sure this was the only kid. No more. He couldn't handle a bunch of screaming brats.

Hannah hadn't believed that he'd joined the Amish church. He really was trying. Their religion was a bunch of mumbo-jumbo to him, but at least he was giving it an effort. She should give him credit for making the attempt.

THE SMALL HOUSE radiated cleanliness. Hannah wondered about that. Most guys didn't notice things like the soap dishes at the sink, but Matt's were spotless. Did he have a cleaning service that kept this place up even when it wasn't rented?

When she went back to the living room, Asia was stretched out on the sofa with her shoes off. Ajax lay beside her, his face a picture of contentment as she stroked his ears. Hannah dropped into the oversized chair and propped her feet on the ottoman.

"Nice place Mr. Detective Man has," Asia said. "Fully furnished too. Wonder why he has a rental?"

"It's pretty," Hannah agreed. "It's definitely a man's place, though. The furniture is oversized and a little big for this room. No pictures on the walls. Nothing on the tables but lamps."

Asia chuckled. "A woman's touch would change that. Still, it's nice. And everything is so organized in the kitchen."

Hannah heard the sound of a vehicle, then a dog barking. Ajax's ears perked, and he got off the couch and stretched before padding to the door. "I think he's back." She went to the door just as it opened.

Matt entered, lugging two cat carriers. His partner came behind him with two more. All four cats hissed when the dog barked. "It's going to be a zoo," he said, setting the carriers down on the tile floor in the entry. He appeared tense, and irritation hunkered in his eyes. "Have I mentioned that I hate cats?"

"Is that right?" It was all Hannah could do to keep a straight face. She knelt before the first carrier and opened the door. With a yowl, Spooky rushed out. Every hair on end, the black cat leaped over Ajax, who was crouched down peering into the cage. The outraged feline disappeared under the sofa.

"He won't come out for hours," Hannah said. "Maybe I'd better take the rest of them to the bedroom and let them out." She lifted the carrier containing Marmalade and started down the hall. Matt followed with the other two carriers. "Thanks for getting them for me," she told him.

He grunted in response, and her smiled vanished. "Look, I know it's a trial to you. I'm sorry. You want us to go to a hotel or back to Aunt Nora's?"

"No, you stay here. It's just that I hate cats."

"I think I heard that somewhere." She smiled. When he didn't respond, she gave a mental shrug. "Why do you have a rental anyway?"

"It was my first house. I got too good a deal to throw it away, so I've rented it out, and it's paid off now. A good investment."

"It's a nice place. But I really don't mind staying with Aunt Nora." Hannah was dying to find out what her aunt knew, but she wanted to give Nora at least a day of grieving space. "Maybe we can go back in a day or so."

"She said something about needing to tell you what's been going on. But what's her role in this?"

It was a piece that didn't fit. "I wish I knew. Reece sent her the picture of the girl, and she mailed it on to me. Maybe he called her or something.

Maybe he threatened her. Like you said, maybe he threw the Molotov cocktail in the window and she knows he did and why."

He set the two carriers on the floor and opened them before answering. The cats poked their noses into the room before stepping daintily out onto the carpet. "I'm frustrated," he said. "I've got no real direction on this murder. The guy who found the body was back at the scene today. I'll follow that and see where it goes, but there's no obvious motive." He glanced at her. "I shouldn't be saying anything about the case, but you're easy to talk to."

The warmth in his gaze brought heat to her cheeks. "Here I thought you hated me."

"I'd like to," he said softly.

The heat in her face kicked up a notch, and she looked away from the interest in his gaze. "About the murder. Maybe it's a case of prejudice. The day I met Reece, some kids were throwing rotten tomatoes at me. He chased them off and took me for a soda." If only she'd known then that his rescuer persona hid a controlling personality as well.

Matt stashed the carriers in the depths of the closet and backed out. "It's possible. But murder is a far cry from pranks." His tone went back to impersonal.

"Arson isn't a prank," she pointed out. "Remember those fires that took place before *Mamm* and *Datt* died? When you're a farmer, that's your livelihood."

They walked to the living room. The back door was open, and Hannah could see Asia outside throwing a stick to Ajax.

"Did they ever figure out who was behind the rash of attacks?" he asked.

"No. This was about a year before my family was murdered. Before you got on at the sheriff's department."

"I'll check out the old records. Maybe there will be a lead."

She gestured to the couch, then curled up in the chair. "Have you reopened the investigation on my family?"

"It was never closed—it just went cold. But yeah, I'm trying to look for similarities. I always thought Long had to have an accomplice." Her lips pressed together, and he knew who she thought that person had to be. "Tell me again about that night."

"Reece was late that night. So late that I was attacked in the bridge."

His head jerked up. "I never heard about that. What happened?"

"He got there in time to run them off." A slight smile lifted her lips. "Always the rescuer." She wanted to tell Matt her suspicions about Reece, but maybe it was anger and bitterness, not truth, that made her wonder if Reece could have been her parents' killer. The more she'd thought about it over the years, the more convinced she'd become.

She eyed Matt. Would he even believe her? "I've wondered if Reece had something to do with the murders. Especially after he began to demonstrate his violent side."

"Long was seen making the cookies," Matt said.

"What about the symbol on the wall and the quilt?"

"What about it?"

"How did that relate to Cyrus? And what was his motive?"

He shrugged, but uneasiness flickered in his eyes. "I don't know. We never found a motive or a connection to the peace symbol."

"Well, I researched it. Wait here a minute." She got up and went to the bedroom, where she dragged out the folder she'd kept all these years. When she got back to the living room, she opened it and flipped through it. "Here. I found the symbol and the Greek word. The word was *anathema*."

"Anathema. Weird word. What's it mean?"

She knew what it meant firsthand, but she kept her tone cool and clinical, though it took major effort. "It's a person or thing cursed and devoted to destruction. It can also be a formal ecclesiastical curse involving excommunication. Early on, the Catholic Church adopted the word *anathema* to signify the exclusion of a sinner from the society of the faithful, but it was pronounced mostly against heretics. And it can mean something that is completely destroyed for the glory of God. I think it's someone who hates the Amish."

"And the peace symbol?"

At least he was listening. She flipped to another page and pointed to the symbol. "It's a peace symbol, like you said. But it's also called Nero's Cross. In this case, I think it's meant as a warning to Christians. Nero used it to symbolize the destruction of Christianity. I think the killer meant it as a warning to exterminate my family."

His eyes widened. "You mean the symbol we use for peace began as a hate symbol against Christianity?"

She nodded. "It was a visual representation of the way Nero crucified Christians upside down."

Distaste twisted his mouth. "That's sick. How did a hate symbol become associated with peace?"

"I don't know, but let's get back to the murder. It fits, Matt. Our people have been victims of misguided people for centuries. I don't expect you to understand."

His hand closed on the folder. "Can I look at this stuff?"

She didn't want to let it go. It was the accumulation of years of searching. "Just be careful with it. Could you make copies and get it back to me tomorrow?"

He rose with the folder in his hand. "I'll go one better. I'll go to the office and make copies and bring it back tonight."

He was more perceptive than she'd realized. And kinder than his gruff voice let on. She remembered Reece had taken credit for getting the younger man on at the sheriff's department. "You knew Reece on the force, right? You were partners?" she asked.

Matt went toward the door without meeting her gaze. "I knew him."

She caught up with him in the hall. "How well did you know him?"

"Well enough, but that has nothing to do with the investigation."

Her warm feelings toward him vanished. "It might if it interferes."

"I'm a professional. My personal life doesn't intrude on my job."

She stood her ground when he started to step past her. "If that's true, then what are you hiding?"

He folded his arms across his chest. "It's not a big deal, okay? He was a foster kid that my grandmother raised. He came back to visit her sometimes, and I met him there. I was a punk kid with an attitude, and he tried to help me." His frown deepened. "Which made it hurt all the more when he ran off with you without a word *and* stole my gun."

Hannah didn't hide the surprise in her voice. "Trudy Beitler is your grandmother? Reece talked about her a lot. He said she was wonderful."

"Have you met her?"

Hannah shook her head. "Her daughter Irene was my mother's best friend, though."

"Irene's *Englisch*."

"My mom was *Englisch*."

"You're kidding!"

She shook her head. "She met my dad when she was eighteen. Actually, Irene introduced them. *Mamm* always said he was worth more than any TV set." She smiled at the memory. "It doesn't happen very often. The Amish are always a little doubtful that anyone who has lived in the world can make that change, but my mom showed them."

"Did you ever meet my aunt Irene?"

"She saw me in a store one day and came up to ask if I was Patty's daughter. I didn't know who she meant for a minute. Everyone I knew called *Mamm* Patricia. Irene told me about their friendship. I saw it in action a few minutes later when *Mamm* saw her and came to chat. *Mamm* was so glad to see her. She even shared some news no one else knew but me and *Datt*. Were you and your aunt close?"

He shook his head. "Nope. She raised my sister, Gina, though. Your mom didn't ever go see her?"

So did he understand the pain of losing parents too? "*Datt* would have been upset with her, and *Mamm* never wanted to rock the boat. Her parents were dead and her only sister had moved to Maine, so there was no *Englisch* family left in town. My mother left that life completely behind her."

"Her friendship with Irene too?" Matt asked.

"I guess so. She wasn't part of my life growing up. Does she still live here?" Maybe she'd reach out to Irene, find out more about her mother's life.

"Yep. In the same house."

"Did you live with your grandmother instead of your aunt?" she asked, curious if he'd answer the question.

He shrugged. "When I was eight, my dad hanged himself. My mom decided she wasn't cut out for motherhood and vamoosed. I haven't seen her since." His voice crackled with hostility. "My aunt couldn't handle a rambunctious boy."

Her maternal heart gave a pang. "A child should know his mother. Matt, have you learned anything about the girl in the picture?"

He grabbed hold of the doorknob. "When have I had time to look? I've been chasing after your cats." His gaze shuttered. He opened the door and exited.

She stared after him. Why wouldn't he help her find the child? His demeanor changed every time the subject came up.

THE OLD PICKUP caught air over the potholes in the road. Reece forced himself to slow down. The old truck couldn't take that much abuse. The Schwartz farm was just over the next hill, and he could barely make out its windmill from here. But his target this evening wasn't Hannah. He pulled to the side of the road and watched the neighboring house.

Ellen Long had to be home, because her black car was in the driveway. He'd wondered why she didn't go to Moe Honegger's funeral. Had she remarried? He'd never heard. A light flickered on in a downstairs room as twilight fell, additional confirmation that the woman was inside. Reece let the truck roll forward and turned in behind the Saturn.

A dog barked at the loud screech the truck door made when he opened it, but it didn't come to challenge him. Too bad. He was in the mood to kick something. Nothing had gone as planned so far. Hannah wasn't staying at her family farm, and he'd lost track of her. He hoped Ellen Long might shed some light on the situation. Of course, all he really had to do was grab the kid, but it wasn't as easy as he'd thought. Taking her from under Matt's watchful eyes would be difficult. Besides, things weren't quite in place. It was one thing to grab the kid and Hannah, and another thing to escape with them before Matt ran him to the ground.

He couldn't tell himself why it was so important that he find Hannah. After all, once he had the kid, Hannah would come to him. But his soul craved the sight of her. He'd been lonely the last five years, and not a day went by that he didn't long for her. He saw himself in her eyes as strong and powerful. Only Hannah had ever truly loved him. She was the linchpin that kept his life together. After she left, everything had gone sour for him.

And he'd blown it. But he'd be gentler this time. He'd keep her with him forever.

He jogged to the side door and knocked hard. From inside he could hear the murmur of the television. He knocked again and finally heard the shuffle of feet on the floor. The white door opened, and a woman peered out. If he hadn't known it was Ellen Long, he wouldn't have recognized her. She wasn't the fashion plate he remembered. Instead, she wore paint-stained sweats. A rubber band caught back her blond hair, and she wore no makeup. Her feet were bare.

"Yes?" she said in a tone that suggested she wanted to get back to her TV.

"Hi, Ellen, how are you?" He put on his most winning smile but also slipped his foot in the door so she couldn't close it. It was a good thing he did. As recognition swept over her face, she tried to slam the door. "I'd like to talk to you for a minute."

"I have nothing to say to you," she spat. "You left town with that little Amish tramp."

His muscles tensed. "Don't talk about Hannah like that. You got what you wanted. Your husband out of the way."

"What good was that when you left me?" Her voice thickened with tears. "I've missed you, Reece. We used to have some good times." She slumped against the doorjamb. Her hard gaze softened. "It's been a long time. You surprised me. Want to come in?" She reached out and touched his face.

What had he seen in this woman? He realized he'd used her, but right now she disgusted him. Being around Hannah's purity had spoiled him for women like this. He recoiled. "I don't think so, Ellen. Did you know Hannah was back in town? Have you seen her around?"

Her eyes glittered, and her mouth twisted. "Can't keep your wife under control?"

"We're separated," he mumbled. "Look, just answer the question."

"No, I haven't seen her." She gave a pointed stare at his foot. "Now get your boot out of my doorway and leave me alone. Unless you want to come in after all? Just once for old times' sake?"

He wasn't even tempted. She needed a lesson about respect. Reece clenched his fists and moved toward her, but a car slowed in front of the house. He glanced behind him and saw its turn signal flashing. There was no time to teach her a lesson. He sent a warning glare her way, then stomped back to his truck and accelerated away. Maybe a cruise through town would turn up some clue as to Hannah's whereabouts.

thirteen

*"The Amish Triangle Quilt is a symbol of all that matters
to the Amish: God, family, and community."*

HANNAH SCHWARTZ,

IN *The Amish Faith Through Their Quilts*

Guilt was an uncomfortable bedfellow. Matt hadn't been able to sleep all night. What was he going to do? The answers were no clearer when the new day got under way.

He glanced at his daughter in the seat beside him. She was more important than anyone else in his life. How could he thrust her into such a terrible situation?

"Why do I have to visit Grandma Trudy, Daddy? She doesn't like me." Caitlin kicked her feet back and forth in the seat. She looked cute in the dress she'd worn to church, a pink lacy number Gina had picked out.

"It's our duty, Caitlin. Duty is important. We don't always feel like doing it, but some things we have to do anyway."

"I thought we were going to see Aunt Gina. I get to stay with her, don't I? I don't have to stay at Grandma Trudy's?"

"No, you don't have to stay there." He wasn't keen on leaving her with Gina either. She'd stayed with him two days, then Blake had sweet-talked her home. She and Blake were likely still fighting, but at least they'd protect Caitlin. He didn't know another place to leave her where Hannah wouldn't stumble into seeing her.

Matt drove out County Road 100E to the narrow lane that led to Trudy's big farmhouse. He parked behind her old car, more rusty than blue these days. A chair with one rocker missing tilted on the porch by the fly-speckled picture window. The porch swing hung crazily at an angle. He'd fixed it last month, but it looked as though the chain had broken again and she'd hooked it up on the next link. He should probably replace all of it. The house was a never-ending money pit, but Trudy refused to move into something easier to care for in town. She wasn't poor by any stretch of the imagination, but she hated to "waste" money on the house.

Ajax woofed in the backseat and pawed at the door handle. "Hold on," Matt muttered. Glancing at the house as he let the dog out, he wondered if Trudy was home. No light shone through the darkened windows. He hoped the old lady hadn't fallen or something, though she was active and spry for seventy-two. She belonged to several clubs in town and drove herself everywhere in that old beater car.

Ajax beat him and Caitlin to the door. The scent of last year's roses lingered around the entry. Pressing the doorbell, he listened to it ding on the other side. There was no answer, so he dug out his key and opened the door.

The odor of stale air and dusty carpet greeted him. "Trudy?" he called, pushing past the dog. "Stay here, Caitlin." He didn't want his daughter to see anything out of place, and the dog would protect her. Shards of glass from a picture frame crunched under his shoes. The frame lay faceup, the photo ripped from it. He struggled to remember what had been in it, but the memory wouldn't surface.

Alarm jangled along his nerves when Trudy still didn't answer his call.

He went into the living room. An upended coffee table barred his path to the living room. "Trudy?" he called again.

He heard a soft groan, then saw the movement of a foot barely showing from behind the sofa. Moving it out of the way, he found the older woman on her stomach. He knelt and touched her shoulder. "Trudy?" She groaned again and tried to get up. "Don't move. I'll call an ambulance." He fumbled to get his cell phone off his belt.

"No, no, I'm fine," she muttered. "Help me up, boy." Her tone was sharp and peremptory. She got to her hands and feet and shook her head as though to clear it.

He grabbed her arm and helped her to her feet. She was a large woman, nearly six feet tall and normally as straight and erect as a general. And just as used to being obeyed. A goose egg was forming on her forehead, red and oozing with blood. She swayed where she stood, and he helped her to the sofa.

She flinched when he touched her head. "Leave it, Matthew. I'm fine." She managed a smile. "Decided you'd been neglecting the old lady a bit? A visit twice in one week. Guilt is a wasted emotion. Get over it."

A strange remark from her when she was such a master at inducing it. "Who did this?"

She waved her hand. Her face was already beginning to regain its color. "Kids looking for drugs, I expect."

"You didn't see anyone?"

"Just a noise, and I went to investigate and slipped. Guess I hit my head in the fall."

He curled his fingers into his palms. "I'll see what I can find. We need to call in backup."

"I don't want a bunch of lawmen running around my house." She smiled up at him. "Present company excluded, of course." Her color was coming back. "Quit fussing—I'm fine. I'm not filing a complaint. What have you been up to?"

"Hang on, let me get Caitlin." He went to the door and called his daughter inside. She had her head down and wouldn't look at him. "Say hello to your grandmother," he whispered. "Be nice."

Her steps dragged, but she went ahead of him into the living room. "Hi, Grandma."

Trudy's gaze went to the backpack Caitlin carried. "Are you planning on staying, child?"

"No, she's spending a few days with Gina. I didn't realize she had it with her." He glanced down at Caitlin. "You can put that back, princess."

Caitlin smiled and went back outside, and Matt knew she'd brought it so she could take it out. It was hard being under Trudy's stern stare—he should know. Still, the woman meant well. She'd taught him discipline, and he was thankful for that.

"Let me take you to the doctor, Trudy. You might need stitches."

"I'll put a comfrey compress on it. I'm fine. Why is she staying with Gina?" Trudy asked as soon as the screen door slammed.

He couldn't tell anyone the full story—especially not Trudy. "I'm going to be working a lot of hours, and it seems easier." The lie rolled off his tongue too easily, but he wasn't about to tell Trudy that Caitlin might be Hannah's daughter. "Want me to fix you some tea?"

She ignored his offer. "Why are you working so many hours? What will you be doing?"

"Searching for the person who killed Moe Honegger." Her gaze sharpened when he said the name. "Have you thought of any new details? You didn't mention the other day whether you knew him or not."

"It's pretty hard not to. I've bought all my flowers and plants at the greenhouse for years."

"I hear you knew the Schwartzes. At least Hannah's mom." Trudy hadn't attended the funeral, he remembered. But then, why would she go? Their contact had been broken decades ago.

"Again, I frequent the greenhouse. But where did you hear I knew Patricia?"

"Hannah Schwartz told me."

Her hand stopped its movement, then continued when Ajax whined outside the front door. "You mean Hannah O'Connor. Where'd you see her?"

"She's here in town. She and Reece are separated."

"Have you seen Reece?"

She had a blind spot where Reece was concerned. In her mind he could do no wrong. It wasn't Matt's place to spoil her fantasy, though. "He's here too. Somewhere around."

"Maybe he'll stop and see me. I've seen her picture. She looks like a sweet girl."

"How did you know Patricia?"

"She was at the house to see Irene all the time."

"What was she like?" Maybe if he understood the dynamics more, he'd be better able to figure this out.

Trudy touched the swelling goose egg on her forehead. "Pretty. Vivacious. All the boys liked her. But once she met Abe, she wanted no one else."

"How'd she meet Abe Schwartz?"

"He worked at your grandfather's lumberyard, and they'd also gone to school together, back before there was a dedicated Amish school. Irene introduced him to Patricia." She rubbed her head again. "Gina's so busy. You can leave Caitlin with me."

"It's already arranged with Gina. Besides, you said you weren't up to taking kids anymore."

"I know my duty."

It hurt that she cared for Caitlin no more than she'd cared for Matt— out of a loveless sense of duty. It was something, but it wasn't enough.

"We've got the arrangements made, but thanks anyway. Are you sure I can't run you to the doctor?"

"I'm fine. Don't be a stranger, Matthew."

"I won't." He left her with a sense of relief. Caitlin was ready to go. She hopped in and fastened her seat belt. He put Ajax in the back of the SUV.

"How long am I staying at Aunt Gina's?" Caitlin asked.

"Maybe a week." A lifetime when he craved time with her. He just had to get things sorted out with Reece and Hannah. Find some proof that Caitlin didn't belong to them.

ALL DAY SUNDAY Hannah moped around the house. She would have liked to attend the Amish service, but no one invited her. Maybe it was better that way. The bishop might have expected her to confess.

On Monday Hannah found herself looking at the picture and beginning to think of the little girl as her own. Dangerous ground. But there was something in the child's sweet gaze that drew her. If only she could talk to her aunt. She'd tried to stop by this morning, but no one was home. She'd been in town five days and still had no leads.

She put the picture on the coffee table when she heard a knock at the door. It was probably Asia. "Don't eat it," she told Ajax. The dog grunted. He was pinned in place by four cats lying on top of him anyway. When Matt said he'd leave the dog with them for protection, she'd expected trouble, but Ajax was a perfect lamb.

She went to the door just as it rang again, two impatient peals in quick succession. Asia would have called out to her. Peeking through the peephole, she saw a woman on the steps. About thirty with long raven hair and eyes as blue as a robin's egg. The V-neck top she wore showed a long tanned throat swathed in pearls. Her expression revealed just as much irritation as her trigger finger.

Hannah opened the door. The woman's eyes widened, and her mouth pressed into a thin line. Her gaze traveled from Hannah's tight bun to her shapeless skirt and flat shoes. "Who are you?" she demanded.

"I'm, um, I'm renting this house. I had the dead bolt locked."

The woman dismissed her with a jut of her chin. "I need to pick up a few things." She started past Hannah, who stood her ground. "Excuse me? I need to get past."

"I think you'd better tell me who you are first."

"Oh, for heaven's sake! I'm Matt's sister-in-law, okay? I left some things in the attic I need. I used to rent this dump."

Hannah thrust her hand into the pocket of her skirt and withdrew her cell phone. She'd programmed Matt's cell number into it.

He answered on the first ring. "Hannah, everything okay?"

"Well, your sister-in-law is here."

"Vanessa? What's she want?" He growled the words.

"She says she left some things in the attic and needs them." Hannah glanced at Vanessa, who stood tapping one high-heeled foot on the porch. She had her arms crossed over her chest.

"Let me talk to her."

Hannah handed Vanessa the phone. "He wants to talk to you."

The woman heaved a sigh and grabbed the phone. "Matt, it's not a big deal. I just need my stuff." She went quiet and listened. "How dare you? There was an Elie Tahari dress in that container. And my favorite pair of Manolo Blahnik shoes."

Hannah could have sworn there were actually tears in the woman's eyes. Evidently Vanessa had some hidden pain to react so strongly to the loss of *things*.

Vanessa handed the cell phone back. "What are you staring at?" she snapped.

Hannah smiled. "You're very beautiful," she said.

The hostility faded from Vanessa's eyes. "Have we met? You look familiar."

"I don't think so. But I was married to Reece O'Connor."

"Ah." Vanessa nodded. "The Amish girl. I remember now. How is Reece anyway?"

"We're separated."

Vanessa's lips curved up. "How delicious. That should cause a stir."

Hannah winced. The woman knew how to place her darts. She said nothing.

"So why are you here? You and Matt having a little fling? If you are, you're a brave woman to tackle Iceman. Since Analise died, he's hardly human." Vanessa opened her bag and withdrew a slim cigarette. She lit it and blew the smoke Hannah's way.

The first puff of tobacco stung Hannah's eyes, and she took a step back. Matt was widowed? "Of course we're not having a fling. I'm his, um, renter." She wasn't about to air her secrets to this woman.

"You're hardly his type. Look, let me come in and just look around." Vanessa's smile was winsome. "Matt might be bluffing about my things."

"In the short time I've known him, I've never seen him bluff about anything." Hannah had seen only quick, decisive behavior.

Vanessa put one shapely foot into the doorway. "Please? Just a minute?" Ajax growled low in his throat and took a step toward her. She hastily withdrew her leg. "That dog didn't like me from day one."

"I'm sorry, I really can't let you in without Matt's permission. You want to call him back and talk about it?"

Vanessa took another draw on her cigarette, then stubbed it out against the door frame. "It's all spite, you know. He never liked me even when he and Analise were married. They were such bores once the kid came along." Vanessa shrugged. "I guess I'll go if you're not going to let me in. Tell Matt he can take a flying leap."

Hannah wanted to say there was nothing between her and Matt, but Vanessa's heels were already clicking along the sidewalk to her car, a cherry-red sports car of some kind. Hannah didn't know much about cars, but she knew enough to recognize something expensive.

She heard a familiar rumble. A glimpse of that tan truck Reece had been driving made her grab the door and slam it. Stepping to the window, she peered through the curtain. The pickup sat idling beside Vanessa's car. Vanessa gestured back toward the house, and Reece took a long, slow look. Hannah jerked away from the window. She peeked out again when she heard a door slam. He was striding up the walk.

She ran to the door and threw the dead bolt. Ajax sensed her agitation and shook off the cats. He padded to her side, and a warning growl rumbled from his chest. "Quiet," she whispered. She peered out the peephole and saw Reece grinning at her.

"I know you're in there, Hannah," he said, his voice calm. "Open the door and let's talk."

"Go away," she shouted through the door. "I have nothing to say to you."

"Look, I know you're mad, honey. I don't blame you. But we've got our daughter to think about. She needs both of us. We can work this out."

"I don't want to be anywhere near you," she said fiercely. "You don't have our daughter anyway. It's a lie."

He rattled the door. "Let me in, Hannah. I've changed. I won't hurt you."

"You pushed me down the stairs!" He'd told her things would be different so many times. She knew better than to believe him.

"It was an accident, Hannah. I think you're remembering it wrong." He rattled the door again. "Come on, let's have some tea and talk. Or we can go out for coffee. You'll be in public and in no danger."

Could he be right? She didn't know what to believe. She could have sworn she'd felt him shove her. And there was no question that he'd hit her. Many times. "Where's the girl, Reece?" she asked quietly. "Tell me that and maybe I'll open the door."

"You're trying to trick me. We're one package. Me and the kid, Hannah. Take us both or neither one. I know what's best."

If she'd heard that once, she'd heard it a million times. She stared at the doorknob. If she could trust him to lead her to the little girl, she would be tempted to open it. Ajax growled again and pushed against her leg. The dog's warning made her back away. "Go away, Reece. I'm not going to talk to you anymore." She rushed from the door down the hall to the bathroom, where she shut herself in and clapped her hands over her ears so she couldn't be tempted to give in.

SIX DAYS AFTER Moe's murder, Matt still had no leads. He leaned back in his chair at the sheriff's department with his hands clasped at the back of his neck. "There doesn't seem to be a clear link between Moe Honegger's murder and the Schwartz deaths."

"Other than they were both poisoned with strychnine," Blake said. "Come on, that's a clear connection. Not the most common method of murder."

"Copycat? It's well-known about the poison," Matt suggested. He pulled the computer keyboard toward him and called up a screen. "There has been only one homicide in the past ten years—a spousal murder."

Blake looked up. "And now Reece is back in town and we have another. That has to mean something. Was he ever suspected at the time of the Schwartz murders?"

Matt's gaze met his partner's. "He was a detective at the time of the first murders, so no."

"And he eloped with the only daughter. You think that ever would have happened if the parents were alive?"

"He was with Hannah when her family was killed." Though Hannah had said he was late. But late enough to have done the deed?

Blake dropped into a chair. "Think about it. He could have helped Long dispose of the quilts, then rushed to meet her at the bridge while the strychnine did its work. We know he was in the area, because he met Hannah at the bridge. The house wasn't far."

"Frankly, I don't know why the quilts were taken. They've never been sold." Matt scratched his head. "It doesn't make any sense. If we could just find those quilts."

"They might have been taken as a trophy. You know how some killers take something belonging to their victims."

"Maybe."

"He was in the area. It wouldn't have taken long to load the quilts. They could have been in the back of his truck all along while you were searching. You must have suspected something."

If only he'd been that observant. Matt shook his head. "I didn't. I noticed how distracted he was, all worried about Hannah. When he ran off with her, I realized it was because he was crazy in love with her."

"Weird, don't you think? An Amish girl like that."

"Yeah."

"What'd she ever see in Reece? She's a looker under those shapeless clothes and scraped-back hair."

Matt had noticed too. Long ago. "You're a married man. You're not supposed to look."

"I'm married, but I'm not dead."

Matt wanted to ask if Blake was having an affair as Gina suspected, but maintaining a partnership with his brother-in-law had become a balancing act.

Blake's face changed as though he'd suddenly been struck with a thought. "What if they did it together?"

"What?"

"Maybe Hannah wanted out from under her parents' thumb and talked Reece into doing the deed. Or *she* did it so she could marry him."

"It would be unusual for anyone Amish to be involved in a violent act."

"But not unheard of. Wasn't there some guy in Ohio who killed his wife or something?"

"Yeah, anyone can snap." Matt rubbed his eyes. "I followed that idea for a while back then, but I was never able to tie Hannah to the purchase of poison. Everyone talked very highly of her. There was no evidence linking her to Long except the fact that they were neighbors. And to tell you the truth, I just don't buy it."

"We can check into her background—see what she's been doing in the ten years she's been gone."

"Focus on Reece. I think that holds more possibilities." Still, Matt didn't want to believe that either. The guy had been his *partner*. And a foster brother. Reece had a temper at times, but didn't everyone? Hannah said he'd beaten her. Maybe you never really knew someone, who they were inside.

Just like the partner sitting right across from him. He had to bring this out in the open between them. "How's Gina?"

"Whoa, where did that come from? She's fine."

Matt pinned Blake with his stare. "She thinks you're having an affair, Blake. Tell me straight up. Are you?"

Blake looked away. "What if I said I was?"

Matt sagged back in his chair. He hadn't wanted to believe it. "Who?"

"Vanessa. Your sister-in-law."

Matt bolted upright. "You've got to be kidding. She's a man shark, buddy."

"Yeah, well, I don't know how it happened. It just did."

Matt clenched his fists. "You idiot! This will kill my sister."

"I know, I know. I'm in a mess. She's pregnant, so what can I do?"

Matt found no pity in his heart for his partner. "You're stupid if you believe that. Vanessa is playing you, man. She came by my house today."

Blake scowled. "What was she doing there?"

"Looking for some containers of clothes and shoes. I gave them to the Salvation Army."

"She'll be steamed. What'd you go and do that for?"

"I don't run a storage service. I told her at least six times to come get them. She moved out of the place over six months ago, and it's been rented out since then. She had plenty of time to get them. Man, you're stupid if you can't see you're giving up gold for pot metal."

Blake wouldn't meet his gaze. "Look, if she says she's pregnant, I believe her."

"Yeah, right. She doesn't like kids."

"I'm trying to figure things out, okay? My marriage is important to me."

"Not important enough to keep your pants zipped." Matt's voice vibrated with anger.

Blake flushed. "Just shut up. It's none of your business."

"Look, we've been friends a long time, Blake. And this is my sister we're talking about. I want the best for both of you. And that's not Vanessa."

"You don't know her that well."

Matt rolled his eyes. "Please. She was a thorn in my flesh for the seven years I was married to Analise."

"She just made you mad over Caitlin."

"Is that what she told you? Ask her how she mocked her own sister after two miscarriages. Or the way she talked about Caitlin as though she were some piece of trash not worthy to be part of our family." If the woman was going around bad-mouthing his family, he'd strangle her. "Let's not talk about her."

"You brought her up."

"My mistake." Matt pulled the mouse toward him and began to look at the evidence again. At least solving crimes was something he understood.

fourteen

"The Drunkard's Path Quilt is a symbol of the journey.
To the Amish, their journey is to live a life pleasing to God.
They believe you can't know your path will end in heaven and that
it's presumptuous to think you can. The decision is up to God."

—HANNAH SCHWARTZ,

IN *The Amish Faith Through Their Quilts*

Quilting calmed her. Occupied by a needle and thread, Hannah's hands had finally quit shaking after Reece's appearance. She studied the block in her hands. The quilt was taking shape. She tied the Triangle Quilt to the three things the Amish held dear: God, their families, and their communities.

Hannah loved the colors. Each set of two rows featured the dark and light opposites of each other—dark blue and light blue, dark green and light green, dark red and light red—all against black triangles that caused the colors to pop. This was the quilt that had to be on the cover of the book. No one could understand the Amish faith without understanding how those three elements shaped their culture.

"I heard from *FOX & Friends*," Asia said. "They were so impressed with their interview, they want to come here for a show. Tape you in the kitchen with some traditional Amish food, film the house and greenhouse, that kind of thing."

Hannah laid the quilt piece in her lap. "No. I told you no publicity while we're here."

Asia rolled her eyes. "Hannah, you have to do this! Do you have any idea how huge this is? We can't turn this down." She folded her arms across her chest. "I already told them yes. They're coming next Friday. Your aunt will let you come out there. And it would be good publicity for your cousin's greenhouse."

"Luca doesn't want publicity. No one here does. Don't you get it, Asia? We are content with what God gives us." Or she used to be. When had the desire for more crept in? When the first awestruck reader e-mailed her? When she made her first TV appearance?

"You owe it to your publisher. You can't turn down something like this. It could translate into tens of thousands of copies sold, Hannah. This is just too big. After this is over, if you want to step back and take a break, I'll go along with it. But we can't turn up our noses at this."

Maybe Asia was right. Didn't she owe it to her publisher to do everything she could to sell the books? But she wanted to be sensitive to her family's beliefs. How could she walk that tightrope? It was hard enough being an outsider. After just a few days of this treatment, she could see why some came back to the Amish faith. She missed the love, the community.

"All right," she said. "But tell them they can't tape Aunt Nora or any other Amish person."

"If you explained it to Sarah, maybe she would let us tape the children. They're so cute."

"No, absolutely not! I won't even ask her." Hannah shuddered at the thought.

"Okay, fine." Asia's voice held disgust as she stood. "I'm going to run downtown. I need to fax some information over to the producer. And I need to e-mail your publicity shot."

"Could you drop me at Aunt Nora's? I really need to talk to her about this whole mess, see what she knows." Hannah rubbed her head. "Oh wait, it's Monday. She always goes to visit her friends on Monday."

"You need to work anyway."

"I need some inspiration. There's a quilt fair going on at the dime store two blocks over. I think I'll take a look."

Asia frowned. "I'm not sure it's safe."

"I'll be in a crowd. Call me when you're ready to come back and I'll meet you at the curb." The cats entwined themselves around her ankles, but she booted them out of the way, then grabbed her purse and joined Asia at the door, locking it behind them.

Asia let her out in front of the dime store, then drove on. Hannah stopped to glance at the quilts in the window. The traditional solid jewel tones shimmered against the black background. Looking at them made her want to keep working on her own, just as she'd hoped.

She slipped into the busy store and made her way to the back, where other women were admiring the quilt display. Some were only for display, but she stopped beside a stack of quilts for sale. Her hand smoothed the top one, its cotton fabric soft and lustrous. She lifted it aside and began to sort through them. It was a habit she couldn't stop. The hope of finding one of her mother's never left her.

After reverently looking through the stacks, she realized there was nothing of her mother's here. Someone had those quilts. Their disappearance was the one piece that didn't fit in the puzzle she'd stitched together convicting Reece of the crime. If he'd killed her family, what had he done with the quilts? If he'd sold them, they would have turned up on the market somewhere. She'd been everywhere, looked online and at flea markets, studied other museums' collections. Not one had ever come to light.

Her obsession with finding them had infuriated Reece. Had he kept them from her deliberately to exert control over her?

She made her way back into the fresh air. Surely he wouldn't have destroyed something so valuable, but she had no other explanation. She was so lost in her thoughts, she nearly collided with a figure on the sidewalk. Strong hands gripped her shoulders and steadied her. She looked up into Matt's face.

"Sorry," he said.

"It was my fault. I wasn't looking."

"I wanted to talk to you anyway."

"Something about the little girl?" The hopeful words sprang from her mouth.

His smile faded. "No, nothing about her. I just wondered if you needed anything. And to say I'm sorry Vanessa bothered you."

He turned and began to walk toward his SUV. "Get in. I'll drive you home."

Such an infuriating man. Just because he thought her quest was a wild-goose chase didn't mean he could ignore her. Maybe she needed to start through town herself and ask everyone she met. She pressed her lips together and got into the vehicle. He shut the door behind her and went around to his side. She called Asia to tell her she had a ride.

She put her cell phone away, then glanced around his SUV. It was neat and smelled clean with a hint of his cologne. The vehicle shifted when he got in. She'd like to ask him about his family. Vanessa's visit had made her curious about him. Would he answer any of her questions? If she got to know him better, maybe he'd help her find the little girl.

He glanced at her. "I hope Vanessa's visit didn't upset you too much. She can be rather . . . overbearing."

"She was larger-than-life," Hannah admitted. "You were married to her sister?"

He nodded. "Analise died three years ago."

"Vanessa told me she'd died. I'm so sorry."

"So was I. Our daughter misses her terribly. Analise was a great mom. And a good wife."

"What happened?"

"She had a brain aneurysm. She was prone to migraines, so at first that's what we thought it was. If I'd taken her sooner . . ." His fingers tightened on the wheel. "Now Caitlin has no mother."

"Guilt is hard to get over. I know all about that." She stared out the window.

He turned his head to look at her. "Are you talking about the lemonade? There was no poison in it."

She stared out the window. "I killed my family."

"The cookies killed them. It wasn't your fault."

"It was my sin God punished." She turned her head to look at him. "You don't think Cyrus killed them, do you?"

"No, not anymore."

"I—I think it was Reece. Except . . ."

"Except for what?"

"What did he do with the quilts?"

"Sold them, maybe?"

She shook her head. "They would have turned up on the market. There's no trace of them."

"Tell me, what about the murder itself? Would Reece have had time to arrange the bodies after you left, gather up the cookies, and help Cyrus get rid of the quilts before he came to meet you? How late was he?"

"Probably fifteen or twenty minutes, maybe even half an hour. I didn't have a watch. The bridge was only five minutes from the house. If he'd been waiting for me to leave, it could have happened that way. When I left the house, I went to the barn to do chores before going to meet him. I was out of the house at least an hour before I went to the bridge."

The SUV rolled to a stop at a light. Hannah couldn't face any more questions. "Look, thanks for the offer to drive me home, but I've got some errands to run." She threw open the door and got out. In the sunshine, the fresh air cleansed the taint of death lingering from his probing. Why had she ever come back here? Her new life might have been boring, but at least grief didn't dog every step. She had to get past this, concentrate on the future. A future that might hold a reunion with her child.

He rolled down the window and called out to her. "Wait, I'll take you where you want to go."

"I'd rather walk. It's not far." She didn't look at him but plunged down the street, dodging the water puddles on the sidewalk. If she cut through some yards, she'd have to walk only a few blocks to the house. Alone time was a treat she craved, time to remember.

A dog barked as she walked through a muddy backyard, and she skirted a freshly seeded lawn to find her way to the sidewalk that fronted businesses along the highway. The sun warmed her face and arms, and she fanned her face with her hand. It would be a hot summer if the spring was any indication. The humidity from all the rain coated her skin.

She glanced at the ice-cream shop, Tammy Twist and Sizzle. Children would be apt to frequent a place like that. She changed her course and entered the store. People of all ages thronged the counter. With so many, her chances of someone recognizing the picture were greater. She fell into line behind a large woman in a pair of red capris.

The lady glanced her way, and Hannah pasted on her most winsome smile. "Excuse me, but I wondered if you've seen this little girl." She produced the picture and watched the woman's expression.

The woman raised her brows and looked Hannah over as if to check whether she might be dangerous. "Why do you want to know?"

"I—I'm looking for my daughter." The words sounded sweet on her tongue.

"Oh, my dear, I'm so sorry." The woman took the picture and studied it. Her eyes held real regret when she handed it back and shook her head. "I'm sorry. I'm not from around here, though. You might try the counter people."

"Thanks, I'll do that." In the meantime, Hannah drifted from person to person and showed the picture, but no one seemed to have seen her. Finally she reached the counter, where she ordered a cup of chocolate-almond ice cream. There was a lull in the line of customers, so she asked the employee, a young girl with a nose ring, if she recognized the child.

The girl glanced at the photo as she was ringing up Hannah's order. "I don't know, maybe. I see a lot of kids." She stared at Hannah with suspicion pulling at her mouth.

"Do you know her name?"

"Look, I'm not a detective agency. I can't tell you anything."

"Sorry." Hannah took her dessert and walked away from the counter. She meandered across the street and cut around a couple of blocks to Sycamore Drive. As she neared the house, she saw a long box by the front door. As she came closer, she saw it was addressed with black marker. The letters were large enough that she could make out her name on the box from a distance. Postage stamps decorated the top right corner.

She reached the door and stood looking down at the box. Her cell phone was in her hand before she realized it. Matt would want to check out this parcel before she opened it. She dialed the number and kept her gaze locked on the box. Whatever it was, it couldn't be good. Five minutes later, Matt's SUV came squealing to a stop by the house.

Blake got out first, then both men jogged to the house. "You think we need to call in a bomb squad?" Blake asked.

"Let me take a look first," Matt said. He pulled out some wipes and carefully went over the box before looking at them. "Seems clean. Is Ajax inside?"

She nodded. "I left him here with the cats when I went to town."

Matt unlocked the door and let the dog out. He led Ajax to the box. The dog sniffed around the box, then sat on his haunches and looked at Matt with an expectant expression.

"I think I'll risk it," Matt said. "Stand back."

Blake and Hannah moved out by the street. Matt took out a pocketknife, slit the brown paper wrapping, and lifted it away from the box. About eight by twenty inches, the box didn't look big enough to contain a bomb. She watched him slide the blade under the tape until the flaps lay loose and ready to reveal the contents.

He gently lifted first one flap, then the next, and peered inside. He jumped back. "Flowers," he said. "Don't get close enough to smell them." He glanced at the dog. "I'd better get Ajax checked out. I'll have the state forensics lab take a look and see if they can lift any prints."

"I'll take it to the jail," Blake said. He jogged back to the SUV and got out a big plastic bag, then slipped on a mask. He slid the box of flowers into the bag and tied the end. "I'll be right back."

Matt put his hands in his pockets. "I'd lay money the flowers are loaded with strychnine. Maybe the killer was counting on you not knowing what killed Moe."

Hannah took a step back and rubbed her palms along the material of her skirt. The attempt on her life left a bad taste in her mouth. "Maybe the killer knew I'd know. Maybe it was a warning he was coming after me."

"Maybe. And now we know he knows where you are as well."

"Reece saw me at the door when Vanessa came by."

"And you're just now telling me?"

"Sorry. I was more concerned with finding the little girl."

He rolled his eyes. "You've got my number. I need to be aware of everything. I've got a murder on my plate to try to solve. Every clue is vital."

"Four murders," she reminded him.

"Okay, four."

Maybe she should just pack up and head back to Milwaukee. Her arrival seemed to have brought more trouble to the people she loved.

"I showed the picture to some people at the ice-cream shop. I think the girl behind the counter recognized her, but she wouldn't say anything. I'm going to start hanging out there."

His lips flattened, and his nostrils flared. His words came out clipped and hoarse. "Just leave it alone. Do you want to hurt her?"

Hannah stared at his face. Was that anguish in his eyes? "You know where she is, don't you?" The air thickened around her, close and still as she waited for his answer.

"Just forget it, Hannah." He turned his back to her and went to unlock the house.

But she knew why he wouldn't look. Her daughter was with someone he knew. But who? She rubbed her forehead. Oh, she was jumping to conclusions. If he knew, he'd tell her. What did he have to gain from hiding anything? She was so used to Reece's games, she questioned everyone's motives.

fifteen

*"The Pineapple Quilt has long been a symbol of hospitality. And the
Amish can welcome you to their home like no others."*

—HANNAH SCHWARTZ,

IN *The Amish Faith Through Their Quilts*

Lights blazed from the house into the thickening twilight. Reece hurtled the fence in the backyard and fell onto his knees in the mud. The
wet soaked through his jeans, and he swore as he stumbled to his feet and
crept toward the house, shaking mud from the steak he carried.

At least the dog didn't come snarling to face him down. The recent rain
had left the yard a mess, and his foot plunged into something soft, followed
by an unmistakable odor. The dog was destined to leave his mark anyway.
Reece bit back the vicious words that wanted to spew out. Someone might
hear. After cleaning his shoe on the wet grass, he finally made it to the window that looked into the kitchen. The wide opening between the kitchen and
living room revealed the women sitting on the sofa watching TV.

The lamplight lit Hannah's loose hair. It had been up when he caught a
glimpse of her through the open door when she was talking to Vanessa. He

loved her locks spread out across her shoulders. The red glinted so brightly. He could feel the texture of her hair in his hand, the silken strands twining around his fingers.

He should have known better than to take the kid from her. He'd underestimated her maternal instinct. If she'd just explained it to him better, he would have made a different decision. He'd only tried to do what was best. His every thought was of her and their love.

They'd be together again, the three of them.

The dog lifted his head, his ears flicking. Reece ducked out of view and moved around to the back door. He'd hide out in the garage until the time was right. Then he would go see Hannah. He longed to feel her softness, to feel her fragrant breath waft over his face. They'd been apart too long. Maybe she was missing him by now. The storm thundered overhead as if in approval.

But first, a minor matter needed his attention. Reece picked the lock with a tool he'd had for years, then opened the door noiselessly. He whistled softly, and Ajax came padding to the rear entrance. He sniffed Reece's hand. "Good, Ajax," he crooned. The dog wiggled with delight and came out onto the porch. Reece pulled out a steak loaded with tranquilizer. "Want to take a little nap, boy?" He dropped the meat on the patio and watched as Ajax gobbled it up.

He wanted to start the ball rolling, but Hannah deserved every possible chance to come with him of her own free will. It was the only way he'd ever fully trust her again. She had to want him. Only him. He had to convince her he'd converted. Maybe he could get his bishop to write a letter.

He settled down to wait until Ajax was out.

MATT RUBBED HIS eyes. The clock on his wall read eight o'clock—he should have been off duty hours ago. He ached to see his daughter. The flowers sent to Hannah today had been chock full of strychnine, but at least Ajax hadn't inhaled enough through the box and paper to hurt him. He stared at the folder on his desk. Matt knew the background check on Hannah might contain anything. Did he really want to know?

"Aren't you going to take a look at it so we can go home?" Blake asked.

"Yeah, sure." Matt flipped it open and began to read. "Did you look at it yet?"

"Yep. Reece was a nasty guy to her, from the looks of it. There are three hospital reports in there, all emergency room visits."

"Broken arm, broken nose," Matt said. "A concussion on one visit."

"The hospital personnel wanted her to press charges on that one and she refused. Said she fell down the steps."

Matt wanted to hurt someone, preferably Reece. Any man who hit a woman was a coward, and Reece had done more than just slap her around. He'd hurt her badly. "She disappeared from the hospital after giving birth prematurely at home, but the fetus was never found. The detectives questioned him, but it doesn't look like a warrant was ever issued."

"So she escaped him. Do we have any idea what she's been doing for the past five years?" Blake asked.

"She told me she worked for a museum. Milwaukee, I think."

"Want me to see what I can dig up in Wisconsin?"

"I don't think it's necessary. It's pretty clear she was running from Reece. Anything new on him?"

"Yeah." Blake tossed another folder on his desk.

Matt glanced through the report. It didn't surprise him. "He hasn't worked anywhere longer than a few months at a time over the past few years. Odd jobs, a stint or two as a guard. He's sure floated around."

"I think he was probably looking for Hannah."

Matt closed the folder. He flipped open the main folder that contained the copies he'd made from Hannah's notes.

"What's that?" Blake peered over his shoulder at the drawings.

"From the first murders ten years ago. The word *anathema* and a peace symbol."

"Seems weird."

"Also called Nero's Cross or the Broken Cross, according to Hannah. We pursued the peace symbol, checking out various groups in the area. I'm not sure how we missed its other meaning. Maybe because it's so obscure."

Blake raised his brows, and his tone was skeptical. "Isn't peace what the Amish believe in? They won't even serve in the military or take any kind of government assistance. Peace or protest. The same symbol represents the annihilation of faith or peace with everyone. Weird, don't you think?"

"Hannah thinks this instance is about annihilation. A declaration of war against everything the Amish stand for. A hate crime."

"You think it's Reece?"

"Why would he hate the Amish? The woman he loved was Amish. He must have seen something good in them. And now he says he's converted, too, and joined a district in Shipshewana in northern Indiana."

"I could check that out. Go to Shipshewana."

"Good idea. Do that." He glanced at his watch. "It's what, four hours or a little over? Head up there in the morning and stay until you find the bishop of his district. See what he tells you."

"Okay, but what if none of this is true? What's Reece want?"

"He wants Hannah to come back to him." His gaze went back to the files. And Reece probably wanted Caitlin too. Matt had to figure out what to do. At least Caitlin was hidden where Hannah couldn't find her. Whether Reece knew of Caitlin's whereabouts was another question. "Any sign of lurkers out your way?"

"Nope. I think Gina was imagining things when she thought someone followed her. But I've got all the security systems activated. And Gina packs that small pistol in her purse. She can handle anyone who tries to mess with her or Caitlin."

Matt wished he could confide in Blake and Gina about why Caitlin had to be hidden. And just who was after her. Carrying this burden alone was wearisome. But he'd do anything to keep his daughter.

Hannah's hope, which had seemed so bright that afternoon, fizzled with the sundown. Hannah began to question whether she was on a wild-goose chase. It looked like the little girl had a loving family. Did she have any right to disrupt that kind of happiness? And her accusation of Matt proved she was getting a little off-kilter.

She needed to get her mind on something else. "Let's cut my hair," she said. Asia had been after Hannah to let her cut it for months.

"What did you say?"

"I'm not kidding. Let's cut it." Hannah jumped up and tugged Asia to her feet. "I'm ready. After I left Reece, I rejected anything that might make me attractive to men. I hated the clothes he made me wear, the come-hither hairstyle. I think I went too far the other way. I've used my professional status as an excuse, but I've always known the real reason."

"Why now?" Asia's sly smile came. "Does the handsome detective have anything to do with it?"

Hannah averted her eyes. "Of course not. *FOX & Friends* is coming next week. I want to look nice."

"Uh-huh, if you say so." Asia turned toward the kitchen. "You don't have to tell me twice. I'll get the scissors. Any idea what you want me to do?"

"I'm in your hands." She grinned at the delight on Asia's face and followed her to the kitchen.

Something outside, a branch or the wind, caught her attention. "Did you hear something?" Hannah tipped her head to one side.

"No." Asia pushed her into a chair. "Come on, let's do it before you change your mind. It won't hurt a bit."

"That's what you think."

"Just a trim." Asia lifted a long lock of Hannah's hair. "It's all thin on the ends. We'll trim a couple of inches and give it a few layers. You'll be amazed at how much better it looks."

Her family already thought she was some kind of heathen. "Do it fast."

Asia sprang into action. "Just close your eyes. I'll be gentle."

Minutes later, locks of russet hair lay around her in a heap. Did she even dare look at it—or touch it? Her scalp felt light as air, an odd sensation. Reaching up, she ran her hand through her hair. She'd been shorn. A smile played at her lips. She should have done this years ago.

"You look amazing." Asia's lips tilted in a smile. "Go look."

Hannah went to the small half bath off the living room. Her hair was still long, reaching just past her bra, but the ends were straight and even. And the long layers Asia had cut into it released the natural curl. It didn't even look like hers. She seemed different, wiser. And maybe she was.

"Can I still put it up?"

"Yes, but you're not going to. You're going to start wearing it down. It's gorgeous and needs to be admired."

"I don't want to draw too much attention to myself." Except from Matt. The stray thought made her cheeks burn. She was still a married woman.

Asia came up behind her. "Now for a little makeup. Though you really don't need it. Your skin is so perfect."

"I think this is enough for one day," Hannah said.

"Nope, we're going the whole hog. Sit still." Asia stroked on eye shadow and blush. "You look amazing. Now for clothes. I want you to see what you look like in something that fits."

"It's nearly time for bed," Hannah said, glancing at her reflection one more time. Was that really her?

"This won't take long. I've got a dress that will look killer on you." Asia grabbed her hand and dragged her down the hall. "Just try it on."

The spare room had a full-length mirror, and Hannah averted her eyes from it. Growing up, she'd been taught it was wrong to dwell on her appearance, and until she'd moved away with Reece, she'd never even seen herself in a full-length mirror. Even now, she found it hard to examine her body.

Asia slid open the closet door and pulled out an umber sheath Hannah had seen her wear once. It was silky beneath her fingers, alluring. "I don't think so," she said, thrusting it back into Asia's hand. She shuddered at the memories that flooded her.

"Just for a second," her friend coaxed. She pushed it back into Hannah's hands.

"Can I go to bed afterward? No more making me over?"

"Okay. For tonight anyway. I want to knock the socks off the producers next week."

Hannah sighed and slipped off her long skirt and blouse. Asia slid the dress over her head, and it fell over her body in a soft shimmer.

Asia's eyes widened, and her mouth dropped open. "Wow. You look amazing."

The hem stopped at the top of her knees. The fabric was more like that of a nightgown than a dress. Hannah ran her palm over her hip. The material barely covered her, and she shivered when the cool air touched her heated skin.

"Here. Put these on." Asia pulled out a pair of strappy tan sandals.

Just get it over with. Hannah stepped into the shoes and turned to look at the stranger in the mirror. The dress fit perfectly, outlining her shape. The color made her skin glow, and her hair seemed brighter by contrast. "I look like a streetwalker," she said.

"Okay, maybe I used a little too much blush and eye shadow. But you look beautiful," Asia said.

Where was the line between tasteful and overboard? Where was the balance? Just like fine quilts, a good life required balance. She hadn't found it yet. This dress wasn't her. Her fingers grabbed the hem and began to yank it upward just as the back door banged. "Is someone here?" She jerked the fabric down to her knees again and rushed down the hall. Reece stood in the doorway.

Dressed in black pants and a white shirt, he looked like a typical Amish man. "How pretty you look, hon. Did you dress up just for me?" He crossed the distance between them in four steps and grabbed her arm. "We need to talk."

The strength left Hannah's muscles. "Reece, what are you doing here?"

Asia grabbed Hannah's other hand. "Let go of her!"

"This isn't your concern," Reece said. "If you know what's good for you, you'll get to your room and keep your trap shut. Otherwise, I'll have to shut it for you."

"It's okay," Hannah said. "I'll talk to him." She glanced from Asia to the phone.

Asia nodded. "I'll be in my room. Call if you need me."

Hannah could still feel Reece's eyes on her, stripping her of her self-regard, exposing her weakness, her guilt. Even with the darkest cloak of night around her, he would find her. She could travel to Tibet and make her home with the monks, and he would know. It was hopeless to dream of a life without his shadow blotting out the sunshine.

She found her voice. "Leave me alone, Reece. I don't want to talk to you."

"Let's sit in the living room." His fingers tightened on her wrist, and he tugged her to the sofa.

She sank onto it, all strength gone. How long before the Rockville police showed up? Or Matt?

Reece settled beside her. "I thought you'd want to hear an update on our daughter."

"Our daughter is dead. You killed her."

"Oh, she's very much alive, Hannah. She's been looking for her mommy. She needs you. I'm not good with kids."

"You—you don't have her."

He coiled a lock of hair around his finger. "Are you sure? Hon, we belong together. You know it too. Quit fighting how you feel. No one has ever loved me like you. I'm lost without you. Come home. We'll settle in Shipshewana. The bishop there has promised to help you repent and come under his guidance."

Hannah wanted to shut out the seductive sound of his voice. He was always able to make her doubt herself. She desperately wanted to know more, but she knew he was playing with her, toying with the scalding emotions that burned her chest. "Where is she?"

"With me. Don't you think she deserves a mother and a father?" His voice dropped to a softer pitch, sweet and gentle. "Come home, Hannah, and we'll forget everything, all the past hurts. I won't hit you again, I promise."

Hannah steeled herself against the pleading tone. "It's a promise you can't keep, Reece. I don't believe you have her. Do you have a picture of the two of you together?" Her hands were shaking, and she clutched them together.

"Not on me."

A siren screamed in the distance, then drew closer. He dropped a kiss on her forehead. "I'd better go. But I'll get proof."

REECE SLAMMED THE door of his truck. She just didn't understand yet. Women were the weaker vessel. Why couldn't she understand he only wanted what was best for her? They *belonged* together. He only felt whole and strong when she was with him. His life had gone down the toilet after she left. Lost jobs, unpaid bills, too much drinking. But she would come back. He had to believe it.

The sirens screamed past him. He'd have to snatch the kid, get a picture of the two of them together. He hadn't wanted to have to do that unless there was no other way. The law would get involved. It would have been better for her to come home, then the two of them could go get custody. But the kid was the only thing that would bring Hannah home.

No matter. He'd have it all—that perfect little family everyone craved. The kid would adore him, and Hannah would rush to meet him when he came home from work.

Driving out to the old homestead, where Reece had grown up, the years slipped away. Matt had never taken care of his grandmother the way he should, but Reece would, just as he always did. He stopped at the farmhouse and slipped an envelope containing cash into the mailbox. That should tide her over for another month. He should go see her, but she would disapprove of what he planned to do.

He drove on to Gina's house. The truck idled in the road as his gaze wandered over the place. They kept it up nice. He couldn't remember who used to live here, but it was always run-down. A shadow passing the front window arrested his attention. He shut off the truck and killed the lights. Darkness hid his vehicle. Moments later the light flipped on and he could see Matt and a little girl enter the room.

He should have realized Matt would stash her here. He wouldn't want to run the risk of Hannah seeing her. Reece grinned. He'd like to be around when Hannah realized how Matt had been lying to her all this time.

He stared at the child. His daughter. An unexpected emotion welled up in him as he gazed at her. *His.* She looked so much like Hannah. Sweet and pure, completely moldable. Why had he thought to give over her training to someone else? Matt could never be the father Reece could. It was up to Reece to raise her to be the right kind of woman. One who obeyed her husband someday. His gaze touched the child's unruly hair again. He'd made a mistake, but he could fix it yet.

Matt carried Caitlin piggyback down the hall toward the bedroom. The evening had gone by way too fast. It was great for Blake and Gina to keep her, but she belonged with him.

He eased his daughter off his back and dropped her in the bed. "I'll listen to your prayers, then I've got to go, princess." He knelt on the floor beside the bed.

She slipped onto the floor beside him and flung herself against him. "I want to come home, Daddy. It's scary out here where it's so dark outside."

"I know. It won't be for long." He kissed her again. "I'll bring you a surprise tomorrow."

"I just want to come home."

Matt found it disconcerting to look in his daughter's eyes, so much like Hannah's. The problem was never far from his thoughts. "Me too. Now let's pray." He was touched to hear her sweet, simple prayer for him and her aunt Gina. And even for Trudy. As she prayed, he added his own plea for forgiveness for the lie he was living. Was it ever okay to lie—even for a good reason? He was Caitlin's daddy. His role was to protect her. But the blow to his conscience was crippling.

Still, he would endure anything for his little princess. He swelled with pride. She was turning out so well, even without a mother.

She had a mother.

He didn't want to think about it. As Caitlin's father, he was responsible for protecting her from people like Reece. She was too young to deal with all this. He kissed her and tucked the quilt around her. "'Night, princess. See you tomorrow."

"'Night, Daddy." Her voice was muffled, and her eyes closed.

He tiptoed out the door. The phone was ringing in the living room when he got there, and Gina answered it. "It's for you," she said. "The captain."

"Hey, what's up?" Matt said into the phone.

Sturgis's voice blared in his ear. "I've been calling your cell for half an hour."

Matt's hand went to his belt. The phone wasn't there. "I must have left it in the SUV. What's wrong?"

"O'Connor picked the lock at your rental."

The alarm that spread up his spine surprised him. "On my way." He ran for the door.

"Gotta go," he called to his sister. "Big problem." She called after him, but he just waved and ran on to the vehicle.

He expected to find the women cowering in the house, but instead, Hannah was making tea. Ajax lay at her feet.

He stared at Hannah. She was dressed in some slinky number that showed off a set of amazing legs. She'd kept those hidden all these years? And she'd done something to her hair. It curled around her face and down her back in a tousle that made her look different, mysterious. Her hair and eyes brought to mind a roused lioness.

Her gaze held determination. "He's not going to terrorize me," she said. "Not anymore."

"What happened?"

She pointed to the door. "He drugged Ajax, then picked the lock on the kitchen door."

Matt knelt by his dog. "You okay, buddy?" Ajax whined and licked Matt's hand, then dropped his head onto his paws again.

Matt clamped down on the anger that rose within him. "We're looking for Reece. He can't hide for long. Every deputy in the county is on the lookout."

"You said you were sending a car by here," she reminded him. "Where was it?"

"The car only comes by every hour." He didn't know what Reece might do, but the man was dangerous. "I'll stay here tonight, talk to the captain."

He went to the back door and examined the evidence. The lock had been jimmied, and scratches marred the brass. Ajax got up and followed, though he was a little wobbly. Stepping outside to the back deck, Matt scanned the dark yard. Reece would be long gone, but maybe he'd left a clue of some kind. He pulled a flashlight from his belt and let its beam sweep the ground. The recent rain had left the dirt soft. The grass was matted down under the kitchen window. The hair rose on the back of Matt's neck. Reece had stood here and watched the women.

What did the man want? Something so simple as wanting his wife back? Matt feared Reece was after more, that he wanted Caitlin too. But maybe not.

He prowled around the yard for about half an hour, then headed to the back door.

The screen door creaked as Blake came through it. "We got a call. Moe's mother, Nora, was run off the road in her buggy. She's dead."

Matt winced. This would hit Hannah hard. "It all seems directed at Hannah's family."

Blake shrugged. "Might just look that way."

"This is very targeted." Could it be that Reece had a vendetta against all of Hannah's family? Maybe he wanted to strip her of all her support except for himself. Abusers isolated their victims, but this took it to a whole new level.

"We've got to pick Reece up and question him."

"When did this happen?"

"About an hour ago."

"But Reece was here, terrorizing Hannah." Unease rustled in his gut. What was going on? "Did you tell Hannah about her aunt yet?"

"Yeah."

The screen door opened again. Hannah's strained face was wet, but she held on to her composure. "I need to be with my family. They'll be hurting about this. I'd like to go out first thing in the morning."

"You all need protection. If we put you together in one place, maybe I can protect you all." He wanted to tell her he was sorry about her aunt, but the words clogged his throat. She'd already been through so much. When he finally got the condolences out, she turned and walked back inside. He knew she wasn't about to let him see her grief.

sixteen

"The Tumbling Blocks Quilt is built piece by piece. It's a picture of how the Amish life is built around community."

—HANNAH SCHWARTZ,

IN *The Amish Faith Through Their Quilts*

Hannah could count the days, the weeks, the months, the years since she'd seen Luca's crooked smile. Ten years, six months, eleven days. An eternity. Yesterday.

Tuesday morning, she sat in the car beside Asia and listened to the tick of the engine cooling. Could he really tear out his love for her, their past, like he pulled up the weeds in the garden? It seemed as though he had. He'd been back for several days and hadn't come to find her.

Maybe he was in the greenhouse. Oh, she was just making excuses. The fact was, he didn't want to see her. If he did, he would have come to find her.

She should have talked to her aunt sooner. Now whatever Nora knew was lost for good. Hannah had thought she had time.

"Are we just going to sit here?" Asia asked. "Reconciliation doesn't come unless you're face-to-face."

"It doesn't matter. He'll do whatever the bishop says." Hannah kept her eyes on the front door. *Please, Lord, let him come to greet me.* A useless prayer. God had forsaken her.

Dressed in an A-line skirt and a sleeveless surplice blouse of Asia's, she felt like a child playing dress-up. And that was the way she wanted it. Maybe she could step outside herself, be someone else, someone who could handle the rejection. Someone who would laugh at the pain.

"Let's go." She shoved open her door and got out. A chicken fled from her feet, then turned and glared as if she were trying to steal the bug it had been after. She let Ajax out of the car. The dog's presence always made her feel safer. The front door remained closed. The breeze ruffled her hair. No noise came from the open, screenless windows, but she sensed the family watched her from inside the house.

Asia was beside her. "Want me to go first?"

"No, I'll go." Hannah walked past the fragrant phlox and mounted the steps to the door. She rapped firmly on the screen door. The seconds ticked by with no one appearing. She knocked again, louder this time.

Asia's fist thundered on the door when again no one came. "We're not going anywhere until we see Luca," she called.

Hannah shot her a quick look. "He won't respond to open anger."

"He's not responding at all right now."

Hannah nodded. "He will." She settled herself onto the top step and waited. Asia shrugged and did the same. A kitten crept near, and Hannah tapped her leg and cooed to the small feline. The scent of horse and hay from the barn blew on the wind.

She'd forgotten the stillness here. No whir of electric appliances, no cars. Just the peace of the past. If she closed her eyes, she could hear her mother's laughter on the wind. The high sound of the wind in the trees could have been her father's call for supper. She could sit here forever and remember.

Nearly fifteen minutes passed before the door creaked open and Sarah stepped out onto the porch. Caught at a disadvantage with her friend towering over her, Hannah scrambled to her feet and smoothed her skirt.

"I'd like to see Luca."

"He's in the greenhouse." Sarah chewed on her lip and didn't meet Hannah's gaze.

"Thanks. I'll be back. I'm going to have to stay here for a while." Hannah didn't wait for Sarah to answer. With the kitten leaping at her feet, she headed toward the greenhouse. She should have checked there first anyway, but she'd been reluctant to enter and see Luca in her father's place.

The fragrance hit her first. Floral scents from the roses by the door were punctuated with the undertones of earth and seasoned with the stink of fertilizer. The scent of childhood. As a kid, her job had been to deadhead the old blossoms. It seemed all her life she'd tended to things too late.

"This is a little creepy," Asia said from behind her. "It's like you could turn around and get lost in here. Or find a dead body on the floor."

Hannah smiled at her friend's fears. This was home to her. "Luca?" she called. She walked the rows and examined the plants. Strong and healthy, they'd thrived under his care.

A head bobbed up by the tomatoes, and Luca turned to face her. He looked different. Older, more tired. Maybe it was just her imagination, but as she neared, she could swear she saw warmth toward her still lurking in his eyes. And at least he was looking at her instead of ignoring her as he'd done at the funeral.

"Hannah." His voice seemed a little thick. "You should not be here." He glanced through the windows down the empty road.

"I had to see you, Luca." The Amish people were not overtly demonstrative, though their love for each other ran deep. Love that cared enough to confront, to correct. And to wound when necessary. "You look . . . good."

His gaze swept over her clothes, then back to her face. "Are you happy with this life you've chosen?"

Happiness. Hannah wasn't sure she knew what that was. "I'm . . . content," she said. "I have a good job, good friends." She pulled Asia from behind her. "This is my friend Asia."

Luca nodded to Asia. "It might have been better for you not to see our disagreement, miss."

"She's missed you every day she's been gone from here," Asia said.

He flushed at the reproof in her voice. "It was her own choice."

"We all make mistakes," Asia said.

But not everyone's mistakes resulted in calamity. "Let's not talk about the past," Hannah said. It would do no good to argue with him. "I need to talk to you, Luca. Explain what's been going on."

"I'm due back for lunch, but I'm afraid you can't eat with us." His voice broke.

Pariah. Anathema. The words pierced her heart. "I need your help."

"Will you talk to the bishop?" he asked.

"I've already talked to him. I can't come back. I think you know that. But I want to stay here. Me, Asia, and a deputy. We're all in danger, including your family. You know someone killed Moe and Aunt Nora. Whoever it is, he seems to be targeting our family. You or Sarah or your kids could be next. The sheriff can only spare one deputy. The detective in charge of the case thought we'd be better off together, and there's not enough room for everyone where I was staying in town."

"We accept whatever the Lord gives from his hand," Luca said. "If God sends us heartache, it was meant to be."

Though his coldness failed to move her, his fatalistic attitude caused her anger to flare. "The killer is evil. I won't stand by and let evil have its way when we can prevent it."

"God's will be done. But in this case, I don't believe we are targeted. You've changed, Hannah. It is as I expected."

His thinly veiled contempt stung. "You have no idea where I've been or what I've endured. And you don't need to know. But I won't stand back and let you or your family be harmed. If I have to, I'll sleep in the barn. But I'm not leaving." She folded her arms over her chest.

Luca stared back at her without expression. "I must talk to the bishop. I'm a deacon now. I have responsibilities."

A deacon. Hannah hadn't heard. No wonder he held back. When those in the congregation strayed, he would be the first to gently persuade them to put away the thing that tempted them. He had to uphold the ban in public especially.

She put her hand on his arm. "We are kin, Luca. It isn't that easy to just toss me aside."

"You left *us*, Hannah." His voice stayed calm and assured. "And we would welcome you back with open arms if you reconciled with your husband and he converted as well." His intent gaze lingered on her face.

Hannah studied his face, the smooth cheeks above the long beard, the brown eyes that used to see everything, the worn hat covering his Dutch boy haircut. Sarah was taking good care of him. A tiny tear on his coat had been expertly mended.

In her sweep of his appearance, she almost missed the meaning of the way his Adam's apple bobbed and the way he refused to look away from her gaze. He was trying to hide his emotions and doing a good job of it. If she didn't know him so well, she might have even bought it.

This was as hard for him as it was for her. He didn't want to turn her away. It was only for love that he was trying to do the right thing. His words came back to haunt her. *We would welcome you back if you reconciled with your husband.* Reece said he'd converted. What if it was true?

"I'm going to get my things and bring them in," she said softly. "You know as well as I do that you can't deny me sanctuary here in my own home. I still own half this house, don't I?"

Red crept into his cheeks. "Yes," he admitted. "I always expected you to come back asking for money."

"I thought you knew me better than that."

"Reece . . ." He looked down at his black shoes. "You have more right to this property than I do."

"Reece never pushed me to get the house. He didn't want me to have anything to do with you. This is one thing that's not his fault but mine. I'll stay out of your way. I will not leave you, Luca."

He sent her a pleading look from under his brows. "Please don't endear the children to you."

Ignoring them would be the hardest thing, but she nodded. Her cousins were darling, and she longed to scoop them onto her lap and tell them stories. She and Asia went to the car and hauled their suitcases to the house. Luca followed.

"I didn't bring the cats yet," she said. "I'll get them later this afternoon."

"Cats?" Luca asked.

"Four of them." She flashed a smile up at him, but he looked away and said no more. "Where do you want us?"

He held the door open for them. "Your old room is now a guest room. I will have Naomi move her toys over to Sharon's room. Wait a moment." He left them standing in the kitchen with their suitcases and disappeared into a hallway. Moments later the heavy tread of his feet went up the steps.

Hannah heard Sarah's voice murmuring, and she could sense the stress in it. Hannah believed that her presence would stop anything bad from happening. Maybe this belief was rooted in a misguided sense of her own control, but her instincts told her she had to be here.

MATT UNDERSTOOD THAT his minutes with Caitlin were drops of water draining through a sieve. Maybe that was fatalistic, but with Hannah showing no signs of leaving soon, it was only a matter of time before the truth came out. Matt wanted to hold his daughter close, treasure every moment.

Frogs bellowed from the creek, a song as mournful as Matt's mood. He sat on the porch swing with Caitlin on his lap. Hannah wasn't going anywhere until she'd exhausted every avenue. All she had to do was show that picture to one other person at the jail, and the jig was up. He should see a lawyer to find out what he could do to avert a tragedy. No way would he abandon his daughter the way his mother had abandoned him. The swing swayed under them, and the gentle movement lulled him.

"Me and Aunt Gina went to visit Grandma Trudy today, and she never smiled at me. Why is she so grumpy, Daddy?"

Why indeed? He'd never figured it out himself. "She's had a hard life."

"How come you don't have a mommy and daddy? Trudy is your grandma, too, isn't she? All the kids at preschool have two grandmas. I've only got one."

She'd asked the question before, but Matt had always managed to put her off. "My dad died just like your mommy. My mom went away, princess."

"Did your mom go away to heaven like my mommy?"

"No, she just went away." He didn't tell her that he'd come home on his birthday to an empty house. He didn't explain how he'd gone through the house calling her name. She didn't need to know he'd fed himself and cried all night for three days until a neighbor called Child Protective Services. "I went to live with my grandma Trudy then." Gina had been luckier. She'd been staying with their aunt over spring break.

He tightened his grip around Caitlin. She would never feel abandoned while he had breath in his body.

"Maybe she'll come back. I'd like to meet her." Caitlin's voice grew softer, and her eyes closed. Rhythmic breathing followed.

"I wish she'd come back too," Matt muttered against his sleeping daughter's hair. She didn't often take a nap. He stood with her in his arms and carried her to bed. His sister was watching her afternoon soap opera. The TV flickered, but the sound was down so low he wondered how she could hear it. He tucked the covers around Caitlin and pressed a kiss against her hair before joining Gina in the living room.

"Sit down, Matt," she said. "You're keeping something from me. Work is always intense, but you've never asked me to keep Caitlin before. You know I love her, but I want to know what's going on."

The need to talk to someone, to confess, gripped him in a stranglehold. "Caitlin's real mother is here in town looking for her."

"Looking for her? What do you mean?"

He shook his head. "Her mother never gave up Caitlin. Someone stole the baby from her and gave her to us." Almost too late, he caught back Reece's name. "We didn't get her in the usual way. Analise heard something at the door, and Ajax was going crazy barking. She opened the door and found a newborn baby girl in a carrier."

Gina pointed her finger at him. "You never told me all this. I only heard a baby had come through for you."

"We didn't want Caitlin to hear about it someday and feel more abandoned than she would when she learned of her adoption. There's something devastating about being tossed on someone's porch. She was all swaddled up against the chill. And we found her immediately, just as the kidnapper thought we would." One peek into her wrinkled little face had triggered love at first sight. He still remembered the way she opened her eyes and looked at him. He and Analise had been trying to have a baby for five years and were just starting to talk about adoption. It seemed Caitlin was a gift from heaven.

With his position at the sheriff's department, it had been easy to keep the circumstances quiet and to put the adoption through. They told friends and family a private adoption had been arranged and they'd gone to the hospital to get her. A quiet search was made for her parents, but no traces of them were ever found. A few months later, the adoption was final.

And *final* was the word. He couldn't give her up.

"Have you spoken with the mother?"

"I haven't told her I have Caitlin, if that's what you mean."

"You don't want this woman to find her. Heck, I don't want her to find her! I love Caitlin. There would be a huge custody battle."

"Exactly." At least he had some support now.

seventeen

*"The Chevron Quilt is an interesting pattern. And one that
has special meaning when you look at the way the Amish
won't wear a uniform or serve in the military."*

Hannah's gaze kept returning to the center of the sitting room where she'd found the bodies of her family. No trace of the symbol marred the walls. The three hours she'd been here had dragged by, hung up on tragic memories haunting every corner and peering from every shadow.

Tableware clanged against plates in the kitchen. Hannah could hear one of her cousins talking to Sarah in German. The guttural tones took her back to her own childhood. Seated on the sofa with a tray, she picked at the food on her plate.

Asia tipped her head and listened. "How well do you still remember your German?" She'd insisted on joining Hannah for dinner.

"I'm a little rusty. I found that out when I tried to talk to the children the last time we were here. Ours is a Swiss-German dialect that's a little different from what the *Englisch* call Pennsylvania Dutch."

"Is Parke County the sect's only home?"

"No, but the majority of the Swiss Amish came to Indiana. Our group came later than those in Pennsylvania. We made our way to the state around 1840 directly from Switzerland. Most Amish people here in Parke County are from Pennsylvania and speak Pennsylvania Deutsch. Most of us here in Indiana who speak the Swiss dialect are up around Berne, but our district was a plant from there."

"Are the languages close enough to understand each other?"

"It's a little challenging." Hannah smiled. "If I were to talk with a Pennsylvania Deutsch Amish woman, it would be easier to speak English. We don't socialize much with the other group either."

Asia studied her face. "You keep saying *we*."

Hannah's laugh felt strained. "I suppose I do. I hadn't noticed. I'll always be Amish at heart."

"How do you mean?"

"Our simple love of family, our neighbors. It's ingrained in me, and I'll always carry it with me. I might carry a cell phone and cut my hair, but inside I'm Amish."

Asia nodded. "I can see that. It's one reason people are drawn to you."

Drawn to her? Hannah had never noticed. She scooped up a spoonful of her cold fruit soup—mashed strawberries, milk, and sugar over bread. She hadn't had anything like it since she left the county, and she nearly smacked her lips over the fresh taste. Sarah was a good cook. The chicken potpie had pastry flaky enough to melt in her mouth, and the homemade root beer rivaled *Mamm*'s.

"I had no idea there was so much diversity among the Amish. You should mention that in the book."

"Each district can be different too," Hannah said. "But most people don't realize there are such distinctions." The noises intensified in the kitchen, and she knew they were finished with supper. She put her spoon down. "I think I'm done too."

"We should help with dishes."

"They won't let me. But I can sit at the table while you help." Hannah rose and went to the kitchen with her utensils. Ajax followed at her feet.

Sarah glanced up quickly, then ducked her head so all Hannah could see was the top of her kapp. The tiny pleats in the prayer bonnet had required hours of ironing. Hannah put her dishes onto the stack by the sink, then retreated to sit at the table. She folded her hands in her lap.

"Can I help you with the dishes?" Asia asked.

"No, thank you. The children will help."

Asia raised her brows and glanced back at Hannah, then joined her at the table. Sarah moved a small step stool close to the sink, and Sharon crawled up to wait for her mother. Sarah took the kettle from the woodstove and poured hot water into the sink. Naomi took a dish towel from the drawer and stood on tiptoes to grab the wet dishes as they were ready to be dried.

"Amazing," Asia muttered, her gaze on the children. "Most kids do everything they can to get out of chores."

The girls' willingness seemed so normal, so right, to Hannah. "We are taught from a young age that work is blessed. Idle hands are the devil's workshop. We enjoy spending time with one another too. The girls want to be like their *mamm*, and the boys like their *datt*. They're eager to begin to learn the chores and to help out. My mother began to teach me to quilt when I was three."

"Do your children ever fight?" Asia asked Sarah.

Sarah smiled and shook her head. "It is not allowed."

"Where's Luca?" Hannah asked.

Sarah's smile faded. "Feeding the horses and chickens."

So far, Hannah had detected no trace of the camaraderie she and Sarah had shared as teenagers. Hannah mourned its loss. "When did you and Luca marry?" She kept her tone light and friendly.

"About a year after you left. Nine years ago."

"Your oldest is only six?" It was unusual for so much time to pass before a child arrived.

"I had a few . . . accidents." Sarah seemed to force the words out.

"I'm sorry."

"The Lord's will be done."

"Of course. And your family is beautiful."

Sarah's eyes finally softened. "Thank you."

"How are your parents, your brothers and sisters?"

"They are well. *Mamm* is dealing with a bit of arthritis, but she has good spirits about it." The smile that flickered across her lips disappeared. "You might spoil everything, Hannah. Don't you care?"

The words pierced Hannah to the bone. "I've always cared," she said softly. "I can't tell you how many times I picked up the phone to call Luca at work. I didn't want to make things worse for him."

"Yet you're here now, aren't you?"

Heat crept up Hannah's neck. It hurt to be so unwanted. It used to be different. She fought to keep her voice from trembling. "I need to find the child."

Sarah turned from the sink and came to where Hannah sat. "Do you really think the child is yours? And what if she is, Hannah? Would you rip her from a family who loves her?"

"I don't know." In spite of her resolve, her voice shook. "You know how important family is to me."

"Not anymore. You turned your back on your family. For *lust*."

"That's harsh," Asia put in. "You don't know what Hannah's been through."

"God chastises his children."

"At least you admit I'm his child," Hannah said in a low voice.

"I admit nothing."

"What are you so afraid of?" Asia asked.

"I'm not afraid." Sarah pressed her lips together.

But Asia was right. Hannah recognized the fear now in the way Sarah's hands trembled. "Are you hiding something, Sarah?"

"Of course not!" The strings on Sarah's cap fluttered as she shook her head.

"Do you know where the little girl is being kept?"

Sarah grabbed up a basket from the counter. "I'm going to gather eggs."

The door shut behind her, and Hannah stared after her through the window. She hadn't answered the question. Hannah followed her.

The night air cooled her hot cheeks. She found Luca and Sarah huddled together near the barn. They stopped speaking when she approached. Was the fear she saw in Sarah's eyes fear of the future? "Look, let's clear the air. I'm not going to throw you out. I don't even want anything from the property."

Luca crossed his arms over his chest. "Half of it rightly belongs to you. I have been setting aside half of the profits every year you've been gone."

"I don't want it." Blood money, that's all it was.

"No. You *will* take it. It's not as much as the greenhouse is worth, but it will be a steady income if you will allow me to continue to manage the business."

She recognized the inflexible tone of his voice but he couldn't stop her from doing what she wanted with it. Maybe she'd set it aside for his girls. "How about we compromise? I'll take what you've got set aside as a final payment. No more after that. That's my final offer." He wouldn't get the reference to a TV show, but she had to say it and smile anyway.

"I cannot do that. The house and property are worth even more."

Hannah glanced back to the house. "Let's break out the accordion, Luca. I haven't yodeled since I left. We'll sing all the old songs and pretend we're kids again."

"I haven't played since you left, Hannah. I'm a deacon now. I got rid of the accordion."

"Is my guitar still in the barn? We can have the kids watch for buggies just like we used to do." She started past him toward the barn, but he grabbed her arm.

"I didn't want to be a deacon, but the vote came to me. Don't make it harder, Hannah."

She stared at him. "Do you still yodel?"

"*Ja.* The girls, they are learning too."

"Could we do that tonight?"

Luca glanced from Hannah to Sarah. "Ja, maybe it would be okay."

Sarah had no expression, and Hannah wondered if he hoped the yodel fest would ease the tension. Did Sarah value her position as a deacon's wife so much that she never liked having fun anymore? The girl she was ten years ago had vanished when the black apron replaced the white one.

MATT RUBBED HIS eyes, bleary from staring at the screen. Blake sat sprawled in a chair on the other side of the desk. His eyes were closed, and a snore rumbled through his mouth. The clock on the wall read only eight thirty, but they hadn't slept since Reece surprised Hannah last night, questioning neighbors, tracing leads. All to find nothing.

Blake had come straight from Shipshewana, and Matt decided to let him sleep awhile before waking him to demand to hear what he'd found out.

He wished he could sleep in his own bed tonight rather than on the sofa at the Schwartzes', but duty called. He hadn't checked his e-mail all day, so he clicked over to it. The in-box contained mostly work-related requests for information or case follow-ups that he'd been copied on. No new burglaries.

He glanced at Blake. He'd been out of town. Coincidence?

An e-mail marked Urgent caught his attention as he was about to click out of the program. The subject line read "Hello Son." The air seemed close and hot, and if he'd had the energy, he would have opened the window or turned up the air. He thought he'd clicked on the message, but then he realized he was still sitting there staring at the screen.

If he didn't know better, he'd have thought he was having a heart attack. A weight lay on his chest, and his arms were numb.

His hand holding the mouse moved slowly, and the cursor paused over the e-mail. For just one second, he wanted to linger and not know. In this case, ignorance might be bliss. He could hang on to the hope just a little longer. He swallowed hard and double-clicked the e-mail. The message sprang onto the screen, and he leaned forward to read it.

Hello, Matt. I heard you've been looking for me. If this is true, please reply to this e-mail. Love, Mom

Could it really be her? How did she find his work e-mail? Wait, he hadn't left town—she had. It would be no problem to get his e-mail. It was listed on the department's Web site. His hands shook as he placed them on the keyboard. He typed a quick reply asking her to meet him. He tried not to sound too desperate. Desperation might drive her away. And did his words sound accusing or judgmental? He reread the note.

Mom, good to hear from you. Can we meet? How about at the coffee shop tomorrow morning at 9:00? Just let me know. Love, your son Matt

Joy exploded in his chest. Whenever he thought of his mom, he was eight years old again, running home to see her. He reminded himself she wouldn't be the same woman he'd last seen. She would be in her fifties, probably with gray hair and wrinkles. Was she remarried? What if she had kids with another man? The thought that she might have loved another child more than him and Gina compressed his chest again.

He warned himself not to get his hopes up. After all this time, if she really was trying to find him, her motive might be to ask for money or something. It wasn't likely she had missed him as much as he'd missed her.

Blake yawned and sat up. His hair stood on end. "Man, I'm beat."

Matt clicked out of his e-mail. "What did you find out?"

"Found the bishop. He claims Reece started coming there a month ago."

"So it's fairly recent. Probably a ploy to get Hannah back."

"That'd be my guess. The bishop said Reece had been faithful to the teachings."

"Except for driving a vehicle."

"Well, yeah, there's that. But the bishop didn't know about it. He said

Reece told him he'd hired a driver for a trip and would come in a few weeks with his wife and child."

The muscles in Matt's belly tensed. Over his dead body. No one was taking Caitlin away from him. "Thanks. You'd better get home to Gina."

Blake glanced at his watch. "Yikes, I told her I'd be home for supper. If I'm late, she'll be suspicious all over again." He bolted from his chair and ran for the door.

Matt followed him outside. He needed to get out to the Schwartz house before they all went to bed. As he drove north out of town, his thoughts kept drifting to his mother's e-mail. Could it be real? He was afraid to hope.

Dim yellow light shone through the windows of the house when he pulled into the driveway. He got out of the SUV and started toward the front door. A warble of some kind came to his ears. Was that yodeling? He stopped and listened. The German song rolled out across the yard, and though it was supposed to be joyous, he heard the undercurrent of a lost time that would never come again, no matter how hard they tried to find it.

THE CHILDREN'S VOICES murmuring their prayers slipped under the closed door. The sunset still glowed in the west, though it was nine o'clock. Indiana had only recently started to follow daylight saving time, and Hannah wondered if her people had adopted the *Englisch* way of changing their clocks.

"You sure you don't mind sharing a bedroom?" she asked Asia.

"We can talk about some publicity." Asia sat cross-legged on the single bed. "How's the quilt coming?"

"You know I've struggled to work on it since we got here. There hasn't been much time. I really want this one for the cover. The triangle is the underpinning of the Amish faith."

"Hannah, the photographer will want pictures of it in a month and a half. You're not even close to finished."

"I know. I'll work on it a little while now." Hannah pulled the large plastic container out from under the bed where she'd placed it earlier. "This room used to be mine." She lifted the lid and rummaged for the last square she'd been working on.

"Homey. What chapter are you on with the book?"

"The one about Chevron quilts."

"What's significant about them?"

Hannah thought a moment as her needle wove in and out of the colorful fabric. "A chevron is a badge or insignia. The Amish believe very much in following secular authority, in leading a law-abiding life. It's very rare to find any lawbreakers among the Amish, and murder is practically unheard of. But the one thing they refuse to do is to serve in the military. In fact, that's why the men don't wear a mustache, only a beard. In earlier centuries only military men wore mustaches, and they associate mustaches with killing. They prize peace and want nothing to do with war."

"So they are conscientious objectors?"

Hannah nodded. "My mother was the perfect example of a soft answer turning away wrath." Though in Hannah's case, those teachings were what had kept her under Reece's fist too long. She focused on making her stitches even and small. She wouldn't think about the sound of her mother's laugh, or the way her mother's auburn hair caught the sunlight. She wouldn't remember the way *Mamm*'s tender hands, rough from hard work, would stroke Hannah's hair at night before bed. The needle blurred in her vision, and she blinked hard.

"Did she only work by hand?"

"No, she had a treadle sewing machine that she used for the piecework. The actual quilting was done by hand. I'll talk about that when I get to the chapter on the Carpenter Patch. We prize things made with hard work, but we use tried-and-true technology. Many use a treadle sewing machine for the piecework."

Asia frowned. "I've always heard quilts made by hand are more valuable."

"When sewing machines first became available, it was a status symbol to have one to use for quilting. Around 1900, during the Colonial Revival period, interest in hand quilting grew, a return to nostalgia. But Amish women are practical. Good quilts are about design and excellent fabrics. *Mamm* always chose her fabrics with care and paid top dollar for them."

Asia glanced around the bedroom. "Does your cousin have any I can see?"

"They were all stolen the—the night of the murders." She stopped. "You know, the quilt that was found over the bodies should still be somewhere. It would have been released to the family once the evidence was collected from it. I'm going to look for it."

Asia sprang off the bed. "I'll come with you."

She followed Hannah down the hall. "This is a big place."

"Four bedrooms up here and another one downstairs. This is another guest room." The large room held a double bed, a dresser, a futon that could be made into another bed, and a crib. Even with all the furniture, it still had floor space to spare.

"Why is there so much furniture in here?"

"An entire family could stay here. We often have visitors who stay a few days." Hannah glanced around the room. She hadn't had time to go from room to room and see what changes Sarah had made. The quilt Hannah sought wasn't on the bed. She opened the closet and pulled out a blanket chest.

Seeing the cedar chest made by her father, she remembered that her mother's keepsake box had always resided inside. She lifted the lid and inhaled the aroma of fragrant cedar. The chest held quilts and an assortment of baby clothes. She began to lift out the quilts one by one. They'd all been made by Sarah. She recognized her friend's favorite Log Cabin pattern.

"What are you doing?" Sarah stood in the doorway. Her brows were raised, and spots of red blotched her cheeks. Hannah refused to let Sarah intimidate her. "I'm looking for the quilt that was over my family when I found them. I wanted to look at it again. I'd never seen it before that night, and it was clearly made by my mother." All of this belonged more to her than it did to anyone else. Even Luca didn't have as much right to the personal effects as she did.

Sarah bit her lip. "It's in Naomi's room. It's a child's quilt. I thought she would enjoy it."

"You gave your child a quilt that had been on her dead relatives?" Asia's voice resounded with horror.

"It was laundered, of course."

A practical response, but Hannah shuddered. They were taught to put others first and avoid conflict, but Hannah could tell Sarah didn't like her snooping by the way she kept biting her lip and clutching her hands together.

"Which room is Naomi's?" Hannah moved toward the door.

Sarah stepped out of the way. "Just across the hall. Please don't wake her."

Hannah reached the other door in five steps and peered inside. She caught her breath at the sight of the quilt on a rack at the end of the bed. The hall light shone on it. Her memory hadn't done it justice. It almost seemed as though the red hummingbirds in the pattern stitching hovered over the black background. It seemed three-dimensional.

Seeing the quilt was like catching a glimpse of her mother. She found herself on her knees by the quilt rack. Pulling the quilt to her face, she inhaled, but there was nothing left of her mother's essence, only the scent of fresh air from hanging on the line. When she got up, she realized her cheeks were wet.

So were Sarah's. The two women appraised each other. In Sarah's eyes, Hannah saw her own helpless yearning for a time that would never come again. A regret for years lost and never regained. A knowledge that there was nothing either of them could do about it.

Sarah averted her eyes and went to the rack. She lifted the quilt, folded it with steady precision, and placed it in Hannah's hands. "This should be yours."

Hannah's upbringing caused her to open her mouth to give it back, but she realized Sarah was right. It *did* belong with her. She was the only child left of Patricia and Abe Schwartz. Even Luca's children weren't their grandchildren.

"Thank you," she whispered. She resisted the urge to bury her face in the quilt again. "What about *Mamm*'s keepsake box?"

Fear returned to Sarah's eyes. "What does it look like?"

"A box about so big." She measured a space with her hands about a foot wide. "It's inlaid wood with a hummingbird design. Her grandfather made it. Have you seen it? It was always in the blanket chest."

"Where did you see it last?"

Hannah could see that the ping-pong of questions was designed to avoid a direct reply to the pointed query. "You have to have seen it, Sarah. I know it was here."

Sarah dropped her gaze. "Yes," she answered. "It's in our bedroom." She turned and left the room.

Hannah exchanged a quick glance with Asia, then followed Sarah. She dropped the quilt off in her bedroom, laying it reverently on the bed, then went downstairs, where she found Sarah in the master bedroom rooting through a shelf in the back of the closet. This was the first time since returning to Parke County that Hannah had been in her parents' bedroom. The same bed with a plain headboard was shoved against the far wall.

"Here it is." Sarah emerged from the closet with her kapp askew. She held the box out toward Hannah.

Hannah reached for it, her fingers grazing Sarah's. The contact made her glance in her friend's face. Sarah looked ashen. Hannah didn't understand what could be so upsetting about the box. "Thanks," she said.

"I must get ready for bed." Sarah bolted for the door.

Hannah carried the keepsake box back upstairs to her room. She couldn't think here with the reminders of her parents all around. Asia was already working on her lists again. She barely looked up when Hannah sat on the bed and raised the lid to the box. A faint melody tinkled out.

Asia tipped her head to one side and listened. "What's that song?"

"*'Land der Berge, Land am Strome.'* It means 'land of the mountains, land on the river.' It's the Swiss national anthem."

"It's beautiful. So is the box."

Hannah stroked the patina of the lid. "It's from Switzerland. My grandfather made it for her when she was a child."

The contents were from another life. Hannah had always loved going through it and having her mother explain everything. There were theater tickets to *Hair* and tickets to a Beatles concert.

Asia picked up the Beatles tickets and stared at them, then glanced at Hannah. "What gives?"

"She was a hippie until she met my father."

"Wow, talk about culture shock. Free love and all that, and then going into the Amish culture."

"I think she relished it. And she'd lived on a commune for three years with no electricity or running water. The structure helped give her meaning, she said."

"Did everyone realize where she'd come from?"

Hannah shook her head. "I don't think so. She was so eager to fit in, to please *Datt*."

"Didn't she ever miss her old life?"

"If she did, she never said so." Hannah sifted through the contents. Letters that she'd never been allowed to read, a tennis bracelet, a Seiko watch, several earrings, and a class ring. She frowned. "I don't see her ring in here."

"What ring?"

"Her mother's engagement ring. She told me it was worth a fortune. She had it tucked away here and never got to wear it. She slipped it on sometimes when we were alone, just to connect with her mother, I think. But she never let me wear it. She didn't want me to yearn for things that had no lasting value."

Hannah lifted everything out of the box and went through each item, carefully shaking out the letters. The ring was gone.

"When did you see it last?"

"About two weeks before she died. It's got to be here."

Could Sarah have taken it? But why? She would have no use for it. She'd never be able to wear it. And Luca wouldn't allow her to sell it. Could one of the girls have gotten in here and taken it out to play with it? It seemed unlikely. Amish children were taught respect from a very early age.

"I'll have to ask Sarah about it." Her gut clenched at the thought. Sarah might think she was accusing her of theft.

She put all of the items back in the box, though she lingered over the letters. She'd wanted to read them for as long as she could remember. "When you're older," her mother had always said. The youth quilt caught her attention. She unfolded it and spread it out on the bed.

"That's gorgeous," Asia said, getting up to take a closer look. "It looks like the birds are about to fly off the fabric. It's a solid black with just stitching as the only other color. I've never seen anything like it."

"All *Mamm*'s quilts are unique. It's the way she uses color. And look at her tiny stitches. I've never been able to match their perfection."

Asia leaned over to examine the quilt. "Oh, it's beautiful. Where did she learn?"

"My dad's mother. *Großmutter* took her under her wing, and *Mamm* was so patient to learn it all. She used to paint before she married *Datt*. Afterward, she poured all her artistic ability into her quilts."

"I wish we had more of her quilts to feature in your book."

"Me too."

Asia went back to her chair. "Is there another one around here? Maybe some of her customers still have them?"

"Oh, of course! We could get some of those. I wasn't thinking. I'd rather feature my mother's quilts if I can find them. She had a magnificent Mariner's Compass one. I think she sold it to the woman who owns the fabric store. We'll check there tomorrow."

Hannah couldn't wait to hold it. Maybe the woman would sell it to her.

eighteen

*"The Double Nine Patch Quilt is one of the most traditional quilts,
which is fitting when you remember that the traditions handed down
through generations are supremely important to the Amish."*

—HANNAH SCHWARTZ,

IN *The Amish Faith Through Their Quilts*

Hannah's cell phone rang after Asia had gone to sleep. She flipped it open and whispered, "Hang on," before tiptoeing out into the hall. She slipped into the bathroom and shut the door. "Hello," she said. She'd been half-asleep and hadn't checked the caller ID.

"Hi, hon," Reece said. "I hope I didn't wake you."

Hannah cleared her throat. "It's after midnight, Reece. Of course you woke me."

"I was thinking about you. Come meet me at the road. We could go for a cup of coffee."

"No. Leave me alone. Our marriage is over."

"Don't say that, hon. I don't want anything . . . bad to happen to you. We have to get back together."

Hannah licked her dry lips. "Are you threatening me, Reece?"

"Of course not. It's just that bad things might happen if I'm not around to protect you."

"Bad things happen when I'm with you. No one has hit me in five years."

His voice vibrated with anger. "I told you, that's in the past. I won't touch you. I've changed. I've converted."

"You're driving," she pointed out.

"It's just temporary. The bishop told me to sell everything. Until I get it sold, I'm driving it."

Hannah barely refrained from rolling her eyes. "What's *Demut* mean?"

"Humility," he said promptly.

Score one for him. "How does that work out in life?" Could he be telling the truth? Some of the districts weren't as restrictive as others.

"Accepting God's will. And God doesn't want us to be apart, Hannah."

"God doesn't want you to beat me either. Or to kill our daughter. You *pushed* me down the steps, Reece."

"You're wrong, hon. I was trying to catch you. I would never hurt you."

"You broke my nose, my arm. Why would I believe you now?" Was she remembering that night all wrong? But even if she was, he'd been liberal with his fists at other times. The loss of the baby was the final, tragic straw.

"I'm warning you, Hannah. You'd better come back home. Where it's safe."

Hannah flipped her phone shut and turned it off without replying to his insistent demand. The hidden threat in his words made goose bumps break out on her skin. She rubbed the raised flesh on her arm. He wasn't going to intimidate her.

MATT DIDN'T WANT to be here. It had been late when he arrived, but even his fatigue didn't help him fall asleep. The lack of outside lighting deepened the shadows in the room. This was a bad idea. He tossed on the sofa. At least the hiss of the gaslights had been silenced. He'd had no idea a lamp like that was so loud.

Now the house echoed with silence. If there were a TV in the place, he'd turn it on and spend an hour of mindlessness. He forced himself to close his eyes and then began to drift. He dreamed of Analise. She was smiling as she ran through a field of flowers. He wanted to warn her not to smell them, but he couldn't speak.

He came awake at the sound of a creak as loud as a shotgun in the dark. Matt thrashed out of the tangle of sheets and leaped to his feet. He listened for the sound to come again. There it was. He rubbed his eyes, and for a second, he thought he might still be dreaming. Then the sound came a third time.

It was the creak of the door in the kitchen. He hadn't heard anyone come down from upstairs. An intruder was in the house. He moved noiselessly across the room. There was no moon tonight, so not even moonlight illuminated the kitchen as he peered through the doorway. He thought he saw a dark figure pass in front of him.

He leaped forward, and his hand touched fabric. There *was* someone here. He wrestled with the figure, neither of them saying a word, until they were both on the kitchen floor. He pinned the intruder to the linoleum.

Only then did he realize he wasn't grappling with a man but rather with the softness of a woman. Grabbing her wrists, he pinned them to the floor above her head.

"Get. Off. Me." Hannah's voice vibrated with anger. "Are you crazy?"

He let go as if the heat of her wrists seared his skin. Scrambling back, he helped her to her feet. "What are you doing prowling around in the dark?"

"I didn't have a flashlight, and I couldn't sleep. I thought I'd have some milk."

He reached over and fumbled to turn on the gaslight. The soft hiss came with the glow. "You could have turned on the light."

"I didn't want to wake you."

She stood in her bare feet. The peach cotton nightgown she wore covered her from her neck to her ankles, but with her hair hanging down her back and her eyes smudged with sleep, he'd never seen a more beautiful sight. He didn't like the way he was noticing things about her—like the way her hair glowed in the light and the way her mouth was shaped. For a second he let himself imagine kissing those full lips.

What was he thinking? He was smarter than to let physical attraction blind him. Besides, she'd never filed for divorce. Anger with himself made his voice gruff. "Oh yeah, I'm sleeping now."

She turned her head away, but not before he caught the glimmer of tears. What a jerk he was. He touched her arm. "What's wrong?"

She pulled away, then brushed past him to open the gas refrigerator. "Want some?"

"Sure."

Taking out a jug of milk, she shook it, then poured two glassfuls. She handed one to him before sitting at the table.

"Why'd you shake it?"

"It's not processed. It's the real thing, so you have to mix the cream back into the milk."

He slid out a chair beside her and took a cautious sip of the milk, finding it creamy and good. Good to focus on something other than watching her bring the rim of the glass to her mouth. She set the glass on the table and licked the cream from her lips. He watched in fascination. "So what's wrong?"

Her sigh was soft. "Everything is so confusing. I don't know what to do, where to go for help. Reece called me a few minutes ago. He swears he's joined an Amish district."

"It's true. Blake went up to Shipshewana to investigate. He talked to the bishop. He's been attending there for a month."

She rocked back in her chair, and her shoulders hunched as though she were protecting herself from a blow. "I can't believe it."

"What did he want?"

"What he always wants. For me to come back to him."

"Are you going to do it?" He'd seen it so often over the years—the abused woman going back to her abuser. He hoped Hannah had more courage than that. Reece would end up killing her, given the chance.

Her head came up. "I'm not going back. I'm done with abuse."

Her voice rang with conviction, and Matt actually believed she meant it. He sensed that a backbone of iron ran through Hannah. Sometimes trials did that—hardened a person enough that they could face new adversity. She was tenacious, he'd say that much for her. She was still here looking for her daughter.

"Good for you," he said softly. He could drown in those golden brown eyes. Leaning forward, he propped his chin on his hand. "I won't let anything happen to you." He was close enough to catch a whiff of her fragrance, a light citrus of some kind, maybe shampoo.

Was it his imagination, or did she move closer by an inch or two? Even as he plucked her hand from the table, he wondered what he was doing. This wasn't professional, but her vulnerability drew him anyway. When was the last time he even went out with a woman? A year? Two? And he was attracted to so much more than her appearance. She was as tenacious as Ajax after a scent. Her soft eyes only masked a will and determination he couldn't help but admire.

She let her hand stay in his, though her eyes widened. Maybe she thought he was just offering comfort. And that's what the gesture was, of course. He didn't mean anything else by it. He encapsulated her hand in both of his. "If you're not afraid of Reece, why can't you sleep?"

"How many foster parents are there in the county?"

"What a question. Lots. I have no idea."

"Can you find out?"

"Sure. But why?"

"You know the picture I showed you of the child?" She waited until he nodded. "The quilt the little girl is sitting on is one that was stolen the night of the murders."

He found his voice. "Interesting, but lots of people bought quilts from your mother, didn't they?"

"Yes, but she'd just finished this one. I recognize the fabric. It was in the cabinet the day she died."

"So you're telling me you think these foster parents had something to do with your family's murder?" He tried to remember where Caitlin's quilt had come from. The information would be crucial. It had been a baby gift, and Analise had kept track of that kind of stuff. Could it be in Caitlin's baby book? But where on earth had he put that?

"It's possible they at least know the murderer. How else could they get that quilt?"

"Maybe he sold them over eBay. Or sold them to any store. There doesn't have to be a connection." What a lame explanation. He was going to have to go home and look for that baby book.

"Maybe." She chewed on her bottom lip.

"I'll try to get a list of foster parents and check them out. It might take weeks, though."

"You'd do that for me?"

He was beginning to think he'd do most anything for her—except turn over his daughter. No wonder Reece was nuts about her. Hannah had a childlike quality mixed in with her beauty. It made a man want to be a hero for her sake. He let go of her hand. If he wasn't careful, he would be as mixed up as Reece.

He rose. "It's nearly two. You should get some rest."

"Of course." The warmth in her voice faded. The chair scraped on the linoleum as she pushed back from the table and rose.

He hadn't meant to hurt her. She turned to go, but he reached out and took her arm. "I—I'll do all I can for you, Hannah." He was closer than he realized. It would only take one small movement for her to be in his arms. Even though he knew it wasn't smart, he tugged on her arm. The next moment her head was against his chest, and he was inhaling the sweet scent of her. He'd been right. The citrus fragrance was in her hair.

Her small, soft form fit in his arms. It had been years since he'd held a woman. Not since Analise. His wife had always been a little tense, looking around like she was about to move on to the next item in her list. There was a stillness about Hannah that soothed him. He ran a hand over her long hair and the heavy locks caught his fingers.

"What's going on here?" Luca stood in the stairwell door. His hair was disheveled, and his shirt was only partially tucked into the waistband of his pants.

Hannah jerked away and smoothed her hands over her nightgown. "I just came down for some milk."

"I thought she was an intruder and tackled her," Matt said. He knew he sounded lame when Luca's glower darkened.

"It didn't look much like a tackle," Luca said, his tone dry. "I think you'd better get to bed, Hannah."

"Of course." Hannah slipped past her cousin, her bare feet pounding up the wooden steps as though she were rushing to escape the devil himself.

Luca said nothing until the bedroom door upstairs shut. "Hannah is vulnerable. Please leave her alone."

"I'm just here to protect her. And find out who's targeting all of you and put him behind bars."

"God exacts justice. It's not our place."

"You don't want him caught?"

"Of course I want Hannah safe. But God will protect her."

"Sometimes evil prevails, Luca."

"That, too, is God's will."

Such a defeatist attitude annoyed Matt. "Then you think we should never work for justice here on earth?"

"We're told to forgive."

"No matter the offense?"

"Yes. That was Hannah's biggest fault. She wanted justice. Even as a child she struggled with this."

"Don't we all?" It was Matt's own desire for justice that had led him to law enforcement. "I'm sworn to uphold the law, to put lawbreakers behind bars. I'm not a philosopher."

"Our beliefs are not about philosophy but about obeying God's command to forgive. Seventy times seven. No matter what the offense. We forgive those who are too weak to stand against the devil and his wiles. There but for the grace of God go we all."

Luca had a point there. Matt knew his own weaknesses. "Aren't you afraid of who is targeting your family?"

"God's will be done. If it is my time, I'll go."

"But your wife, your children."

Luca grimaced. "It would be hard, but I know God is sovereign. And I accept that. Even pain can be for the glory of God."

"He's not going to get to any of you. Especially Hannah."

"You're *Englisch*. You know nothing about the things that matter most to her."

The jab hurt. "And you do? You're not acting like it."

Luca's color mounted. "I do only what's best for Hannah's soul."

Matt believed him. He could see the man's earnest love for his cousin. And who was he to say Luca was wrong? Matt now recognized he was beginning to want her for himself. Hannah had an unrest in her, a sadness that might be cured only by returning to the bosom of her family and friends.

Would meeting his mother tomorrow bring rest to Matt's soul?

WEDNESDAY MORNING. SHE'D been here a week. It seemed longer. From where she sat in the sitting room, Hannah could see her cousins at the kitchen table with Sarah. Their blond heads bent for silent prayer with their small hands clasped together. How often had she done the same around the table with her parents? It was one of the things she missed the most.

The children took their breakfast dishes to the sink and climbed the stools to wash them. Hannah forced herself to stay in the sitting room. Luca had already gone to the greenhouse, and Hannah hoped for a chance to talk to Sarah. Asia was upstairs working on a press release, and this morning would be the perfect time once Naomi and Sharon went outside. She didn't see Matt anywhere, and after last night's embarrassment, maybe that was best.

Hours later, she still longed to experience the strength of his arms around her. But look where that had gotten her last time. She needed to keep her distance. Besides, she was still married, at least legally. She'd hoped Reece would initiate divorce proceedings when she disappeared, but she should have known better.

The girls finished the dishes, and Hannah heard Sarah tell them to go gather the eggs. Before Sarah could start another chore, Hannah hurried into the kitchen. "Can I talk to you for a minute?"

Sarah's glance held a trace of wariness. "*Ja*, I suppose. I have laundry to do. I am two days late with it, and Luca has no more clothes."

"Oh, we can talk over laundry. It was always our favorite chore to do together. Remember how we used to throw suds at each other? *Mamm* was so mad the day we had more suds on us than on the clothes. What were we—thirteen or fourteen?" Hannah had to smile at the memory.

Sarah's lips twitched, but the smile never reached breaking point. "I cannot accept a favor from you."

Hannah's smile vanished. "It's a favor to me that you would allow me to do my laundry too. I didn't bring many clothes with me, and most of them are dirty."

Sarah still looked uncertain, but finally she nodded. "Get your clothes."

Hannah flew up the steps to gather the laundry. She yearned to see Sarah smile, to resurrect some tiny part of their friendship again. She took Asia's clothes with hers in a basket she found in the hall closet upstairs. By the time she got to the laundry room, an enclosed back porch, Sarah had already fired up the gas-powered wringer washer.

Hannah dumped the clothes onto the concrete floor and sorted them.

Sarah kept glancing at her from under her lashes. She almost looked . . . scared. Hannah wondered if Sarah feared she'd ask about the missing ring.

The gasoline-powered washer chugged along, stirring up a fresh batch of suds. Before Hannah could talk herself out of it, she plunged her hand into the cold water and scooped up a handful of foam. She flung it onto Sarah's head, then started back for more. Giggles burst from her at the bewildered expression Sarah wore.

White bubbles dripped down Sarah's hair onto her forehead, and she wiped them slowly. She didn't crack a smile, and Hannah became aware of how inappropriate her actions had been. She opened her hand and watched the suds slide back into the washer. "I'm sorry," she said.

Sarah reached over and grabbed a dish towel lying on the pile of towels. She dabbed at the top of her head.

"Here, I'll help you." Hannah took the towel and cleaned the suds from her friend's head.

Sarah still hadn't said anything. Maybe she was too shocked. After all, they were a sedate thirty-two years old. Matrons didn't behave like giddy teenagers about to enter their *rumspringa*.

Something cold hit her neck and slid down the back of her blouse. She stepped back to find Sarah with the suds still in her hand and a wicked smile on her face. "You suckered me in," Hannah said. She dove for the washing machine again, and ten minutes later, there was more water on the floor and on each other than in the washer.

"Oh my," Sarah said, collapsing onto a cane-backed chair in the corner. "I'm glad the children didn't see their mother acting *dumm*."

"It's not foolish to have fun." Hannah wiped the suds from her cheeks. She pulled the chair from the other corner over next to Sarah. "I've missed you, Sarah."

"*Ja*, and that is why you've come to visit so often and sent so many letters." Sarah turned her back and began to run one of Luca's shirts through the wringer on the washer. She dropped the garment into a basket and reached for another.

"My husband wanted me to break all ties. He thought you'd coax me back. He knew how many times I cried to know I was shunned. And I wanted to please him, to be faithful to him."

"Yet still, you left him." Sarah's voice held censure.

Divorce was not accepted in the Amish community. A woman who left her husband would be shunned. Hannah stared into Sarah's face. "He beat me, Sarah. He shoved me down the steps on purpose so my baby would die," she said, her voice hard. "Would you accept that? Just say it's okay and go on living with him, sharing his bed?"

Sarah bit her lip and looked away from Hannah's gaze. "It is required by the *Meidung* to be faithful and respectful to my husband."

"He would have killed me if I'd stayed, Sarah." Hannah watched Sarah's face, but the other woman said nothing.

Hannah hated divorce. Hated that she was separated. In a perfect world, a man cherished his wife and put her above himself. In a perfect world, a man was gentle yet strong toward his wife. In a perfect world, marital strife never happened. Too bad the world wasn't perfect. Hannah wished she could live in a world like that.

Hannah decided to change the subject. "*Mamm* had a ring in the keepsake box. Do you know where it is?"

The sympathy on Sarah's face vanished. "I don't know." She stood and grabbed a towel from the heap on the floor and began to mop up the water left around the floor drain.

The goodwill had fled the room. Sarah's cheeks were red, but Hannah saw no reason for such agitation over a perfectly reasonable question. The ring had to be here somewhere, and she meant to find it.

nineteen

"The Amish didn't invent quilts, but they brought
their own unique style to the craft.
Only solid colors in hues worn in clothing are used,
and the bright colors are often paired with black."

HANNAH SCHWARTZ, ON PBS'S *The Art of Quilting*

Any trouble over the weekend?" Matt asked Sturgis, who leaned out the window of his car with a cigar clamped in his teeth.

"Quiet both nights," he said. "Any new leads?" Sturgis had dark circles under his eyes. "The media has been hounding me for news. And there's nothing to throw to them to get them off my back."

Matt nodded. "I brought hard copies of all the data we've collected. I'll go over it again. I don't think the family will be in danger during the day. There are too many people coming and going at the greenhouse. I'll sleep here at night and work the investigation by day."

"Ah, I see. And Blake?"

"I'm meeting him at the coffee shop to prepare new questions for some of the family. Anything else happening?"

"Another burglary."

Matt frowned. "Where?"

"John Deere. Some electronics taken, computers, things easily sold for hard cash. The camera didn't pick up a thing. It looked like it was switched off. But I've got detectives looking over the scene for anything we missed on the once-over."

"The fourth one in three months. He's getting bolder." He hesitated, unsure whether he should voice his suspicions. "What if it's one of us, Captain?"

Sturgis sighed and leaned his head against the window frame. "I haven't wanted to think about it, but the thought crossed my mind."

"The guy has to be local. He knows when to slip in and how long to stay before getting away. He knows just how long before the canaries show up."

"Anyone special you suspect, Detective?"

The things Blake had been buying flashed through his head: a fancy sports car for Gina, a gift to the spa, that five-thousand-dollar ring that probably went to Vanessa. All guilt gifts. Was it possible? He pressed his lips together and shook his head.

"Check it out, Beitler. I run a clean department, and I want it to stay that way. If you suspect anyone specific, I want to know."

"No one specific," he muttered. He couldn't turn Blake in without evidence. As if Matt didn't have enough to worry about. The captain drove off, and Matt glanced at his watch. He was supposed to meet his mother in an hour. If it really was his mother who had e-mailed him. "Come on, Ajax." He whistled to the dog lying under the tree with three cats sleeping atop him, but Ajax just lifted his head and briefly looked at him before plopping down again.

"Traitor," he told the canine. "You're an insult to dogdom." Ajax stretched as if to show him just how little his condemnation hurt. "Stay here, then." He didn't think Hannah would need the dog during the day, but just in case, it wouldn't hurt to let Ajax stay. Just when he'd made the decision to leave the animal, the cats scurried away. Ajax got up and trotted over to stand by the rear door of the SUV expectantly. Matt let him in.

Hannah stepped to the back door of the house just as he climbed behind the wheel. "Is there a McDonald's around? I'd love an iced coffee—vanilla."

"Nope, no McDonald's. But Rockville has a Burger King. They've got a pretty good iced mocha. And there's a coffee shop in town."

"Thanks, I'll check it out." She disappeared inside again.

He drove to his place in Rockville. He hadn't been back to the house since Friday. He parked at the street and let Ajax out. The dog chuffed at his feet and whined. "You miss your toys, boy?" Matt unlocked the door and opened it, and stale air rushed out. The dog went inside ahead of him, and by the time Matt shut the door, Ajax had returned with his stuffed cat.

Matt went down the hall to his bedroom and packed a small suitcase of clothing before shucking his jeans and taking a long, hot shower. With his hair still wet, he padded in bare feet and jeans to the living room. Caitlin's baby book used to be in a drawer in the coffee table. He sat Indian-style on the carpet and pulled everything out of the drawer but didn't find it. His gaze studied the bookcases behind the sofa. No sign of it.

Caitlin liked to look at pictures of her mother. Maybe she'd taken it. He got up and went to her room. They'd left in such a hurry he hadn't made her bed. He straightened the pink ruffled spread and put her shoes in the closet. He glanced around the room but saw only dolls and toys until he got on his hands and knees and looked under the bed.

He pulled out the slim volume that chronicled the advent of his daughter into his life. Sitting with his legs straight out in front of him on the floor and his back against the bed, he began to flip through the pages. Ajax flopped down beside him and put his head in his lap.

"I miss Caitlin too, boy," Matt said. "Look, here's her first picture with you." The photo showed Caitlin two days after they got her. Her tiny face was screwed up as Ajax licked her cheek. His muzzle had been pure black then instead of laced with gray like now. "She loved you right from the start."

He turned the page. Ah, here was what he was looking for. The baby shower. Seeing the photo of Analise holding Caitlin made him pause. She looked so happy. Two years of bliss as a complete family followed Caitlin's arrival. "You big ham, you're in this picture too," he told Ajax. The dog woofed as though he understood. Most of their church family was there, standing in for the lack of grandparents. Analise's parents lived in Florida and rarely came to town.

There was a picture of the quilt with Caitlin lying on it. Ajax sprawled beside her. The next page held a list of the gifts, but there were several holes regarding who gave what. At least half of the items were not attached to a name, and he remembered why. Analise had given the job of making this list to two little girls from church who wanted to be included. Their childish scrawl showed their age. They'd been about ten.

If only he could remember. Maybe Gina would know. He'd ask her about it. He glanced at his watch and realized he'd better get moving. His heart thumped against his ribs.

AT THE COFFEE shop, he had trouble finding a place to park. For just a moment as he stepped onto the walk, he became that frightened eight-year-old boy. He shook off the sensation and strode with all the confidence he could muster to the door. The aroma of coffee and cinnamon rolls lingered in the air when he stepped inside.

He made a quick perusal of the room. Two women sipped frappés at a table in the back. Too young to be his mother. A man and a woman old enough to be his grandparents were standing at the counter arguing over how many shots the man usually took in his latte. Two men occupied a table by the door, no help there.

His stomach plunged. She wasn't here. Glancing at his watch, he saw it was barely nine. Maybe she was just a little late. And maybe he was just a sap.

He ordered a black coffee and took it and the newspaper to a table by the window at some distance from the other coffee drinkers. Opening the paper, he noticed his hands were shaking a little. For half an hour he sat pretending to read the paper and jerking to alert status anytime the bell on the door jingled. He checked in with Blake, then settled in to wait.

At nine thirty he folded the paper and laid it on the table. He'd wasted half an hour he could have spent with his daughter. As he stood, a woman stepped into the room. He appraised her appearance. About sixty, so the age might be close. Her hair looked dyed. Her height seemed about right.

Ajax whined at his feet, and he put his hand on the dog's head to calm him. Or maybe to calm himself. He wasn't aware of standing. She looked around and caught his gaze. With an uncertain smile, she approached and looked up at him. Her tongue darted out to wet her lips. Seeing her nervousness gave him courage.

"Are—are you Frannie Beitler?"

"Yes. Are you Matt?"

Her low, modulated voice struck him wrong. He'd remembered a higher pitch. But that was a long time ago. Age roughed up vocal cords. "Sit down. Can I get you some coffee?"

"I'd love a mocha." She fussed with her bag, opening and closing the latch.

He ordered the coffee and stood watching her from the corner of his eye. Had her hair been so straight? He used to wrap her curls around his boyish fingers. But maybe she'd had it straightened. The barista handed him the mocha, and he carried it back to their table.

His head on his paws, Ajax lay watching her. Matt wished the dog could tell him his impression. Matt handed her the drink, then picked up his own coffee. The strong, hot liquid fortified him.

"How did you find me?"

"Through the Web site," she said. "I was surprised to find you still looking."

"Why did you leave, Mom?" The words burst out of him. "You just walked out on us and never looked back."

She stared down at her hands, tightly clenched in her lap. "I wasn't cut out for motherhood."

"Don't give me that. You were a great mother until the day I came home and found you gone." His voice vibrated with passion.

"Let's not talk about the past, Mattie."

She'd never called him Mattie. Not ever. He studied her face. The nose wasn't right. His gaze dropped to her chin. He looked for the scar she'd received from falling on ice when he was seven. Her chin was smooth. "You're not my mother."

Her gaze shot up and collided with his. She grabbed her purse and started to rise, but he caught her wrist. "Let me go," she said.

"Why did you come here and try to impersonate my mother?"

"I—I—please, you're hurting my wrist." She twisted to try to break free, but his grip was too tight.

"I'm a detective. You didn't contact me through the Web site. You used my personal e-mail at the sheriff's department. I'm going to arrest you unless you tell me why you did this." He got no joy from the terror in her face, but she'd come here with an agenda, and he meant to find out what it was.

"He—he paid me."

"Who paid you?"

"The guy. Older than you. Going a little bald. We started talking at a bar in Broad Ripple. He said he wanted to help a friend and he'd pay good money for it. It seemed harmless enough. Make you think your mom wanted to see you so you weren't so obsessed with finding her."

Harmless. The disappointment devouring him was anything but harmless. She obviously had no idea what it was like to long for someone the way he longed to find his mother. "Was his name Reece?"

"He never told me his name."

It had to be Reece from the description. What kind of sick puppy would do this to him? He shook his head. The same kind who would beat a defenseless woman.

He let go of her wrist. "Get out of here. Count yourself lucky that I don't arrest you."

She scurried out the door without a backward glance while he sat back down and wondered what Reece's motive had been. If he just wanted to inflict pain, he'd managed that. The region around his heart still ached. But what if Reece had something bigger in mind? Was he trying to divert Matt's attention from the murders? If that was his goal, he'd only made Matt more determined to find evidence that implicated him.

He needed Caitlin's arms around his neck. He drove out to the covered bridge and across it to Blake and Gina's house. As his SUV rolled up the driveway, he watched for the sight of Caitlin's bright head.

There she was. Pigtails flying, she came bounding down the steps with her smile brighter than the sun overhead. She was small for her age of five, but the doctor had said not to worry. He pushed the guilt away. Caitlin belonged to him, not Hannah.

He flung open his door and opened his arms. Caitlin leaped into them and wrapped herself around him like a monkey. She smelled of soap and Cheerios. He buried his face in her neck and nuzzled it until she giggled.

Ajax was about to have a seizure in the backseat. Matt opened the door, and the dog leaped out. Jumping against Matt's hip, Ajax licked every part of Caitlin he could reach. She laughed and rubbed his ears. Matt put her down so she could say hello to the dog properly.

"I've missed you, Red," he said, touching her bright hair. He couldn't lose her.

"My hair's not red, Daddy." She looked up at him as she rubbed Ajax's ears. "It's titian."

"And where did you learn that word?" Every day was an adventure with her. He couldn't miss out on watching her grow up. Hannah didn't even know her. He took her hand and started toward the house.

"My teacher called it that. Did you come to take me to preschool?"

"Not today. How's Aunt Gina this morning?"

Caitlin's face stilled, then the smile vanished. She put her hand over her mouth and whispered through her fingers. "She was crying. Uncle Blake yelled at her."

Matt curled his fingers into his palm. "It's grown-up stuff. Nothing for you to worry about. Are you being good?"

Caitlin nodded. "I help her. Yesterday I brought in all the eggs and made my bed."

"You're a great help, I'm sure. Stay," he told the dog. He pushed open the screen door and entered the house. "Gina?"

"In the kitchen."

Matt patted his daughter on the bottom. "I need a new picture colored for me to put on my bulletin board. Will you do one for me?"

Caitlin's smile came out again. "Okay." Her bare feet slapped along the wooden floor, then she disappeared into the living room.

Matt turned the other direction, into the kitchen, where he found his sister seated at the table snapping green beans. She didn't turn her face toward him, but he caught the glimmer of wetness on her cheeks. "Got any fresh coffee?"

"In the pot."

He poured a cup of coffee and joined her at the table.

"When is this going to end, Matt? Every time I think it's over, I find out he's still seeing her."

He could have wrung Blake's neck. "He told you he was having an affair?"

"Yes, he admitted it." She swiped at her eyes. "I'm just tired of it. I'm going to go see this woman myself. I can't handle any more lies."

"When?"

"As soon as I'm not needed for Caitlin. I hate having her see me upset. When do you think her mother will be gone from town?"

"I don't know. She isn't showing any signs of leaving yet. You could go one evening when I'm here with Caitlin."

"No, I'm being selfish. Your problem is worse than mine. Caitlin belongs to us, not some woman she's never seen. This can wait a few more days."

She snapped another bean, and the sound was like the crack widening in Matt's heart, a crevice that let the terror surge into this throat. He'd do anything to keep his daughter. Anything.

TWO DAYS LATER, a big truck parked in the driveway. The side read *FOX & Friends*. Hannah wanted to wring her hands. Why had she ever agreed to this? It went against everything she'd been taught and was a symptom of the pride she'd allowed to creep into her life.

"What's going on?" Sarah peered out the window at the truck as men began unloading video equipment.

"It—it's a TV show that's going to interview me." Hannah wanted to cringe from the judgment in Sarah's eyes when she explained. "I wrote a book that has sold really well, and I've become something of an expert about Amish quilts. A morning TV show wants to get some footage of me here."

Spots of color appeared on Sarah's face. "We will stay inside, me and the girls."

"Of course." Hannah bolted for the door to avoid her censure. Asia followed. Out on the porch, Hannah leaned against the railing until the crew called her. "I should have canceled this," she said.

"It will be over soon," Asia soothed. She took out a notebook and went down to greet the hosts of the show.

But it wasn't over soon enough for Hannah. Two hours later, she'd been photographed sitting in the buggy, leaning against the barn, standing by the laundry line, and smiling by the ham hanging in the smokehouse. Limp as the overalls flapping in the breeze on the line, she wanted nothing more than to forget the morning ever happened. The crew and hosts were wonderful, but she knew the interview had been wrong for her, for her family.

Once the trucks and cars departed, Hannah wanted to get away. Asia drove her to town, where Hannah pointed out the coffee shop. Plenty of residents would be there. Asia parked the car and they headed inside.

The aroma of coffee beans roasting burned Hannah's throat as soon as she stepped in the door. She glanced around the room. None of the people sipping lattes and checking e-mail paid her the least attention.

"You sure you want to do this?" Asia whispered. "Do you know any of them?"

Hannah was about to say they were all strangers when a man looked up and their eyes locked. Panic fluttered into her throat, and she took an involuntary step back. Noah Whetstone rose from his chair and came toward her. He wasn't smiling. She wanted to flee, to hide in the bushes outside the door where she didn't have to see the betrayal come into his face again.

She watched him approach. He wore a long beard, no mustache, and smooth cheeks, so he'd kept the faith. And he'd taken a wife, another woman, someone who deserved him. The beard was a symbol of his married status. His pants were a little dusty as though he'd already worked awhile at the sawmill this morning. And he likely had. It was after ten.

After what seemed an eternity, he reached her. "Hannah. I heard you were back in town, *ja*."

"You—you look well, Noah." Hannah forced a smile, lifting her chin to look him in the eye. He didn't have to know her perfect life had crumbled around her like a rotted board. There was no need to let him know she still carried the shame of how she'd treated him.

"And you." He cleared his throat. "There is room at the table next to mine, if you'd like to sit." He glanced at Asia. "This is your friend?"

"Oh yes. Asia, this is Noah Whetstone. A—a friend. Asia is my good friend and assistant."

His gaze held reproach, but he said nothing about their former relationship. "You want coffee? I will get it."

Asia plopped into the chair as though the air in the place hadn't just thickened to the consistency of molasses. She said, "I'll take a mocha."

"You probably shouldn't do that, Noah. It might look as though we're sharing a meal."

He frowned, then shook his head. "You are still under the ban, *ja*? But no matter. I will get it. You can sit at the table next to mine and we can still talk though I honor the shunning."

"I'll take an iced coffee, then." Hannah sank onto the chair he'd pointed out. Her hands were shaking. Noah had moved on too. It wasn't as though she'd ruined his life. Still, it hurt to come face-to-face with her failures. She watched him take out his cell phone and place a call, then put it back. Maybe he was calling the bishop to come confront her.

"You all right?" Asia asked. "You look like you're about to faint."

"It was just a shock, seeing him."

"I gather he's more than a friend?"

"We were engaged. I hurt him when I ran off with Reece."

Asia studied the young man standing in line. "You left him for Reece? He's cute, especially if you could get him to shave off those whiskers."

"I like the beard," Hannah said. She'd grown up admiring her father's.

Noah came back holding two cups of coffee. He set one in front of each of the women, then took his own seat again.

"Thanks." Hannah took a sip of her coffee. "Who did you marry, Noah?" Hannah knew it would be someone she knew.

"Katie Stoltz. She has been a *gut* wife."

Hannah was relieved he'd done so well for himself. "I always liked Katie." Katie's dad owned the sawmill where Noah worked. "You're still at the sawmill then?" She smiled and pointed to the dust on his jacket.

"*Ja*. Katie's father retired a year ago."

"Children?"

"Four." His smile grew broader.

"Wonderful!" She hoped her envy didn't show.

"What about you, Hannah? You are happy, *ja*? Children?"

"I'm so sorry, Noah," she burst out. "I hate what I did to you. I hope you can forgive me."

His warm eyes studied her. "I have a *gut* life, Hannah. You did me no lasting harm. I forgave you long ago."

And she knew he had. The Amish way wasn't to wait to offer forgiveness until asked. It was freely extended regardless. She fingered the picture in the pocket of her skirt, then slowly drew it out and reached across the aisle to show it to him. "Do you recognize this child?" A line crouched between his eyes, and she could tell he wanted to ask more questions, but he took the picture and gazed down at it.

"*Nein*," he said finally. "But she has the look of you. Who is she?"

"I don't know for sure, but since she looks like me, I thought . . . she might be related."

He studied her face, then nodded. "Your cousin Mary, she lives here in town. Might the child be hers?"

Hannah's memory went back to the day of Moe's funeral. When Hannah had asked Mary about a husband or children, sadness had tugged at her mouth when she said she was single and childless. Could it be she'd given one up for adoption? Mary and Hannah looked enough alike to be sisters. But how would Mary's child have gotten the quilt?

MATT SAW HANNAH sitting with Asia near an Amish guy as soon as he entered the coffee bar. What did he have to be jealous about? He'd never even kissed her. But all the rationalization in the world didn't make the hot squeeze in his gut go away. Especially when he caught the intent expression on her face.

She was tucking that dratted picture back into her purse. His first lie had started him on a slippery slope to perdition. If he'd been honest the first time he saw the picture of Caitlin, what would have happened?

The barista handed over his coffee. Hannah still hadn't seen him, so he walked over to be introduced. As he approached, he recognized the man's face under the straw hat as one of the guys who worked the counter at the lumberyard. Matt struggled to remember if he'd ever taken Caitlin in with him.

"Mind if I join you?" he asked.

Hannah finally noticed he was on the planet. Her smile seemed strained, and he wondered if she'd felt anything when he'd held her. Maybe the attraction between them was all on his side. But he didn't think he imagined her response.

He slid into the seat beside her. Once he set his coffee on the table, he reached across to offer his hand to the guy. "Matt Beitler, sheriff's detective."

"Noah Whetstone. I've seen you in the lumberyard."

"Yeah, I put a deck on the house last year."

The conversation fizzled as Matt tried to think of what to say without mentioning his daughter. Before he could think of a safe topic, Noah rose. "I must get back to work. Say hello to your cousin, Hannah." He nodded to Asia and Matt, picked up his coffee cup, and left.

"I didn't mean to run him off," Matt said. Liar, liar. That was exactly what he'd hoped for. He'd have liked to put a hedge around Hannah and keep every other guy at arm's length. Maybe that was why Reece acted so possessive.

"You didn't."

"It looked like you were deep in conversation." He nearly winced when he saw Asia grin. Even if Hannah was too innocent to recognize his interest, her savvier friend saw everything.

"I've known him all my life."

"They were engaged," Asia put in. Her smile widened, and she glanced at Matt as if to see him squirm.

"That was a long time ago. He's married with four kids now."

It almost sounded as though she didn't want him to worry. Matt couldn't help but smile. Maybe she was transparent too. And Asia understood.

She stood. "Listen, Hannah, since Matt is here, I'm going to go back to the house and call the producer to see if they got all they needed today. Why don't you have Matt take you over to see Irene? You've been wanting to go. She's probably got some of your mom's quilts. See if you can borrow them for a few days for me to photograph them."

"But I should go back and work on the quilt too."

"Yeah, you should, but you're not going to, so just get your sleuthing out of your system. See you two later." Asia grabbed her coffee and sashayed out of the coffee bar.

"You sure you don't mind taking me over to Irene's?"

How was he going to get out of this one? Irene would recognize Caitlin in one glance. "Not a problem. I need to question Irene myself. You just need to borrow quilts?"

"I was going to ask her about the little girl, but now there's no need." She blinked rapidly at the moisture flooding her eyes.

"Why not?" Was she giving up?

"One of my cousins. We look a lot alike. I think the girl might be hers. She might have given her up for adoption."

"I'm sorry." He reached across the table and took her hand in both of his. He rubbed his thumb along her palm.

One part of him was rejoicing that he wouldn't be found out, and the other was responding to the touch of her hand. An impossible situation. He didn't dare explore his feelings for her when it would all come crashing down the minute she found out the extent of his deceit. Besides, she'd never filed for divorce.

Her fingers clutched his hand, and her eyes held a naked appeal for him to make it all better. But he couldn't. Not without destroying his daughter and himself.

twenty

"The Mariner's Compass Quilt reminds me that in murky times,
the Amish rely on the Word to steer their course."

—HANNAH SCHWARTZ,

IN *The Amish Faith Through Their Quilts*

The desire to be certain burned Hannah's veins. "Could we stop and see my cousin Mary before we go to your aunt's?" she asked as Matt pulled out of the parking lot. Rain drummed against the top of the vehicle and sluiced over the windshield.

"Do you think she'll talk to you about such a personal matter?"

"I don't know. But I have to ask. If I know she gave a child up for adoption, I'll know for sure that Reece is lying to me. It will put my mind at rest. And if she knows who has the child, that might lead us to important information. The little girl is on my mother's quilt."

"You're sure about that? The picture isn't that big."

He seemed determined to disbelieve her. "I'm positive. I'm a quilt expert, remember?"

"I'm just not sure the quilt means anything more than that the killer finally started selling them off."

She didn't want to admit he might be right. Craning her neck, she pointed out an older house in Nyesville. "There's her place." Matt parked at the curb, and Hannah got out as soon as the SUV stopped rolling. She dashed through the downpour to the porch. When she knocked, the door opened immediately.

Mary's face lit when she saw Hannah. "I didn't think you'd really come." She opened the door wide. "Come in out of the storm. I just put on a fresh pot of coffee. And I made some peanut butter cookies. They're still warm." She led them into an immaculate living room decorated in blue and yellow. The chintz fabric on the sofa and overstuffed chair looked new.

Hannah settled onto the sofa. "I hope you don't mind us barging in without calling first."

"I'm tickled to death to see you! There's no one left on my mom's side of the family. My parents live clear across the country, and I get lonesome for family sometimes."

Her cousin's eager welcome made Hannah want to crawl under the sofa. She should have come sooner. Her gaze lingered on some pictures on the table. Standing beside her mother, Cathy, Mary smiled out from the photo.

"How about that coffee and cookies?" Mary asked.

"I'd love some," Hannah said, even though the thought of more caffeine didn't appeal. Her cousin was so eager to please. "You need some help?"

"No, you wait here. I'll be back in a flash." And she was. Two minutes later she returned to the room with coffee and cookies on a tray. "There's creamer in the little pitcher, and sugar as well," she said.

Hannah stirred creamer into her coffee and tried to think how she might bring up the subject of children. Maybe just show Mary the picture. She could ask if Mary had seen the child. She sipped the coffee, then put it down on the table and picked up her handbag. "I wondered if you might be able to help me." She pulled out the picture and handed it to Mary.

Mary took it and glanced at it. Her smile turned plastic. "What a cute little girl. Who is she?"

"That's what I'm trying to find out." She launched into the story of how she came to have the picture. Mary listened intently, but her expression didn't betray what she was thinking. "I've got to find out if this child is mine," she said. "Do you have *any* idea who she could be? You said you didn't have children?"

Mary handed back the picture. "Not now. I had a little boy, but he died when he was a week old."

Which explained the sadness in Mary's face when Hannah had first asked. So this little girl *might* still be Hannah's daughter. Elation made her voice raise. "Have you ever seen this child?"

Mary shook her head. "I'm sorry, no. Do you believe Reece? He would have needed help hiding the baby from you and the police."

Had Reece been with her every minute after her tumble down the stairs? She vaguely remembered drifting in and out of consciousness, and he'd been by her bedside every time. "Maybe he had an accomplice. I'm going to ask him to explain it the next time he calls."

She and Matt finished their visit, then managed to get away from Mary after promising to come back when Hannah could stay longer.

"You ready to go home?" Matt asked.

"I want to go see Irene," Hannah said. "We've still got enough time." A frown crouched between his eyes, and she wondered what had made him so quiet and grumpy.

"I guess," he said. "But let's not stay long. I've got things to do this afternoon." He hesitated. "Just to warn you, Irene can be a little strange. She's got some mental issues and may seem a bit off now and again."

Hannah nodded. She hadn't seen Irene in over ten years and had never known the woman well. "I might ask her about my mother as well as using the quilts," she said. Ajax thrust his nose in her hair, and she rubbed his muzzle.

"I've been wanting to talk to her about the murders," Matt said. "She knew all the victims well. I didn't realize that until recently."

Matt parked on the street in front of a two-story house with a rounded brick turret on the front. Oak trees shaded the quaint house, and hyacinths lined the brick walk to the front door. Hannah's pulse quickened, but she didn't know why. There should be nothing dangerous about talking to Irene.

Matt let Ajax out, then went around to Hannah's door, but she'd already exited the vehicle and stood looking at the red front door. Before they reached the door, it swung open and a smiling Irene knelt to pet Ajax, who had leaped forward to greet her. With a final pat, she stood. Nearing sixty, she had only a little gray at the temples of her short dark hair. She was still slim and attractive in her capris and sleeveless top. She had a greenhouse in the yard like so many people in the area did.

"What a nice surprise," she said, hugging first Hannah and then Matt. "I didn't even realize you two knew each other."

"We've known each other for over ten years," Matt said.

Hannah glanced at him, then away. That was stretching it a little, but maybe only a little.

"Come in. I just made chocolate chip cookies, and they're still warm." Irene led them to the living room and went to kitchen.

"I'll help you," Matt said. He hurried after her.

Hannah heard the low tones of his voice but couldn't make out any of the words. He sounded intense. The exchange wasn't any of her business. Clearly he wanted to talk to his aunt in private. She glanced around the room. Pictures from years ago covered one wall. She got up and studied them. One in particular caught her attention. Irene, Nora, and Hannah's mother stood with their arms around each other. They all had hair that reached their waists, parted in the middle and held in place with a headband that encircled their foreheads. They wore caftans.

Someone had drawn red horns on Hannah's mother's head. Hannah gulped, then found her voice. It would probably be rude to mention the horns. Maybe a child had gotten hold of the picture. "Why isn't Aunt Nora dressed Plain? Was this during her *rumspringa*?"

"Yes, her brief stint with freedom." A flush ran up Irene's neck and cheeks as she and Matt came back. She didn't look at Hannah. "Here we go. Would you like some coffee? Or maybe milk?"

"I just had coffee. Two cups, in fact. A cookie is fine." The day was going to make her gain five pounds. Hannah gestured to the picture. "Where was this taken?"

"We had a commune out near Sugar Creek." Irene came to stand beside her. "We lived there for about a year. It wasn't a free-love kind of place like you hear about. We grew our own vegetables, were one with nature."

Hannah peered closer. "Is that a peace symbol on the shed in the background?"

"Yes. We thought if everyone lived as we did, there would be no war." Her smile turned sad. "We were so young and naive."

Hannah turned to go back to the sofa and caught sight of another photo out of the corner of her eye. The two young people weren't touching in the photo, but Irene was gazing at Hannah's father, Abe, with longing. Hannah said nothing. The last thing she wanted was to embarrass Irene.

Hannah selected a cookie and bit into the warm chocolate. "Do you have any of my mother's quilts?"

"No, I'm sorry, I don't. I have four of your grandmother's, though, one for each bed plus an extra. I bought them when your grandmother was still making quilts. Why do you ask?"

Hannah barely remembered her grandparents. They and Luca's parents had died in a buggy accident when she was five. "I'd love to photograph them for an Amish quilt book I'm working on." They would be a nice addition.

"I read your first one. Lovely book. I was so proud of you. What a lovely tribute to your father. And, ah, your mother." She cast a wary glance at Matt.

Surely he wouldn't have told his aunt not to talk to Hannah about her mother. Hannah frowned at him, but he smiled in her direction.

"I'm sorry about your cousin and aunt," Irene said. "Such a nasty business. Why do people show such prejudice? The Amish are good people, the best. Remember that time someone torched your barn, Hannah?"

She didn't care to revisit that memory. Something about Irene's tone seemed flippant too. "My rabbits died in the fire," she said. Even now, her chest hurt when she remembered it.

"But you forgave the kids who did it."

"Only because *Datt* made me," she blurted out. It should have been a clue to her true nature. "I'm still angry about it. It was so senseless."

"That's terrible," Matt said.

She pressed her lips together. "About Moe and Aunt Nora. Aunt Nora sent me a picture." She fumbled in her purse for it. "I realize she's likely not my daughter, but when Nora sent it, she knew it would draw me back here. She suggested later that she shouldn't have sent it, that someone was angry she had." She held the picture out to Irene.

The picture trembled a little in Irene's hand as she looked at it. She handed it back. "Darling child." She didn't look at Matt or Hannah.

What was wrong? Hannah couldn't figure out the tense air swirling in the living room. "Yes. But about Moe and Nora. What could Nora have known that she wasn't supposed to tell anyone? Could it be something she knew about this child that caused her death?"

Irene shrugged. "I don't know, Hannah. Your mother and I went our separate ways long ago. And I rarely talked to Nora once she returned to your community."

Hannah sighed. "I'm more inclined to think Nora's secret might be from long ago. You've known her a long time. My parents too."

"That's true. I met Abe before he was baptized Amish." Irene stood. "I need to throw some clothes in the dryer."

The initial welcome had worn off, but Hannah wasn't quite sure why. She stood. "We'd better go anyway. I need to get to work on a quilt I'm trying to get finished. Could I take a quick look at the quilts?"

"They're in the bedrooms. Help yourself." Irene walked away quickly.

Hannah exchanged glances with Matt. "Do you know the way?" she asked.

"Sure."

She followed him down the hall past other pictures from a lost era. She lingered a moment to look. There were so many of her father. She paused to look at one last picture. "Does Irene have any children? She looks pregnant in this picture."

"No kids. Maybe she just gained some weight."

Hannah didn't argue with him, but Irene looked clearly pregnant. Hannah followed the sound of his voice and found him in the first bedroom. A beautiful quilt in royal blue and black lay on the bed. "It's gorgeous. The colors will look great in the book. Any others in the closet?" She went to the closet door and shoved it aside. It held only clothing and boxes.

"The other spare room is across the hall. I'll get the quilt out of there." Matt stepped across the hall and pushed open the door.

He closed it behind him, but not before she caught a glimpse of a crib and a wall covered in pictures. He closed the door too quickly for her to see who was in the pictures. Maybe Irene didn't like people in there.

When Matt came out carrying the quilt, she asked him about the room. "I thought you said she didn't have kids."

"She didn't, but she was a foster mother to many," he said. "She had this set up for when she took in babies."

"Oh right, that makes sense." The crib quilt looked a little like the one that had covered the bodies of her family. Same design but pink instead of black. Maybe Matt hadn't noticed. It didn't matter anyway. This must be a design her grandmother had taught her mother.

"Could I see the pictures? Maybe there are some of my mother."

"There aren't," he said in a clipped voice. "And the master bedroom is here."

Hannah followed him to the last large room. Austere with nothing on the walls and only plain wooden shades on the windows, it could have been a room in her parents' home. The quilt on the bed made the room, though. Breathtaking. One of her grandmother's masterpieces. The intricate Mariner's Compass radiated in all directions in vivid colors. Another quilt, a pure white one with hummingbird stitches, was on a rack at the foot of the bed. It was equally gorgeous.

"I've never seen this one," she said. "It looks like my mother's work."

"She wasn't the only one to make hummingbird stitches," Irene said from the doorway. She dumped a basket of towels on the bed, then disappeared through the door.

What was Irene's problem? Hannah's gaze caught on one last photo by the bed. A smaller one of the same pose with Irene and Hannah's father. "I think she never got over my dad," she said. "Maybe that's why she never married."

"Makes sense." He took her arm. "Let's get out of here."

They went to the door just as Irene came back to the room.

"Come back and see me sometime," Irene said in a voice that suggested the opposite. Matt left the Tumbling Blocks Quilt with Irene before they left.

Back outside, Hannah glanced at Matt. "She dated my dad. I'm shocked he was interested."

"Why?"

"I always thought my parents had eyes only for each other."

"Maybe they did once they met."

"Maybe." Something didn't sit right with her, and she couldn't figure it out. Was it jealousy that had broken up Irene's friendship with Hannah's mother? That could explain why her mother had always grown quiet when Irene's name was mentioned. Shame at stealing away a man Irene loved, maybe? But why would Irene have bought Abe's mother's quilts?

Hannah couldn't think of a thing to say on the drive back to the farm. The rain continued to come down in buckets. They slowed to pass a buggy, but she didn't know the occupants, not even the half-drowned children peering out the back. Her gaze lingered on them, taking in their features, searching for auburn hair.

"You okay?" Matt asked.

"Sure. Just—just disappointed. I'd hoped to find out more today about the girl." Her voice hoarsened on the last word. She'd never even held her, never kissed her downy head. Never said good-bye. "I wonder if there's a grave back in Wabash."

"For your daughter?"

"Yes, could you check?"

"Sure, I'll make a call." He cleared his throat. "Do you really think she is your daughter? Deep down?"

"I don't know. I've tried not to get my hopes up, but I guess they rose anyway. She looks so much like me. If you could see pictures of me . . ." Being here had made her realize how much she missed her childhood, the community, the simple way of life.

"I bet you were a beautiful little girl with such bright hair."

What if she went back to the Amish life? The thought hovered in her mind. The thought of being welcomed home made her eyes burn. For ten long years she'd moved like a tumbleweed blown from one town to the next, never staying very long, never believing she belonged. Always trying to stay one step ahead of Reece, yet knowing he would find her someday. She longed for the love of her community, the constancy of their love and commitment, their calm certainty about life.

"Your wheels are turning. What are you thinking about?" Matt asked.

"Going home." He'd think she was crazy. Most of the world didn't understand the peace of their faith, didn't understand how putting the focus on God and others made life so much better, so much more meaningful.

"Back to Milwaukee?"

"No, home. My place with my family. Go back to my roots, my faith."

"I can see the draw. Your cousin's family is wonderful. So much love and commitment. It's compelling. But I couldn't give up my computer, TV, my car."

"The car would be hard," Hannah admitted.

"I don't get it anyway. They pay people to drive them, so it's not like they think cars are evil."

"Cars can be a status symbol, and we believe in the common good and not putting one person above the other. And look at our modern world, how people run around with no time to sit and eat meals together as a family. Cars have been largely responsible for the splintering of the family. If an Amish man hires a car, it's for a specific reason—often for a trip for his family or something equally important."

"If you say so. But I'm not giving up my SUV." Matt's grin was cheeky.

"I'm probably not either. I'm just thinking out loud. Sometimes I wish I could go to sleep and wake up to find all that's happened was only a dream."

"Don't we all? Life isn't like that. Good and bad are part of the human existence."

"You sound very philosophical."

Matt's grin widened. "I actually think about life now and then."

Hannah's cell phone rang. She grabbed her purse and looked at the caller ID and winced. Maggie Baker was her editor. The last thing she needed right now was more pressure, and she didn't want to hear what Maggie might have to say. Whatever it was, it would likely entail more work. She called occasionally with a suggestion to include a certain chapter or to find out about this or that technique. Hannah didn't want to deal with it, so she shut off her phone.

Asia came flying out the door when they pulled up to the house. She was on her cell phone and mouthed, "Maggie," at her. It had done no good not to answer the phone. Hannah knew she would hate whatever Maggie was saying. Why had she ever agreed to hire a publicist? She thought of Asia as a close friend, but at times like this, she wished she answered to no one but herself.

"What's wrong?" Matt asked.

"It's my editor."

"Is that bad?"

"I'm not sure." Hannah got out of the car.

Asia hung up and shot her a panicked look. "Um, she wants your deadline moved and the book turned in two weeks from today."

"Two weeks! I hope you told her it was impossible." Hannah saw the stubborn set of her friend's mouth. "You *did* tell her, right, Asia?"

Asia opened her mouth, then shut it again. She shook her head. "I couldn't say no. It was too big."

"Oh, Asia, don't tell me you agreed. There is no way. None." Hannah stopped by the farmhouse and banged her forehead on the siding three times. "Just shoot me now."

"Don't stress, Hannah—it will be worth it. She's got a major promotion planned, but the book has to be done in time to launch it for the event."

"I have to finish the quilt for pictures!"

"Well, yeah, but you can work on it in the evenings. It won't take as long as you think."

"No, it will take longer than you think. I've made enough quilts to know it always takes more time than you anticipate. I've got at least one hundred hours of work left on it."

"If you work three hours every night, that's, uh, that's . . ."

"A month. Thirty days. And we've got two weeks." Hannah rarely lost her temper, especially with people she loved, but she felt she was in a pressure cooker about to blow its top.

"You can maybe work every morning and evening?" Asia's tentative voice lost steam as she finally got what Hannah was saying.

Staring at her friend's pleading face, Hannah's ire faded. "I'll try, Asia. But we might not make it. What's the big hurry anyway?"

"There's a big quilt show coming up in New York in six months. Maggie got the producer of *Good Morning America* to agree to have us on the show talking about the book. But we've got to have it releasing that week."

Hannah was shaking her head before Asia finished talking. "I'm not going on TV again. This morning was too hard. You can handle that, my friend."

"They'll want you to talk about the quilts. You're the expert, not me."

"I'm not doing it. I'm sick of publicity."

"Oh, we'll worry about it when the time comes. Right now we've got to get the quilt and the book done."

"Irene says we can have a photographer come over and take pictures of her quilts too. I saw them—they're gorgeous."

"Wonderful! Thanks for asking her."

Hannah nodded. Maybe it was just as well. Filling her time would keep her from obsessing over the little girl. She couldn't help sneaking one last glimpse of the child's face in the photo in her hand. Her child. She was beginning to believe it. She tucked the picture back into her bag.

She looked around for Matt and saw him pushing Naomi and Sharon on the swing under a cloudy sky, though the rain had stopped for now. Watching him with the children, she knew his daughter was a lucky little girl. His entire attention was focused on the kids.

Up near the house, she saw a buggy in the drive. Luca and Sarah must have company. She hoped it was no one she knew. All she wanted to do was rush to her room and have a good cry. Now she'd have to paste on a smile, at least for a few minutes. She stopped in the yard and turned toward the barn. Maybe she could hide out there for a little while.

"Where are you going?" Asia asked.

"I thought I'd—I'd check on my old horse." Hannah bolted for the barn. She heard Asia call after her, but she didn't stop. Shoving the barn door aside, she stepped into the cool darkness of the barn. The familiar scent of hay and horse enveloped her in a warm, safe embrace.

Lucy nickered, and Hannah ran to her. She should have come to see the animal sooner. How amazing that Lucy remembered her. She stroked the old appaloosa's soft nose. Lucy had to be twenty by now but was still working.

As a child, Hannah had spent many hours in the hayloft with a book and a secret radio. This was her place, her refuge. She eyed the ladder to the hay-mow, then gave Lucy one last pat and went to stand at the base of the ladder.

Looking up, she realized the top wasn't as high as she remembered. Hannah put her foot on the first rung, then went hand over hand up to the haymow. Stacks of hay bales filled the loft. She balanced across the tops of the bales to the back corner. Once upon a time, she'd had a little nest back here, a cocoon she'd carved for herself from bales of hay.

It was probably long gone, but she couldn't help shoving aside a few bales just to see. She wiggled back to where she'd made the opening to her small space. There it was! Hannah couldn't believe it. The rough hay tore at her hair and clothes as she dove into the "house" she'd built over twenty years ago.

The space seemed smaller, but she was an adult now and time changed her perception. The area measured about six by six and five feet high. She crawled in on her hands and knees and peered out the window into the yard. *Datt* had put the window in just for her when she was ten. From this perspective, she could see the whole yard, the house, and the greenhouse area.

Asia wasn't in the yard anymore. She must have gone inside. Hannah could be alone and enjoy the solitude. Hugging her knees to her chest, she settled back against the hay. A smile tugged at her lips, and the tension eased from her neck and shoulders. She could forget her problems here.

Until she heard someone calling her name. She wanted to clap her hands over her ears and refuse to respond. Then she recognized Matt's voice. It sounded as if he was in the barn below her. She scrambled from her hidey-hole and moved over the uneven bales of hay to the ladder.

"I'm up here," she called. When he looked up and their eyes met, an unseen bolt of energy connected them. An invisible umbilical cord tugged her toward him. The last time she'd experienced a connection like that, she'd run away from everything she knew and loved, ending up in a heap at the bottom of the stairs with her baby's blood seeping out of her.

twenty-one

"The Amish prize objects that are made by hand, well-made items
that will last for generations, just as their faith has lasted through the
decades. That's why I prize the Log Cabin Quilt so highly."

—HANNAH SCHWARTZ,

IN *The Amish Faith Through Their Quilts*

The sun illuminating Hannah's hair through the windows of the barn made it look like a coil of copper. She had it up again, and if Matt were bold enough, he'd grab the pins and shake it loose just to see it in the sunshine. She'd probably slap him for his trouble. Just for a moment when their eyes had locked, he could have sworn he saw something in her eyes. Awareness, need, something. It was gone too quickly to name it as more than interest.

She swayed as though she was dizzy. "You okay?" he called up to her.

"I'm fine." Her hand swiped straw off her cheek. "Stand away from the ladder and I'll come down. I have a skirt on."

He should be so lucky as to see her legs. He walked over to lean against the door frame, but he had to resist the temptation to peek. She brushed the hay from her clothes, but the yellow stuff sticking from her hair stayed untouched. She probably had no idea how pretty she looked with the hay in her hair and a flush on her cheeks. He was mightily attracted against his own will and annoyed with himself enough to grit his teeth.

"You can turn around now," she said.

She looked just as prim and proper as her voice. Except for the fact that the hay in her hair made her look as if she'd just tumbled in the haymow with someone. Before he could stop himself, his fingers were in her hair, and he was plucking out bits of hay. Thick and lustrous, her hair invited him to plunge his fingers in deeper.

He dropped his hands before he could be tempted further. "You in here feeling sorry for yourself?"

"Maybe." She bit her lip as though she was sorry she'd said anything.

She swayed again as though she'd like to lean against him. It was probably wishful thinking on his part. "Anything I can do to help?" he asked.

"Not really. I'm just disappointed. I knew Reece loved to play mind games with me. But I thought maybe this time would be different. I'm no closer to finding out what happened to my daughter than I was when I came last week. Even here, I'm an outsider. I—I wanted so much for my daughter to be alive. I tried not to count on it." She looked up at him as though he could make her wishes come true.

He stilled—his blood, his breath, his entire being. He should tell her. He knew it was the right thing to do, just as if God had whispered it into his heart. He could imagine the joy breaking over her face, could see the shine in her eyes. But once she realized the full story, he'd lose his daughter. He couldn't give up Caitlin, wouldn't give her up. The adoption wouldn't be legal because Hannah had never signed away her rights. Any court would give Caitlin back.

"Aren't you going to say anything? Some platitude about it being God's will that I'm alone? I've already got that, believe me. I know he's rejected me."

He found his voice. "I'm not going to help you have a pity party. You're young and healthy. You can have more children."

"I *can't*." She shoved him with the palms of her hands. "The trauma made it impossible."

"I'm sorry, Hannah." Talk about heaping guilt on his head. He was in possession of the only child she'd ever have. Something told him to trust God with the outcome, but putting such a dangerous thought into action proved too difficult. "God still loves you. Your grief is all that's making you hold him at arm's length. It wasn't your fault. Evil will always be around. It had nothing to do with you." Her eyes showed her pain. He cupped her cheek in his palm. "You'll find the right guy, Hannah. Your marriage to Reece was over long ago, the night he threw you down the steps. Get him out of your life once and for all. You don't have to be alone."

She rested her face against his hand in a trusting gesture. "No?" she whispered.

He knew he was playing with fire, but his gaze went to her lips. She leaned forward ever so slightly, but the movement entranced him. This couldn't be love. You didn't fall in love with someone in two minutes. But he could imagine what it would be like to gather her close, to inhale the sweet scent of her, to taste her lips. He could see her in his house, could anticipate how exhilarating it would be to come home to her every day. She'd make a wonderful mother. Did he have the right to deny Caitlin such a wonderful mother?

He pulled away and looked down into her face. Her long lashes fluttered against her flushed cheeks. The words "I love you" trembled on his tongue, but it couldn't be true. He was reacting to the physical attraction between them. Besides, once words like that were spoken, there was no going back.

A heavy veil fell between them, the weight of it palpable. The weight of the truth, the weight of deception. Dropping his hands from her shoulders, he stepped away.

"I think I'll get some coffee." If he looked back at her face, he would lose his courage. He nearly ran for the door.

A CHILL FILLED the vacuum around Hannah that was created by Matt's departure. She wasn't so naive she couldn't recognize how her soul longed for him. He was drawn to her as well. If he hadn't gone, she might have kissed him. In his arms, she'd be wrapped in safety. Secure. His wife had been a lucky woman. She clasped her arms around herself. She had no right to even think like this. At least not until she was free of Reece.

She sighed like a silly schoolgirl. *Don't think about him.* He would drive her crazy. The thought of loving someone again scared her to death. But Matt was nothing like Reece. She had to remember most men would never hurt their wives the way he had hurt her.

She shut the barn door behind her and headed for the house. The sun had begun to slip down the horizon. Three cats came running to meet her, and she stooped to pet them. "Where's Spooky?" she asked them. Marmalade meowed as if to tell her all about it, and Hannah smiled. She called to the missing cat, but the black ball of energy didn't appear. He was probably off chasing a chipmunk.

Supper was nearly ready when she left the cats and went inside, but she knew better than to offer to help. Matt stood talking to Luca about fishing, and she let her gaze rest on him a moment. It didn't matter if her expression reflected her feelings. He wasn't paying attention.

When she turned away, she found Asia watching her. The amusement in Asia's eyes made Hannah's cheeks burn. "I think I'll run upstairs and wash up," she muttered.

"I'll come with you." Asia trotted after her. She caught up with Hannah at the top of the steps. "What's going on with you and Matt?"

"Nothing." Hannah went to their room and began to search for a fresh blouse.

Asia jerked a plain white blouse out of her hand. "Don't wear that." She began to rummage in the closet. "I'm not stupid. I can see how much you watch him, and he does the same to you." She pulled out a taupe blouse that wrapped and had a V-neck. "Wear this."

"I can't wear that." Hannah frowned as she held it up.

"It won't show your boobs or anything. It will just flatter your shape and your coloring. Try it on. You want Matt to notice you, right? Aw, you're blushing. You're not used to going after the man you want, are you?"

Hannah pressed her palms against her hot cheeks. "If he wants me, he can take me the way I am. Besides, I'm still tied to Reece."

"Legally, yes, but you're never going back to an abuser. It doesn't hurt to put a little chocolate on the fruit." Asia jerked the blouse down over Hannah's head. "Were you in the haymow with him?" She plucked a strand of hay from Hannah's hair.

"I was in the haymow, but not with Matt."

"Too bad." Asia's grin was sly.

"You're terrible."

"Just honest. Has he kissed you yet?"

Hannah ducked her head and didn't answer. She tugged on the blouse and tried to look down to see how it fit. At least it didn't show any cleavage.

"He *has* kissed you, hasn't he? I bet he's a great kisser."

"No, he hasn't! He's got more integrity than that. I'm still married." Hannah laughed it off, but her cheeks and neck felt as if they would burn up any minute.

"Okay, okay. Sit down on the stool a minute and let me do something with this mop of yours. You've got hay and chaff all through it."

Hannah sank onto the stool. In minutes, debris littered the floor around her. She reached up and touched her hair. "I should put it up."

"No, you should not. I didn't cut it so you could wind it all up and hide it. You look terrific. Let's go eat."

A model on display couldn't be any more self-conscious. Hannah followed Asia down the stairs. "Smells like beef and noodles with brown butter," she said.

"It is." Sarah didn't look at her. "The table is ready for you and the children in the sitting room."

Matt had seen her. His gaze followed her, and she hoped he didn't think she was trying to attract him. Oh, who was she kidding—of course he knew. The whole family had to know. The new outfit was as blatant as a neon sign flashing "Look." She practically ran from the room.

The children had their hands in their laps. "Naomi, would you like to pray?" Hannah asked in her rusty German.

Naomi nodded, and both little girls clasped their hands and bowed their heads. Hannah listened to the silence and remembered her own family. Luca had asked her not to endear the children to her, but she found it impossible not to talk to them and interact. By the time the meal was over, they were chattering to her as though she was their best friend. They helped her carry the plates back to the kitchen.

Luca stopped at the sink and glanced at her. "It's good you have come back, Hannah. If there's anything that belonged to your parents here, feel free to take it."

Hannah wondered if he might know what had happened to the ring. "Luca, would you happen to know—"

"Hannah, could you hand me those plates?" Sarah broke in with a desperate edge to her voice.

Hannah blinked but handed over the plates stacked on the table in front of her. Sarah was accepting a favor? As Sarah took the plates, Hannah saw the plea in her eyes.

"Thanks. Matt, I've got some scraps you can feed the dog." Sarah gave the bag to Matt.

Sarah didn't want her to talk to Luca about the ring. Hannah decided to hold her tongue, but only until tomorrow when she could talk to her friend alone. Maybe Sarah would finally tell her what was going on.

"I'm going to go out and feed the cats," Hannah said. She grabbed the cat food from the back porch and carried it into the yard. Three of the cats came running, but Spooky was still missing. Matt followed her, but he didn't say anything and walked off toward the woods.

Did he suspect someone was out there? She hurriedly finished feeding the cats and went back inside.

"Have you seen Spooky?" she asked Asia. Through the window, the trees drew shadows against the backdrop of night. Her family had already headed to bed.

"Not since this morning," Asia said.

"Maybe Matt has him." Hannah stepped to the back door and peered out to where he stood staring off into the woods. His stance conveyed loneliness. Had he been watching for intruders or just craving some alone time? Interacting with the big family could be an intense experience. She couldn't read his expression in the darkness. The backyard swallowed up any hint of illumination from the stars, and there was no moon. She slipped out to join him.

"Something wrong?" he asked.

"Have you seen Spooky?"

"Like I'd be looking for a cat."

She'd forgotten how much he hated cats. "Maybe he's with Ajax. Where is he?"

"On the step." He pointed out the dog, who had pricked his ears at the sound of his name. Ajax rose and stretched, then padded over to nuzzle her hand.

Hannah didn't want to admit to her worry, but her mild misgiving ramped up to alarm. "He never stays away at mealtime. He loves his food."

"Did you try calling him? Maybe he's lost in the woods."

Hannah didn't want to admit something might have . . . eaten him. "I'll go look."

"Look, it's a cat. He'll be fine. Don't tell me you're one of those who think cats will climb a tree and then not be able to get down."

"He's a good climber. I'll go find him."

"Not without me. Reece could be out there. I'll grab a flashlight." Matt went past her into the house and returned moments later with a flashlight and a kerosene lantern. He gave her the lantern. "You take that since you know how to work it." He called his dog to him. "You got anything of Spooky's?"

"His bed." She took the lantern, then ran to grab the pad from the back porch. "Here it is." She handed it to Matt.

He held it under Ajax's nose. "Find Spooky, boy." The dog whined, then put his nose to the ground and began to pull Matt toward the woods. Matt flipped on his flashlight and went with the dog.

Hannah followed the wide beam cast by Matt's flashlight. "Here, kitty, kitty," she called. "Spook-man, where are you? *Pur-r-r*." She made the purring sound that usually had the cats running to her.

"There's a wild patch of catnip over this way," Matt said, pointing to the left. "Ajax is leading that way. Let's see if he's there." He unhooked Ajax's leash, and the dog bounded ahead.

Hannah raised the lantern high and let its beam radiate through the trees as they entered the woods. The cool, damp air smelled of moss and dead leaves under the new vegetation. She stumbled over a fallen log and nearly fell. Stopping to catch her breath and her balance, she listened for a plaintive meow but heard nothing but frogs in the pond and the whir of mosquitoes dive-bombing for her skin.

Matt was a few feet ahead of her, and some whisper of alarm made her hurry to catch up with him. "You see anything?" she asked when she touched his arm and found it hard and tense.

His other hand covered hers. "Shh, I thought I heard something."

She held her breath, listening to the night sounds of the forest. Then a faint sound reached her ears. A meow, she was sure of it. Ajax leaped from Matt's side, and they heard him rustle through the weeds before the sound of his movement faded away.

"Ajax, come back here!" Matt called.

Hannah ran after the dog. "Maybe he can lead us to Spooky."

"Not if he goes too far too fast." Matt caught her arm. "Don't go rushing off. It might be a trap."

"A trap? It's a lost cat."

"Maybe. Your cats are used to roaming and coming home. So why didn't Spooky?"

She tugged on her arm. "Maybe he's hurt."

"Maybe. But it's my job to protect you."

For some reason the bald words stung. She wanted him to protect her because he cared, but that was stupid. The interlude in the barn this afternoon must have meant nothing to him. She managed to pull her arm free, then moved forward, finding her way through the brambles and vines that tried to trip her up. The light from her lantern wavered and bounced, making the twisted branches and low shrubs look menacing. Matt's paranoia was affecting her.

"Spook-man?" she called again. "Here, kitty, kitty." The meow came again, an outraged sound that bounced off the trees. He was still some distance from her location, and she couldn't quite tell which direction to head.

Matt caught her arm again. "This way." He pulled her to the right. A small creek barred their way. "Careful, the rocks will be slippery."

Hannah stepped out onto a rock. Cold water soaked through her shoes. The rocks almost seemed to roll under her feet, but it was only moss trying to shed her from its surface. Balancing with her outstretched arms, she tottered across the stream and only fell to her knees with the last leap onto the wet bank.

"You okay?" Matt hauled her up as if she weighed no more than his dog.

"Fine." She brushed at the wet mud on her skirt. The cry from her cat came again. "He's over this hill."

"Yeah." He took her hand and helped her up the slippery hillside.

The warm embrace of his hand around hers made it seem they were actually partners—and congenial ones at that. What might their relationship become if they could get past their previous hurts and move on to a new life? She was such a coward—she hadn't even wanted to face the trouble of divorcing Reece.

Matt battered through some arching brambles and held them out of the way for her. She stepped into a small clearing with him. Holding her lantern high, she turned in the meadow. Metal caught a beam from the light and bounced it back at her. Eyes glowed through the wire. A cat's eyes.

Spooky paced a small cage placed in the center of the clearing. His plaintive cries rose to a crescendo. Ajax circled the cage and whined his sympathy. He pawed at the door. Hannah started forward, but Matt grabbed her arm.

He grabbed a stick and prodded the air and the ground with it before he approached the cage. Ajax began to bark, obviously thinking it a fine game.

Hannah started to follow Matt, but a hand smelling of onions clapped over her mouth. An arm came around her waist and pulled her back, dragging her into the bushes. She thrashed against the man and dropped the lantern. She tried to scream, but the animals were making so much ruckus that her muffled screech didn't get past the strong hand. She thought she heard Matt calling her name in the distance. Reaching out, she grabbed at branches, but they were too thin and weak to support her and she was left with leaves.

"Sh, Hannah, don't make a fuss." Reece's lips touched her ear, then traveled down her neck in a trail to her shoulder.

She shuddered when she realized who held her, then began to struggle more wildly. If only she could get her teeth into his hand. He dragged her farther away until she could barely hear the bark of the dog in the shrouding trees.

He shook her. "I said be quiet. I've got a gun, Hannah. Want me to shoot Matt?"

Hot moisture burned her eyes, and she blinked rapidly. She wouldn't give him the satisfaction of seeing her frightened tears.

"Good girl," he crooned. "I've missed you, Hannah. The smell of you, the taste of you."

He nuzzled her neck, and bile rose in her throat at the sensation of his whiskers. A tear escaped and rolled down her cheek. He licked that up too. Matt called her name from somewhere.

"Sweet Hannah," he whispered. "I know you've missed me. Our little girl misses her mother. We can be a family, my love, the perfect little unit. Just come home with me now. I'm going to take my hand away if you promise not to scream. Do you promise? Remember, if Matt comes running, he's a dead man."

She nodded. If he didn't take his hand off her face soon, she'd faint. He nuzzled her neck again, then raised his hand from her mouth. Before she could react, he flipped her around to face him. He dragged her tightly against him and buried his face in her neck again.

She managed to get both palms against his chest and shoved hard enough to gain a few inches. "Get your hands off me. You're a murderer. You killed my parents, and Moe and Aunt Nora. I have *proof*!"

He pinned her arms to her sides. "What proof?" His voice went harsh.

Now that he was in front of her, hatred swallowed her fear. He was still lying, still manipulating. "The picture you sent. The little girl is sitting on one of my mother's quilts. That means you had access to them when you got rid of her."

Now that she was in his presence, she knew. Her soul recognized the evil in him.

"No one will believe you. Besides——" He broke off and shut his mouth. "Never mind."

"Where is she?" Hannah demanded. She began to strike at him with her fists, but she was no more effective than a kitten pawing at a tiger. Her hands struck his suspenders. "Where is my baby girl?" The words choked off. She could see him smiling in the faint glimmer of light through the trees now that her eyes had adjusted.

"Have you asked Matt about her?"

"What's Matt got to do with this?"

Before Reece answered, Matt called Hannah's name again. His voice sounded closer. Reece released her. "Ask Matt if you can meet his daughter. See what he says." His hands fell from her body, and he melted into the shadows.

Hannah stared into the darkness. Where had he gone so quickly? Matt yelled for her again. "I'm here," she called.

He broke through the underbrush and found her. "What happened?" He carried the lantern she had dropped. Ajax loped at his feet.

"Reece grabbed me." Hannah wrapped her arms around herself. The shakes began then, shuddering through her frame. She swiped at the wetness still on her cheek. Disgusting.

Matt lifted the light and came to her side. "You okay?"

"I'm fine."

"Which way did he go?"

"I—I'm not sure." The darkness and trauma had left her disoriented. "Don't leave me." She hurtled into his arms. Before she realized it, she had wrapped her arms around his waist and was nestling against his chest. She fit nicely. His chin just touched the top of her head. She liked the scent of his cologne, something spicy and masculine.

"You're shaking," Matt said. He grasped her shoulders and pulled her away. "Let's get in the house. I want you safe." He handed her the flashlight and lantern, then returned to fetch Spooky.

She shone the way with the flashlight. Safe. With him she was safe. But she'd thought that once about Reece. She wasn't a good judge of men.

They were back at the house none too soon for Hannah. Asia had gone upstairs.

Matt pressed her onto the sofa in the sitting room. "You need some water?"

"No, I'm fine." And she was. In the rays of the sputtering gaslight with home around her and Matt here with her, she knew Reece could never touch her.

Matt sat beside her. "You're pale."

"It's okay. He wanted to scare me."

His arm came around her and pulled her to him. "What did he say?"

"Nothing, really." She shuddered. "I told him I knew he'd killed my family. I'm sure the girl is my daughter. The quilt under the child connects him to the murders. Reece had access to the quilts only if he killed my parents."

Matt stilled. "Anything else?"

She wasn't about to tell him that Reece had insinuated Matt might know something. Reece had sensed her feelings for Matt and was trying to destroy them. She leaned her head against his chest and fell silent.

Heaven. The scent of his breath, the hard muscles of his chest under her palm as it rested against his shirt—this was heaven as she'd never known it. It had been so long since someone looked at her as if she was a real person.

Hannah realized this emotion she'd been fighting for days was love. Matt was the kind of man she'd always longed for. Peace and safety settled around her until she realized the position she'd put them both in as she sought comfort. She wasn't divorced.

"Ask him about his daughter."

Why would Reece say that? Was it only to twist her emotions about Matt up in knots? Did he think Matt wouldn't want her to see his daughter? She didn't want to think. She straightened and pulled away from his embrace. He immediately released her. Reece never would have done that. He would have taken it as a personal challenge to force her to yield to him.

"I'm sorry. I'm moving too fast," he whispered. "I care about you, Hannah. I want to see you, to take you to dinner. Make you laugh. See your hair on your shoulders in the candlelight. When you're free to do that."

What woman's heart wouldn't be stirred by those poetic words? But maybe he was just practiced at it. Hannah swallowed past the lump in her throat. She should ask him about what Reece had said, but she didn't want to bring strife into the room with them. She wanted to cup his dear face in her hands and kiss him. But the question had to be asked. She had to know what Reece meant.

"Could I meet your daughter?"

Matt went still, and his smile faded. "Where did that come from?"

"Reece said I should ask you about your daughter. What did he mean?"

The warmth blinked out of Matt's eyes. He rose from the sofa and turned his back to her. "Who knows what a madman thinks? We'd better get to bed."

"Could I see a picture of your daughter?"

"I don't have one with me." He stood and held out his hand. "Let's forget tonight ever happened."

Forgetting about it was the last thing she wanted. Was he hiding something?

twenty-two

"*The Amish Center Diamond Quilt is beautiful in its simplicity. It captures in a lovely image the belief that God should always be at the center of all decisions and life choices, that he is supreme.*"

—HANNAH SCHWARTZ,

IN *The Amish Faith Through Their Quilts*

Matt sponged himself off with warm water heated on the woodstove. He towel-dried his hair with a vengeance, then jerked on jeans and sneakers to dash to the outhouse and back. The sun was peeking through the window as he went back to the sitting room and folded his sheets. He hadn't gotten much sleep last night with the ferocious thunderstorm that had crashed overhead until early this morning.

He should have known better than to let himself care. All he had to do was keep his distance and wait for Hannah to leave, but no, he'd had to go make a fool of himself. He was weak, and even worse, he was a fool. She had the power to rip his world apart. He needed to keep her at arm's length. For all his preaching to Blake about the sanctity of marriage, he'd ignored the fact that she was legally bound. Where did the boundaries lie with God? Surely God didn't want her to go back to an abusive man, one who might even be a murderer.

Being with her was like peeking into a different world—a place where he might actually find love again. But it couldn't happen, not now. He'd never give up his daughter, and Hannah would never forgive his lies.

The rest of the household stirred overhead. Floorboards creaked and a door scraped open. The steps groaned under someone's weight, then Hannah stepped into view. Dressed in a denim skirt and yellow blouse, she looked as bright as a daffodil.

"Sounds like your family is up," he said.

"I'd love to make pancakes for them this morning before we go to Aunt Nora's funeral, but they won't accept any favors from me." She wasn't looking at him.

He knew he should shove his feet into his shoes and get the heck out of Dodge, but instead he stepped closer to her. "Hey, I'm a mean wielder of the spatula. How about you mix it up before they get down and I'll do the cooking. They won't say a word."

Her smile turned hopeful. "You cook?"

"You question my culinary ability?"

"Of course not. I know you can do anything." She smiled, and a steady faith burned in her eyes.

She made him believe he was Superman. How did she do that? He followed her to the kitchen and made coffee while she put on an apron and assembled her ingredients.

"I wish they'd let me make them a shoofly pie."

"Hey, you can make me one." He grinned and pulled up a chair. Hannah began to mix the ingredients in a large yellow glass bowl. His grandmother had an old bowl like that. "I like your family. I used to think the Amish were just a strange sect, almost a cult or something. But they're good, honest Christians. The peace here in their home is almost enough to make me give up my SUV."

She smiled and cracked an egg into the batter. "It's good to be back." She wiped her hands on her apron, then untied it. "Your turn." She had him stand up and swathed him in the dark blue apron.

"Do I have to wear this?"

"You look more official."

She was standing close enough when he turned around that he would only have to bend over slightly to kiss her. Her golden eyes captivated him. The expression in them was as soft as the color. He was too weak to resist even though he knew the pain was coming. He cupped her face in his palm. "What are we going to do about us?"

"Is there an us, Matt?"

"I love to hear you say my name. Say it again."

"Matt," she whispered. "Don't hurt me."

"I wouldn't." He wanted to kiss her, but he heard the steps creaking. With reluctance, he turned to the stove and began beating the batter. Stupid, stupid. There was no way to fix this. For a second he allowed himself to dream of what life might be like if the truth were out in the open and she forgave him anyway. It couldn't be, though. No mother would forgive what he had done. And there was still her tie to Reece to contend with.

She put her hand over his as he whipped the batter. "Not too much," she whispered. "It won't rise." She retreated to a chair at the table. "Good morning," she told her cousin.

Luca nodded. "*Gut* morning." He sniffed as the batter touched the hot oil in the skillet. "Pancakes?"

"Yep," Matt said. He kept a close eye on the edges of the batter.

Luca went to the coffeepot and poured himself a cup. "I am hungry. The family will be down soon. It is kind of you to feed us all on such a busy morning."

"Your cupboard provided the ingredients. I'm just doing the cooking."

"*Gut* coffee. You made it?"

"Sure did." He wondered what Luca would do if he said that Hannah had made it. Or if he said that she'd mixed up the batter for him. Would he refuse to eat the pancakes? Spit out the coffee? He cooked three pancakes and flipped them onto a plate for Luca.

Feet pounded down the steps, and Sarah burst into the kitchen. She jabbered something in German that made both Luca and Hannah leap for the door. "What's wrong?" Matt asked, running after them. But when he reached the door, he needed no translation. "The barn's on fire!" He grabbed his cell phone and dialed 9-1-1.

By the time he jammed his phone back onto his belt, Luca was dragging a hose toward the barn. Flames were beginning to shoot through the roof.

"The horses!" Splashing through puddles left by last night's rain, Hannah ran toward the barn.

Matt sprang after her. "Hannah, no!" But she paid him no attention. Shoving open the door, she disappeared into the black smoke billowing from the opening. The air from the open door fueled the fire, and the flames shot higher through the roof as if straining to torch a few lazy clouds passing by.

Luca sprayed the water onto the barn, but the flames just danced higher. Matt reached the billowing smoke, and the harsh heat struck his lungs. He coughed and plunged into the darkness of the superheated barn. "Hannah!" he shouted, still coughing. It was like an image of hell. Flames and smoke billowed around him, the fire eating up the dry tinder of the old barn. Horses screamed, and he leaped in the direction of the sound.

He burst through what seemed to be a wall of flames into an area the fire hadn't reached. Hannah hadn't noticed him. She fought to control an appaloosa who reared in terror. Two other horses bucked and snorted in the pen behind her. He ran to the other horses and entered the pen. Grabbing their halters, he led them out.

"Hannah, this way!" he screamed over the roar of the flames. On the wall behind him he saw something that made him gasp in more smoke. A broken cross had been painted on the wall in red paint above her head. Had she seen it?

She turned toward him. Dragging the horse with her, she started in his direction. He plunged through the way he'd come. Sprinkles of water dotted his face, and he blessed Luca for continuing to focus the water toward where it was most needed. It was all he could do to keep hold of the horses. They bucked and whinnied, but he dragged them toward the barn door, past the fire devouring everything in its path.

Then he was out. He released the horses and turned to go back to help Hannah, but she was behind him. Her clothes were blackened, and so was her face. A flicker of flame caught his attention. "Your skirt is on fire!" He leaped at her and bored her to the ground. She thrashed and fought him. "Lay still." He scooped dirt onto her, then batted at the flames with his bare hands. He considered tearing her skirt from her, but one last roll and the flames were gone. Her skirt was seriously mangled, but she was alive.

He helped her up. They probably both smelled of soot. "Are you okay?" he whispered. He cupped her face in his hands. Even streaks of soot couldn't mar her beauty. He'd almost lost her. He kissed her, and she showed no signs of wanting to pull away.

"Your poor hands." She lifted one to her lips and kissed it.

"It doesn't hurt." He looked down at the torn and burned flesh. It would hurt like the dickens when the adrenaline wore off.

With his arm around her, they stood and watched the roof crash in. Luca had given up the fight with the hose now that they and the horses had reached safety. By the time the volunteer fire department arrived, the barn was nothing more than a smoldering pile of rubble.

They walked back toward the house and let the firemen do their job of extinguishing the embers. Luca and Sarah followed with the girls and Asia. No one had much to say. Such a traumatic event had left them drained. And it was no accident. They had to be told.

Matt reached the front door and opened it. "Could you send the children inside for a minute?"

Luca shot him a quick glance, then gave the girls a short order in German. They scampered past Matt into the house. He shut the door behind them. Sarah stepped closer to Luca as if for courage.

"I don't think this was an accident," Matt said.

Hannah put her hand to her mouth. "You saw the symbol?" She shuddered and clutched her arms around herself.

"Yep. On the wall."

"What symbol?" Luca asked. "I saw nothing."

"The Broken Cross, or Nero's Cross, or whatever you want to call it. The same one that was on the wall in the house when the Schwartzes were murdered. Someone painted it in red inside the barn. And I smelled kerosene."

"We keep kerosene for our lanterns and such," Sarah put in. "The heat could have caused a container to explode."

"It looked like an arsonist burn pattern," Matt said. "A row of flames where the accelerant had been poured. Someone torched your barn. The firemen will confirm it, I'm afraid." He had no doubt about it. He would tell the fire chief what he'd seen and smelled.

"Who?" Hannah asked. "Reece?" Her voice was hoarse from smoke inhalation. Tears pooled in her eyes and slid down her cheeks, leaving streaks in the soot.

"That would be my guess. He's trying to force you to go back to him. What better way than to target your loved ones, box you into a corner?"

Asia put her arm around Hannah. "Well, he can't have her."

Exactly Matt's sentiments. The only problem was, he hadn't figured out how he was going to keep her for himself once she knew the truth.

THEY'D MISSED HER aunt's funeral, and Hannah never got to say good-bye. Tears burned the back of her throat as she glanced out over the collapsed barn. The shrill chirp of her cell phone was as unwelcome as the smell of smoke in her hair. She knew who it had to be.

She pulled out her cell phone and looked at the caller ID. Reece's number. She didn't want to talk to him, but she forced herself to flip open the phone and hold it to her ear. "Reece, how could you burn down the barn?"

"I didn't burn down the barn. I saw it was on fire, so I'm just calling to make sure you're all right. Why do you always suspect me first?"

"Your track record speaks volumes," she said. "I don't believe you." But his denial was so earnest.

"I know how much you love your horse. Lucy, isn't it? Is she okay?"

Hannah closed her eyes briefly. Did she dare believe him? "If you didn't torch the barn, who did? The Nero's Cross symbol was painted on the barn." The phone fell silent in her hand. She couldn't even hear him breathing. "Reece?"

"I'm here." His words were clipped. Angry. "I think I know who did it. But it wasn't me. You have to believe me."

Hannah found herself nodding. She could hear the truth in his voice. If not him, then who? "How did you get the baby here? After I fell down the steps?"

"Aw, hon, don't hash up all that. Isn't it enough to know she's okay and we can get her back?"

"It would have taken at least six hours to drive from Wabash to here and back. I thought you were with me the whole time."

He sighed. "I guess it doesn't matter anymore. One of my drinking buddies helped me. That's all you have to know."

Hannah curled her fingers into her palm so tightly her nails bit into the flesh. Her heart pounded against her ribs as she imagined that wild ride in the dead of night with a crying baby. A daughter crying for her mommy. A baby who had been ripped from loving arms and placed in another home. Did her baby know she was adopted?

"Hannah? You there, hon?"

Hannah couldn't choke out a sound. She closed her phone and turned it off.

BY NOONDAY, BUGGIES packed the driveway and yard and lined the road leading to the house. Their Amish friends came bearing food, shovels, and other tools to begin clearing away the debris as best they could with the intermittent downpours of rain. Dump trucks from various businesses they owned began to appear to haul away the wreckage. By breakfast the next day, much of the heap had been cleared and lumber began to arrive. Helpful Amish swarmed over the farm like busy ants intent on doing good.

Hannah had watched this scene play out many times, but her heart always warmed at the generosity of her people.

"I thought I would make coffee soup for breakfast," Sarah said.

"What?" Asia gave a shudder.

"It's good." Hannah's mouth watered at the thought. "She'll pour coffee over saltines or bread—I like it best with saltines—then pour on milk and sugar. Wait until you try it."

"I can wait. It sounds nasty. I like my coffee in a cup with cream and sugar."

"It's better than it sounds." Hannah accepted the first bowl of coffee soup and carried it into the living room. The Amish flooding into the house jabbered in a mixture of German and English, and the familiarity brought her childhood flooding back. *Mamm* always fixed coffee soup for her birthday. She could still remember the first time she'd been allowed to have it— on her fifth birthday. She finished the coffee, milk, and crackers that made up the soup and asked for more. Her mother had obliged. The caffeine had kept Hannah chattering to her mother far into the night.

Even Asia admitted the coffee soup was pretty good. Hannah finished her food and pulled out her last quilt square. Asia put down her word processor, and her dark eyes studied Hannah.

"I shudder to say anything, but should I just call your editor and tell her you're not going to make it?"

"I don't see any way I'm going to get it done in time. The quilt still needs to be assembled and all the quilting done. Ask her if she'd be willing to use my grandmother's quilt. The big one on Irene's bed."

"That won't work. She wants one of your designs. I'll just tell her you'll make your original deadline."

Sarah came to the door. "Don't do that. The women will be here in a few minutes to do it."

Hannah's head came up to snare Sarah's gaze. "I don't understand. Why would they help me?"

"Because I asked them to." Sarah held Hannah's mother's keepsake box in her hands. "I am going to confess at the next meeting."

Hannah waited to hear what Sarah meant. They'd been through enough already—she didn't want to drag Sarah into more turmoil.

"I took the ring, Hannah. I'm so sorry. Can you forgive me?"

Hannah's needle stilled in her hands. "You took my mother's ring? Why?" Wasn't it bad enough that her family had been stripped from her? Did Sarah and Luca have to begrudge her small mementos? She tried to keep her anger in check, but her foot began to tap restlessly.

"It was worth a great deal of money," she said. "When we were engaged, Luca talked of nothing but expanding the greenhouse, of what he could do once he saved enough. I had nothing but love. I was here cleaning after the murders and I found it. It did no one any good in that box. I thought your mother would have wanted it to be used for something worthy. I sold it. I told Luca it was my dowry and he never asked where the money came from."

"I see," Hannah said. "You had no right." Hannah had looked at the ring many times. It belonged to her. Her mother would have wanted her to have it.

"I know. Can you forgive me?" Sarah asked again, advancing into the room. "I'm so sorry, Hannah. I judged you when I should have judged myself. Maybe I didn't want you to expose what I'd done."

Hannah wanted to hold on to her anger. "Does Luca know?"

Sarah sniffed. "Not yet. I'll tell him tonight. I wanted to beg your forgiveness first."

"You lied to him. Won't he be angry? I have to be honest, Sarah—I'm angry. And I'm hurt." Hannah found lies the hardest to forgive. They struck at the core of any trusting relationship, and since Reece, trust came hard to her. The lies about the ring had slipped off Sarah's tongue all too easily.

"Yes, but he loves me. He will forgive me."

"Can you get the ring back? I really want it, Sarah."

Sarah's eyes clouded. "I'm sure it's been sold by now. You haven't said if you forgive me."

Hannah tried to struggle past the anger that still simmered. Sarah had no right to sell her mother's ring. It was easy for Sarah to ask for forgiveness. She was the thief. But saying "I'm sorry" wouldn't bring the ring back to Hannah. It was one thing to ask for forgiveness, but could Sarah extend it as easily as she asked for it?

"Sarah, what would you do if you'd married a husband who beat you?" she asked. She'd thought her friend would answer quickly and tersely, but she kept silent and pondered the question.

"I don't know," Sarah said after Hannah began to think she wouldn't answer at all. "I would not want my girls to see such a thing. I would not want to experience anything like that. I hope I would try to love the violence out of him."

"Some people can't be loved enough," Hannah said. "I tried. Reece was too far gone."

"Not for God," Sarah said quickly.

"But I'm not God," Hannah said. "And I did my best." But had she? She'd been quick to slip out to sales to look for quilts in spite of his orders. Had she ever put him first? She'd been so lonely in the early months, so ill equipped for marriage. At least half the blame was probably hers.

Sarah put her hand on Hannah's shoulder. "I'm not going to judge you, Hannah. I don't know what shoes you've walked in." She released her and went to pull out the quilting frame. "Now let's get your quilt finished. The others are coming. We can talk later. But please, I so want your forgiveness."

The hard coil of bitterness began to unwind in Hannah's heart at the desperate plea in Sarah's voice. "I forgive you." She said the words not knowing if she meant them.

Hannah heard them then, women talking and laughing as they poured into the house with their needles and thimbles. Thunder rolled and rain swept the windows all afternoon, but none of them minded. By suppertime, the quilt was finished, and Hannah knew love never died. It just sometimes went underground.

MATT HAD NEVER seen anything like the busyness going on outside two days after the fire. Sunday had been the Amish day of rest, but they tackled the job with gusto on Monday. No wonder Hannah missed the warmth and love of these people. He turned to work on the pancakes he was making for the crowd eating at tables outside.

"We'll have a new barn up by the weekend if the rain holds off," Luca said over breakfast. "When the tornado struck southern Indiana a few years ago, Amish friends from all over had the mess cleaned up and barns rebuilt in a couple of weeks."

"I believe it," Matt said. "The storm coming through here over the next few days is supposed to be ferocious with heavy rains and flooding." Hannah stood beside him as he worked. His movements were awkward because of his burned hands. "Hannah"—he spoke too softly for anyone but her to hear—"I checked on the cemeteries in Wabash. No luck."

She inhaled softly. "Thanks for checking. It is as I suspected. He told me one of his drinking buddies brought my daughter here and gave her away."

More of Reece's lies? A grave would have proved his daughter wasn't hers, but Matt's hope had faded fast over the past week. His cell phone rang as he poured more batter into the skillet.

Hannah tried to take the spatula from him, but Luca shook his head and took his place instead. Matt shrugged and glanced at the caller ID. His grandmother's name rolled across the screen. "Hey, Trudy," he said. He noticed he had missed two calls this morning. Must have been when he was in the shower.

Her voice was at a near shriek. "I can't find Caitlin!"

"Wait, I don't understand. Caitlin is at your house?"

"Gina dropped her off this morning for a few hours, said she had something she had to take care of. She said she'd call you to come get her. I fixed Caitlin's breakfast, and when I called her to come eat, I couldn't find her. I've looked everywhere."

For the rest of his life, Matt would remember how this moment felt: the way his blood seemed to freeze in his veins, then pulsed to his feet, leaving his vision swimming. Time slowed to a standstill. He could hear the oil sizzling, Luca clearing his throat, Hannah sipping her coffee. Every muscle in his throat spasmed, and he couldn't force out a word.

With a supreme effort, Matt got his tongue to work. "Trudy, calm down." *Stand back. Think this through.* It was up to him to rescue his daughter. What would he do if he got a call about a missing child? "When did you see her last?"

"She was coloring on the porch. About half an hour ago."

"When did you notice she was missing?" He was aware of Luca and Hannah looking at him with wide eyes.

"I called her for breakfast. When she didn't come, I yelled again, then went to the porch. I couldn't find her anywhere. She's not in the barn either."

Matt forced himself not to react, to hold his composure. "I'll be right there. I'll call headquarters."

He turned his back on the Schwartzes and called Captain Sturgis. He promised to send out a deputy to meet him at his grandmother's. When Matt slipped his phone onto his belt, he turned to face Hannah and Luca. "My daughter is missing. I've got to go."

Hannah put her hand to her mouth. "I'll come with you."

He needed all the help he could get. Caitlin needed to be found quickly. She was more important than his reputation with Hannah. "Thanks."

"I will come also," Luca said. "Will you drive us?"

"I'll get Asia too. We'll round up other friends to help search. Maybe she wandered off."

Matt's eyes burned unexpectedly. He'd heard about the way the Amish rallied around folks in need, even those who weren't part of their church, but this was the first time he'd seen it firsthand. "Thanks," he mumbled, unable to get out more than that.

Hannah sprang for the steps. "Asia, Sarah, come now. We need to help look for Matt's five-year-old daughter."

Hearing the words spoken out loud by someone else was almost as painful as hearing them the first time. A missing child. Every parent's nightmare. He'd been on the other end a time or two—the deputy talking to parents in such a situation. He should have been more compassionate, more sympathetic. Now he knew what it was like to hear the world shatter in a moment.

Focus. He had to focus. "The others can follow in Asia's car. I need to go now," he told Luca. He called Ajax, and the dog came running.

"I'm ready." The other man grabbed his black hat and slapped it over his Dutch boy haircut.

Luca followed Matt to the SUV. Hannah rushed to join them. "Asia will bring Sarah and any others with her." She got in the front seat with him, and Luca got in the back with the dog.

The tires shrieked in protest when Matt tromped on the gas pedal. It echoed the scream building in his own head—a babbling plea begging God to spare his baby girl. Hannah tried to talk to him, to pray with him, but the words didn't penetrate the pain blocking out all coherent thought. He knew he should confess everything, but he couldn't get his mouth to work.

The clouds released a burst of heavy rain. Matt barreled through the downpour to his grandmother's. As he pulled in the drive, he heard the sound of a siren screaming toward them. Never before had he experienced the way that familiar sound could seem so ominous, a harbinger of personal, devastating pain.

He slammed on the brakes and hurtled from the vehicle into the driving rain. The last time he'd seen her, Caitlin had come running to meet him. Taking the steps in one leap, he flung open the door and rushed into the house.

His grandmother was wrapping sandwiches in the kitchen. "You'll need these," she said, thrusting a bag of food into his hand.

As if he could even think about eating until his daughter was safe in his arms. He took the bag but put it on the counter. "Was she upset this morning?"

"Yes. She said she wanted to go home." Trudy's voice held censure. She stared at Hannah, then glanced at Matt. Her gaze lingered on Luca standing by the door with his hat in his hands. "What are you thinking to bring one of *them* here?"

Matt didn't have time for her prejudices. Ajax pressed his nose against his leg and whined. Matt swallowed his turmoil. He had to focus.

Car doors slammed, and moments later a fist pounded on the door. "Sheriff's department," Blake called.

"Come on in," Matt yelled.

Blake and another deputy joined them in the kitchen. "You okay, buddy?" Blake asked.

"Caitlin's gone," he told the deputies.

"Could she have run away?"

"Maybe." He could only hope and pray that was what had happened and he'd find her dragging her backpack along the road. People around here were decent people. Maybe one would stop and help. The thought of his daughter in this storm was too much to bear.

Matt stepped onto the porch where the toys lay. Her backpack was here too. So much for hoping she'd run off to find him. Ajax went to the pack and whined. Matt wished he could do the same. The wind blew rain onto the porch, and droplets pummeled him.

Hannah followed him. "She didn't take her backpack of toys. If she was running away, wouldn't she take that?"

"That would be my guess."

"How long has she been here?"

"My sister brought her this morning." Gina was probably one of the calls he missed. He'd been too upset to listen to her message, but he'd better. What if someone took Caitlin and left a message? "I had some messages." He pulled out his cell phone and called up his voice mail. Both were from Gina saying she was going to go talk to Vanessa. She asked him to go get Caitlin from Trudy's.

He put his cell phone away and glanced at Hannah. Confession trembled on his tongue. But nothing would be gained by causing that uproar now. It would only take the focus off finding his daughter. He made himself go through her backpack. It contained only her doll, Jenny, and the doll's clothing.

"If someone took her, wouldn't they be likely to take her toys to keep her quiet?" Hannah asked.

Reece would. Matt realized he had to tell the truth for law enforcement to be able to help him. He had to tell them to put out an APB for Reece. And to do that, he had to tell them why.

twenty-three

"The life of the Amish is summed up with the Amish Sunshine and Shadows Quilt. They are taught to accept whatever comes from God's hand—good or bad."

—HANNAH SCHWARTZ,

IN *The Amish Faith Through Their Quilts*

The storm battered against the house while thunder boomed overhead. Hannah gazed out across the yard at the black clouds. The porch was little protection. The little girl surely shouldn't be out in this. She wanted to help Matt, to comfort him in some way, but she understood that nothing could bring solace but finding his little girl. Even though she still believed she might have a daughter out there, she also believed the child was with a family that loved her. The picture had shown a happy, smiling child. Hannah had no sense that the girl was in danger, that someone might have taken her.

Matt was looking at her strangely. His gaze held a plea she wasn't sure how to read. And the twist of his lips almost made her think he was defiant about something. "Is there anything I can do, Matt?" she asked when he just stared without saying anything.

"I have to show you something," he said. His voice trembled. He dug into his pocket and pulled out his wallet. Flipping through the photo section, he stopped and stared at a picture. He tugged it from its sleeve and handed it to Hannah.

"This is Caitlin?" Hannah asked as she took the picture.

"This is my daughter." He put the emphasis on the word *my*.

Such a proud and loving father. Hannah glanced at the picture. And froze. The little girl smiling back at her with her arms around Ajax could have been herself at five. Auburn ringlets cascaded down Caitlin's back, and her golden brown eyes smiled as much as her lips. Hannah's gaze traced the familiar features, the happy smile as she looked with love at whoever was taking the picture. Probably her father.

"You've had her all along," Hannah whispered. "All this time when I've been looking for her. You lied to me."

It was all clear in an instant. All those times she'd asked him for help. All those times he'd listened to her fears about whether it might be true she had a daughter. He could have set her mind at ease so easily. All he would have had to say was that he had a child who looked like that. Why the lie? Unless he'd adopted her. But then he could have just said he adopted her. But maybe he didn't know who the mother was. Her thoughts jumbled wildly, nothing making sense.

Matt's voice was low. "I know, and I'm sorry. It's torn me up inside. But we'll have to talk about it later. For now, we have to pull together to find her. I think Reece took her."

Hannah gasped and put her hand to her mouth. But why, if Caitlin was Matt's own child? "But why would he take your child? Unless he thought he could convince me she was mine?" The thought of that precious little girl in Reece's control made tiny beads of perspiration break out on her forehead.

He raked his hand through his hair. "I didn't want to get into all this, but you have to be on board with me. We've got to get everyone looking for Reece." Matt drew a deep breath. "I think he put her on my doorstep five years ago. My wife and I tried for years to have a baby, but we learned she could never conceive. One night we heard something at the door. Analise opened it and found a baby in a carrier."

"She's not yours?" The ramifications began to seep into her consciousness.

Matt was still talking in a monotone. "Caitlin seemed heaven-sent. With my position in the sheriff's department, we were able to pull some strings and adopt her without turning her over to Child Protective Services. The pediatrician estimated she was only hours old, not more than a day or two."

A day or two. Hannah couldn't breathe, couldn't think. Could Reece really have taken her baby and just deposited her on a doorstep? Yes, he could. He was capable of anything. "She—she's mine?" Hannah couldn't breathe for fear this might be a dream. Joy vied with terror.

"I suspect so. I don't know for sure."

"Could she belong to someone else?"

He hunched his shoulders. "Why would she be put on my doorstep? Reece had a connection to me."

Hannah studied the photo again. "She looks just like the picture Reece sent me." Her gaze traced the smooth roundness of the child's cheeks, the gentle curve of her lips. "She's beautiful."

"Yes, she is." Matt's voice held anguish. "We have to find her." He disappeared inside.

Through the screen door, Hannah heard him telling his suspicions to the other deputies. Through a fog of confusion, she was aware they were calling for more help, putting out a warrant for Reece. With the thunder rolling over her and the lightning flashing overhead, a bubble of disbelief surrounded her. This couldn't be happening. She'd begun to love Matt, to trust him. He'd proven to be no different from Reece. He wore a smiling mask that hid the true man. And now her daughter was in Reece's clutches. She shuddered.

She'd tell the deputies Caitlin belonged to her. When she was found, she'd have her daughter and she'd never have to look Matt Beitler in the face again. She rubbed her forehead. That wouldn't work. Matt had friends, connections. He had adopted Caitlin. Sorting out the mess would be no easy matter. And if Reece really had Caitlin, finding him might be impossible.

She knew what she had to do. Call Reece and, to rescue Caitlin, go crawling back.

Her cell phone rang. Of course. She didn't have to look at the caller ID to know who it was. In a dreamlike state, she dug it out of her purse and flipped it open. "Hello, Reece," she said in as sweet a voice as she could muster. "I've been thinking. I want to come home."

"Wh-what?" Reece's voice quivered.

"We're attuned to one another. I was sure it was you when the phone rang. You're right. We have to work things out. I miss you." It was as if she stood outside herself listening to her lies. God forgive her, but she had to save Caitlin.

"I'm so glad, hon." His voice grew stronger. "And when you get here, I have a wonderful surprise for you."

A cold stone formed in her belly. He had Caitlin. An unnatural calm descended on her. She wasn't the same weak woman Reece once knew. He would find a bitter adversary. And she would protect Caitlin with her life.

"Where should we meet?" she asked in a soft and low voice that was sure to attract Reece.

"I'll pick you up at the coffee shop. Have your Asian friend drop you off and leave us alone. No tricks," Reece said as though he suddenly thought she was setting a trap.

Hannah didn't intend to tell anyone what she planned. The safest thing for Caitlin would be for her to go in alone, then slip out with the child the minute Reece went out to the store or to work. The problem would be that Reece might expect a lot from her until that time. A real marriage. He'd always had a strong sex drive. The thought of him touching her made bile rise in her throat, but she forced it back. She could do this. She had to do it.

"That sounds wonderful."

"What's brought about this sudden change of heart?" Suspicion vibrated in his voice.

"Being with my family, being back where we met. It brought all the love back." The words nearly gagged her, but she put tenderness into them.

"I should have made sure you stayed in touch, then." He chuckled then, a self-satisfied sound.

"I've missed you. I can't wait to see you. When can you come get me?"

"I—I've got something to take care of. Your surprise. Give me two hours. Don't be late," he said.

"I'll be early," she said. She put her phone away. Somehow she had to slip away without raising suspicion. Get her things from the house, get to the coffee shop. In a fog, she went inside and listened as Matt barked out orders. Every time he looked at her, she glanced away.

In the end, it was surprisingly easy to arrange. When Asia arrived, Hannah told her she needed migraine medication and needed to run home for it. The detectives were out slogging in the mud and searching the woods behind the house for Caitlin. Hannah simply told Asia she'd be right back, then drove to the house, packed her things, and went to wait at the coffee shop with her suitcase. She bound her hair up in a bun on the back of her head, then sat at a table by the door to wait.

"Hannah?"

She looked up at the sound of a woman's voice. Ellen Long stood in the doorway. The old anger surged at the sight of the woman's face. Hannah had always believed Ellen knew more than she would admit to. "Ellen."

"Mind if I sit down a minute?" Without waiting for an answer, Ellen slid into the chair across from Hannah. "I'd heard you were back in town."

Hannah laced her fingers together in her lap. The woman had lost the bloom of beauty she'd had the last time Hannah had seen her. She was dressed in too-tight jeans and a top that revealed ample cleavage, and her features had a hard cast. "I've been back a couple of weeks."

"I was hoping to run into you, see how you're doing. I never got a chance to tell you how sorry I was." Ellen's words spilled out but held not an ounce of emotion. It was as if she'd memorized them and waited for the chance to spew them out.

Hannah held her tongue as her resentment grew. She had enough to worry about without listening to Ellen cry alligator tears.

Ellen fidgeted when Hannah didn't reply. "Reece stopped to see me the other day. He says you've left him. That's too bad."

Why had Reece stopped to see Ellen? For the first time, Hannah wondered if Ellen and Reece were connected in some way. The thought hadn't crossed her mind.

"How well do you know Reece?" Hannah asked. A secret smile flitted across Ellen's face so fast that Hannah wasn't sure it had come at all—until she saw the self-satisfied expression in the woman's eyes.

"His mother introduced us."

"His mother?" Reece had been a foster child of Trudy's.

Ellen nodded. "I was taking quilting lessons from Irene Beitler. I met him there."

Irene was Reece's mother? Hannah wanted time to process the news. He'd never told her, yet he'd told his mistress? Even Matt hadn't seemed to know. Even though Hannah longed to be free of Reece, the thought scalded her. "And had an affair?" Hannah could see it was true by the way Ellen looked away. "So why are you telling me this?" Her rage nearly choked her.

Ellen shrugged. "I just wanted to clear the air. Let you know Reece and me go back a long way. Make sure you're not longing to reconcile. I don't want to play second fiddle again."

"I think Reece might have a say in that. What makes you think he wants you back?" Hannah heard the roar of a truck. Glancing out the window, she saw Reece behind the steering wheel. "I'll ask him about it now." She rose and walked past Ellen's shocked face toward the truck.

Everything she thought she knew wasn't true, and she couldn't see through the deep water to the bottom. She reached the truck. When he grinned, she nearly fled, but she forced herself to return his smile and climb into the truck he was driving—one she'd never seen before. He took her cell phone and tossed it out the window. She was alone with him, and she didn't know if she'd live to see tomorrow.

Rain dripped from the brim of his hat, and Matt lifted a mud-coated boot from the muck. No one had located any sign of his daughter. Even Ajax hadn't found a scent. That had to mean she'd been taken somewhere in a vehicle, and the realization made his mouth dry up.

He glanced at his watch. Nearly noon. His baby girl had been gone an eternity. He'd prayed all morning for God to keep her safe, to keep her from being frightened. He motioned to Blake. "I don't think she's out here. Any word on Reece?"

"No one has seen him. He might have ditched the truck and gotten another vehicle."

"Let's call off the search out here. I'm sure he's got her."

"You're probably right."

Matt and Blake tramped through the mud back to the farm. Buggies and cars lined the road as far as he could see. The Amish community had poured out to help him. He'd never look at them the same again. Matt saw them as friends now, friends who cared.

Everyone was coming back to the yard now that the search had been called off. He found himself searching for Hannah's bright head. He knew the news had rocked her hard. And it had probably ended any future they might have had. Instead, they would engage only in a long, bitter battle over Caitlin's future.

His fear and deceit had ruined everything. He didn't like the person he'd become. He'd always told himself he feared nothing, but instead of trusting God to work things out, he'd run scared, told countless lies, and put his daughter in harm's way. And he'd been stupid to boot.

He didn't see Asia's familiar red car. Asia stood talking to Sarah and Gina under the shelter of a giant tulip tree, but rain still dripped onto their heads.

Gina rushed to him, and he embraced her. "Oh, Matt, I'm so sorry!" She was sobbing so hard she could barely talk. "A friend from church called me." She swiped at the tears on her cheeks. "We've got to find her, Matt."

"I will. I'm calling off the search in the woods, though. I think Reece has her." A foggy disorientation muffled his thoughts, but he focused on his sister's face. "You went to confront Vanessa?"

"Yeah, but Blake was there, Matt. And I saw a bunch of stuff in her garage. I think she and Blake are behind the robberies in town. I just turned around and left. I'm leaving him."

Matt found no joy in discovering that his suspicions about Blake were true. "I'll tell the captain."

She put her face against his chest. "If only I hadn't brought Caitlin here!"

"It's not your fault, Sis. If Reece has her, he could have taken her from your house just as easily." It was his job to keep his daughter safe, and he'd blown it. He glanced around the yard again. "Where's Hannah?"

Asia wrinkled her nose. "I've been wondering that myself. She left here two hours ago to go get some migraine meds. I thought she'd be back in fifteen minutes. Maybe she had to lie down a few minutes."

Matt knew Hannah well enough by now to know she'd crawl on bleeding knees to help those she loved. "I can't see her doing that." Something was going on, and every nerve in his body tightened in response.

"Me neither, to tell you the truth. I was trying not to worry." Asia pulled her cell phone out of the purse slung around her shoulder. "I've got a good signal here. So if she had a breakdown, she could have called me."

"I hope Reece didn't find her," he said. His pulse galloped as he thought it through. "If she thought Reece had Caitlin, would she go back to him?" Even before he saw Asia's face change, he knew the answer. "Of course she would," he said. "In a heartbeat." He wanted to hit something. "Reece would call her and taunt her with the fact that he had their daughter."

"*Their* daughter," Asia said. "Do you think it's really true?"

"I think so. I've got to find Hannah." He called Ajax and ran to the SUV.

IN THE WASH of daylight, Reece looked older, harder. His hair was grayer and coarser, especially the straggly beard he'd grown. His jowl seemed softer too, but the same hard light shone in his eyes. Hannah had to look hard for it, though. His jovial smile would have masked it completely from someone who didn't know as well as she just what he was capable of.

"You look good, hon," he said. "Take your hair down."

"Not now," she said before she thought.

"Take it down *now*."

The hard tone of his voice and the way the amiable mask vanished told her to obey. Slowly, she reached up and began to pull the pins from her hair. She'd thought he would hide his true colors at least for a little while. His eyes spoke of a further slide into madness. When her hair lay on her shoulders, she leaned forward to grab her bag from the floor and drop the pins into it.

Reece's fingers plunged into her hair and wrapped around the locks. "No one has hair like yours. I've told you never to wear it down for anyone else."

Using her hair as leverage, he dragged her across the bench seat until she was close enough for him to release her hair and slide his arm around her.

Her scalp stung, but she said nothing. He seemed calm at the moment, and she didn't dare complain. With the overpowering scent of his familiar cologne nearly asphyxiating her, Hannah's strength and courage waned. What made her think she could outwit him? Whenever she was around him, he sapped her will and determination. Her life would slide into the same old nightmare, and she would be helpless to prevent it.

No. She had Caitlin to think about. The little girl needed her protection. Hannah saw no evidence of Caitlin in the vehicle. Could he have merely used the situation to bait Hannah? She prayed that was true. It would be eas-ier to escape if she wasn't frozen with fear for her daughter.

"So where are we going?" she asked in a bright voice. From the corner of her eye, she saw his quick glance as though he couldn't figure her out.

"You'll see. I've got a surprise for you. Things are going to be different, Hannah. You're going to obey me this time. We're going to be the model family."

"Family? Are we going to go find our daughter?" The words nearly gagged her, but she got them out in a loving tone.

"Maybe."

"Why did you take her away from me, Reece?" The words poured out of her in spite of her resolve not to annoy him. "I wanted her so much."

"I didn't want to share you with anyone else. Now I see I was wrong about that."

The craftiness in his glance frightened her. He had some kind of plan, and she feared for Caitlin. Where was the little girl? Surely he hadn't left her alone somewhere.

"If she's been adopted, how can we find her and get her back?"

"You leave that up to me." He reached a dirt road that was only wide enough to allow a single car to navigate. "Where were you when I called?"

"At the farmhouse. Working on the quilt." The lie came too easily to her lips. What kind of a Christian was she that she could smile and lie without compunction?

"Liar!" His fingers squeezed her arm hard enough to leave bruises. "I followed you. I know you were looking for Caitlin. You know I have her. That's why you came, isn't it?"

"No!" She tried to pull away, but his grip was too tight. "Do you have her? We thought she just wandered off into the woods. That's where Matt was looking. How do you know Caitlin?" She thought her subterfuge had worked when he didn't ask why she lied.

But his attention was on something else. Glancing in the rearview mirror, he accelerated around the curve, then whipped the steering wheel. "Did the detectives follow you?" he snarled.

"No, of course not. I was careful to make sure I was alone."

The truck fishtailed in the mud, then slid into a wide spot between some shrubs. Ahead was an abandoned covered bridge. He drove over the grass toward it. "Hang on," he said. His grip fell off her shoulders.

This bridge had never been restored, and Hannah immediately spotted the missing planks and rotted girders. Any minute she expected the truck to plunge through the floor of the bridge and into the creek below, running deep with cold water from the storm. She'd never seen the water so high. The tires rumbled on the planks, then Reece wrenched the wheel to the right and rode the passenger side tires up onto the side, where the frame looked stronger.

Hannah caught another glimpse of the water below through gaping holes in the structure of the bridge. She gripped the armrest on the door. Her pulse pounded in her head. They weren't going to make it. The openings in the bridge passed by in a dizzying blur when Reece accelerated. The light at the other end grew larger, then the truck lurched over the last of the uneven boards. The tires found purchase in the rocky dirt at the other end and gave the truck traction through the last few feet.

Reece guided the truck to a stop in the shelter of underbrush. "Lost them," he said with a smug grin.

"I never saw anyone."

He stretched his arm across the top of the battered bench seat. "You haven't kissed me yet, Hannah. That will tell me how sincere you are."

Her stomach roiled. How could she cover her revulsion? She'd known it might come to this. The distance between her lips and his wary smile seemed as vast as the Pacific Ocean. Her muscles froze in place, pressing her back into the safety of the cracked leather seat. Any minute he would reach across the chasm and grab her. It would be all she could do not to scream, and he would know. Know she'd rather die than touch him.

A siren blared in the distance. His head whipped around, and he peered back through the trees. "We'd better get going. This can wait until tonight."

Somehow she would have to find a way to get Caitlin to safety before then.

twenty-four

*"Religious services are held every other Sunday in a
different home. Each family takes a turn hosting the congregation.
It adds to the sense of community."*

—HANNAH SCHWARTZ,
IN *The Amish Faith Through Their Quilts*

Matt saw Asia's car parked outside the coffee shop and breathed a
sigh of relief at the sight of it. But why would Hannah stop to get
coffee and spend hours there? The panic came again, and he knew something was wrong.

He and Ajax went to the car and peered inside. The locks were down,
and the car held only a computer bag in the back, probably Asia's. Inside the
coffee shop he saw only two men with an open briefcase between them at the
back table. The barista had just come on duty and hadn't seen Hannah. Not
good. Matt didn't want to face the truth, but he knew it.

Reece had Hannah.

No doubt in his mind. But how to find them? He'd tried her cell phone half
a dozen times, but she had it switched off. Reece had been a detective. He knew
how to evade law enforcement. Chances were, he'd ditched his truck and

gotten other wheels. Matt drove to the jail and went to his office. He checked the list of stolen vehicles. Most would likely turn up once the kids who'd taken them for joyrides sobered up. But one stood out. An old red pickup. It had been taken two days ago. About the time Reece would have been making his plans.

Matt put out an alert for the vehicle, but it was a long shot. Several hours had already passed. Parke County was only minutes from Illinois. Reece could have taken Hannah and Caitlin and crossed the state line already. He sat at the desk with his head in his hands. *Think!* He knew Reece well, knew his likes and dislikes, his way of looking at the world. There had to be some clue he was missing.

He wanted to bang his forehead against the desk. Ajax whined and pressed his nose against Matt's leg. "I'm okay, boy." Matt rubbed the dog's ears. Reece had no family. Like Matt, he was a throwaway kid. Reece's mother had given him to Irene, who had raised him for a time. When she couldn't handle him anymore, he'd gone to Trudy. She'd be sorely disappointed in Reece. Most kids who passed through her doors went on to live decent lives. Reece was fond of Irene too. Maybe she'd have an idea where he could look. He and Ajax hopped into the SUV and drove out of town.

Reece used to go see her once a week. Maybe he resumed that tradition when he returned. It couldn't hurt to run out and talk to her. She might have some idea where Matt should look. Something had happened between his grandmother and his aunt, and rather than ruffle his grandmother's feathers, he'd avoided Irene. It was just easier that way. Keeping his grandmother pleasant could be a full-time job.

He rolled to a stop in front of the big old Victorian house. Irene's yellow dress was a bright splash of color against the red of the rose garden she labored in. The fact that she wore muddy Wellingtons ruined the perfect picture. Her hair was unkempt as well, and when she turned around, her gaze was foggy. It must be one of her bad days.

Most days her medication held the darkness at bay, but once in a while, the fog rolled in and took her into its murky depths.

He let Ajax out of the SUV, and his aunt came to meet him. "David, what are you doing here?"

It was worse than he thought. "It's Matt, Irene. Not David."

Her gaze drifted away from his face and out over the fields. "Of course it is. I should get the meadow tea in and make you some. You've always loved my meadow tea, David."

Matt gripped her shoulders and turned her to face him. "Listen to me, Aunt Irene. I need your help. Caitlin's in trouble."

"Your mother?"

"No, Caitlin. My daughter. Remember her?" He folded his arms over his chest. "Have you seen Reece O'Connor?"

Her hazel eyes clouded. "A few days ago. He's not a good son."

Who did she think he was talking about? When she was like this, it was almost impossible to get any sense out of her. "Did you take your medicine today?"

Her hand went into her pocket, and she withdrew a pill bottle. "No medicine, all gone," she said in a singsong voice.

"I think Reece has taken Caitlin. And maybe Hannah Schwartz," he said. She stared at him as though she'd been expecting something like this. "Did he tell you he planned to take her?" She wouldn't meet his gaze. She rocked on her feet, picking petals off a rose like some lovesick girl from the turn of the century. "Did he tell you?" he repeated.

"Caitlin puts me in mind of Hannah," she said. "You made me lie to Hannah the other day. She's Caitlin's mother, isn't she?"

"Yes. Look, I don't have time for this. I've got to find my daughter before he disappears with her. Or hurts her."

"Reece can't be trusted. That's why I turned him out."

Matt didn't have time to try to decipher her ramblings. "I think he killed the Schwartz family. And he threw Hannah down the steps so she'd lose the baby. Only the baby didn't die. And he left Caitlin on my doorstep."

She still showed no real reaction. He'd thought his accusation would incite her to protest or something. "Things aren't always what they seem. Mother knows everything, sees everything, punishes everything," she said in a singsong voice.

"Trudy knows all about it. Reece took Caitlin from her front porch. She didn't hear a thing. She didn't even know Caitlin was gone until she tried to call her for breakfast."

"Mother knows. Don't worry."

He clenched his fists. "She's five years old! Not worry about it? We've had a doozy of a storm all morning too."

Still plucking petals, she exhibited an unnatural serenity. He wanted to rip the roses out of her hands and fling them to the ground. She *would* tell him what he needed to know if he had to drag her to her feet and shake it out of her.

"I've got work to do." She tossed the flowers to the ground. "I hope you find her."

He blocked her path. "Where would Reece take her?" Her eyes cleared, and he saw sharp intelligence gleaming in their depths.

She shook her head. "This isn't about Reece, David. It goes much deeper than that. Much further back. You'd better start with Mother."

"You're not making any sense. Trudy doesn't know anything about this."

"No?" She smiled, a grimace that only made her eyes look sadder. "Everything that goes around comes around. This evil goes on and on. I think there's no end to it. At least none that I can see."

"Start with the truth."

"The truth? It depends on how you look at it."

Matt couldn't make heads or tails out of her babbling. He jerked his thumb toward the SUV. "Let's go," he told Ajax. "There's no help for us here." He'd do what she said, go talk to his grandmother. Just in case he'd missed something. He had to find his daughter. The urgency rumbled in his chest like thunder, but he took the time to call Gina and asked her to go check on Irene and make sure she got her meds.

Rᴇᴇᴄᴇ ʜᴜɴᴄʜᴇᴅ ᴏᴠᴇʀ the wheel as the truck zoomed along at breakneck speed. He had said nothing for the last fifteen minutes. Hannah huddled on her side of the seat. "Where are we going?"

"You'll see."

Some of the area looked familiar. She vaguely remembered picnicking once at the top of the hillside the truck climbed. This part of Parke County had steep hills and hidden ravines. It had been all their horses could do to pull the buggy up here. Those were happy days, filled with love, discipline, and godly training. She hadn't appreciated it fully at the time.

The truck left the gravel road and turned down a cow path, a faint depression in the grass that led through a break in the raspberry bushes. She thought they might be taking a back way into Turkey Run State Park. The truck bogged down in mud several times, but Reece managed to power it on through. Vegetation brushed against the side of the vehicle and tore at the side mirrors. The trees blotted out the light, and the thick foliage made it as cool and dark as midnight, cocooning them from the world. The tires rumbled over fallen logs and muddy ruts in the ground before coming to rest in a small clearing.

A cliff covered with vines and weeds loomed over them, blotting out even more light. "Honey, we're home," Reece said. His chuckle fell flat.

"Wh-where are we, Reece?" Hannah didn't want to get out of the truck. Menace coated the air.

"You'll see. Hop out, hon." He got out and removed her suitcase from the back.

Hannah shoved open her door and stepped out into the clearing. No birds sang here. A twisted tree raised dead branches into the air. No frogs croaked, no wind ruffled the leaves, and Hannah could not even hear the hum of insects.

She tightened her grip on the shoulder strap of her purse. "Now what?"

"Follow me." He struck out along an impression of beaten-down grass. Fighting his way along the base of the cliff, he held back brambles and bushes for her. The underbrush grew thicker and the silence more oppressive. Hannah wanted to turn and run for the truck. Reece seemed too smug. But Caitlin was somewhere back here, so she trudged on.

In the distance, she heard the roar of rapids, probably Sugar Creek. With the heavy storms the past few days, it would be in full flood stage. The roar of the water grew louder with every step until they arrived at a battered shack on the shores of the creek.

He unlocked the padlock on the door. "Step into my parlor," he said.

"It's a sugar shack." She tried to peer in the window, but it was too dirty and fly-speckled.

He grabbed her arm. "Hurry up. We don't have all day. The kid is inside."

In a frenzy of movement, Hannah shoved open the door. An old rug had been thrown down on the floor, and inflatable furniture made it seem almost homey. A cot was on the far side of the space, and a little girl lay curled up on it with an afghan thrown over her. She appeared sound asleep. A chain dangled from one small ankle to the cot.

Hannah moved to the side of the bed. Her vision narrowed and her heart galloped. She looked at the child for the first time. Her child? The unruly auburn hair, the tiny hands fisted, the shape of the toenails and feet. Even the curve of her cheeks and the length of her lashes held an uncanny familiarity for her. She told herself not to let the lid off her hopes. "Is she ours, Reece?"

"Sure, hon." Reece put his arm around her, and they stood looking at Caitlin. "I was wrong. I know that now. I want her too. It will be great now that the three of us are together."

Hannah wanted to move away, but she didn't dare. "All these lost years. Why did you give her to Matt?"

"I heard from Trudy about all the trouble his wife was having getting pregnant. It seemed right that someone should have her who would love her." His tone suggested he'd done something heroic, something praiseworthy.

Hannah drank in the sight of her child. She wanted to touch the soft hair, kiss the round softness of Caitlin's cheek, smell the little-girl scent. She wanted to pull the child onto her lap to experience her weight for the first time. She wanted to recapture every moment that had been stolen from her—the first tooth, the first word, the first stumbling step. Gone—it was all gone. Stolen. Destroyed. It would never come again.

She whirled and curled her fingers into fists. "How could you, Reece? How could you destroy our family like this?" Leaping at him, she tore at his eyes. Her hands grabbed fistfuls of hair. Kicking and pummeling, she wanted to inflict as much damage as she could. Nothing she did to him would ever be enough to pay him back for what he'd done to them all.

He grabbed her in a bear hug and wrestled her to the floor, where she lay pinned under him. Panting, she tried to wrench her arm free. "Let go of me," she spat. Hatred black as tar and just as immobilizing filled her heart.

"I will, just as soon as you calm down." Blood trickled from his mouth, and a red lump formed on his forehead. "You've turned into a little spitfire. You're going to have to learn to obey me, Hannah. Just settle down. I knew you'd be upset once you saw her. She's cute, isn't she? Looks like you. Doesn't seem to have anything of me in her at all." His eyes narrowed. "Maybe she's not even mine."

"Oh please. You kept me shackled to the house. Who would I have had an affair with?" Strength seeped from her bones and into the cold stone beneath her. What was the use? He always won. He was bigger, stronger, smarter. She lay still and stared up at him.

With tears blurring his face in her vision, she could almost imagine he wasn't the monster she thought he was. Maybe everything was her fault. If she'd been a better wife, with a gentler, more submissive spirit, their lives wouldn't be in this mess. "What do you want from me, Reece? I gave you all I had, and you trampled it."

He brushed his lips across hers. "I want you to be a good wife, Hannah. To put me first like you should. I want us to grow old together, to raise our little girl to be a good, obedient woman. Think you can do that?" He released her arms and lifted his weight from her but continued to loom over her body. His stare seemed to prod into her soul as he searched for the truth in her face.

She breathed in courage. She reached up her hands and cupped his cheeks in her palms. "I'm sorry I hurt you," she whispered. "It was such a shock. All those wasted years . . ." Tears slid from the corners of her eyes and ran down to soak the hair at her temples. "We could have had this time with her and with each other, Reece. I would never put her first. I know it frightened you, but you always came first with me."

The hard stare of his gaze softened. "Ah, Hannah, that's all I ever wanted. For someone to love me and put me first. You don't know what it was like to grow up knowing no one really cared."

"I'm sorry, Reece. You never talked about it."

"It hurt too much," he admitted.

She put on a stern expression. "I am your wife. I'm here for you to share those things with me. Don't keep anything from me again."

"We'll have lots of time together, the three of us." His lips brushed hers again. Before she could react, he rolled off her and got up. He held out his hand to her and hoisted her to her feet. "I think our daughter is awake. But then, who wouldn't be with the way you were yelling." He wrapped a curl of her hair around his finger.

Hannah's insides trembled, but she didn't dare show how he terrified her. She smiled up at him until he released her hair. Then she let go of his hand and turned back to the cot. Caitlin sat with her small feet dangling over the edge of the mattress. Her eyes were round and fearful, and her lips trembled. She twisted her hands in her lap.

"Don't be scared, honey," Hannah said. She approached the bed and knelt in front of the little girl. "I won't let anyone hurt you."

Caitlin touched Hannah's hair. "You have hair like mine. I've never seen anyone with hair like mine. Daddy says it's fairy hair."

Hannah managed a smile. "Maybe he's right. My name is Hannah."

"I'm Caitlin Beitler. My daddy is a sheriff's detective. He'll be mad that bad man took me." She pointed at Reece. "Can you take me home now?"

"Soon," she whispered too softly for him to hear. She craned her neck to face Reece. "Take off the chain. Give me the key and I'll let her go."

He shrugged. "Just make sure she doesn't bolt. I don't want to have to hurt her." He dug into his pocket and found a small key that he dangled in the air above her head. "Say please."

"Please, Reece." She made a grab for the key and missed. He laughed. Forcing a smile, she grabbed his forearm. "You're such a tease. Hand it over."

He grinned at her sweet tone and dropped the key into her hand. "Thanks!" She stabbed the key into the lock and had Caitlin free in moments. Lifting the child in her arms, she relished the weight of her, the smell of her even through the stink of wet mud. Caitlin's long hair brushed against Hannah's arms and mingled with her hair. It was hard to tell whose locks were whose. Caitlin looped her arms around Hannah's neck, and the trust in the movement nearly buckled Hannah's knees. She sank onto the cot and held the child close.

She would never let her go. Never. And she'd kill anyone who tried to take her.

twenty-five

"A pure white quilt with excellent stitching is always prized.
My mother was a master of the quilt, and she told me white
was her way of imagining heaven. The Amish strive to lead
pure and holy lives in order to reach God."

—Hannah Schwartz,

in *The Amish Faith Through Their Quilts*

His grandmother had to know something. It all made a kind of weird sense. Matt gripped the steering wheel and gunned the SUV through the water standing on the road. Ajax whined in the seat behind him. How could Caitlin have disappeared the minute Trudy got her unless she'd called Reece to come get her? He skidded to a halt in front of the house.

He and Ajax went to the front door. He didn't knock. "Trudy?" he called, stepping inside. The house was empty, silent. Now that he thought about it, he hadn't seen her vehicle outside. Sometimes she kept it in the backyard.

He walked through the house to the back door. Glancing through the window, he saw no sign of his grandmother's old blue car. "Maybe she went to the grocery store," he muttered. Ajax woofed as though he understood what Matt said.

He wandered down the hall toward Trudy's bedroom. Irene had told him to ask Trudy about what had happened between them. How could that matter? He glanced around Trudy's bedroom. Austere with white walls and bedding, it was immaculate. A prominent wardrobe stood in one corner, one he'd never peeked inside. Maybe now was the time. He stepped to the wardrobe and opened the doors. Stacks of quilts were inside. He pulled one out. It had a hummingbird pattern on it.

Could they be Patricia Schwartz's quilts? What would Trudy be doing with them? They certainly resembled the ones he'd seen. A large family album caught his eye. Matt carried it into the kitchen under the light and set it on the counter. Irene had hinted that the seeds of this situation were in the past. Maybe this album would give him some clue.

He started at the front. The first black-and-white picture showed a young couple staring stiffly into the camera. He recognized Trudy. He assumed the man was his grandfather, though Matt had never seen him. He flipped through more pages and saw his father and Irene at various ages. He'd never realized he looked so much like his dad. He'd study these pictures later. Right now he had to find his daughter. There had to be something here.

He turned the page and stopped at a picture of Irene. Hannah had been right. His aunt was clearly pregnant. She looked as though she was ready to give birth any minute. On the next page, the pictures continued as though her pregnancy had never occurred. He studied the previous picture. From the clothing and hairstyle, Matt guessed the date to be in the early seventies. She still wore the long hair and caftan of her hippie days.

He studied the location. The setting looked familiar to him, but he couldn't put his finger on where it was. Billie Creek, maybe? Matt tried to remember what his aunt had said about where her commune had been. "Sugar Creek," he said, snapping his fingers. "That's what Irene said. But where?" It would be a place to look. Maybe Reece knew about the place.

Matt turned a few more pages and came to another picture taken by the big creek, which more accurately was as big as a river. He studied one of the women in the photograph. She had the look of Hannah, but the clothing was all wrong. This picture would have been snapped before she was born.

Maybe Hannah's mom? He studied the other couple in the picture—Irene and an Amish guy. Must have been Hannah's dad on his *rumspringa*. The two sets were clearly paired up by the way they stood. It looked like his dad was seeing Hannah's mom. He'd never heard that before. He thought back to the arguments in the house before his dad killed himself. It seemed his mom was always unhappy with how much time Dad spent in the barn and away at the greenhouse. Could it have been the Schwartz greenhouse?

"This is a weird tangle," he muttered. Ajax whined at the stress in his voice, and Matt rubbed the dog's ears. Maybe Reece gave the quilts to his grandmother, and she'd been covering for him. Maybe she'd even handed Caitlin over to him. He flipped through more pages of the album and stopped beside a newspaper clipping of his grandmother in her mid- to late forties. She was standing with a proud smile beside a white quilt. The caption read "Trudy Beitler Takes First Place at the State Fair with Her Hummingbird Quilt."

Matt carried the album into the light so he could see the quilt better. It looked exactly like the pattern Hannah's mother was famous for. Had she imitated Trudy's pattern—and found even more success with it? Was that part of the reason for his grandmother's hatred of the Amish?

He heard a vehicle in the back and rushed to look out the window. His grandmother's old car was rolling over the ruts. He started toward the door, but Trudy got out, grabbed a cooler, and hopped back into the vehicle again. What was she doing? He decided not to let her know what he'd seen just yet. He'd follow her and see if she led him to Reece and Caitlin.

Matt grabbed the photo album and ran for the SUV. Her car had rumbled away down the back lane, which meandered across an abandoned covered bridge. Where could she be heading? He waited until his grandmother's old car disappeared into the trees, then set out along the lane in the direction she'd gone.

There wasn't much out this way. Forest and steep hills. No real roads even. The land bordered Turkey Run State Park, and his grandmother had turned away every developer who'd come calling. He had time to ensure he wasn't seen. Trudy owned nearly five hundred acres out this way. He used to hike back here—until she found out. She didn't like anyone back here but her. And even then, he could count on one hand the times he'd seen her trek this way.

The SUV rumbled over the bridge, but he wasn't sure the old structure would hold up anything coming back. The thing was falling down. If Trudy wanted to keep it, she'd have to do some repair. Rather, he'd have to do some repair.

He came to a fork in the road. "Now which way?" he said to Ajax. The dog whined. Matt got out and looked at the muddy track. "That way," he said, pointing to the left. "Toward the creek."

Matt got back in the SUV and turned the vehicle onto an even narrower lane logged with water. He was surprised his grandmother had the nerve to drive this way by herself in a car. The route begged for a four-wheel-drive. She could get stuck back here and never be seen again. The trees encased Matt like a tunnel. The maples and walnut trees grew so high they met above the SUV and turned the landscape to twilight. He could only go five miles an hour without bottoming out.

The road, if you could call it that, came to an abrupt end. Trudy's battered blue car was parked just ahead. She wasn't in it. Matt peered inside the vehicle, then turned back to his SUV and let Ajax out. He took the dog to the driver's side of Trudy's car. "Find her, boy."

The dog's nose plunged toward the ground, and his tail began to wag. The jerk on the leash nearly toppled Matt, but he regained his footing and followed along with Ajax on his run to the south. The surroundings were as dark as if it were nine o'clock at night. The mosquitoes began to descend in hordes, and he wished he'd taken the time to put on some repellent.

The dog led him down ravines, and they splashed across creeks swollen with rain. "I don't know how she had the strength to go this far," Matt said, panting when they paused to catch their breath. Ajax was straining at the leash again, so they were probably close behind her. "Let's get our bearings before we go any farther."

SUNLIGHT FILTERED THROUGH the dirty windows of the old shack. Hannah sat on the cot with Caitlin on her lap. The creek outside had crescendoed to a roar, and vibrations of water hitting rock rattled the wooden structure.

"When are we leaving, Reece?" she asked.

"Soon."

He seemed nervous, checking his watch every few seconds and going to look out the window. Hannah wondered what he was waiting for. He had her and Caitlin, and there seemed no reason to hang around while the flood-waters rose. Though this old place had been here for years, the forecasters had warned of near-record flood conditions all over the county. Hanging around Sugar Creek seemed a stupid thing to do.

She rose with her daughter in her arms. "Let's go now. I'm hungry, and I'm sure Caitlin is too."

His eyes narrowed. "What about me? I haven't eaten either. You never think about me, Hannah."

"I'm sorry to complain. I know we're all tired, hungry, and grouchy." She smiled up at him. "I'm just eager to get out of here and start our life together, the three of us."

His glare softened. "Soon." He turned when the door opened.

Trudy Beitler stepped into the shack. She shut the door behind her. Mud caked the Wellington boots she wore, and debris littered her old jeans and checked shirt. She could have passed for a lumberjack except for the long gray braid hanging over one shoulder. Her gaze perused Reece, then moved on to Hannah, who stood with Caitlin wrapped around her like a little monkey.

"Grandma Trudy!" Caitlin unwound her legs from Hannah and slid down to run to her grandmother.

Trudy shoved her away. "Go back to your mother."

"Come here, Caitlin." Hannah held out her arms. The older woman wasn't here to rescue them. Hannah didn't know how this whole plan was going to play out, but she realized Trudy was no ally.

Her expression confused, Caitlin glanced back at Hannah, then up at her grandmother. "Are you going to take me home, Grandma?"

"I told you to go to your mother. No, I'm not taking you home. You're right where you should be." She dropped the small cooler she carried onto the wooden floor.

"Where were you?" Reece asked. "I did what you said and brought Hannah here. I thought you'd be here to say good-bye. I need to get going before Matt tracks us here."

"I think not. Sit." She pointed at the cot. "You've done well, Reece," she said. "You did everything I asked of you."

"Thanks for helping me figure this out, Trudy. But I didn't need the kid after all. Hannah came back to me of her own free will." His triumphant smile beamed from above his beard.

Trudy glanced at Hannah, and the chill in her gaze froze Hannah's veins. "I need you to run an errand, Reece. I forgot the money at the house. It's in the cookie jar on top of the refrigerator."

"I've got enough. I don't need it," he said.

"I want to make sure you have enough for a fresh start. Run get it, and then you can disappear. It won't take long."

Hannah didn't trust the other woman. She wanted to beg Reece not to leave her alone with Trudy, but he shrugged and went to the door.

"I won't be long."

Trudy nodded. "I'll be here waiting."

Silence stretched out in the sugar shack. Hannah tried to make sense of it all. Why would Trudy help Reece get Caitlin and lure her here?

THEY WERE ATOP a hillside, so Matt planted one foot on a fallen tree and stared through the gloom in all directions. He caught a break in the trees. "I think there's a cabin over there," he said to Ajax. He took out his topo map and consulted it. The map said there was an abandoned sugar shack this way.

"Let's check it out." Matt and Ajax plunged down the hillside. "Quiet, Ajax," he told his dog. He didn't want any barking to give them away.

As they neared the structure, he recognized it from the pictures in Trudy's album. He started toward a window, intending to peer inside and see if Trudy was there, but the door opened and Reece stepped out. Matt ducked out of sight, watching as the other man went up the trail toward where Trudy had parked the car. Great, maybe Matt could slip in and rescue his daughter and Hannah without any gunplay.

When Reece was out of sight, he rose and moved toward the shack. The door opened again, and his grandmother stepped out. With a gun. His gaze went to the weapon in her hand. It was pointing at him. "It's just me, Trudy. You can put that peashooter away."

"I don't think I can, Matthew. Ease your gun out and drop it on the ground."

The hard, inflexible voice she used struck Matt in the heart. "Trudy, what are you doing?"

Her finger tightened on the trigger. "Do what you're told. You're too much like your mother, always questioning things. Next time I'll shoot out your kneecap. Now do what I say."

Matt struggled to make sense of this world gone mad. His grandmother held him at gunpoint. He'd stepped through a rabbit hole into another dimension. He glanced down at Ajax. Would he obey an attack command?

Probably not. The dog had been trained to protect his grandmother, not attack her.

"Drop your gun," she said again. "And if the dog moves, I'll shoot him."

Matt pulled out his gun and dropped it into the mud. "What's this all about?"

Trudy stepped away from the door and gestured with the gun. "Inside."

Matt let his contempt show in his eyes. He strode into the shack and stood in the doorway while his eyes adjusted to the dim light. Ajax trotted close beside him.

"Daddy!"

He swung toward his daughter's voice. He'd never heard such a sweet sound as her voice in that moment. "Caitlin?" Moments later, she was climbing his legs. He swung her up against his chest, and she clasped her arms around his neck. Ajax barked and danced around them as if he wanted his turn with her. "Quiet, Ajax." The dog stilled and lay down under the window.

"I knew you'd find me, Daddy."

He buried his face in her hair and fought the sting of tears. "You okay, princess?"

"I want to go home." Caitlin began to cry.

"We will." He glanced around and saw Hannah on the cot. He turned to face Trudy. "What's going on here?"

"It's the final act in a long play, Matthew. I'm sorry you got caught up in it." Trudy beckoned to Hannah. "I can't let her continue the Schwartz tradition of destroying my family. Come here, girl." Hannah's eyes widened, but she got up and moved slowly to where Trudy stood. "Tie up my grandson."

Matt couldn't let that happen. He'd be helpless to protect his daughter and Hannah. Backing away, he started for the door. Trudy wouldn't shoot him.

Before he got more than two feet, a shot rang out, and a bullet creased the skin on his arm. "I don't want to shoot you, Matt, but I will if you force me to," Trudy said. "Sit in the chair." She gestured to a rickety wooden chair.

Blood trickled from his arm. He lowered himself onto the chair. "What is going on, Trudy?"

"Shut up. Hannah, tie him up."

Hannah bit her lip, then picked up the rope on the floor and moved to the chair. She began to wrap the rope around his wrists.

"Get his ankles too," Trudy ordered. "I'm going to check the bonds, so get them tight."

Matt flexed his wrists to give himself the most give as Hannah tightened the rope, then looped it down to his feet. Trudy stepped over to test the give, and he kept his muscles flexed until she nodded with satisfaction.

She turned back to Hannah. "You, come with me. Leave the kid here with Matt."

Hannah glanced up at Matt with an apology in her eyes. Matt had to delay Trudy until he could get free. "I found a photo album. Some things are starting to make sense to me. My parents were never happy. All I remember as a kid was how unhappy my mom was. Dad never smiled. He killed himself. I think he was in love with Hannah's mother. But that's not Hannah's fault."

"Her family has blighted mine for decades. But no more," Trudy said.

Hannah was frowning. "What are you saying?" she asked Matt. "I thought my dad dated your aunt."

Matt kept talking, straining at his bonds the whole time. Was there a bit of give? "There once were four friends. They all met in town, where they worked together at a local café. Patricia and David—your mom and my dad—were dating. Irene had a crush on the Amish boy—your dad, Abe— and the four of them double-dated. Your grandparents probably didn't like that, but it was Abe's *rumspringa* and they hoped he'd grow out of it. But something went very wrong. Abe fell for Patricia and stole her from David. David never got over the loss, even though he married. The marriage was unhappy, and he eventually took his own life. Did I get all that right, Trudy?"

"Shut up." Trudy grabbed Hannah's arm and dragged her toward the door. "Patricia was a cuckoo in our nest. And so is her daughter. You're just like her, batting your eyes and enticing men into your web. First Reece and now Matthew. I won't allow it to continue."

Hannah managed to tug her arm free. "Did you kill my parents?" Her eyes grew round with horror.

"Of course I did. You didn't think I would let them get away with destroying my family, did you? Hannah here told Irene her mother was finally pregnant again. That was the final straw. Patricia didn't deserve a child after all she'd done. Then Hannah took my first grandson and ruined his life. She has to pay."

"Irene is Reece's mother," Hannah said.

Trudy scowled. "How did you know that?"

Hannah went pale. "I ran into Ellen Long today. She mentioned it."

"Who's his father?" Matt asked. He saw horror dawn on Hannah's face.

Trudy laughed. "It's not Abe, if that's what you're thinking. I would have stopped that soon enough. It's some loser who stayed at their commune a few months, then moved on. Irene had a nervous breakdown, so I took him."

"I thought he was a foster kid."

She waved the gun in the air. "A smoke screen."

"What about Cyrus?"

Hannah answered. "I think he was just a dupe. His wife was having an affair with Reece. I'm guessing Reece mixed poison in with the sugar, then asked him to make cookies and deliver them to my parents when he went to pick out a quilt. The trail would lead back to the bakery, and it would look like he got caught up in his own murder plot."

Trudy squinted at her. "That Ellen is—"

Hannah backed away from Trudy. "Why did you take my mother's quilts?"

"Jealousy," Matt answered. "I saw a picture of you, Trudy. You were beside a quilt that looked like Patricia's famous hummingbird quilt. She imitated your pattern and had more success than you ever dreamed of."

"All because she was *Amish*," Trudy spat. She grabbed Hannah again and dragged her to the door. "But it all ends today." She pulled her captive through the door and closed it behind them.

Matt began to strain at his bonds. They didn't give much, but he had to get free. Wrenching and twisting his wrists, he stretched and moved the rope until he began to feel a bit of give, but it still wasn't enough to slip his hands free. "Caitlin, come here. I need your help."

He could only pray his daughter had enough strength to loosen his bonds. When she was at his side, he instructed her to find the end of the rope and trace it back to the knot, then try to push the end through. She wasn't accomplishing much. Finally, five minutes later, he felt it give and his hands began to pull free.

THE MOSQUITOES CAME in hordes, eager for their blood. Hannah could see the same bloodthirsty intent on Trudy's face. Trudy marched her down a muddy path toward the raging creek, fifty feet across at its widest point. The current had torn trees up by the roots, and giant sycamores rode the dirty waves in the churning water. The swollen creek had nearly reached two beached canoes.

They skirted the water, and Trudy turned toward a small path that circled back toward the shack. An open cistern yawned in front of them, obviously just uncovered. It was about four feet in diameter.

She stopped in front of the open hole. "Time to say good-bye, Hannah."

Hannah froze. What could she do? She cast her gaze back and forth across the area, but there was no place to hide. Trudy raised the gun, and Hannah expected the bullet to plow through her any second.

"Trudy, no!" Reece's shout rang out through the trees.

Hannah saw him rushing up the path toward them. His eyes wild and his face white, he was not the savior she'd hoped for. He carried a gun in his hand. Trudy turned toward her grandson, her scowl deepening.

He reached them and stopped by his grandmother. "You said we could leave, go our way. Hannah came back to me of her own free will. She had nothing to do with her parents' sins. You promised you'd help me get her back. You never said anything about killing her."

Trudy slapped him. "You fool! She's got you totally flummoxed. Can't you see she only came because she was sure you had the brat?"

Reece put his hand to his cheek. "You didn't have to do that."

"Do what I say, Reece. I've been working years for this minute."

Over Reece's shoulder, Hannah saw Matt and Ajax running up the path. She didn't see Caitlin, so she prayed the little girl was on her way to safety. Trudy must have seen the expression on her face, because she turned to look.

She pressed her lips together and raised the gun to point it at Hannah. "If either one of you moves, she's dead." She pointed to the hole. "You've been looking for your mother, Matthew. Come say hello."

Matt came toward them, clenching his fists. "You killed my mother?" His face took on a stricken expression.

"She killed my son."

"No, she didn't—he killed himself."

"Because she wasn't the wife he needed," Trudy spat.

Matt couldn't engage that kind of irrational thinking. "You had Reece hire that woman to pose as my mother. Just so I wouldn't look anymore, right? Did you think just any woman would pass for my mother? I remember her too well to fall for that masquerade."

Trudy waved her hand. "Hannah is about to join her. She can give her your greetings."

twenty-six

"There have been cases of prejudice against the Amish in some communities. They are the perfect targets for hate crimes because they don't fight back—they are peace-loving and gentle."

—HANNAH SCHWARTZ, ON *The Early Show*

Trudy gestured with the gun again. "Would you like to say hello to your mother, Matt? She's right down there if you'd like to stop in for a visit."

"Stop it!" Hannah shouted. "Just stop being such a cruel witch."

Trudy's brows raised. "The mouse roars?"

This was where bitterness led. Hannah got it now. Forgiveness was much more beautiful when contrasted with this vengeful woman. How had she been so blind? She found it hard to look away from that twisted mouth, those eyes filled with hatred and judgment. Had she looked like that to Ellen earlier today? Is this what Reece saw when he looked in her face?

"Why, Trudy? Why all this hatred to people who never even hurt you? What did Moe ever do to warrant death?"

"That was his own fault. The flowers were meant for his mother." Trudy glared at Reece.

"My aunt was a wonderful woman," Hannah said. As long as she could keep Trudy talking, they might have a chance of being rescued.

"She was a busybody. She came to see me after your parents' funeral, all the way in her little buggy as if I would be impressed. She told me she'd seen Reece coming out of Ellen's house when Cyrus wasn't there. She suspected Reece was a killer and came to tell me to be careful of him." Trudy smiled. "She didn't tell the police. She wanted to leave justice in God's hands."

"And of course she had no idea you were involved," Hannah said slowly.

"When Reece told me what he'd done to lure you back here, I knew Nora would have to die. She wouldn't keep that information to herself." She glanced up at Reece as though seeking his approval. "I put you first in everything."

"She never told me. You didn't have to kill her."

"She would have." Trudy's voice was matter-of-fact. "Shoot her, Reece. You need to do it to be rid of her in spirit." Reece shook his head and dropped the hand with the gun to his side, but she seized his arm. Her voice rose, and even the wind didn't drown it out. "If it hadn't been for me, you would have been out on the streets, Reece. We're in this together too far for you to back out now. It has to be done."

"Let me keep Hannah." His voice was weak and pleading.

"You're so weak, boy. Would you fight me again? Want to knock me down like you did when you first got back? You're pitiful."

Hannah's gaze went to Matt, and she saw from his expression that he had heard Reece too. His nostrils flared, and his lips thinned. She could see his coiled muscles waiting to spring into action. They weren't going down without a fight.

"You've got my gun," Matt said. "This time use it for a good purpose. Save Hannah and Caitlin."

"Shut up, Matthew!" Trudy transferred her glare from Matt to Reece. "Reece, you'll do what I say."

Trudy finally seemed to badger Reece into submission. He brought the gun up and aimed it at Matt. "I'll put your gun to good use, all right. You want to go first, big guy? See your mother?"

Hannah stepped in front of Matt. "Let's leave now, Reece. Just go away, you and me. Matt can keep Caitlin. That's all she knows anyway." She didn't think Reece would be able to shoot her. He never destroyed his possessions. Matt made a grab for her to shove her out of the way, but she evaded him and began to walk toward Reece. "You don't have to listen to her, Reece. Look at me. Let's leave here, start a new life. You'll never have to see her again."

"Reece, we have to end it here," Trudy said, her voice steely and commanding. "She'll never stay with you. You know that. She's sacrificing herself for her daughter. I'd shoot her myself, but you need to do it or she will always haunt you."

The tremble in Reece's hand was nearly imperceptible, but Hannah caught the slight movement. She sidled closer to her husband. She had to find the courage to forgive him, truly and from the heart. He would only recognize truth.

She reached into the depths of her soul and found the courage. "I forgive you, Reece. I forgive you for every slap, every harsh word." She was shocked to realize she meant it. She could look at him and see past his brutality to his pain. She'd never dreamed it would be possible to give him grace.

There was no way she'd be able to get the gun out of his hand, but he might leave with her. If he'd lay down the gun and let Matt and Caitlin go, she'd honor her promise. It would be a small price to pay for the life of her daughter and the man she loved.

Trudy never gave her the chance to find out. "You're so weak, Reece. I even have to save you from yourself." She brought up her gun and aimed it at Hannah. "You're just like your mother—a user." Her finger tightened on the trigger. "She ruined everything that ever mattered to me."

Hannah stared down the bore of the revolver. The muscles in her legs coiled to spring away, but she knew at this close range, she had little chance of escaping. Before she could make the leap to death or life, Reece turned toward his grandmother. Everything moved as though in slow motion. Hannah heard him shout Trudy's name. She saw the puff of smoke and heard the gun bark in his hand. The revolver recoiled, and Trudy began to fall.

Matt hurtled past Hannah. "Run!" he shouted, tackling Reece. He bored the other man to the ground. "Get Caitlin from the shack!"

Ajax barked and danced around the struggling men. Hannah rushed away. Her gut told her to stay and help Matt, but Caitlin was depending on her. She darted down the path toward the shack, but before she got there, Caitlin stepped in front of her. The little girl saw her and ran toward her. She was crying.

Hannah grabbed her hand. She heard a shot ring out in the trees. Daring a glance back, she saw Reece stagger toward her, brandishing his revolver. His presence cut off their escape that way. The water was the only way out. Hannah raced toward the creek.

She was an expert at canoeing, but with Sugar Creek so turbulent, it would be dangerous. Matt couldn't be dead. She wouldn't believe that. If she could get to town, she could send back help. If only she had her cell phone, but Reece threw it away. She deposited Caitlin into the bottom of a canoe. "Don't move," she said.

As soon as the end of the canoe hit the water, the current grabbed it. She nearly didn't make it into the canoe herself before the water flung the vessel into the middle of the creek. Too late, she realized how hard the waves would be to navigate. Caitlin sat on the bottom of the canoe. "There's a life vest under the seat—put it on," she called to her daughter.

Caitlin grabbed the vest and slipped her arms into it. Hannah glanced behind to find Reece in the other boat, coming after them. In the back of the canoe, Hannah dipped the oar into the water and used it to try to steer the vessel around the worst of the rapids. If she could guide them around this bend toward land and hide the boat, Reece would go on downstream looking for them.

A covered bridge loomed ahead. The water tore at the underpinnings, and the bridge began to bob. Her gaze searched frantically for a way through. If they hit the bridge, they'd be capsized. A small gap in the side near the south bank caught her eye, and she aimed for it. The rapids intensified as she neared the bridge. The churning water smelled of mud and dying vegetation. The swiftly flowing water raised the canoe as if taking aim for the gap. With one final heave, the canoe hurtled for the spot.

And flew into the bridge, which had now come loose from its grip on the land. The canoe skidded across the planks and came to a stop. The bridge swirled in the water, and waves licked over the side. "We've got to try to crawl to shore!" Hannah shouted. Caitlin nodded and began to crawl on her hands and knees across the canoe toward the bridge floor.

Hannah followed her and prayed.

PAIN PURIFIED THE soul. If that was true, Matt figured he was nearly an angel. The gunshot wound felt like hot metal in his gut. His grandmother lay half in the cistern, but he spared no thought for her. He staggered in the direction Hannah and Caitlin had gone. Reece had Matt's gun and would catch them. He had to help.

Ajax limped beside him. Matt could see blood on the dog's paw. Maybe he'd been shot as well. Matt stuffed his fist against the blood seeping from his stomach. Death might be calling his name, but he wasn't going out without a fight. He wouldn't leave Hannah and Caitlin defenseless.

When he reached the water, he realized both canoes were gone. Hannah wouldn't have taken Caitlin out onto the water unless she'd had no choice. He clawed his cell phone out and flipped it open. Thank God, he had a signal. He punched in 9-1-1 and called in the incident as he stumbled downstream in search of Hannah and his daughter. The dispatcher promised to get an EMT chopper out ASAP. He asked to have a vet standing by for Ajax.

His vision faltered. Barely aware of his surroundings, he kept going.

Was that a canoe up ahead? Before he could decide what he'd seen, he stumbled to his knees. As he fell facedown onto the mud, the roaring in his ears intensified and darkness sucked him into a vortex that went down to a bottomless pit.

THE FLOODWATERS ROARED their fury in her ears. The little girl scampered across the rough-hewn boards. She made the final leap across the water to shore before Hannah was fully out of the boat. Hannah crawled across the bridge floor after her daughter. She heard a crash and looked back to see Reece's canoe fly into the air and land upside down. What had happened to him? She crawled back to the end of the floating bridge closest to Reece and searched the water.

The muddy water churned with flotsam: tree limbs, pieces of metal roofing, old tin cans, and car parts. Then Reece's head broke the surface, and he gasped for air. "Hannah, help me!" His arms flailed.

He'd saved her from Trudy. She had to help him. Hannah searched for a branch to hold out to him. There, a loose one poked up from the mass of limbs and trees lodged against the bridge. She tugged it free and reached out to Reece. The desperation in his face made her lean too far, and she nearly toppled into the water with him.

She tried again, flinging the end of the branch into his face. He grasped it in one hand, and she began to pull him toward the bridge. The nearer he got to her, the more the waves crashed over his head. At this rate, she would drown him. She pulled harder. A surge of water covered him again, then he popped up several feet closer. He'd lost hold of the branch, but he managed to grab a limb that protruded from the blockage.

His gaze on her, he began to crawl up onto the logjam at the base of the bridge. Hannah turned and sidled away from him, toward her daughter and safety. He could fend for himself now. Her conscience was clear. She reached the other end of the bridge. The gap between the bridge and the shore had widened. Could she make it? She coiled her muscles and sprang for the shore. Her outflung hand grasped a tree root, and she hauled herself up with it until she lay face forward in the mud.

If she had the strength, she'd kiss the ground. Her vision darkened, and she fought to stay conscious. They weren't out of the woods yet, literally. She had to get Caitlin to safety and send back help for Matt. She became aware that Caitlin was shaking her and rolled onto her back to stare up into the beautiful face of her baby girl.

"Miss Hannah, the bad man is coming," Caitlin whispered. "You have to get up."

Hannah managed to sit. Pain gripped her back, her legs. Blood ran from her knees from crawling along the rough logs. She bit back a groan. A sound behind her caught her attention, and she turned to see Reece standing on the collapsed bridge. The structure bucked like a wild thing and began to break apart. He wore a victorious grin that widened when he saw her watching him.

"I'm coming, Hannah. Wait for me."

"Run, Reece!" Hannah screamed. "It's falling apart." She knew she should grab Caitlin and run as fast as they could, but she couldn't move, caught by the drama playing out in front of her.

The surging water intensified as a new round of flotsam hit the bridge. The structure shuddered. Reece's victorious grin morphed into wild-eyed terror as the boards under his feet rolled. He tried to drop down and grab a board, but the thing bucked again. He flipped into the air and came down hard. Hannah heard something crack when he hit the beams. The next instant the bridge splintered, and pieces of wood flew in all directions. Reece's hand flew up in a silent plea, then the debris rained down on him and he disappeared under the onslaught.

Hannah sank to her knees and put her face in her hands. There was no way he could have survived that. She was free, she and Caitlin. Free to live their lives out from under his cruelty. But she ached for the man he might have been. And if not for Reece, she would lie in the cistern with Matt's mother.

She staggered to her feet again. "We've got to find your daddy," she told Caitlin.

They looked up to hear the *whop-whop* of a chopper overhead. How did the EMTs know where to find them? Her blood surged at the knowledge that Matt had to have called it in. She raced back along the bank with Caitlin. Around the curve and through the mud with the creek roaring its triumph. She could see the shack in the distance, then she heard Ajax barking. He sounded frantic, but weak, too, and her initial joy began to drain.

Then she saw Matt. Crumpled in the water. Ajax barked again, then took hold of the collar of Matt's shirt and tried to tug him from the water that sought to claim him. The dog was losing the battle. He looked battered and weak from the effort. Hannah put on a burst of speed and reached Matt's side. She grabbed him under the arms and, with Ajax's help, managed to get him out of the water's grasp.

She rolled him onto his back and saw the awful wound in his belly. All the while she waved her arms to flag down the chopper, she knew she was going to lose him.

twenty-seven

"Children are treasured by the Amish. They take however many children God chooses to give. They're never considered a burden. Happy is the man who has his quiver full of them."

—HANNAH SCHWARTZ,

IN *The Amish Faith Through Their Quilts*

Equipment choked the room at the IU Med Center. Hannah sat close to the bed and watched the monitors. Not that she understood them, but if sheer force of will could keep Matt's vitals good, she would stare at the things until she went blind.

Asia peeked in the door, and Hannah went to meet her. "Any change?" Asia asked.

"No, he's still unconscious."

"Any new update from the doctors?"

"They still say it will be a miracle if he pulls through." Hannah clutched her hands together. "How's Caitlin?"

"Gina has her. She's asking for her daddy."

"I don't think she should see him like this. Hannah glanced back at the battered man in the bed. He hardly looked like the Matt she knew and loved.

"But what if he dies, Hannah? Wouldn't you want a chance to say good-bye if it were your daddy?"

The question hit Hannah hard. She did wish she could have kissed her parents one last time, could have smelled her mother's hair to imprint it on her memory. She didn't have the right to keep Caitlin from her father. She resituated her grip on her hope. "I won't let him die."

Asia put her hand on Hannah's cheek. "He's been shot in the stomach, girl. He's got liver damage, intestinal damage. You've got to face facts."

"I'm facing facts. I *know* he's not going to die. Listen, I've got to get back to him."

"What about Caitlin?"

Somehow the thought of letting Caitlin see her daddy like this made Hannah grit her teeth. She would not give up. "Not yet," she said. "Maybe when he wakes up."

Asia squeezed Hannah's arm. "I'll bring you a sandwich this evening. You want anything now?"

"No, I'm not hungry." The thought of food made her shudder. She just wanted Matt to open his eyes and look at her with that gaze that told her he could swallow her whole. The expression that said he saw *her*. Just as she was, warts and all. And loved what he saw.

She'd just returned to the bed to take his hand when she heard another tap at the doorjamb. This time the doorway crowded with Amish friends and family: Luca, Sarah, the bishop, cousins, friends. At least twenty people stood outside in the hallway.

Hannah stepped to the door to greet them. "What's going on?"

"We've come to pray for Matt," Luca said. "He's a good man, Hannah."

She could hardly speak past the boulder in her throat. "Yes. Yes, he is," she managed. When she stepped to the side, the group filed into the room and surrounded the bed. When she joined them, they made room for her at Matt's side. She held his hand while her friends gathered round and stood in silent prayer.

They had to have hired several drivers to bring them here. Even by car, Indianapolis was an hour away. She closed her eyes and prayed too, asking for forgiveness for all the bitterness she'd carried, for her unforgiving spirit. And she especially prayed for Matt. When she opened her eyes, only she and Matt remained in the room. The Amish had left as quietly as they'd come.

She squeezed his hand. "Open your eyes, Matt." His lashes didn't move. The machines continued to hum and beep around her. She laid her head on the bed beside his hand. She was going to lose him, and she deserved that kind of loss. But Caitlin deserved more. What could she offer God in exchange for Matt's life? She would give her own happiness for his. Didn't God always demand a sacrifice? What better sacrifice than giving up her daughter?

Raising her head, she stared at Matt's face. No change. Stepping into the hall, she pulled out her cell phone and called Asia, who tried to argue with her, then finally agreed to do what she wanted.

"HANNAH, DON'T GO through with it." Asia paced the hall outside the hospital room.

"I have to." Hannah scribbled her name on the paper and handed it to Gina, who stood watching them.

"He wouldn't want you to do this," Gina said. She put the paper in her purse. "I don't understand."

Gina looked drawn and exhausted. In addition to Matt's tenuous grip on life, her husband and Vanessa had been arrested for theft. The woman's pregnancy was a lie as well.

Hannah squeezed Gina's hand. "He loves his daughter. She's his more than mine. I—I'd like to say good-bye, though."

"She's in the waiting room with Irene."

"I want to explain it to Matt. I'll be there in a few minutes." Hannah left them and went back to the room, where he still lay unresponsive. After three days, the doctors held out little hope. His skin had begun to take on a yellowish cast. She couldn't delay much longer.

She took his hand and brought it to her lips. "I love you, Matt. You've taught me so much about honor and unconditional love. I've signed Caitlin over to you. She's yours free and clear." Her voice broke, and she leaned closer to take one last whiff of his male scent, to brush her lips across his. "I've made a deal with God. We Amish believe in putting other people first. Sometimes I've forgotten that. But this time, I'm going to do it right. I'm putting you and Caitlin first. I believe if I make this sacrifice, he'll let you live. I'm going to leave here, and you'll never find me. Don't try, my love. Something terrible might happen if you make me break my promise to God. I know you'll give our daughter a good life. A happy life."

Her vision blurred, and she found it hard to keep going when all she wanted to do was bury her face in his neck and never leave. She wet her lips. "Good-bye, Matt. You deserve the best of what life has to offer. Be happy. I'll always love you." She pressed another kiss against his skin and turned to go before she could change her mind.

She thought she heard something, so she stopped and looked back, but he looked just the same. Pale, motionless. Dying unless she did something. Squaring her shoulders, she went out of the room and down the hall to the waiting room, where she stood for a moment and watched her daughter color. Caitlin sat at a child-sized red table and chair set.

Was there ever such a beautiful child? Hannah thought not. So sweet and unassuming too. Matt had done a wonderful job with her. She tore her gaze from her daughter and went to sit beside Irene and Gina. "I'll call in a couple of days and see how he is, if you don't mind."

"Of course," Gina said.

Hannah glanced at Irene. "Did you know about your mother?"

Irene sighed and rubbed her head. "I suspected. Her bitterness grew after I had Reece and ended up in a sanitarium for two years. Then when David killed himself, she fell apart. It got harder and harder to be around her. I'd go over there and all she'd talk about was how terrible all the Amish were and how the Schwartzes would get what they deserved someday. When their barn burned back in the late seventies, I suspected she had something to do with it. Then ten years ago when she heard Patricia was pregnant again, all her anger came spewing out. We had an argument, and we never spoke again." She looked up. "Bitterness is a terrible thing. It eats a person alive." She chewed on her lip. "The darkness comes sometimes and even I can't fight it." She plucked something off her blouse.

"It was nice getting to know you, Irene." She hugged the older woman, then held out her hand to Gina. "Thank you for taking care of my little girl. I'll call and check on her from time to time, if you don't mind. Maybe you could e-mail me a picture once in a while."

"I'll do that." Gina embraced her. "I wish we'd had time to get to know one another better."

"Me too." Blinking back the tears, Hannah put a smile on her face and stepped closer to her little girl. "Hey, Caitlin. Is that picture for Daddy?"

The little girl nodded without looking up. "He loves princesses. I'm his number one princess."

"Of course you are. You're the most important thing in his life." Hannah touched her daughter's unruly hair, then knelt. "I have to go away. Do you think I could have a hug?" Caitlin put down the crayon and came willingly into Hannah's arms. "Are you coming back?"

"No, honey, I'm not. I have to leave you here with your aunt Gina. She'll take good care of you until your daddy is well. And he'll be well very soon."

"I thought you were my new mommy. Your hair is fairy hair like mine." Caitlin's small fingers caressed Hannah's thick locks. Over Caitlin's shoulders, Hannah could see Gina, Irene, and Asia weeping. It took every ounce of strength Hannah possessed to give her daughter one last fierce hug, then turn her loose. "I love you just as much as any mommy could love a little girl. I'll pray for you every day. You take care of your daddy, okay?"

Caitlin nodded. "I always take care of him. We bake cookies. Chocolate chip are his favorite." She went to her backpack and rummaged through it. Lifting out her doll, she carried the battered toy back to where Hannah stood. "Will you take Jenny? I'll be busy taking care of Daddy, and she'll need a new mommy."

Tears flooded Hannah's eyes. "I'd be honored to take care of her for you. Are you sure, sweetheart?"

Caitlin nodded. "Don't let her forget me."

"I won't." Hannah couldn't take much more. "You'd better finish your picture. Daddy will be awake soon and you'll want to give it to him."

"Okay." Caitlin sat back down at the little table and bent her head.

Breathe. In and out. Hannah hugged Irene and Gina, then followed Asia out to the car.

"You didn't have to do this," Asia said, her tone fierce.

But Hannah knew better. "Let's get out of here," she said. "I need to go home and pack my stuff. Get my cats."

"But where are you going?"

"I'm not sure." Just away from the pain.

"You'll keep in touch with me, won't you? I'll be working on publicity for the new book. The editor is really happy with it."

"You have to promise not to give in to Matt's questions when he comes looking for me." Hannah knew Matt. He'd look for her and keep looking even though the letter she'd left explained everything and told him not to. Even though she'd warned him.

"I'll keep my mouth shut."

Though Asia sounded sulky, Hannah believed her. "Let's go."

They collected her cats and her belongings and headed to Milwaukee. Hannah had a plan, nebulous though it was. At least the challenge would give her something to think about instead of all she'd left behind. It would take hard work, but that's what she needed now—something that left her too exhausted at night to remember a set of blue eyes that told her she was special.

twenty-eight

"The Double Wedding Ring Quilt has been loved by all generations.
Amish weddings are most often held on Tuesday or Thursday. A sure-
fire way to tell if a daughter is getting married is to check out the gar-
den. An overabundance of celery signals upcoming nuptials."

—HANNAH SCHWARTZ,

IN *The Amish Faith Through Their Quilts*

Six months, six days, three hours since she'd left him. Matt leaned away from his computer at the sheriff's department and rubbed his eyes. Every spare moment when he wasn't working, he searched for Hannah, but she'd vanished without a ripple. How could she have disappeared so completely? She hadn't appeared on any TV shows or been featured in any magazines. Her publisher wouldn't divulge her address. Even with his contacts, he'd been stymied.

Asia knew where she'd gone, but she wouldn't tell him. Meanwhile, her daughter was growing up without her mother. And he longed to see Hannah's face. Grabbing his winter coat, he stepped out into a driving snowstorm. The weatherman was talking about the worst blizzard in Indiana since 1978, and the storm had already dropped six inches of snow, with another eight to ten inches forecast.

It was a good night for staying in and eating popcorn with Caitlin, but he wanted to drive to Milwaukee and force Asia to divulge Hannah's whereabouts. He managed to uncover his car and drove slowly through the clogged streets to his house. The snow in his shoes melted, freezing his feet by the time he got home. He let himself into the house and heard Gina's voice on the phone.

"Oh, Hannah, it's so good to hear from you," she said. "Caitlin is doing well. She started kindergarten, and she's reading already." She fell silent while she listened. "I'll e-mail you the picture from school. She's probably grown two inches since you've seen her."

Gina had kept this from Matt. He'd had no idea she was still in contact with Hannah. He stayed where he was, listening quietly for any clue, but nothing Gina said gave away any possible location.

When she hung up the phone and turned around, she stopped and put her hand to her throat. "Matt, you scared me."

"Have you been in touch with her ever since she left?" He stepped closer, and she backed away.

"Look, she didn't want you to know, okay?"

"Where is she, Gina? I have to find her." He grabbed the phone from her and checked the caller ID, but the call had come in as unknown.

"She doesn't want to be found. And maybe she's right. The doctors said you were a goner. They were shocked when you made the turnaround the day she left."

"God doesn't make deals." He turned and headed back to the office. "Show me her e-mails."

"Matt, don't do this. Marriage isn't all it's cracked up to be anyway."

He stopped and grabbed her shoulders. "Don't let your views about marriage keep me from being happy. I'm not Blake. I love Hannah, and I'm going to find her. Caitlin needs her too."

Her cheeks paled. "Do you blame me for being bitter? He was a thief as well as an adulterer."

"You have your health. Me, your friends. You've still got good things in your life if you'll just accept them. Don't you want me to be happy, Gina? Are you afraid I won't need you if I'm married, that I'll toss you out of the house or something?"

The color came rushing back. "That's a mean thing to say."

"Then help me find her." He released her and stomped off to sit in front of the computer.

Gina followed more slowly. "I've saved her e-mails." She went to the Gmail sign-in screen and showed him the messages. "I'm going to go check on supper."

He began to read through them. Hannah's e-mails were so much like her: caring and thoughtful. She often asked how Gina was dealing with her divorce and advised her about taking care of herself. Her concern showed through every message. He ached to see her, to touch her hair. How could she have left him like that? Didn't she realize how much he needed her—how Caitlin needed her?

He opened the next message and began to read. She mentioned a festival going on called Swiss Days. He checked the date and opened another Google screen. Bingo. It was held in Berne, Indiana, last July. He called up MapQuest and checked the distance—185 miles. A little over three hours in good weather. It was six o'clock. Surely he could be there by midnight, even with the storm. The highway crews would be out plowing the roads, and besides, he could take his four-wheel-drive with the blade on the front.

He checked stats about Berne. The population was only a little over four thousand. All he'd have to do is show her picture around town. Small towns could be protective of their own, but he wasn't above flashing his badge if necessary. He went down the hall to his bedroom and packed his bag, then carried it to the hall.

Ajax whined from his spot on the rug when he saw the suitcase. The dog stood and stretched and padded over to nuzzle Matt's hand.

Gina's gaze went to the suitcase in his hand as well. "Where are you going?"

"Berne. That's where she is. I'm going to camp out at the McDonald's. She loves their coffee. I'll find her."

"You'll be driving all night. Why not head up tomorrow morning?"

"We may be snowed in by morning."

"You may get stuck out on the road tonight."

"The worst of it isn't supposed to hit until after midnight. I want to go now. I've wasted enough time without her."

Caitlin came from the kitchen. "Are you going somewhere, Daddy? Can I go?" She ran to hang on to his leg.

Matt started to stay no, then caught himself. Why not? He could use all the ammunition he could get. Even if Hannah refused to marry him, their daughter needed to have a relationship with her. Now that he knew where she was, he could make sure Caitlin understood how much Hannah loved them both.

"Go pack your things," he told her. "Take enough for a week."

"Where are we going?"

"To bring your new mommy home."

Caitlin's eyes widened. "Yes!" She ran back to her room.

"Are you sure you know what you're doing?" Gina asked.

"I've never been more sure of anything in my life."

"I'd better go help her, then."

Matt glanced at his watch. In only hours, he'd look into Hannah's beautiful eyes again.

THE SNOW CAME nearly to Hannah's knees. The cold wetness soaking her legs nearly took her breath away on the north wind. Carefully tucking the locket that held a picture of Matt and Caitlin inside her parka, she zipped it clear up to her neck and put on her gloves. She opened the trunk and removed the shovel, then made a path to the door of her office. Though it wasn't likely anyone would come out in the weather until the plows came through, she wanted to be ready if she was needed. The battered women's shelter needed to be welcoming no matter what was going on elsewhere. She'd only made it to work because her apartment was over the office.

It took nearly an hour to uncover the walk to the office. She backtracked to the car to put the shovel away. Standing at the trunk of her car, she watched a big four-wheel-drive truck with a blade on the front approach. The driver was probably going to bury her car with the drifts he was plowing. A large drift barred his way. He backed up, then came at it twice before parting it. Snow blew over the hood of the vehicle.

She stepped off the road and onto the walk. She thought she heard someone call, "Hannah!" but she had to be wrong. People here thought her name was Sonya Fearnow. The wind picked up, and she stuck her hands in her pockets and hurried toward her office door. The shout came again, and this time there was no mistaking the word.

She turned to see the big truck pulling to a stop in the middle of the snow-clogged main street. A man leaped out, then lifted a little girl in his arms. A dog leaped from the truck and began to bark. The man stumbled through the snow toward the walk. Hannah drank in the sight of Matt in his heavy coat and Caitlin in her pink parka and boots. She'd hungered to see them both, to hear their voices.

They reached the sidewalk. Matt's gaze never wavered from her face. He put Caitlin on the sidewalk, and she broke into a run. "Mommy!" she shouted. Ajax barked and raced up the walk with her.

Hannah crumpled to her knees at the word. She opened her arms, and Caitlin hurtled into them. Ajax licked her face and nuzzled in her hair. Hannah hugged Caitlin tight to her chest and slung an arm around the dog. The sweet aroma of baby shampoo still clung to Caitlin's auburn hair. Tears rushed to Hannah's eyes.

She looked into her daughter's face. "Caitlin, what are you doing here?"

Caitlin pulled away. "We comed to take you home with us. You have to pack now." She said the words matter-of-factly, as if Hannah had no say in the matter.

Matt reached her. Hannah released Ajax and rose with Caitlin in her arms. "How did you find me?"

"I overheard you talking to Gina yesterday. I made her show me your e-mails and I figured it out."

She fell into the bottomless love in his eyes. Drowning, she fought her way to sanity. "You shouldn't have come."

"You shouldn't have left." He held out his arms for Caitlin. "She's heavy. Let's go inside."

Hannah handed her daughter over with reluctance. Only then did she become aware of the subzero wind howling around her neck. Lost in his gaze, she'd felt only heat. "It's warm inside."

"I'm not cold, but Caitlin might be." Carrying his daughter, he followed her inside with Ajax at his heels.

The austere surroundings brightened in the presence of the ones she loved. "Have a seat," she said, pointing out the sofa and chairs.

He dropped Caitlin onto the sofa. "What is this place?"

"A shelter for abused women and children." Hannah watched Caitlin's gaze land on the toy box. The little girl glanced up at her, and she nodded. "Go ahead. You can play with them."

Caitlin hesitated. "How is Jenny?" she asked in a voice that was too casual.

"She misses you. She's upstairs. If you want to go up there, you can have her."

Caitlin's smile was as bright as the sun beating off the snow outside. "Okay."

Matt's gaze had never wavered from Hannah. She couldn't look at him or she was lost. "This way." She led them through the hall to the back stairway and up to her tiny apartment.

The living room wasn't any bigger than a bedroom, and the only item on the coffee table was a picture of Caitlin and Matt smiling into the camera. A baby quilt nestled Jenny in the rocking chair in the corner. Caitlin ran to crawl into the chair with her doll. She took off her coat and nestled under the covering with the doll. All four cats came out to investigate. They milled around Ajax, and the dog flopped down. The cats climbed onto the dog and began to knead his fur. He wore an expression of bliss.

Hannah clasped her hands together. "Would you like some tea? I've got milk and cookies too."

"Chocolate chip?" Matt asked, his eyes crinkling at the corners.

She could look at the way his dimple flashed forever. "Actually, they are," she said. "I made them last night when the snow started falling." She rushed past him to the miniscule kitchen. The plates rattled in her shaking hands as she took them down. When she turned around, he was standing in front of her. Close enough to touch. Close enough to kiss if she dared.

She backed up with her palms flat against the edge of the counter behind her. "It's a little tight for two people."

"I don't mind." His hands came down on her shoulders. "Look at me, Hannah."

She didn't dare. "I—I need to get Caitlin some cookies."

His warm fingers lifted her chin, but she still refused to lift her gaze. His lips brushed hers. The touch she'd longed to experience. A sob burst from her, and she wrapped her arms around his neck and put her heart into answering his kiss.

She'd missed him so. Longed to hear his voice, to bury her face in his neck and smell his aftershave. She'd ached for his touch. She tore her mouth away.

He tipped her chin up. "Look at me, Hannah."

She finally dared to raise her gaze, locking it with his. "Don't do this, Matt." The pleading in his eyes broke her heart. She had to be strong for his sake.

He cupped her cheek in his hand. "I heard every word you said the day you left. I tried to tell you not to go, but I couldn't get the words out. I've looked for you every day since you left. I need you. Caitlin needs her mommy. You can't desert us."

"I thought she would forget me, but she called me . . . Mommy." Was there a more precious word in the human language? Hannah's shields were crumbling, and she didn't know how to shore them up.

"I've shown her your picture every day you've been gone and talked about you. So she wouldn't forget."

The thought of his taking the time to do that made her want to cry. "How'd you find me here in town?"

He grinned. "It took us until two this morning to get here, and I went to McDonald's as soon as it opened in case someone there knew you. I told her you'd order an iced vanilla coffee. A woman behind the counter told me where you worked, so we came to take you home. If you can forgive me for all the lies."

"I forgave you long ago. But I can't come with you. Something might happen to you," she whispered.

The light in his eyes intensified. "God doesn't make deals like that, love. He's never stopped loving you, just like I've never stopped. The forgiveness you were taught is only a shadow of what God gives. You just have to take it. Quit beating yourself up." He pulled her close again.

Oh, if only she could believe him. But she was afraid, so very afraid. "You have to forget about me. I want only good things for you and Caitlin."

"You were made for us. Who would love her more than her own mother? Do you want her to deal with some wicked stepmother?"

Hannah laughed, but the thought unsettled her. It was painful to imagine someone else reading her daughter a bedtime story. Or even worse, yelling at her. Her thoughts shied away from imagining Matt with another woman. But wasn't that what sacrifice was all about? And God had honored it—here he stood, whole and strong.

"I can't break my pact with God," she whispered.

"'To do righteousness and justice is more acceptable to the LORD than sacrifice,'" he said. "Proverbs 21:3. Don't you think it's right to raise your own child? To love the man God created just for you?"

Could it really be that easy? Her defenses crumbled around her feet.

He gripped her shoulders in his hands. "I'm not leaving here until you agree to marry me, let me make an honest woman of you. Isn't that justice?" His dimple flashed.

"An honest woman?"

"You don't want Caitlin going around telling everyone you're her mother and we've never been married." His blue eyes smiled again.

A small hand insinuated itself into hers. "When are we going home, Mommy?"

Hannah looked down into her daughter's face, then back to Matt's. Happiness was in her reach. All she had to do was accept the good things God had sent her way. Was that so bad? Certainty enveloped her. "How about we go home right now?"

She knelt on the floor and embraced her daughter. Matt joined her with cookies in hand, and they devoured the sweetness of life together.

Acknowledgments

Dear Readers,

Many of you ask how I come up with an idea. In this case, my agent, Karen Solem, and I were talking about the Amish school shooting in Nickel Mines, Pennsylvania. Karen said, "I wonder what would happen if something really horrific happened and a member of the church couldn't forgive?" The idea for *Anathema* evolved from her astute question.

I have some Amish friends whom I dearly love, and I so admire their homes and their children. I tried to present a balance in this story, though much of Hannah's longing for her Amish family springs from my own peace when I'm in their home. They have such contentment there. Watching their children interact with only love and no fighting is a real joy. So thank you, my friends (you know who you are), and I wish you God's blessings always.

I couldn't create the stories you enjoy, Readers, without my Thomas Nelson family: fiction publisher Allen Arnold, Superman to those of us who love him, and even more than that, a man who lights up the room he enters; senior editor Ami McConnell, who had fabulous insight and suggestions for this book, as always, and who blesses me with her awesome ability and friendship; editor Natalie Hanemann, my friend and a budding Ami with an eye for good fiction; marketing director Jennifer Deshler, who is the most creative marketing person I know and a friend who is always looking out for my best interests; marketing specialist Bekah Quillan, who partners with Jen and me in coming up with great ideas; fabulous cover guru Mark Ross (you *so* rock!), who works hard to create the perfect cover and does it every single time; fellow Hoosier Lisa Young, who lends a shoulder to cry on when needed; my sweet Amanda Bostic, who is still my friend even though she doesn't work on my books anymore; and my freelance editor Erin Healy, whose magic touch on my books is the glue that holds us all together. I love you all more than I can say. And I'm thrilled that Erin is writing! Look for her name on a book with Ted Dekker soon and *buy* it.

I had some great input on the Swiss Amish by Joe and Frances Schwartz— they even yodeled for me! Thanks so much for your help. My thanks to the Rockville Sheriff's Department for answering stupid questions.

Writing can be a lonely business, but God has blessed me with great writing friends and critique partners. Kristin Billerbeck, Diann Hunt, and Denise Hunter make up the Girls Write Out squad (www.GirlsWriteOut. blogspot.com). I couldn't make it through a day without my peeps! And another one of those is Robin Miller, president of ACFW (www.acfw.com), who spots inconsistencies in a suspense plot with an eagle eye. Thanks to all of you for the work you do on my behalf and for your friendship. Special thanks to Karen Solem, Mel and Cheryl Hodde (Hannah Alexander), Cara Putman, Denise Hunter, and Diann Hunt, who helped me brainstorm this book one crazy night at CBA Advance in Indianapolis. The title was Mel's brainchild.

I have a super supportive family that puts up with my crazy work schedule. My husband, Dave, carts me around from city to city, washes towels, and runs to fetch dinner without complaint. Thanks, honey! I couldn't do anything without you. My son and daughter-in-law, Dave and Donna Coble, and my daughter, Kara Coble, as well as my new grandsons, James and Jorden Packer, love and support me in every way possible. Love you guys! And thanks to my parents, George and Peggy Rhoads; my brothers, Rick and Dave Rhoads; their wives, Mary and Teresa; and my "other parents," Carroll and Lena Coble. One of them is often the first to hear a new idea, and they never laugh at me. Love you all!

Most important, I give my thanks to God, who has opened such amazing doors for me and makes the journey a golden one.

I love to hear from readers! Drop me an e-mail at colleen@ colleencoble.com and check out my Web site at www.colleencoble.com. There's a forum to chat about books, and I try to stop in often, since books are my favorite things in the world. Thank you all for spending your most precious commodity—time—with me and my stories.

Reading Group Guide

1. Why do you think guilt is such a powerful motivator?

2. What actions did Hannah take as a result of guilt?

3. How big a role does tradition play in your own life?

4. An unforgiving spirit can lead to a string of bad decisions. How many can you name from this book?

5. Do you ever long for a simpler time? What sounds the most appealing about it? What would be the most challenging in living that simple life?

6. Have you ever felt the pressure of prejudice? How should it be handled?

7. Do you think Reece was ever sincere about wanting to change or was it always a ploy to get Hannah back?

8. Is it ever okay to tell a lie—even to protect someone else like Matt did? Why or why not?

9. Is there any difference between an outright lie and subtle deceit?

10. Which quilt analogy to the Amish faith was your favorite and why?

11. Why do you think one lie leads to another?

12. Based on what you've read, what do you think is the strongest cord in the Amish faith?

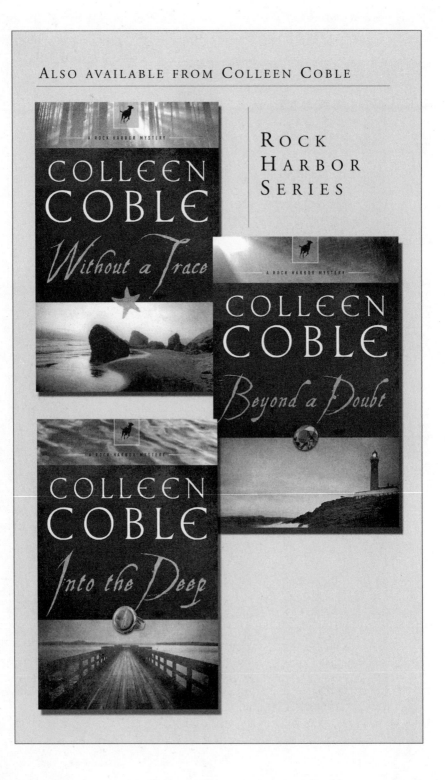

An Excerpt from *Abomination*

P r o l o g u e

NIGHT CREPT OVER THE HILLS, SMOTHERING THE LANDSCAPE in a cocoon of darkness that would hide him in a few minutes. He'd abandoned his real name for one more fitting of his strength and intellect. Gideon was what he called himself when clouds hid the moon and the shadows gathered. Gideon, the Destroyer of Evil.

Before the moonlight could fade completely, he flipped down the sun visor and stared into the face of his wife, Miranda—a photo of her as she had once been.

As she would be again.

The blare of a horn startled him, and he slapped the visor back into place as a gray SUV careened past where his car sat on the narrow shoulder. The vehicle splashed water from a mud puddle over his car. He bit back an expletive, knowing such words ill befit a man of his intellect. He twisted the key and heard the car engine purr to life. Easing onto the road, he hunched over the wheel and stared into the fog. The turnoff to the lake was just ahead. No car lights illuminated the road ahead or behind. He turned the vehicle onto the muddy track and rolled down the window to let in the fresh scent of the water. The lane was meant for tractors, and visitors rarely trespassed. The owners would never even know he'd been here.

The lake reflected the golden orb of the moon. He parked and turned off the car. The cacophony of crickets and tree frogs paused, then started up again as he stepped into the mud and went around to the trunk. The lid sprang open at his touch, and he looked down into the woman's face. As with the others, preludes to the grand finale, he'd stripped her of beauty. This one would never lash a man with her tongue again.

Securing the gray wool blanket around the body, he hauled it out and dumped it on the ground. He tucked a partial peanut butter sandwich under the sinner's blouse. He took hold of the end of the blanket and pulled the bundle down to the water.

Reaching the small pier, he paused and listened, then stepped onto the rickety boards. The body slid easily across the worn wood. Once he reached the end of the dock, he dropped the end of the blanket and settled onto the weather-scoured boards to wait. He pulled his GPS from his pocket and noted the coordinates. Close enough. He didn't plan to go far from shore.

A hint of pine mingled on the night air with the scent of water. The chilly night began to creep into his bones. Loons called, and he straightened and stood to stamp his feet.

Then the angels came.

Gideon held his breath as they glided into the shaft of moonlight. Silent and beautiful, they moved as one along the placid surface of the water. He counted one, two, ten. The largest one's wings spanned at least eight feet.

He shoved the body into the bottom of a small boat, where it lay amid the flotsam of tackle boxes, tarps, and fishing poles. Gideon hurried to the shore, where he gathered rocks in a bucket. Carrying his burden, he went back to the boat and set the bucket into the boat as well. The boat tipped when he stepped in, but he was quick on his feet and moved to the center, where he settled onto the seat.

Years of use had worn the oars smooth, and they fit into his palms as if they'd been carved for his hands. His muscles flexed, and he dipped the oars into the water. The boat moved smoothly through the ripples. They barely noticed his approach. Their voices raised the hair on his arms and back.

About five feet from them, he laid the oars back against the sides of the boat, then crouched beside the body. Opening the blanket, he piled rocks from the bucket inside, then tied the ends with the rope he'd brought.

They moved around him. One bent her neck and looked at him. Something about the way she held her head made him catch his breath. She glided nearer. They would wait with him, patient, long-suffering, until he secured the ultimate prize. Then one rose into the air. The others soared heavenward as well, and he was left alone with a single feather wafting toward him on the shifting fog. He caught it in his hand and brought it to his face. He brushed it over his lips like a kiss. A benediction.

His gaze lit on the body. Frowning, he put the feather in his pocket. He balled his fists, then stooped and heaved the bundle over the side. The water rippled, then closed over the space. He turned around and began to row back to shore.

The house was quiet when he got home. He peeked in on his daughter, Odette. Seventeen years old with a soul as old as Moses, she slept with one hand on her cheek. So innocent the sight made his heart swell in his chest.

What would happen to her if he were caught?

His lip curled. They weren't smart enough to find him. Besides, he was surrounded by a mantle of protection. He was invincible as long as his angels stayed with him. Pressing a kiss on his daughter's hair, he went down the hall to his office and entered, shutting the door. The computer screen lit as soon as he lifted the laptop's lid. He launched the browser and went to the geocaching site.

After he put in the GPS coordinates, he typed:
ABOMINATIONS WILL FIND YOU.